RUNNING FROM REGRET

Author, Richard Jan

ISBN

Hardback: 978-1-964289-74-8

Paperback: 978-1-964289-73-1

'**Running from Regret**' is the fifth book in the series **Dying To Succeed**. To date twelve books make up a series filled with thrills and adventures, love and hate, success and failure.

God willing and the spirit strong, I hope to offer many more new books in the future.

Other books in this series are titled:

Book 1, Winds of Success
Book 2, Living with Death
Book 3, Pretending to be Alive
Book 4, Presumption of Sanity
Book 6, Longing to Go Home
Book 7, Afraid to Hope
Book 8, Waiting in Infinity
Book 9, Chasing after Wind
Book 10, Casualties of Words
Book 11, Traveling into Chaos
Book 12, Snow of Fear

As I wrote these books, I often played music. May I suggest that you do the same.

This book, like all the books in this series, is a continuation of the main character's story. Reading the preceding books is not a requirement, but it does make it easier to understand. Unlike most books which are divided into chapters, it is series of episodes identified by place and time, along with the name of the person speaking.

Should you have questions or comments after reading the book, please feel free to email me at rhoekstra@sbcglobal.net.

Richard Jan

Contents

AUTHOR'S NOTE

Although I am familiar with the colored gemstone industry from having worked in it for ten years, I don't pretend to be an expert on any level. My knowledge can best be described as that of a man traveling through a city without ever stopping for an extended period of time to experience the living conditions up close. And yet, as I contemplated my journey after it came to an end, I thought it was interesting and perhaps worthy of being a wonderful subject for a book.

But what I discovered as I wrote was that the real story was not the gemstone industry but how the cast of characters reacted to the challenges they faced, challenges similar to what we daily endure. And it is my hope that knowledge gained from existing for a time in their shoes as you read this book; may encourage you to live a fuller, more purposeful life.

ACKNOWLEDGEMENTS

It is only fair that I acknowledge the help and encouragement that I received from New York Book Publishers. I went to them initially looking for guidance in editing, cover design, marketing, and distribution. They promised me that they could fulfill my needs. I accepted their proposal and began working with them virtually while living in the Midwest with their company's resources located in New York City. Our journey together has been an adventure; one not taken lightly, but traveled with some trepidation and concerns. Special thanks go to Victor Hughes, who guaranteed me they would not let me down. And thanks to my daily contact, Serena Hoffman for understanding my concerns and assuring me that everything was progressing as it should. And to Jim Bannister who took the time to talk to me when I needed a conversation. And to the many editors and artists who have contributed greatly to the final product. Thanks to them all for helping me achieve what I had hoped for when I first contacted this New York Book Publishers.

Page Left Blank Intentionally

BANGKOK, THAILAND, DATE AND TIME UNKNOWN, LUANG

A sudden blinding desperation washed over the old patriarch as he slept. A desperate anger so dark and penetrating that it felt as though his body had been hit with the driving force of a lethal weapon.

Murky streams of intense rage instantly penetrated his troubled soul as warm blood began to seep from a wound in his chest. Luang stumbled backward from the force of the blow, falling against the rough bark of an old oak tree and sliding down until he was sitting upright against the tree trunk on the ground. Slowly, through crying pain, his eyes adjusted to moonlight reflecting off silky sheens of dew hanging from spider webs in nearby bushes. Gray moon shadows of majestic pines and oaks fell over a dark, dense residue of decaying leaves covering the ground where he was sitting. Vague images of men illuminated by intermittent flashes of light burst all around him, accompanied by the sound of gunshots echoing through tall trees as shadowed figures ran and fell, screaming in fear and anger.

In the middle of all this anxious chaos stood a man quite still, his face only sporadically visible in the flashes of gunfire. Luang sensed he knew this man, but he could not say his name. A heavy metal gun fell from the man's hand, but the man seemed not to notice the loss of his weapon. He simply stood quietly in the middle of the mayhem surrounding him and stared down at Luang with no pity in his eyes, no anger... nothing. Luang smiled back at the man. It was as if they were blood brothers now, sharing a common bond.

The noise of gunfire slowly eased as overhead clouds cast dark shadows over the palely lit scene, obscuring the light of the moon. Lost in this world of vague images, a place where light could not penetrate, Luang sensed he was dying, but he was not afraid. He felt only peace, a sad, lonely peace. The rhythmic sound of waves breaking softly over a nearby shore offered him comfort. He closed his eyes. His time on this earth was now done.

When he woke up, Luang was sitting in his favorite chair on a deck overlooking his beautiful flower garden. The sun was brightly shining, and for a few brief seconds, he remembered nothing of his dream before it returned to him with great intensity. His eyes grew wide. Terror filled his heart. He immediately understood that he had experienced a vision. A vision telling him his nephew was dead.

And he had seen the face of the man who killed him.

AMBERGRIS ISLAND, BELIZE, FRIDAY, JULY 24, 1998, 8:10 AM, JOHN

Something was different.

That much was obvious. My relationship with Ilana was not like before, not like when I never wanted to leave this island paradise. Now I can't stay here for more than a few weeks at a time. Something begins to tug at me when I am here, calling me, driving me to abandon my beautiful lover and her island home. It is as if a sad, ugly gloom settles over my soul, accompanied by memories of that night. The night I killed that man. In my mind's eye, I am once again in a dark forest, staring at the smiling face of the man I killed.

I see a murderer whenever I look at my reflection in the mirror of her beautiful eyes.

It isn't that I don't love her, don't want the best for her. I still love her, love her deeply. It's just that I don't think I can be with her anymore. Because every time I am with her, I see the man I have become. Being with her is a constant reminder of what I did, a deed I will never ever be able to forget, a night that has changed my life forever. I am not the man I was before, and I don't think I am right for her anymore. I am a different man now, a murderer. She deserves someone better.

Or so I reason... or rationalize... I'm not sure which.

We don't talk about our future anymore, not like before. She doesn't introduce the subject of a future marriage, and neither do I. It is as if we have a tacit agreement to avoid the subject. Marriage is not a word on our lips or on our minds, not like before. Oh, she still wears the ring I gave her. But it does not represent the future as it was once intended. Now, it is simply a reminder of a time in the past that no longer exists for either of us.

She, too, seems to be a different person.

Not for the same reason as me. It's not about what she did. More about what she didn't do. What she held back from me. What had been bothering her. About how she was being harassed by a South American for information. She kept that from me. I wish she had told me that a member of my board of directors was the same man who had originally paid her to spy on me. But she kept this information from me, and I believe it could have changed everything if I had known.

Oh, I understand her reason for not telling me, her fear for her brother's life. And I have forgiven her in my heart. But still, a void exists, a hole that may never heal. She should have come to me and told me what this man was doing to her. She should not have held that back. I think she knows this now.

So, she is different, too. She also carries a heavy weight in her heart because of what happened on an island off the coast of South Carolina. She knows it could have gone very differently if she had confided in me... But she did not.

And I did what I did. Something I should not have done. Now, we both live with the guilt of our actions.

I know she doesn't like it.

Ilana doesn't like it when I leave her island, leave her behind. She has told me this many times. But she also does not wish to travel to the States with me anymore. She prefers to stay in Belize, where she feels safe. This is her home, this island where she was born. She doesn't want to go to that place up north where it is always cold and rainy, the place where I live, the place that has caused her so much pain. She is done with that place. She has made that perfectly clear. And she has also told me on more than one occasion that I should stay with her in her place, on her island. Why not stay, she has asked. I have money, more money than I can ever spend. I don't have to work anymore. I don't need to return to the cold, lonely place where all the trouble began.

'Why don't you live here with me, John? Do you not like it here?' she asked again as I was packing to leave.

I shrugged my shoulders, half-conscious of the real question she was asking, asking why I did not love her enough to stay.

Ignoring her veiled question and all its implications, I grabbed the handle of my suitcase and headed for the door. I didn't look back because I knew if I turned around, I would want to stay. The soft breezes of this Caribbean paradise would pull me back. And her smile, her wonderful smile, and the mischievous look in her big brown eyes, she would lure me to stay. Her soft round body and flowing black hair, everything wonderful which was her would hold me, capture me in this house by the sea.

But this life is not for me, not anymore, only for short stays maybe. But not forever. It can't be forever. This is her world, not mine. That much is clear. She and I are different now. We come from different worlds. We look for peace in different worlds. We can be friends. We can even be lovers. Our bond is deep. But it is a bond that needs space.

This place is no longer my home.

THE ATLANTIC OCEAN, 2:45 P.M. JOHN

The constant low-level droning inside the cabin of an airplane traveling at speed can be very annoying, filled with noisy vibrations capable of penetrating your bones.

This is not the experience you imagine when viewing white jet trails crossing a clear blue sky. A shining silver bird flying in the sky appears to be little more than an afterthought resonating through a lonely void. So, it would seem logical that flying inside one of these wonderful mechanical birds would be an effortless silent journey; the sounds of its jet engines lost far behind, the whisper of its wings hushed like a sharp knife cutting through the air; the experience nothing more than a graceful rip through the high reaches of space.

But in reality, jet plane travel is nothing like this. It is constantly accompanied by grinding friction and low caustic noises filled with busy vibrations. Nothing is smooth and effortless about jet plane travel. When flying, you are continually aware your mechanical bird is forcing its way through the air, making a hole in the sky allowing the plane to pass. The air pushes back in anger, pressing hard against the skin of the plane, expressing its discontent in a din of noisy complaints, unhappy with the presence of a foreign object in a place where it does not belong. It is as if the air will only be content again when it has closed the door behind the unpleasant trespasser and can return to its former free-flowing ways.

Don't get me wrong, I like to travel by plane. It is efficient, and it is easy. But I am never really content while flying. Most of the time, I read or work to free my mind from unease. Sometimes, I write in my journal. I had not written a word for some time. In fact, the last entry in my journal had been months ago. But something significant has occurred since then, something very ugly. Something I don't want to think about but something I need to process.

In one momentous moment of my life, so much danger existed that it should have put an end to my time on this earth. Call it a day, call it a life, call it whatever you want. Nothing more was required, nothing more to think about, nothing more to write because the truth was, given the circumstances, I should have died, been killed instantly by gunfire.

But life is not always predictable. And even though what happened was terrible, it didn't kill me. My time on this earth has continued as if that awful event had never happened. But that doesn't mean it has been easy. In fact, it has been hard and difficult to understand, but it is my life.

In an acknowledgment of my new reality, I have decided I would be good to start writing again, hoping this might help me understand what happened. Because even though it may have been better for my life to have ended in the forest where I killed a man, this was not what happened. I lived. And it is difficult to stop living when you are not dead. You sleep, you get up, you eat, because you must. You don't have a choice, none of which makes sense some days. But that doesn't mean that things don't change. How we live can be different, very different after a tragic event.

In my case I have been going through all the motions, but not really living.

The real truth is that all I have been doing is running, running mentally as hard and as fast as I can from my past. Running from the memory of the man I have become, the man who is a killer. I don't like this man. I don't want to be this man. But I am this man. I am him every time I stop running. But this doesn't stop me from running, running as fast as I can to get away from this man. Running anywhere, any place which might prevent the man I have become from finding me.

But it never takes long for my killer friend to catch me once again.

CHARLOTTESVILLE, VIRGINIA, FRIDAY, JULY 31, 5:55 PM. JOHN

I was in my office on a Friday afternoon.

It was after five-thirty, almost six. I had nowhere to go. And no one... specifically, no one of the soft feminine gender, was waiting for me in my apartment. I was alone. My office was empty. The staff gone home. Helen, my secretary, had left a few minutes earlier after I forced her out by telling her I wouldn't need her services anymore today.

'Go home, Helen, and enjoy the weekend. See you on Monday.'

But I don't think Helen enjoys time off from work any more than I do. She is a loner like me. Her husband is dead. Her only daughter is married and living in another city. Grandchildren are shielded from Helen by a son-in-law who doesn't like her. I have been told that this is the result of some conflict in the past, which keeps them apart except for short visits. It is the sort of thing that can happen in any family. As a result, her job is her life. I understand, but I can't help her any more than I can help myself.

And I need help. I know I need help. I have not been very civil to her or to any of my other employees since returning from Belize. Mostly, I have holed up in my office and worked with a genuine lack of enthusiasm or humor, just putting in my time.

Charlie came into my head at that moment. Don't know why I thought about him, just needed someone to think about. It was possible he was still in his office in Langley, Virginia, home of the CIA. He was a workaholic like me. I decided to call him. After his phone rang hollow in my ear several times, I became convinced he had gone home for the day.

However, before I could put my phone down, he answered. 'John.'

'Charlie, you're still working? Don't you have a life?'

'Not any more than you.'

'So, it would seem.'

'What can I do for you?' he inquired.

'Oh, nothing, just thought I would call.'

'No hair-brained schemes on your mind, I hope?'

I assumed he was referring to my plan to catch my adversary in a lie. It didn't go well. In fact, it had all gone wrong. I killed the man instead.

'No.'

'So why call?'

'Don't know. Can't a couple of buddies talk?'

'So, are you my buddy now? Because most of the time when you call, it's because you want something. Why don't we cut the bullshit, and you just tell me what it is you want?'

'I don't want anything.'

'John.'

I paused before saying, 'It's just... I don't have anyone to talk to... you know... about what happened. Someone like you who could understand.'

'Are you okay, John?' his voice suddenly sounded serious.

'No, probably not.'

'Be serious for a minute.'

'I am being serious.'

'What's going on John?'

Pause... I didn't know how to answer him. In fact, now I wished I hadn't called him. I suddenly wanted to hang up. 'Nothing really, sorry... I shouldn't have bothered you.'

'How's Ilana?' he asked, changing the subject.

'Oh, she's fine.'

'Is she with you?'

'No, she's in Belize.'

'Are you two still together?' he probed.

'No, I guess you could say we broke up.'

'Why, I thought you were getting married?'

'No, not anymore. It didn't work out.'

'I thought you were in love?'

'Charlie, it's personal.'

He paused. 'It's because of what happened, isn't it?'

'I guess you could say that.'

'How you sleeping, John?'

'What's that got to do with anything?' I started to feel like he was digging too deep. It was time to end this conversation.

'Just answer the question,' he demanded. Charlie was Charlie. He was direct, if nothing else.

'Not well. And now that we have finished discussing my sleeping habits, hey, thanks for taking my call. It's been great talking to...'

'Don't hang up, John.'

'Why.'

'Look, John, I have seen this before in some of my colleagues after they had a tough experience, shot someone or got shot. That kind of thing takes a toll. Sounds to me like you have a problem. And John, it can be serious. You need to get help.'

'I'm fine, Charlie.'

'I doubt that. You should see someone.'

'Like you.'

'No, like a shrink.'

'I don't need a shrink.'

'I think you do.'

'It's been great talking to you, Charlie.'

'John, take my advice.'

'Have a good weekend, Charlie.' I hung up.

SATURDAY, AUGUST 1, 5:35 PM. JOHN

Bored and irritable may seem like an unlikely combination of emotions, but it was how I felt that Saturday afternoon.

I didn't sleep well Friday; up most of the night, watched TV, and tried to read a book; nothing worked, nothing took my mind off my call to Charlie, what he had said about seeing a shrink. That was the last thing I wanted to do because what could I tell a shrink? Should I tell him I had shot a man to death? How would he ever understand a thing like that? Because I didn't. I didn't understand it. So, how was I going to explain it to him? I was both ashamed and afraid at the same time. Ashamed of what I had done and afraid the cops were going to come and put me in jail for my crime.

Seeing a shrink was out. Charlie was wrong. I would just have to deal with my problem my way, determined to get through this thing on my own terms.

The telephone in my apartment rang, interrupting my thoughts.

The caller must have thought Saturday afternoon was a good time to call when I wasn't busy and in my apartment alone. But the caller didn't know me, didn't know I wouldn't pick up, something I seldom did in my apartment. But that afternoon, the caller was rewarded. I was bored. I answered the telephone.

'Hi John,' Ilana said.

I didn't respond immediately. I wasn't sure I wanted to talk to her.

'You there, John?' she questioned.

'Yes, I'm here.'

'How are you?'

'Fine, I guess. How are you?'

'I'm good, John, but I am missing you. When are you coming for a visit?'

'I wish I could tell you. I've been busy at work, you know.' I lied.

'That's not the real reason you won't come, is it John?'

'No... I guess you know it isn't.'

'Yes, I know.'

'I'm sorry, Ilana.'

'I'm sorry too, John.'

'I wish it hadn't happened.'

The face of Nue immediately came to my mind's eye, his smiling, dying face, telling me I was like him now. I was a murderer, just like him. You are just like me now, John Van Laan, he said with a smile. I had tried to look away from his face, but I didn't, not till it was too late. Now, his image was sharply engraved on my mind. His eyes and his smile continued to grin at me from beyond the grave.

'We can't change what happened,' Ilana observed.

'I know. I wish we could.'

'Will you ever come to see me again?'

'I don't know, Ilana. I don't really know. I'm sorry.'

'I understand. And I am sorry, too. I wish I had told you...'

'Ilana, stop. Please stop. I don't blame you. You know that.'

Our conversation was becoming more irritating the longer it continued. It was time to end it. She instinctively understood.

'It was good to talk to you, John. May I call you again sometime?'

'Of course.'

'Will you call me?'

When I didn't reply immediately, she said, 'Goodbye John.'

'Goodbye, Ilana.'

My phone went silent.

I poured a glass of whiskey in the kitchen and took it to my back balcony to spend some time outside, alone with the trees behind my apartment as my only companions.

BANGKOK, THAILAND, MONDAY, AUGUST 3, 2:20 P.M. LUANG

The old patriarch slowly climbed the stone stairs leading to the formal entrance to his family's mansion.

Two grand wooden doors carved hundreds of years ago waited for him to open and beckoned him inside, welcoming him once more into his former home. Luang remembered all the days he had climbed these steps in the past. First as a boy, then as a young man, and finally as the person who ruled this house. So many experiences, so much of his life was tied to this old mansion and its many stately rooms. But even though he loved this place, he was not happy to be returning.

Not today, not ever.

His legacy was seriously out of order. No former head of the family had ever returned to live in this mansion after leaving it. They were either buried after dying in this place, or they lived out their life somewhere else, their time in this mansion over, their life's work completed; their duties to their family and their country entrusted to someone else, someone younger and stronger who now lived in the mansion. Luang didn't like what he was about to do. He didn't like breaking with tradition. It was a bad omen. But this was a bad time. He knew it was necessary.

His nephew, the current ruler, was dead.

Luang had been informed by US authorities that his nephew and bodyguards were killed in a helicopter crash somewhere off the coast of America in the Atlantic Ocean. Their bodies had not been recovered because their helicopter had crashed in an area of deep water and sank quickly to the bottom of the ocean with all on board, too far down to be retrieved.

However, the old patriarch did not believe what he was told. A vision had offered Luang a different explanation. Every detail of this horrible vision was deeply engrained in his mind. In the vision, his nephew was shot to death. And the killer was a free man, never charged with his nephew's murder, never confronted by the police.

Luang had no way of establishing the truth. An investigation might uncover the facts, but to his knowledge, no investigation was being conducted. Even though Luang had pleaded for an investigation through diplomatic channels, all his efforts had been in vain. Not that it mattered. Luang was convinced he knew the truth. He believed his vision. It gave him all the evidence he required. The truth was that his nephew had been killed in cold blood.

Luang had always attempted to live by the law. The law was his guide, his life conducted under the rules of law, international law. He was an honorable man. But in this case the law had failed him.

So many questions needed to be asked and revenge exacted. The man who was responsible must pay for killing his nephew. The murderer must die. But this was work for another day. Today, he had more pressing business. The death of his nephew created a power vacuum at the top of the family. No one was currently in charge. His nephew's son, the legitimate heir to the seat of power, was too young and inexperienced in his early twenties. The young man had much to learn before he could be given control. The old patriarch appointed himself a mentor to his nephew's young son. Until the young man was ready, Luang would assume the position of power.

The family had agreed.

For this reason, Luang was returning to live in the old mansion, the symbolic seat of power. The move solidified his right to be in control. In addition, his nephew's son lived in the mansion. It would allow Luang to work with the boy. Help the boy learn what he needed to know for when it was time for him to assume the chair of power at the end of the long conference table.

Luang climbed the steps leading up to the carved wooden doors with mixed emotions. This had been his home in the past, a place he had always enjoyed, where he had lived comfortably.

Now, the mansion was to be his home again, but nothing was as it should be.

GRAND HAVEN, MICHIGAN, USA, TUESDAY, AUGUST 18, 3:55 P.M. JOHN

She saw me before I saw her.

It was one of those picture-perfect days in Western Michigan, which only occurs a few times each year in the summer. The sun was bright in a cool blue sky devoid of clouds with a gentle, warm breeze to keep the air temperature from becoming too hot.

I had flown from Charlottesville to Grand Haven, Michigan where I own a cottage on Lake Michigan. It is my connection to my past, my hometown. It is where I go to relax, to get away from the grind of work and problems, especially problems I did not want to think about, like the problems I was currently facing. I had hoped a change of scenery might alter my mood and offer me some relief. Besides, August is normally a slow time of year in the gem business. With not much to do and too much time on my hands, I figured I was better off somewhere other than my office, anywhere else. My cottage on Lake Michigan seemed as good a place as any. But it wasn't really working. Unfortunately, my problems had traveled with me despite my intention to leave them behind.

Driving into town was my required task for that day. I needed supplies. Even though I don't like to shop, I have discovered that food is essential to life, and it doesn't appear out of thin air. Supermarkets are apparently a convenient place to find food, but you have to go there, walk the aisles, sort through vast quantities of goods on endless shelves, make proper decisions, meaning no junk food... and avoid eye contact at all costs. Too many people know me in this small-minded town from my younger days; too many don't hold a very high opinion of me. I have been told that I have Phillip Palmer to thank for this. Apparently, false rumors and back-biting gossip about me had been initiated on his lips. But I couldn't control him, and I didn't intend to try. Instead, I try to be efficient when I am in the public eye, like locating the essentials I need in the store quickly and getting out fast.

After filling my cart with the food on my list, I went in search of a better lamp for my desk. I often work at night. Even when on vacation. My job has some demands, and it is easier to work after the sun goes down. Besides, I don't really mind. It's something to do, to fill the time. For this, I needed a good desk lamp, and mine had died, which was frustrating because finding a good lamp took time. Finally, I threw one my cart and headed for the worst part of the shopping experience: waiting in line for checkout because I hate to wait.

After successfully completing my necessarily unpleasant shopping excursion, I decided a reward was in order, like a drive into town for an ice cream cone. Under a disguise of sunglasses and a large brimmed straw hat, I joined a nameless throng of tourists and natives walking a sidewalk parallel to the channel. It was an easy stroll, the scenery pleasant, and a cooling breeze off the lake made it a joy.

The channel is a waterway connecting the Grand River to the vast open waters of Lake Michigan. On stormy days, it is a roller coaster ride of huge gray lake waves crisscrossing between concrete retaining walls. But this day, it was a gentle, placid, smooth ribbon of blue water occupied by speedboats sporting sleek white fiberglass hulls along with a few gas-guzzling cruisers with gleaming flying bridges in an endless parade as they meandered through a designated no-wake zone leading to Lake Michigan. They were the envy of us poor, boatless channel strollers.

After buying an ice cream cone from a vendor situated along the channel, butter pecan, my favorite, I took a break. An unoccupied bench overlooking the channel under the shade of a tree looked inviting. Plus, the local female scenery presented entertaining viewing. Dressed in scantily attired short shorts and tightly wrapped halter tops, the young lovelies elicited memories of days when my high school buddies and I trolled the channel in outboard motorboats in hopeful anticipation of luring unsuspecting female beauties into our boat for some innocent fun in the sun.

While licking my ice cream cone with memories from my youth pleasantly circulating in my overcooked brain, she appeared like a dream out of the past, a dream that couldn't be real. I must have looked dumbly startled when I first saw her, staring with my mouth open and ice cream dripping from my chin, mesmerized by the thought that she was a figment of my imagination.

She gave me a sly smile, which I knew from the past meant nothing but trouble, and sat down beside me without saying a word, waiting in the warm sunshine for me to say something, anything even slightly intelligent.

A tall blonde with beautiful features, she had a sense of the world that seemed to inhabit her space, making everything around her good and sweet and naturally alluring. When we first met in high school, we instantly fell in love, or at least I did. Puppy love is what I guess it was called at the time. We were young, seventeen, but we thought of ourselves as adults. In our undeveloped brains, love was certain and pure. Perhaps we would eventually marry and live happily ever after. Why not? Wasn't this the natural course of events?

Well, it didn't exactly work out as we fanaticized, mostly due to our naivete. I guess we were not quite ready to marry, but we sure as hell were ready to have sex. Or, more accurately, I was ready to have sex. She, on the other hand, simply thought it was as it should be. Sex was a natural thing, wasn't it? She understood. We had good times and pleasures I have never forgotten.

But unhappily, our ideas of love and everlasting romance contrasted wildly with the ideals of our parents. And in the end, nothing but trouble came from our adolescent mussing. She, I, and love lived on one side of the contest. Our parents and religious negativity existed on the other side. Of course, we lost this battle. I was forced to walk away. Not that I ever totally let her go. I loved her even after we separated. And I had never really stopped loving her, even as time and space separated us.

In retrospect it was probably best we separated. Or maybe not. Perhaps she was my one real soul mate, and I should have never let her go. I don't know. Does it matter what happens in the past? Does time diminish the importance? I am not sure. Anyway, I was so shocked to see her I just stared at her without saying a word until it was obvious even to me that she was not a dream.

'Sandy Voss?' I finally exclaimed.

'John Van Laan, it has been a long time,' she responded serenely.

'So, it really is you. I'm sorry,' I apologized. 'I just never expected to see you here. Don't you live in California?'

'Yes.'

'So what are you doing here?' I asked witlessly.

'I'm here to visit my sister.'

It wasn't until that moment I noticed the gorgeous dark-haired woman standing next to her. The last time I saw this tall beauty, she was Sandy's little sister in pigtails and I never imagined she would grow up to be so pretty. Two tow-headed kids were next to her, pulling on her arms.

'Karen.' I stood up to greet her.

'Hi John,' she replied.

'Wow, you sure have grown up. And kids too?'

'Yes, Betsy and Johnny,' she quickly added. 'My son is named after his father.'

'Oh, of course.'

'Mom, you promised me an ice cream cone,' Johnny wined, staring at my cone.

'In a minute,' Karen responded while her daughter waited patiently, peeking around her mother's tan legs.

'As you can see, I have to go,' Sandy interrupted. 'Nice to see you again, John.' She took the little girl's hand.

'Are you staying long?' I asked quickly.

'A few days.'

'Can I call you?'

'Of course, silly. Do you want my number?'

I didn't have a pen, and little Johnny appeared to be ready to throw a tantrum if he didn't get an ice cream cone immediately, if not sooner. I took a business card out of my wallet and lamely gave it to her. It had my cell phone number.

I asked her to call me when she had the time.

WEDNESDAY, AUGUST 19, 2:35 P.M. JOHN

A hot wind blew whitecaps across the restless waters of Lake Michigan as beach grass on shore danced to the steady rhythm of the breeze.

The escalating wind off the lake offered only minimal relief from the heat as I sat mesmerized by aggravated waves near shore rising up in mighty, majestic walls of smooth green water before spilling over in disintegrating shows of fiercely rushing whitewater. The constant roar of the crashing water was mentally disconcerting, as if something terrible lived near the shore, something which wanted to take you into its arms and trash your tender body in the mayhem that lived in the lake.

My day had been a wash.

Nothing of importance had been accomplished in the way of work, nothing good. Even though I had earlier promised myself I would get some work done, I was just not motivated. Every time I went into my cottage office to accomplish something, I couldn't concentrate.

I thought of calling my good buddy David, who lived in town. Maybe ask if he and his family would like to come for a swim after work. But that didn't make much sense. The lake was angry, the waves large. Lovely Mary, his wife, would never allow their boys to swim in the currents. It was too dangerous. An undertow lived in the aggravated water, a strong current that could drag a young swimmer unwittingly into the lake to drown.

So, I didn't call David, and I didn't accomplish anything constructive. Mostly, I simply wandered around in my cottage looking for something to occupy my time, my mind, anything to keep from becoming depressed. I tried reading a book but couldn't. Again, no concentration. My mind was somewhere else, somewhere out in the restless waters of the lake. I put the book down and wandered out on the deck to watch the waves break over hidden sandbars. A storm was coming. I could feel it in my bones. Nothing on the horizon yet, but it was out there.

Thoughts of my beautiful Ilana raced in on the storm winds. I couldn't help but remember thinking of her and how I had survived a tropical depression while sailing together in the Caribbean. I'm not sure I would have made it without her. At the time, I was sailing away from men who had tried to kill me, hired killers who had blown up a house I was renting by the sea. I had been lucky. I had been outside at the time of the explosion on a dock. I escaped by sailing away while watching my house burn, smoke, and fire leaping into the night sky. I could still see the scene clearly in my mind: a house burning red against a black night sky filled with gray smoke. A sick feeling of Paradise Lost settled slowly into my gut as I sailed out beyond the sheltering reef off the coast of Belize to where my boat could not be identified from shore. The next morning, a storm arrived, and we almost drowned in the wind and waves.

The coming storm over Lake Michigan brought back these memories. Ilana is on my mind again. And with her was the man in the forest. She was there the night I killed the man who had tried to kill me. He was on my mind, messing with my head, bringing me down. Filled with an ugly depression, an inky-black sadness that was difficult to escape. My nights had been bad lately, filled with bloody nightmares of dark forests and the sound of guns. And days when I accomplished nothing, brooding hours when all I wanted was to be alone. Time lost to doing nothing, a downward spiral into a world covered with fear.

I badly needed to stop thinking about that man and start thinking about something else, something more pleasant. I deliberately decided to think about Sandy instead, about how she had innocently sat down beside me on a bench by the channel, her blonde hair blowing in the breeze, her big blue eyes, and her sly smile. And I thought about how lame I had acted in her presence, how she had caught me off guard. I wasn't ready for her. But then, I was never really ready for that woman.

And I wondered why I gave her my card instead of getting her phone number. That was stupid. Because I wanted to call her, but I didn't have her number. I knew she was staying with her sister, but I didn't know her sister's married name, so I couldn't exactly look up her number in the telephone book. Perhaps my friend David who lived in this town would know. I could ask him for her sister's name. But for some reason, I didn't really understand; I didn't want David to know about Sandy. I wanted to keep Sandy for myself for now. So, I didn't call David.

All this meant I had to submit to waiting for her to call me. It was sort of like being in high school all over again. Like when I was afraid to call girls for dates for fear of suffering the humiliation of being shot down. And girls didn't call boys; most girls didn't, not in those days. And this meant I spent much of my early teens time fantasizing, dreaming about girls instead of doing something constructive, like studying.

And that's why the best part about my teenage love affair with Sandy was we instantly knew we liked being with each other. We established a bond early. I never had to endure that time at the beginning of a relationship with Sandy that was like other romances, that time of wondering if my puppy love would be rejected or accepted. I wasn't forced to live with that unsettling feeling of wandering around helpless in a desert of whimpering need searching for water. I never liked this stage in a relationship. So, when it quickly became apparent that she and I shared a kind of restless understanding, nothing deep, but at a minimum, something comfortable, it was great. From the beginning we seemed to form a kind of metaphysical bond, as if we alone existed in the world, a world we shared with no one else. It was our world. We easily concluded this meant we were in love, which may or may not have been true. It was possible we had simply found someone we enjoyed. Existing for a time in a world we did not understand and did not understand us, nothing more. Or perhaps it wasn't love at all, only a convenient bond that allowed us to spend time together, share common experiences, and develop a common language only we understood, words only we knew the true meaning of. Just being with her, holding her hand, kissing her lips, seeing her smile, times stolen from the closely controlled world imposed on us by the nihilistic society orchestrated by our parents, our school, our church; a system completely out of touch with what we desired.

Unfortunately, our ideal relationship quickly became too intense for our immediate adult supervisors, our parents. They didn't understand.

This is a common theme for teenagers. I know. I understand. But in our case, it was true. However, in our parent's defense, we did nothing to ease their anxieties. For example, we enjoyed making out in school halls between classes. Something which was not considered proper behavior by our authoritarian teachers. And when it was reported to our parents, they expressed no appreciation for how much fun it was.

Same for when we stay out too late, not a behavior acceptable to our parents. But staying out late was fun. Making out was fun. And she was beautiful, and I was young and horny, and well... do I need to say more. She was irresistible. But this activity became much too problematic. And in the end, the powers of the church and the adult society were destined to overwhelm us. We were not allowed to continue together. They hounded us until we drew apart. We were too young and too weak to stand up to their pressure.

Anyway, I kept thinking, hoping she would call me now... or maybe not. Maybe I would never hear from her again. This time, everything was different, and it was possible she had no reason, no interest in calling me now. Maybe she didn't want to see me again. Maybe she was already in a relationship. Maybe this time was not like the first time. Just because I wanted to see her again did not mean she wanted to see me. I didn't know. Did she, or did she not? Would she call, or would she not? It was just like when we used to pick petals off a dandelion one at a time until the last petal gave us an answer to our question: did she love me or did she not?

Waves rolled on shore in endless succession from across the lake as I sat on the deck of my cottage, wave after wave falling in crashing confusion before rolling up the beach. As I watched, temporarily engrossed in the vast, wild, wet scenery that stretched out below me from one end of the horizon to the other, I had an odd sensation of being in high school again. Wanting her, wanting to be with Sandy every minute of every day, only content when we were together.

That's how it was then. And it was how it was for me now. Because I knew I badly needed something, someone who could rescue me from a depression that was threatening to take over my lonely existence.

And I had this strange and irrational thought that she might be the only person in the world who could do that for me.

3:15 P.M. JOHN

The unwelcome intrusion of a ringing phone abruptly interrupted my afternoon reprieve from anxieties, which had become my world.

I had fallen asleep on a couch after again trying to read a book, anything to take my mind off my troubles. Half in anger, half in jest, I picked up the offending instrument responsible for this mildly criminal act. My first impulse was to give the harassing apparatus a toss. I didn't really want to talk to anyone. By this time in the afternoon, I was happy to be alone. If Sandy had wanted to call, she would have done it by now. So, I put her out of my mind. I decided I had enough problems. One woman was more than enough for me. I didn't need another complication. I decided it was best this way.

'Hello.'

'Hey, old buddy,' David said to my relief.

'David, I was just thinking about you,' I lied. 'How's it going?'

'Good. Say, any plans for tomorrow?'

'No, why don't you and the kids come over?' I asked.

'Sure, thanks,' David responded. 'You read my mind. The weather is supposed to be better tomorrow. The kids would like to go swimming, and well, I could use an afternoon off. And it would give us time to catch up.'

'Sounds great.'

'Swell, Mary gave me explicit instructions to tell you we will bring food. You don't need to do anything.'

'Hey, I have food, you know.'

'I know, but you know Mary. She likes to be in charge. So, let her do her thing,' he half pleaded.

I understood. Mary never felt completely comfortable around me. David and I had a friendship that began in grade school. Mary showed up later in high school. I always sensed she felt she needed to earn her way into our established relationship. Maybe she still did. Or maybe it was just being around me. I'm single. I don't fit her world and life view.

'Sure, David, have Mary bring food. I'll be here.'

'Say around eleven then? We'll come for lunch.'

'Great.'

He hung up.

Almost immediately, the phone rang again. I had an urge to ignore it, get up instead, and go for a swim. The wild lake was calling me. Something alive in the water was beckoning. I wanted to be a companion to its violence. The rushing, angry waters mimicked my mood, inviting me to join in the fun. Something to occupy my mind and my time, live with the wind and the waves for a while, and just let the breaking waves wash over my disturbed anxieties.

I hesitated, looked at the phone, hesitated again, and began to walk away. But at the last second, I answered it. Seemed like the socially responsible thing to do.

'Hello,' I replied, hoping it was the wrong number.

'Hi John,' she said, her voice soft, controlled, confident, tinted with a sweet smile of self-confidence.

Immediately, I knew it was her. Something in the sound of voice never failed to excite me.

'Sandy?'

'Who else would it be?' she answered. 'How many women call you on this line?'

'Well, I'm not sure I should answer that question.'

'Why not?'

'I wouldn't want you to get the wrong idea.'

'Why does it matter what I think about you?'

It didn't take her two minutes to push me into a corner. If I answered yes, then it might appear as if I was too interested in seeing her again. But if I said no, it might seem I had no interest. Either way, I was doomed. I decided to be honest with her. Something buried deep in my memory banks told me anything, but the truth would be a mistake when dealing with this woman.

'Yes, it matters,' I replied.

'Why would it matter, John?'

As soon as the words escaped my mouth, I knew she had me, and she knew it, too. So, I said the only thing I could say under the circumstances. I said. 'Because I'm still in love with you.'

'Oh,... I see,' she replied cautiously.

My comment slowed her down, but not for long.

'Well, I'm not surprised,' she responded.

I decided to go on the offensive. Retreat was never an option with this lady. 'Why are you not surprised?' I asked

'Because you have always been in love with me. I know that.'

'So what are we going to do about this?' I replied.

'I don't know. Should we do something about it?' she answered innocently.

'Of course, when two people are in love, they always know what to do.'

'But I haven't said I'm in love with you,' she replied.

'Are you?'

'I'll have to think about that.'

'How long will it take you to think about it?'

'I'm not sure.'

'I see. Well, what should we do in the meantime?'

'I don't really know, but I guess I could have dinner with you,' she suggested. 'Do you think you would like to do that?'

'Yes, I think I would. How about the Kirby Grill at seven?' I suggested before I could consider the consequences. Deep inside my muddled brain, I knew I might be making a mistake. But why? How could it hurt to have dinner with an old friend?

'Make it six if you don't mind.'

'Sure, see you there.'

5:35 P.M. JOHN

A bullet shattered the driver's side window, propelling finely dispersed shards of transparent glass like shooting stars into the air, passing inches in front of my eyes before exiting through a newly formed hole in the windshield.

Instinctively jerking the steering wheel away from the loudly abrasive assault caused my Corvette to fishtail wildly sideways, tires screaming over the concrete highway under anti-lock braking, and my foot jammed hard against the brakes in panic. Searing pain immediately spread across my forehead as blood poured freely from deeply embedded shattered glass wounds over my eyes.

Visibility was quickly lost in a murky red blur as I rubbed my eyes in a vain attempt to extricate reality from mass confusion. I was nothing more than a passenger in an out-of-control automobile wildly fishtailing down the road in the path of a big, bright red semi-trailer loaded with gasoline coming up fast behind me. The semi driver was helpless, unable to stop in time. Onrushing momentum of tons of truck metal and contained liquid gas crushed the left rear quarter panel of my Corvette, sending it like a projectile headed straight for the deep ditch separating competing four lanes of a divided highway. My head bounced hard against the headrest from the unanticipated impact with the truck; my status was reduced to a stunned participant on an unauthorized thrill ride. Releasing a clenched white-knuckle fist from the steering wheel to wipe the blood from my eyes, I didn't like what I saw. The other side of the highway across the deep grassy medium was coming directly at me at high speed. An all too brief moment of silent reprieve followed as my Vette flew innocently suspended in midair over the ditch before violently hitting the opposite bank in a blast of exploding dirt, dust, and gravel. The car bounced, careening out of the medium into oncoming highway traffic as an old lady in a white Oldsmobile Aurora headed directly for me. I don't think she ever hit the brakes. All I saw was the startled look on her face.

Turning the steering wheel hard left towards the shoulder, praying no traffic was in the right lane, I barely avoided her Aurora. Tires of my Vette dug into the soft gravel in a vain attempt to correct the slide, and for a moment, I thought I had won the battle, but then the rear end came loose again as I fishtailed uncontrollably onto the pavement into a lucky gap in oncoming traffic, providing a welcome opportunity to safely turn into the slide across two lanes of the highway, tires screaming in derision, finally slowing and pulling off the road onto a gravel shoulder. I came to a stop just as a car passed from the opposite direction, its horn haughtily blaring at my wrong-way intrusion onto its side of the highway.

Breathing deeply while trying to regain control of my panicked emotions, I wiped the blood from my eyes. Turning the visor down and sliding open the vanity mirror to view the damage to my face, I was not a pretty site. I looked bad, blood everywhere, the collar of my blue denim shirt a coagulating red mess. Wiping the blood off my forehead with the sleeve of my shirt revealed a few cuts on my forehead above my sunglasses, streaming blood. I had to constantly wipe away the mess of blood in order to see, but the wounds didn't hurt much, considering all the blood.

I was only vaguely aware of a Ford Taurus completing a U-turn at an intersection up the road before heading my way, causing a random concern that quickly crossed a barrier from my subconscious to my consciously confused brain, forcing me to consider that perhaps this was the car I had seen in my side mirror before a bullet hit my car. I concluded I didn't have the luxury of waiting around for an answer. It was time to go. If the guy with the gun was in that car, I didn't want to give him an open shot. He probably wouldn't miss the next time.

Pedal to the metal with the Vette's crushed rear quarter-panel fiberglass wounds flapping in the wind; thankfully, the damage didn't affect the rear suspension, and my car was still operable. Headed the wrong way down the highway, I bounced down the gravel shoulder, swerving to avoid the Taurus bearing down on me. He may have taken another shot. I wasn't sure, but nothing hit me as I sped past him. Turning at the first intersection, crossing quickly to the proper side of the divided highway, I accelerated towards the police station in Grand Haven.

6:25 P.M. JOHN

Leaving the scene of an accident is a criminal offense.

I had some explaining to do after arriving at the police station. But after the law enforcement officers examined my broken car and saw where a bullet had shattered the windshield and another had dug a hole in one of the fenders, they finally took pity on me and agreed to drive me to the hospital to get my forehead cleaned and stitched.

And it wasn't easy to get a hostess at the restaurant to agree to find her. Apparently, she was too busy to help me when I called. She had other more important work to do. It took my asking my new cop friend to get on my cell phone while I sat in the back of his patrol car on the way to the hospital. The cop convinced her. He told her I had been injured in an automobile accident. And given my rather dire circumstances, it might be nice to help me by finding my date.

The hostess said Sandy was still in the restaurant and agreed to get her on the phone.

'Yes, John.' Sandy replied with less than her normal enthusiasm.

I couldn't blame her. I was currently twenty-five minutes late for our dinner date. 'I had an accident on my way to the restaurant,' I tried to explain.

'Are you okay?'

'I'm fine,' I replied, momentarily reliving the horrific moments of the crash with the sounds of gunshots still echoing in my bruised brain. I was physically okay, well mostly, no major damage, but mentally I was a mess. Adrenalin had by now drained from my body, and the reality of my circumstances was descending on me like a load of heavy, wet cement. I needed some relief, anything to take my mind off my troubles. Sandy's smile seemed like the perfect solution to my situation. I subconsciously knew it was wrong to involve her in my mess, but I couldn't think of anything else that might keep me from sliding into a deep mental pit of inexhaustible sadness.

'I don't think I'm going to be able to have dinner with you tonight,' I said through a mental haze.

'That's okay John, some other time maybe,' she replied as if it was no big deal.

Now, this wasn't exactly the response I had been hoping for. Sympathy was what I wanted instead. After all, I was badly shaken up. My car was severely damaged, and I had almost been killed. But worse was the fact that my personal nightmare was becoming a reality again. Just when I thought all the nasty business of someone trying to kill me was behind me, apparently, it was happening again, this time with a new and improved vengeance. The man in the forest, the man I had killed. It was as if he had come back to life from the dead to haunt me. He was after me again.

I hadn't had enough time to absorb the full extent of my situation. I didn't completely understand it, but one thought was perfectly clear. I didn't want to go through any more near-death experiences. I had done that before, and I didn't know if I had the strength to deal with them anymore. However, at that moment; all I wanted was to forget about all that and spend some time with her. So, I did what any normal male would do under the circumstances, I begged.

'Sandy, I know this is asking a lot, but could I ask a favor?'

'Depends.'

'Depends on what?'

'Depends on what the favor is, silly,' she said.

'Could you meet me at the hospital? Drive me home?'

'That's a lot to ask, John.'

'Not really. I have a nice place on the lake. We could see the sunset.'

'Is that all you want?' she asked mischievously.

I temporarily ignored the implications of her comment and went on begging. 'Look, Sandy, I had a really bad experience tonight. I was almost killed. I could use some company. It would mean a lot to me.'

'What happened, John?'

'I'll explain when I see you.'

'I don't know John. I've had a very busy day.'

'For old time's sake. Please, Sandy.'

BANGKOK, THAILAND, SATURDAY, AUGUST 22, 6:15 A.M. LUANG

The old patriarch put down his phone very slowly.

He had been concentrating, intent on listening every word of his phone conversation. As a result, he had not noticed the young man come into his bedroom.

The young man was twenty-two years of age. Sophon Nue was his name. Taller than his dead father with the same black hair and piercing eyes, he was better-looking, almost beautiful like his mother; not pretty, but a handsome young man.

The old patriarch was very proud of the boy. In fact, in many ways, Luang felt closer to the boy than to his father. Luang had never married. After his brother and wife were killed in an unfortunate automobile accident, his brother's son, known simply as Nue, became the rightful heir to the seat of power, the person who would one day run the family's businesses. For this reason, Luang asked Nue and his young family to live with him in the mansion until the time when Luang was ready to give up control. Nue's child, Sophon, had grown up in the mansion and became like a grandson to the old patriarch.

When Sophon heard the phone ring in the early hours of the morning, the young man came into his great uncle's bedroom. Sophon wasn't sleeping at the time because he knew what was happening, and he had been waiting impatiently for the phone to ring, afraid to sleep, wanting to hear it was done, wanting to know his father's murderer was dead.

The boy knew the truth. He knew how his father had died. Luang told Sophon about a telephone conversation he had recently had with a man named Phillip Palmer. Phillip confirmed the real cause of his nephew's death. Phillip established the truth of Luang's vision. So, the truth was known, and the boy knew the truth. The boy wanted revenge for his father's death.

Sophon anxiously scanning his great uncle's face for a sign after his Uncle hung up his phone. Sophon saw nothing, nothing to tell him what he wanted know. His uncle's face appeared to be made of stone, expressionless, with cold, hard eyes.

'He's not dead?' Sophon questioned. 'The man who shot my father, he is not dead?'

'No, I am sorry. He survived,' Luang replied in a trance of regret.

'I should kill this man myself.' Sophon reacted.

His great-uncle looked at him. 'No. You will do as I say. You will stay in this house until it is your time.'

'No, I am going to kill this man, and you cannot make me stay. You are not my father.'

Luang watched Sophon turn to leave the room. It was obvious the young man was very angry. The old man decided to wait to talk to him. Morning would be soon enough. Let him calm down first. Everything would look different after the sun came up. Luang turned out the light beside his bed and lay down.

But as he rested, he sensed the boy was no longer inside the house.

GRAND HAVEN, MICHIGAN, 8:05 P.M. JOHN

An occasional flash of lightning emblazoned a line of churning black clouds near the horizon over the lake.

The sun had disappeared early, and the sky over the lake was dark.

I poured her a glass of wine, trying to keep my hand steady. It wasn't easy. I think she noticed.

She had agreed to meet me at the hospital and drive me home, but she promised nothing more. Unfortunately, my medical stay at the hospital had taken longer than anticipated. The ER docs were busy. I was not a high priority. Other patients arrived more critically hurt than me. Eventually, a doctor got around to removing the broken glass from my forehead and putting in a few stitches. She said it wasn't that bad and said I should heal nicely with no major scars. I told her I was already ugly, so it didn't really matter. She smiled and said I would look a lot prettier when the cuts healed.

I wasn't sure Sandy would still be in the waiting room when I was finally released, but thankfully, she had waited.

She smiled when she saw me.

'Still willing to drive me home?' I asked.

The bandages on my forehead and dried blood on my shirt must have made me look like a war refugee. Perhaps this was the only reason she agreed. Her motherly instinct took over. I didn't care why. I was just happy she was willing.

A police car followed us down Lake Shore Drive to my cottage. I wasn't sure the cops totally believed the story I told them when they took my statement at the police station, but they had agreed to keep an eye on my cottage for a few days as a courtesy. I didn't know what Sandy was thinking when she looked in her rear-view mirror, but I assumed she didn't think having a cop following us was a normal everyday event. However, she didn't ask why, and she didn't complain. She just listened to my directions as we drove in silence.

None of this was as I had imagined. I had been looking forward to having a casual dinner with her, maybe some reminiscing about our youth, maybe even talking about getting together again before she flew home. But to be honest, I hadn't thought beyond this evening. I only wanted to enjoy our meal.

She looked good. She was still the same tall, blond, blue eyed Dutch girl I remembered; older now, but with the same smooth skin. We grew up together, went to the same church, and played on the same school playground as the other children. I guess I always knew her, but it wasn't until high school that I really started to notice her. This was after she grew tall, had long legs, a beautiful smile, and a kind of shy, sly way of looking at me and the rest of the world.

Her family was not rich. I think this made her feel inferior when she had no right to feel this way. Or was it possible something in her family wasn't quite as it should be? I never really knew. Her father acted strange sometimes. But then, we were teenagers. All grownups seemed strange to us. I didn't pay too much attention. He wasn't really important. She was. She was a knockout, the prettiest girl in school. At least, this was my opinion.

'So, are you going to tell me what happened?' she asked after accepting my invitation to come inside my cottage for a drink.

'It's a long story. Sure, you want to hear it?' I replied while opening the glass sliders to the deck overlooking the lake for some fresh air. It was getting dark. The wind was picking up, and a few streaks of bright lightning could be seen in dark storm clouds racing toward shore.

She settled on a couch in the living room with a glass of wine. A stone fireplace in the middle of the room between large sliding glass doors was the only visual barrier to viewing the storm over the lake. Floor lamps cast warm light over the casual, brown cloth cushions covering wood-framed furniture. American Indian-styled rugs covered a wood floor. Driftwood gathered from the beach decorated simple wood tables covered with scattered magazines and books. I hadn't anticipated her visit. The place was a mess. But in my frazzled, accident-scrambled brain, I barely noticed. I was simply glad to have survived the latest attempt on my life.

'Well, it looks like rain,' she replied. 'A walk on the beach is probably not advisable. So I guess we could talk. Or did you have something else in mind?'

I couldn't help but laugh. She hadn't changed in the years since I last knew her. She still had the same sly sense of humor, which always put me on the defensive. And there was always something overtly sexual about her, like the way she walked, the way she smiled. She immediately took me out of my comfort zone.

Or maybe it was just me. Maybe the memories of those high school nights in the back seat of my parent's car were returning to haunt me. Like the first time she took off her bra... Didn't seem like a big deal now, but back then, well... we were young, and she was so beautiful. And she was still beautiful now, maybe fuller and rounder than before. But she still had the same tall, statuesque figure and good posture of a runway model.

'We could make out,' I joked.

She smiled, 'Why don't we start by you telling me what happened to you this evening and why it was so important I come to the hospital and drive you to your cottage? You were very persuasive, you know.'

'I wasn't persuasive. I begged. You know it, and I know it.'

'Is that what you call it?'

'I'm sure I'm not the first male to beg you.'

'I guess not.'

'Well then, don't act so surprised.'

'Did I say I was surprised?' she asked with a smile.

'No.'

'Okay then.'

'Okay, what.'

'Okay, tell me why you begged.'

'I told you before. I'm in love with you.' I managed a smile even though my forehead hurt. The anesthetic was beginning to wear off.

She looked at me. 'Okay, we have been down this road before. Let's go back to you telling me why your face looks like you have been in a fight. And why a cop car is presently sitting in your driveway?'

Black clouds from the approaching storm raced over the lake toward shore as we sipped wine and ate cheese and crackers. I began by recounting my most recent near-death experience, the one that happened that afternoon when I drove into town to have dinner with her. As I talked, the wind increased in velocity. Occasionally, I had to stop, interrupted by a loud clap of rumbling thunder. We took a break to go out on the deck to view a black line of fuming storm clouds rushing on shore as the wind whistled through the trees surrounding my cottage. Rain coming down sideways in a wet, drenched mayhem drove us back inside, pelting the glass sliders, occasionally accompanied by tingling bits of icy hail. The high winds of the storm were intense but gratefully short-lived.

After the storm front passed, I continued. It took time to tell her the story. I didn't embellish, just the basic facts, the truth. And she didn't ask questions. Just let me ramble on, smiling occasionally.

The death of my girlfriend, Monica, and a man who I thought was responsible for her death was the first installment of the story. I explained how my company was at the heart of the problem. It affected the man's family business in Thailand. They had, for generations, dominated the world of colored gems, sapphires in particular. My work had changed. The man from Thailand wanted to take control of my company and, with it, retain revenue, which for hundreds of years had belonged to his family and made them very rich. And apparently, he was willing to kill me to keep it, like this afternoon when he almost accomplished his mission.

I guess I should have told her the stories in some kind of chronological order. But I couldn't do that. My mind was too traumatized by the accident. Remnants of my recent past came oozing out in no particular order, just one episode after another, some ugly, some good. I told her about a woman I met in Belize. Admittedly, she was beautiful, and she had helped me get over Monica's death. I could have told her more and probably shouldn't have told Sandy anything about Ilana, but something inside my damaged brain wanted Sandy to know my story. I wasn't sure why. Just thought it was important. Even though I didn't know if I would ever see her again after that night, I wanted her to know my story.

Towards the end, I told her how I killed the man responsible for all my problems and shot him to death. Again, not sure why I told her that. I wasn't proud of killing him. And I certainly had not intended to tell her about him when I began. It just came out.

I also admitted the shooting was covered up. This was not my idea. The CIA did it. The man's family thought he died in a helicopter crash. Or maybe they didn't believe what they were told. Because why else would someone try to kill me today? Or it could be they just wanted me dead so they could take over my company. Nothing changed, just different characters with the same goals. Truth was, it didn't matter why they wanted me dead. It only mattered they were once again trying to kill me.

It was late by the time I finished. I was mentally and physically exhausted. I stood to stretch my legs and open the front sliders. The world outside was shiny and wet. Stars sparkled in a black night sky interrupted by a few swiftly flying overhead clouds, remnants of the storm. The sound of waves crashing on the shore was overwhelming, one roller after another rising up to crash before washing up the beach. Whitecaps rode the lake to the horizon, illuminated by shafts of moonlight shining through breaks in the clouds.

By this time, we both had too much to drink and not enough to eat. I didn't know about her, but I was tired.

After telling her my story, I felt strangely calm for the first time in a long time. I couldn't really explain it. Perhaps telling someone my story was a natural catharsis, calming my nerves. Or maybe it was simply being in her presence again. I didn't know. I only knew I felt more relaxed than I had felt since the day I killed that man.

She looked at me with her big blue eyes, those eyes which always seemed to be able to see right through me like no one else ever could.

'Well, John Van Laan,' she said. 'That certainly was an interesting story.'

BANGKOK, SATURDAY, AUGUST 22, 5:10 P.M.
LUANG

Luang couldn't sleep after receiving the phone call that told him the American had survived.

Not because the phone call was bothering him but because he was worried about Sophon. With the morning light, Luang got out of bed and immediately went down the hall to a door outside the young man's bedroom. He knocked on the door, hoping Sophon was in his room. But as he feared, only silence greeted his inquiry. When he opened the bedroom door, he noticed that Sophon's bed was undisturbed and clothes in his closet were missing, along with a suitcase.

The old patriarch shut the door and returned to his normal morning routine. He took a bath, got dressed, and went to his garden for tea and breakfast. Nothing in the routine needed to change. He read the morning paper as he sipped his tea before attending to his duties for the day. It was only in the evening after his work was complete and he had read the afternoon newspaper while sitting in his garden; only then, only after the tasks that consumed his life were accomplished, did he take time to think about Sophon.

He knew Sophon had the means to travel. He had money, his father's inherited money. But Luang had options. He could send men to bring Sophon home. He was presently the head of the family. The boy would be obligated to return if his great-uncle sent men to return him. Once the young man was home, Luang could talk to him and try to convince him to allow someone else to deal with the problem. But as the heat of the day cooled in the evening, he decided it would be better to do nothing. The young man was old enough to make his own decisions, make his own way in life, and learn lessons that could only be taught through experience.

Perhaps this was as it was meant to be. If not, the desire to kill the American might linger in Sophon's brain, poison his mind, fill it with evil, and dog him until he is consumed with anger. Perhaps the fact the American had not been killed by a hired assassin was as it should be. Perhaps it was something Sophon needed to do for himself.

It would be what it would be.

Luang made a mental note to contact his man in the States. The assassin would receive new instructions. The hired gun would be told not to kill the American, only to keep an eye on him and wait for further instructions.

Luang poured a glass of wine while resting in his beloved garden. He loved living in the family mansion again. He decided he would not leave this place ever again, except in death. This was his home, and this was his garden as it had been in the past.

He would live out his days here.

GRAND HAVEN, MICHIGAN, FRIDAY, AUGUST 21, 10:10 P.M. JOHN

She took me by the hand, just like when we were in high school, and I needed someone to show me what to do.

It was what I badly needed and wanted... because I would not have done it on my own. I was still in shock after the accident. And I had too much to drink. The wine had calmed my nerves, but not completely and not forever. Bad thoughts were beginning to filter into my traumatized brain. It was starting all over again; my nightmares were beginning to reassemble their vulgar shapes in my subconscious. Guns, wrecked cars, and near-death escapes were becoming a routine in my life again.

The painkillers administered to my bandaged forehead had begun to wear off. My head hurt, especially my forehead. Stabs of pain pulsed through the bruised tissue in my body from the accident. I didn't feel the pain at first, but now, as my strained muscles tightened, I hurt everywhere. I think she knew I was a broken man, both mentally and physically. It was like before, like when she could see inside me as no one else ever could. So, she did what she thought was right. She took me by the hand.

'You have a bedroom in this house, don't you?' she asked innocently.

'Yes, several,' I smiled, suddenly aware that maybe something good might come out of this brutally terrible day.

I used to dream about making love to her when I was a teenager. Just the thought of being naked with her would send me into euphoria. And I don't know why I felt the same emotion at that moment. I thought I was older and wiser, not so needy now. But I guess I was wrong. Or perhaps it was because my world looked so bad again, my life once more filled with disaster, guns, accidents, and cops. She was the only bright light in a room filled with darkness. So when she asked where the bedroom was, the question made me feel like I was young again, like this was going to be the best thing ever.

Sitting on my bed, I was able to unbutton and remove my blood-stained jean shirt without her help. But my black tee shirt was a problem. It had dried blood around the collar. My left shoulder was very sore and tight. I couldn't raise my arm past my shoulders. She cut the t-shirt at the neck with scissors, widened the opening, and slipped it over my throbbing forehead. I didn't mind. It was nice to have assistance.

She continued to be of service by undoing my belt and unbuttoning my khaki pants, slipping down the zipper, and letting the pants fall to the floor. After stepping out of the pants and standing only in my underwear and socks, I tried to give her a kiss, feeling the one part of my body which didn't hurt, react to all this fun activity.

She stiff armed me, held me back, 'Woe, big boy, now go to the bathroom and do whatever it is you do before you get into bed.'

Assuming she was asking me to get ready for sex, I dutifully followed her command and went to the bathroom to look for a condom. When I returned, she had rolled back the bed covers and was sitting on the edge of the bed, still fully dressed. Something in my feeble brain suggested this might be a sign that what I thought or hoped would happen was not in my near future after all. But I quickly dismissed this errant thought and lay on my bed as she instructed, assuming she would get undressed and join me under the covers.

'Did the doctor give you anything for pain?' she asked, sounding more like a nurse than a lover.

'Yes, but I don't think pills are what I need, nurse,' I replied.

'Where did you put them?' she asked, ignoring my weak attempt at verbal foreplay.

I sensed her question was not leading to the desired result, but I played along, still hopeful. 'They are in the bathroom on the counter,' I replied.

She returned with two pills and a glass of water. Handing me the glass and the pills. 'Now take these,' she instructed. 'This should help you get through the night.'

I looked at the glass and then at her. Her big blue eyes sparkled. A sly smile curled the corners of her lips. She had me, and she knew it.

'But nurse, I would sleep so much better if you lay down beside me,' I pleaded.

'You need to rest tonight, Mr. Van Laan. Now, take your medicine, say your bedtime prayers, and try to get some sleep. I will check on you in the morning.'

So, it wasn't going to happen. This much was very clear. But did she just promise to be here in the morning? I took the pills with some water.

'So, nurse. You will check on me in the morning?' I questioned, wanting to be sure I had heard her correctly.

'I will check on you in the morning,' she smiled.

I was tired, sore, and beaten. I wasn't sure she was telling the truth. In fact, I assumed she would be gone in the morning, but I let her tuck me in. Then she did something unexpected. At least it wasn't an activity nurses normally do. She kissed me hard on the lips. I tried to say something, but she simply put her finger on my lips to stop me from talking. Then she got up, turned out the lights, and closed the door.

Just as well, I thought. Sex with her would only complicate my life. She will be gone in the morning. Good, because it would not be wise for her to become involved with me. My life was a mess. What little life I still had to live. It was becoming increasingly obvious that my days were numbered. She was better off without me.

I rolled over to sleep, but every time I moved, something hurt.

GRAND HAVEN, SATURDAY, AUGUST 22, 4:05 A.M. JOHN

Sleep came fitfully.

Pain pills helped, but not enough. Finally, when it was obvious sleep was not happening, I turned on the light next to my bed. A book was on my nightstand. I got out of bed and sat in a chair to read the book, but nothing registered. I would read a sentence, blank out, and try to read again, only to blank out again. The words were nothing more than blurred ink on a page. I couldn't concentrate. Eventually, I returned to bed and said a prayer, repeating the Lord's Prayer from memory. Then I tried to sleep again while trying not to think about what I recently thought about every night, about the face of the man I had shot to death. Seeing Nue's face smiling at me in the moonlight, his shirt seeping blood, his dying eyes staring at me, accompanied by the sounds of gunfire and flashes in the dark.

I tried to stop thinking about that horrible night, about how I held Ilana in my arms, about how she had leaned against my chest like a hurt, lost child. She had been brutalized, both mentally and physically, by Nue and his henchmen. And when they were done abusing her, Nue had ordered the murder of her brother. Not because it served a purpose but because he wanted to do it.

Nue had justified it by saying it was necessary because she lied to him. He wanted her to feel responsible for her brother's death. Her brother was to be killed to teach her a lesson. Some of this was true. She did lie to him. But I also had lied to him and asked him to come to a meeting for what I knew was not true. So, I believe the real reason he wanted her brother killed was to teach me a lesson, not her. He was ordering her brother's execution in retribution for what I did.

I tried to stop him and begged him not to do it. But Nue would not change his mind. He was intent on making me pay for my sins. I couldn't let that happen. I couldn't be responsible for something that terrible.

I shot him to stop him.

That's how I have rationalized the killing in my mind.

But I'm not sure that's true, and I have been obsessed about what happened that night ever since the shooting, and I'm still not completely convinced I was justified. I may have been able to prevent the death of her brother another way, a way which would not have required killing him. Charlie, my CIA friend, and his gang were with me at the time, hiding behind some bushes. His men were armed, trained CIA operatives. They may have helped if I had asked. But I did not. I took the matter into my own hands. So, the idea I killed him to prevent the death of Ilana's brother is weak. And I now suspect the real truth is I shot Nue in a moment of insane anger. I lost control. I lost my temper. I shot him, and then I watched him die. Just stood in front of him and watched him die.

I don't want to believe I was temporarily insane when I did it, but that's probably closer to the truth. I just don't want to admit to it.

I have tried to eradicate the image of his dying eyes and smile from my memory ever since it happened. I have asked my God for forgiveness, asked for mercy, asked for peace, and grace, and asked for it over and over again until it is my mantra, repeating the words until eventually, I go to sleep. That's what I did that night but like most nights. But sleep brought me no rest. Speeding cars and loud gunshots permeated my dreams until I woke up in a sweat with crashing noises reverberating through my tortured brain.

When the first dim light of dawn appeared in my bedroom window in the morning, I stumbled out of bed, relieved that night was finally over. Moving gingerly to avoid stressing any painful injuries from the accident, I walked like an old man. Every muscle in my body rebelled in hurt. After putting on jeans and a sweater, a Jim Harrison book caught my eye, sitting on my nightstand by the bed. It was the book I had been trying to read that night but with little success. I wondered if I could read it now. A glass of milk sounded good. I was thirsty. I decided to take the book into the living room to read while waiting for the sun to wash away the last anxious remnants of what had been a dark, confining night.

Night is not my friend, never has been. I am a day person. I need light.

I grabbed the book and headed for the kitchen to retrieve some milk from the fridge. I wasn't trying to be quiet. I assumed Sandy was gone.

A light from my bedroom cast dim shadows over the furniture in the living room as I walked to the kitchen. The big lake outside the front sliders in the room was gray. A dark sky stretched in graduated shadows from one end of the horizon to the other. The lake was a welcome sight, something familiar, something to contemplate other than the tortured images in my brain.

I reached for the light switch in the kitchen but then hesitated.

An irregularly shaped object on the couch had registered somewhere in my brain as I walked through the living room to the kitchen. I hadn't really taken notice of it. I was looking out the front window at the lake at the time. Somewhere in my subconscious, an unaccustomed object on my couch had registered in my brain.

Without turning on a light, I returned for another look.

A curl of blond hair carelessly falling across a pillow appeared to shine In the dim light from the window with a pale iridescence glow. The shape of a woman's body was lying on the couch, her eyes closed in sleep. She looked very peaceful. I was instantly happy as I stared at her, finding it unbelievable she had not gone away as I assumed.

As I silently gazed at her lovely form, alarm bells began going off in my head. This was not good, her being her. My life was already an overheated mess, which didn't require the addition of another female. But I did what I usually do in situations such as this; I rationalized, deciding I deserved some joy in the middle of all my pain. Hopefully, she could bring me a few hours of relief from the downward spiral of suffering that had become my arduous existence.

I remembered how Sandy had once told me she always slept easy and peaceful. And she certainly looked contented in the faint light of early morning. I stood very still, hoping not to wake her, simply relishing in the reality of having a gorgeous woman in my house.

She must have heard me because eventually, she opened her eyes. 'What are you staring at?' she asked.

'An angel is in my house, a beautiful one with blond hair and big blue eyes.'

'It's only me, silly.'

'Am I dreaming?' I asked, gingerly kneeling down beside the couch and gently brushing the hair off her forehead.

'You're not dreaming.'

'Surely you jest, my angel. You must be an angel sent to keep watch over me, protect me from the horrors of the night,' I replied, attempting to sound Shakespearean.

She smiled, 'Nope, just little old me.'

'Prove it. I think you're an angel.'

'And how would I do that?' she asked, playing along.

'Well, I suppose you could start by kissing me. I don't think angels are kissers.'

Before she could react, I leaned over and kissed her gently on her mouth, long and slow.

'So, are you convinced now?' she asked after I allowed her to come up for air. 'Do you still think I'm an angel?'

'It's hard to tell. You certainly kissed like an angel.'

'You said angels don't kiss.'

'Well, most don't. But you certainly do. I'm not sure we have proved anything yet.'

'What further proof do you need?' she asked with a sly smile crossing her face.

I assumed by now she knew exactly where this game was leading.

'Well, let's begin by checking for wings,' I said as I reached beneath her blanket.

She didn't resist at first. Just let me run my hand down her back and over her round bottom. It was as I remembered touching her body when I was a teenager, feeling the soft curves, her smooth thigh, her long, narrow ankles, and her feet. Every inch of her was full of wonder and mystery. She had removed her outer clothes and was sleeping in her panties and a tee shirt. The soft touch of her stomach and the round curves of her breasts were exactly as I remembered: absolute, undeniable exaltation.

She took my hand when I gently pinched a nipple and asked. 'Well, Mr. Van Laan. Are you satisfied now I'm not an angel?'

'You sure feel like an angel to me,' I replied, holding her hand and smiling. 'I'm not quite satisfied. Just a few more tests...'

She didn't allow me to finish my sentence. Sitting up on the couch, still holding my hand, she declared. 'I think perhaps we could conclude your examination under more comfortable conditions.'

She led me like a young boy to my bedroom. After removing my clothes, she examined my bruised, black, and blue body with her eyes. 'You sure you want to do this? We could wait until...'

'I've waited long enough.'

MONDAY, AUGUST 24, 8:55 A.M. PHILLIP

'Just thought you might like to join me for lunch,' Phillip Palmer said into his cell phone.

Sitting at his favorite table in his designated restaurant, he was having his usual breakfast of eggs, toast, bacon, and hash browns. Last night's paper was spread out on the table in front of him. He had thoroughly perused the local news, looking for a particular headline. But no murders had been reported, no deaths from gunshot wounds, only the usual nonsense gossip, standard fare for a local newspaper. He was disappointed, although not overly surprised. His archenemy seemed to have been blessed with nine lives.

Phillip had been informed, alerted by an overseas phone call, and told to be in the public eye yesterday afternoon and evening. This was the advice he was given. Nothing more was said over the phone, nothing that might implicate him in a crime. He had previously warned them that his phone might be tapped.

It didn't take Phillip long to understand what was in the wind. He assumed it involved John Van Laan because he knew John was in town. In fact, it was Phillip who had called and told the Thai that John was currently staying at a cottage on the lake near Grand Haven. Phillip had passed on this information because he was under the impression it was only a matter of time before the Thai would try to kill John. Either here in his hometown or somewhere else, it didn't matter where. It only needed to happen. Phillip knew John was a dead man. It was this thought that had been Phillip's salvation, the one thought that kept him motivated after what happened on the island.

Phillip had been at the scene the night John killed Nue. Afterward, Phillip was transported off the island in a CIA helicopter to Langley, Virginia, where he was vigorously questioned for forty-eight straight hours. No sleep, no food, no nothing. It was torturous, but he had given them nothing. He was tough, and he was smarter than they were. He knew they couldn't break him. They hadn't really tried that hard. Truth was they just kept him for a couple of days. When they were done, they let him go and told him to keep his mouth shut, or he would be charged with a crime and locked up for a long time. They drove him to an airport and watched him walk away a free man.

None of this was right in his mind.

He knew it wasn't right because he was a material witness in a murder case. A man had been shot to death in his presence. Phillip knew all the details of what happened. He knew who had been killed, and he knew who the shooter was. He had seen John Van Laan pull the trigger to kill Nue. And Phillip was more than capable of testifying against John. In fact, he was eager for the opportunity. Problem was, it just did not happen. Instead, the CIA had warned him to talk to no one about the crime.

At first, he couldn't understand why. Then it hit him. It was a cover-up. No one was going to be charged. John Van Laan was a free man. And Phillip could do nothing about it, nothing. Because who could he tell, the local police? They wouldn't believe him without solid evidence or someone to corroborate his story. He needed someone like Manuel to testify. Manuel was with him that night. Manuel, the dirty little emerald dealer from Columbia. Manuel knew what happened. But Manuel had disappeared, maybe even dead. So Manuel was no help.

The only other person present besides Phillip who could testify to the truth was John's girlfriend. She could back up Phillip's story. But would she do it? Would she accuse her boyfriend, John, of killing the man who had ordered the death of her brother? Phillip didn't think so. Truth was Phillip had no one to corroborate his story, no one to back him up.

Phillip personally couldn't believe John had pulled the trigger. He didn't think John had it in him. Never figured John could kill anyone. But then, you never know.

After Phillip returned home, he did nothing for a while and did as he was instructed by the CIA. But it was not like Phillip to keep his mouth shut forever. Phillip liked to talk. More than anything, Phillip liked to talk. He liked to stir the pot and make things happen. And what could be better for Phillip than to be in possession of an incredibly valuable piece of information? Eventually, he could not keep silent. He had to tell someone. He placed a call to Bangkok. He bought a burner phone that couldn't be tapped and called a telephone number the dead man had given him in case of emergency.

After several rings, a young girl answered in Thai. Phillip gave her his name and while speaking English, he told her he had been instructed to call this number by Mr. Nue in an emergency. Phillip carefully explained that the reason for his call was information concerning Mr. Nue's death.

The young girl asked him to wait, speaking English very well.

Finally, a man who called himself Luang Nue took his call. He said he was Nue's uncle. Luang asked Phillip who he was. Phillip answered and said he was a friend of Nue. Then he told Luang he knew how Nue died. Phillip told Luang the whole story.

Remarkably the phone call had not been very satisfying. Phillip thought Nue's family would be happy to know what really happened. Phillip hoped perhaps something good would come from telling them. He thought Nue's family might even reward him for the information. But Luang did not react as Phillip expected. Luang exhibited almost no emotion over the phone and acted almost as if he was disinterested like he already knew what Phillip was going to tell him. In fact, as soon as Phillip finished his story, Luang abruptly thanked Phillip for the information and hung up. Their conversation had been a complete disappointment for Phillip.

In fact, the phone call was just another disappointment in a long line of disappointments in Phillip's recent history. Phillip had hoped John would be charged with murder and executed by the state. Not because Phillip cared about the man John shot. Nue had double-crossed Phillip and made promises he did not keep. No, Phillip wanted John dead because Phillip thought John had stolen the life that Phillip believed belonged to him.

John and Phillip had been associates at one time. They came from the same hometown. Phillip was older. They weren't classmates in school. They didn't really know each other in their childhood years. But they had a common history. So, when they later met through their work, they connected. They worked for the same client, a colored stone dealer with a string of retail jewelry stores. John was an advertising executive assigned to the client. Phillip was the client's hired gemologist/geologist. At the time John had been eager to learn about gems to better serve his client. Phillip had obliged him and taught him about colored gemstones in after-hours drinking conversations. So, in a way, Phillip had helped John get started. When their client's business failed, John took what he learned and started his own company, effectively denying Phillip what Phillip thought was rightfully his, what Philip wanted: all the wealth, all the power, all the glamour that went with being a fabulously wealthy international businessman. John had taken everything from Phillip, the life Phillip wanted. He was now determined to get what was his, and he was willing to work day and night until he got it.

Phillip considered John's death to be the first step in this process. After John was out of the way, Phillip was convinced everything would naturally come to him where it rightfully belonged. So, when he received a phone call from Thailand telling him to have an alibi, Phillip made a point of being in public places where he would be seen, first a haircut at the local barber shop and then to a local car dealership shopping for a new car he did not need. And finally, a visit to a restaurant for a long dinner. He took his time and even invited a lady friend to share his meal.

All this social activity was uncommon for Phillip and expensive, too, but he assumed it would be worth the cost. Kind of like a celebration dinner. Revenge would be sweet. And to make it even better, he didn't need to lift a finger to make it happen.

He bought a bottle of expensive wine at dinner and enjoyed the night with his lady friend because he knew morning would bring him the beginning of his new life. When he returned home from dinner, he watched the local news on TV for a story confirming his celebration. He saw nothing, nothing which would jumpstart his new life, nothing. In the morning he called his buddy, Russ, who was a member of the local Ottawa County Sheriff Department and asked him if he would like to have lunch.

Russ was Phillip's inside guy when Phillip wanted to be updated on all the local dirt. Russ loved to talk almost as much as Phillip. Russ liked to be the center of attention. He had this in common with Phillip. And this made Russ an easy mark when Phillip wanted information. Russ' mouth was like an open sewer line filled with criminal waste. He knew everything there was to know about the lurid and ghastly lives of the local citizenry.

'Sorry, old buddy,' Russ replied, 'just too busy for lunch today, maybe tomorrow.'

'No problem. Tomorrow would be great. Say... what's so important you can't come today? Any interesting stuff going on?' Phillip inquired.

'No, nothing unusual,' Russ said. 'Lots of paperwork. I'm just backed up today, that's all.'

'No messy murders or drive-by shootings or stuff like that?' Phillip asked, not wanting to be too specific.

'Nope, this is Grand Haven, Michigan, not Detroit. Nothing ever happens here. You know that.'

'Okay,' Phillip said, trying not to sound disappointed.

'Oh, one thing did happen last night. And come to think of it, it happened to your old friend, John Van Laan. Claimed he was shot at. His car was damaged, hit by a gasoline truck. The guy is lucky to be alive. I think the State Police are handling it.'

'Really?'

'Yes, State guys are looking into it. That's all I know.'

Phillip didn't respond. He didn't want to give anything away or express an emotion that might implicate him, so he shut up.

'So where were you last night?' Russ laughed like it was a joke.

Everyone in the small town of Grand Haven knew about the bad blood between John and Phillip. Their history was common knowledge. Russ had to ask Phillip. It was the natural thing to do. He was a policeman, after all.

'I was out to dinner with Linda, if you must know. I can't believe you asked me where I was.'

'Just kidding old buddy,' Russ replied; happy to hear his friend Phillip had an instant alibi.

10:40 A.M. JOHN

'Charlie, they are after me again.'

I was outside on the deck of my cottage overlooking the big lake with my cell phone in my hand. An earlier call to my friend David had been a letdown. I didn't want to call him, but I had to. He had been planning to come over today. I had to tell him that was probably not a good idea. I had been in an accident last night. I was okay but pretty beat up. Then, I reluctantly told him the rest of the story. He was my friend, after all. He knew my history. I said I was sorry, but someone had taken a shot at me, and I didn't want his family in danger in case the guy was still in town. I knew he would understand. I asked him if I could call him later so we could talk more in detail. He said, sure and hung up.

I didn't mention Sandy to him. He knew Sandy from high school. He knew about our teenage romance. And I don't know why I didn't tell him. Just didn't want him to know she was at my cottage; not yet... maybe later.

Speaking of Sandy, I didn't want her to overhear my conversation with Charlie. I didn't want her to worry. That was why I was outside. The sound of waves crashing on the shore made it difficult to hear Charlie. I had my finger in my left ear to blunt the noise of the surf while my cell phone was plastered against my right ear.

'Where the heck are you calling from?' Charlie asked. 'You sound like you're inside a factory or something. I can hardly hear you.'

'Outside my cottage on Lake Michigan, I didn't want anyone to hear our conversation.' I fairly yelled into the receiver.

'No problem. I, for one, can't hear you,' Charlie shouted.

'Okay, okay, hold on a minute.' I walked around to the other side of the cottage, where I was out of the wind and away from the sound of the waves. 'Is this better?'

'Well, if you are asking if I can hear what you are saying, then yes, it's better. But I doubt there is anything good about what you are going to tell me.'

'So, do you want me to hang up?'

'Sure.'

I didn't respond.

'You are not going to hang up, are you?' Charlie finally asked.

'Don't you want to know what happened to me last night?'

'Not really, but you're going to tell me anyway, aren't you,' Charlie replied.

After I finished telling him about the incident on the road to Grand Haven, he was silent. Finally, I had to ask him if he was still on his phone.

'I'm here,' he said without enthusiasm.

'I just thought you would like to know.'

'No, I don't think you want me to know. I think you want to know what I can do to help you. Because you don't know what to do, do you, John? But you know you need help. That's why you are calling me, right?'

My friend Charlie was a black African American who worked at the CIA. He was direct, if nothing else. We didn't always get along. But that didn't matter because, in the end, he never let me down when I needed him. It was Charlie who had covered my butt when I killed the man on the island. Charlie was the reason I walked away clean. He said it was too complicated. He decided not to report it. He said people, including me, would be hurt if the shooting was reported to the local authorities. I assumed one of the other people hurt might be Charlie. He had been trying to help me at the time. He was deeply involved, and I'm not sure he or the CIA wanted a full-scale murder investigation to see the light of day. That's why he did the next best thing. He had the killing scene swept clean. The local police were never told. And no report exists anywhere today except in a confidential file buried somewhere deep inside CIA headquarters at Langley.

The body of the man I killed was buried at sea. His relatives were told he and his bodyguards had died in a helicopter crash off the coast, bodies never recovered. It was an unfortunate accident, so sorry.

And Nue's friend Manuel, the Columbian emerald dealer, was at the scene when I pulled the trigger. He's now serving a life sentence for conspiracy to commit murder, kidnapping, and numerous other crimes. Apparently, the Columbian government had wanted to lock him up for some time. They only needed an excuse that was given to them by the CIA.

The only other person at the scene was a former business associate from my hometown, a man named Phillip Palmer. He had been set free. It was assumed Phillip would keep his mouth shut. He had been told that if he tried to raise the issue, he would be implicated in a crime as an accomplice of Manuel and imprisoned. So Phillip was lucky. Had the shooting been reported, Phillip would probably be in prison today.

The only other people present were my girlfriend Ilana and Charlie's CIA crew. They would not talk. That was the end of the matter. Or at least this was how Charlie viewed it. Case closed. The man who had been trying to kill me was dead. I had killed him instead. No more problems.

So, it was understandable when I called Charlie. He didn't want to hear what I had to tell him. And I was pretty sure he hoped he would never have to deal with me again. Unfortunately, now he knew that wasn't going to happen.

'John, what do you want me to do?' Charlie finally asked after a pause. 'The best advice I can give you is to hire bodyguards and start acting like a man who is on someone's hit list. Apart from that, my hands are tied. You know what happened the last time I tried to help? It was a disaster.'

Nothing I could say. I got him in trouble the last time. That was my fault. He was probably lucky to still have his CIA job after our last debacle. I knew he was right. I was on my own.

I took a deep breath, 'Right, Charlie, sorry, I guess I shouldn't have called.'

'John, I don't mean to sound negative. You just caught me off guard. Look... let me read the local police report and call you in a couple of days. Okay?'

'Sure, sorry.'

'Who's in charge of the case?'

'Michigan State Police.'

'Good, that helps. I would rather deal with them than the local yokels.'

'Thanks.'

'And John, do what I said. Hire bodyguards and start acting like a man on a hit list because that's exactly who you are.'

'Okay?'

'One more thing,'

'Yes.'

'Did you get the help I suggested the last time we talked?'

'You asking if I went to see a shrink?'

'Yes.'

'No, what am I going to say to a shrink, Charlie? Do you really want me to tell him about the man I killed?'

'No, but you have other stuff you could talk about.'

'I suppose.'

'So, are you going to go?'

'I'll think about it.'

'Not good enough.'

'Charlie, I have more pressing problems right now.'

When he didn't respond, I asked when he would call back.

'I think I said a couple of days.'

'Okay, thanks.'

I closed my cell phone and sat on some steps behind my cottage, alone and once more very afraid.

4:45 P.M. JOHN

Her overnight bag sat innocently on a chair in the living room.

The black and brown bag was made from a soft leather bag and zippered at the top with two black shoulder straps. The leather pattern on the bag looked like something only nature could replicate, kind of like dried leaves on a forest floor in the autumn. Its size was ambiguous, bigger than a handbag but not as big as a suitcase, and that made it very difficult to determine if enough clothes and other necessary supplies were contained in the bag for a stay of a day or perhaps a week.

Earlier Sandy had gone to her sister's house to retrieve some clothes. When she returned, the bag come with her. I didn't ask her what was in it. I was just happy she had returned.

As the day wore on, my injuries from the accident became more and more problematic. My body hurt everywhere. Bruises on my legs made it difficult to walk. One knee was injured so badly I could put very little pressure on it, not enough to climb stairs. I hopped up steps instead, using my other good leg. And my left shoulder was killing me. A solid pain ached deep inside. And if this wasn't enough, I looked like a mess. My forehead was covered with bandages, and one of my eyes had turned a little puffy, black and blue.

However, my injuries weren't my real problem. The real problem was inside my head. I now knew my enemy was coming for me again. And this time, I didn't think they would fail. I was a dead man effectively, and I knew it.

The cops said they would keep an eye my place for a few days. After this I was on my own. I would have to hire bodyguards. Okay, I could do that. I had the resources and I done it before, but I wasn't sure that was a good long-term solution.

The only positive to come out of this mess was her. The fact that Sandy felt sorry for me. Like I said before, she could read my mind. I didn't have to tell her anything. She knew I needed her. I didn't have to ask her to stay. And I didn't ask her how long she would be staying with me. I was simply happy to have her company. Nothing more was said, and I didn't think beyond that. Probably should have, but I didn't, didn't want to. Just wanted to enjoy this day.

Swimming was out of the question for me, as I was hanging around on the beach due to the difficulty of climbing the steps leading to the water. Instead, we sat on the deck under a couple of umbrellas for shade. More correctly, I sat under an umbrella while she soaked up some rays on a lounge chair dressed in a skimpy white bikini. After a while, I climbed inside to get her a soda with ice. It was a hot day. Drops of sweat had formed on her tan body under the sun as I handed her the drink while taking the opportunity to observe firsthand her beautiful long curves. She was in great shape. This much was beautifully obvious.

After a while, she went down to the beach for a swim to cool off. The wind was blowing, and waves were rolling in, remnants of last night's storm. She spent more time dodging incoming breakers than she did swimming. I sat on the deck and kept an eye on her like a lifeguard. It was great to be with her again. But it also brought back all the old needy feelings from high school. However, this time was different. This time, we were adults. We didn't need adult supervision, and we didn't need anyone's approval. We could do what we wanted. And I knew what I wanted, more of what I had in the morning.

She climbed the stairs after a short swim still wet from the lake. I gave her a towel and turned on the hose. She sat on a deck chair as I ran water over her feet, gently removing beach sand. She looked down at me as I performed this ritual ceremony of subservience, the washing of her feet.

The hot August sun relentlessly beat down, warming and drying her skin. And in a way, it wasn't my fault. I just couldn't resist the thought of washing her long tan legs with the cool water from the hose while running my hand up her thigh.

'Hey, that's enough,' she said.

'Doesn't that feel good?' I laughed, keenly aware the water was cool. Pointing the hose directly at her with my hand firmly on the grip of the nozzle, ready to release a shower of cold spray. 'Would you like a refreshing shower?'

'Don't even think about it.'

I sent a short spray of water her way as she ducked and ran for cover, opening the sliding screen door and disappearing inside the cottage.

Fun over, I turned off the hose and stared at the lake for a moment. The waves were big, and the day was perfect for a swim. But my emergency room doc had warned me to stay out of the water until my forehead was healed and the stitches removed. Instead I headed inside to look for her. She was in the kitchen searching in the refrigerator for something to eat. Her swimsuit was still wet and dripping on the ceramic floor.

'Hey, didn't anyone tell you it's against cottage rules to walk around in a wet swimsuit dripping water all over the floor?'

She looked down at a puddle forming on the tile beneath her feet. 'So what am I supposed to do?'

'Take off that wet suit immediately,' I said with a smile.

She smiled back at me while slowly taking off the bottom of her suit. After untying and removing her top, she placed the offending, dripping articles of clothing in the kitchen sink.

'So, is this okay?' she asked. 'I mean, do the cottage rules allow for walking around naked?'

'Nothing in the cottage rules prohibits beautiful ladies from walking around naked. There is, however, a prohibition against ugly, beat-up men from being naked. That is unless a beautiful woman waives the rule.'

'In your case, consider it waived. I guess I can put up with one ugly guy running around naked.'

I didn't need a second invitation. But it wasn't easy getting undressed. My shorts and underpants were no problem. I simply let them fall to the floor. But my tee shirt was a different challenge. I couldn't raise my left shoulder. I had to beg her assistance. Even then, it was difficult, but my shirt finally came off with her help.

All this activity in close proximity to her naked body offered its own kind of pleasure and opportunity. Before she could get away, I embraced her around the waist with my one good arm, feeling her smooth, round body move against me. She didn't resist; she simply kissed me softly on the mouth.

The windows in the cottage were open. A warm summer wind blew in, cooling our overheated bodies. Every nerve in my body was alive, excited by the soft caress of the wind and the sweet closeness of her body. I reached down to touch her. She brushed the hair off my forehead and simply let me stroke her, responding softly, gently moving against my hand, finally reaching down and holding the one appendage on my body that did not hurt as a little explosion of delight ran through my troubled mind.

At this moment, nothing hurt. I had no problems. No one was trying to kill me. It was just the two of us.

I turned her around and gently pressed her upper body over the counter and entered her from behind, running my hand up her back and over her neck and through her hair as the summer wind rushed around and through the canyons of my mind, taking me to a place I had not been for years, a place where only she could take me.

NEW YORK, NEW YORK, TUESDAY, AUGUST 25, 5:45 P.M. SOPHON NUE

The young man took a piece of paper from his billfold where it had been stored during his flight to America.

After carefully unfolding the precious cargo, Sophon Nue simply stared at the paper for a long time while letting his thoughts wander. It was late in the day, and he was sitting at a small desk in his hotel room on the twenty-ninth floor next to a window. A vast exhibit of elevated edifices to man's ingenuity, grand structural intrusions rose high into the sky outside his window, hard evidence of the anxious energy of metropolitan New York City. However, the young man did not appear to be overly interested in the remarkable skyline as he stared blankly out into space. Sophon had other, more important issues on his mind.

He had never been in the United States before. His father had promised him a trip to this country someday... but someday had never come. His father was always too busy. And now his father was dead. So, it was a bittersweet experience to finally come to a country he had longed to visit, but never imagined coming to alone and not for the reason he was now here.

He carefully dialed the telephone number written on the piece of paper in his hand, not wanting to make a mistake. Too much depended on this call. The numbers were instantly displayed on the phone. He checked their accuracy against the numbers written on the paper before pressing the call button. In the back of his mind, he feared it might be too late in the day to make this call. If this was a business number, employees would be gone home for the night. No one would answer. That would be his fault. He had put off making his call, probably because so much depended on who answered it and what this person might be willing to tell him. He had procrastinated all day, walking the busy streets of New York in a mental fog.

He didn't know why. Maybe it was jet lag, his biological clock off. Or maybe it was this city, a place so full of people, so much money, tall buildings, and big shiny cars. It was like Bangkok but different, so different in many ways. He was having trouble adjusting. Not because he couldn't speak the language but because he spoke English very well. This wasn't the problem. Something else was bothering him. Something unpleasant seemed to linger on the streets and down the back alleys of this city, a sadness that walked these lonely sidewalks with him. He could feel it everywhere. It was not what he assumed he would find in this city. He had assumed everyone in America was happy. The city was rich. The people must be happy. That's what he assumed. However, he discovered that not all Americans were wealthy. Dirty, unkempt bums walked these streets, sleeping in its alleys, peeing on its walls. He wondered where all these poor people came from. And why did they live on these streets? Why in this city of wealth? Why did they not have homes? Why were these sad people walking these streets carrying bags filled with their sorry belongings? Why did they exist in this city, walking side by side with their rich neighbors? And why did the rich and the poor not see each other? Almost as if they were blind to their neighbor's existence.

With so many questions on his mind, he strolled the sidewalks of the city looking and listening and wondering. And thinking about the phone call he would soon place to the man whose name was written on the piece of paper in his wallet. He wondered if the man would talk to him. If not, what would he do? He had no one else he could ask for help?

He knew where his father's murderer lived. He assumed he could travel to the city and kill the man without help. But it would be far easier with assistance. He hoped the man whose name was written on the piece of paper would help him. He had questions he wanted to ask, questions his uncle could not or would not answer. Almost as much as he wanted to kill his father's murderer, he wanted answers, answers to why his father had died.

The young man had originally been told his father had died in a helicopter crash in the Atlantic Ocean. This he did not want to believe. It didn't seem right. He badgered his uncle until he got the truth. And he was right. It wasn't an accident. His uncle finally told him the truth. His father had been murdered.

So why did the American authorities lie about his father's death? Why were people always lying? And did he really know the truth now, the whole truth? Or was there more to his father's death that he needed to learn? So many questions remained.

He had cried the day he learned his father had been murdered. He had sat in his father's chair, at his father's desk, and cried long and hard. The door to his father's office was closed at the time. He didn't think anyone had heard him. He didn't want anyone to hear him. He didn't want to think he was weak. It was the only time he cried.

His father's telephone book lay on his desk that day. Sophon had opened it and looked through it until he came to a page where names of men who lived in America were listed. The name of his father's murderer was written on this page: John Van Laan. His father had traveled to America to meet with this man for business. According to his uncle, this was when his father had been murdered.

Above John's name in the book was Phillip Palmer's name, the name of the man who had told his uncle about his father's murder. Beside Phillip's name was a phone number. Sophon knew his father had business with this man, Phillip Palmer, but he didn't know what business.

Other names were also in the book. Beside each name was the name of a business and an address. John Van Laan's business was called Gemstone International Inc. Charlottesville, Virginia, address and telephone number. But not Phillip Palmer; only a name and a number, no address, no business name. This seemed very odd because the young man knew his father had talked to Phillip many times.

Sophon had always been fascinated by the business conducted in his father's office. He knew that someday he would sit in his father's chair. So, it was only natural for him to be interested. He had often asked his father questions about his work. His father mostly put him off, saying he was too busy. They would talk later. Later never came.

Sometimes, Sophon stood outside his father's office and listened. On several occasions, he heard Phillip's name. These phone conversations were often late in the day or at night. This was strange, not normal for his father. Business was for business hours.

He also heard his father take a call from this Phillip Palmer a few times when he was in the rooms of their residence. These calls came at all hours of the day. And his father didn't always seem happy to answer the calls, but he did anyway. So this Phillip Palmer must have been important.

Sophon had torn the page out of his father's book, the page which contained both John Van Laan and Phillip Palmer's information. He folded the page carefully and put it in his wallet because he knew he would make a call one day to ask this Phillip about his father's death. Now was the day and the time. He waited, listening to a phone ring somewhere in America. Finally, a voice answered, a loud voice, a very clear voice.

'Hello.'

At first, the young man found it difficult to speak. So much depended on this conversation. He hesitated.

'Hello,' the voice repeated. 'Answer, or I am going to hang up.'

'Don't hang up, please,' the boy finally said. 'My name is Sophon Nue. I want to talk to you about my father's death.'

Now, it was the other man's turn to be silent.

Sophon waited. 'Is your name Phillip Palmer?' he asked.

'Yes, I am Phillip Palmer.'

'Did you know my father?'

'Yes, I was a friend of your father.'

'Will you tell me about my father's death?' Sophon asked. Then waited for what seemed like an interminable time. 'Will you help me?'

'Nue never told me he had a son,' Phillip finally replied. 'How do I know you are who you say you are?'

Sophon was not prepared to answer this question. He knew he could tell this man many things that might prove he was who he said he was. But there was only one way which was indisputable. He took a big chance. 'You can call my uncle in Bangkok and ask him who I am. My uncle's name is Luang Nue. I can give you his number.'

Phillip did not reply immediately. Sophon asked him again if he would like to have his uncle's number.

When Phillip did not reply immediately, Sophon asked him again if he would like to have his uncle's number.

'I am in New York. Will you talk to me if I can prove to you who I am?'

'Yes,'

Sophon held his breath and asked the question he had traveled so far to ask, 'Will you tell me why father was killed?'

'Yes, I was with your father when he died,' Phillip replied after a long pause.

GRAND HAVEN, MICHIGAN, MONDAY, AUGUST 31, 7:35 P.M. JOHN

Her brown and black leather overnight bag had moved several times during her stay.

Each time it moved, it got closer to my bedroom. But sadly, it never made it all the way inside. Currently, it was lying on the floor of my bathroom, where Sandy had placed it for easy access to items like her toothbrush or hair dryer.

Just once I suggested she hang her clothes in a closet of my bedroom, put her toiletry items on a shelf in the bathroom and store the leather bag in a closet.

Sandy ignored me.

Well... not completely, she did acknowledge my suggestion, but with a definite lack of enthusiasm. She looked at me, smiled one of her bemused sly smiles as if she was tacitly saying, 'Silly boy, what makes you think I want to get settled here? You don't have me yet.'

I never made that mistake again. Just let her do what she wanted; let her brown and black bag sit wherever she wanted to put it. It was enough to have her stay with me for a while. I didn't push.

The weather remained hot through the end of August. And as far as I was concerned, this was a good thing. Because it meant she spent most of her time in little more than a bikini, sometimes covered with a sheer see-through shirt. When I complemented her, said her bikini looked good on her, she smiled.

I was physically beginning to feel much better. Aches and pains from the accident were becoming less bothersome. A few stitches still occupied my forehead, but the bandage was off, and I was headed to the doctor in the morning to have him remove the stitches. My black and blue eye was mostly healed. Sunglasses were no longer required in public. So, my condition was looking up. But my relatively quick recovery didn't exactly make me overly happy. My over-strained brain began to worry. I began to think that she would leave as soon as I was healthy. When her services were no longer needed, there would be no more reason for her to stay, no more pity required, no more nursing necessary, and finally... no more sex available.

However, I had not raised this thorny issue. I did not venture to ask her about her plans. Mostly because I was afraid of what she would say. And as if to confirm my suspicions that this topic of conversation would not turn out well; our morning had been pathetically lacking in the area of casual conversation. A disquieting silence seemed to have taken over our existence. I guessed it was because we both knew we needed to talk, but neither of us was willing to initiate the conversation.

She finally asked me if she could take one of my cars into town.

I offered her my white Mercedes convertible, which I had previously purchased to be used as a summer cottage car. The crashed Vette had been a later acquisition. I always wanted a Corvette, and I had spotted one in a used car lot while driving around Grand Haven one day. I guess I was bored at the time. Took it for a drive and fell in love; that is, if you can fall in love with a car. It was trash now. Insurance company had called and said it was a total loss. Parts were probably worth more than it cost to fix it.

She said she wanted to spend the day with her sister. On the way back to the cottage, she promised to stop at a grocery store to replenish my meager supply of food and booze. I thanked her and watched her drive away with the top down looking good, blond hair blowing in the wind.

After she was gone, it was lonely hanging around the cottage without her. Seemed I had gotten used to having her around. I spent my time doing mostly nothing in the way of productive work. However, I did manage a call to my office. Helen, my secretary, said she didn't have anything pressing. My guess was Helen was giving me a mental 'time out' after my accident. She was probably saving work for when I returned to the office.

I had planned to be in Grand Haven for only two weeks. But after the accident and most due to Sandy's wonderful attention; well... it seemed prudent to put off returning to Charlottesville. Besides, it was August. Nothing important usually happens in

August. Everyone is on vacation. The mass confusion called work would start up again after Labor Day. Or so I reasoned to justify my extended stay at the cottage.

Sandy returned late in the afternoon. It was a hot and cloudless day with little relief from a breeze. The sun beat down on the placid lake waters, making it almost unbearable to be anywhere near the beach except in the water. She went for a swim while I acted as her lifeguard from the deck, sitting under an umbrella, relaxing with a beer in the shade, keeping an eye on her beautiful body swimming effortlessly in the calm, clear waters. We drove into Holland later in the evening for a dinner of fish and chips. I was beginning to feel comfortable in public again; I just needed a baseball hat to cover the embarrassment of my healing forehead.

The hat I wore had an orange V logo. It was something I had purchased at the University of Virginia Law School bookstore while taking a walk. When I'm in Charlottesville, sometimes I walk for fresh air and exercise. My former dead girlfriend, Monica, was an alumnus of the law school. I often wander the campus and think about her, spending time where she had gone to school, thinking maybe it would help me to feel close to her again. But it doesn't work. Still, it is a nice place for a stroll, gardens, and wonderful architecture.

Monica's death was an accident, but not really. Nue and several of his goons had forced his way into a hotel room where we were staying. He came because he wanted to take control of my company. Offered me a large amount of money for my stock and then informed me he would kill me and her, both of us, if I didn't accept his most generous offer. Honey or hell, money or a casket; this was the choice he gave me. It was an interesting method of doing business and very effective. I was ready to sign. Money seemed a better option than death. I reasoned it would be better to live to fight another day when I wasn't being threatened. A pen was in my hand, ready to sign when Charlie decided to mount a rescue. He and his CIA buddies stormed the room. A gun battle ensued. Monica was accidentally shot in the head and died in my arms.

I blamed Nue for her death even though I never knew for certain who fired the shot that killed her. As far as I was concerned, that evidence was irrelevant. Nue was the person who created the situation which caused her death. That made him guilty in my mind.

Anyway, I wore the University of Virginia hat into the restaurant with Sandy even though I felt slightly uncomfortable wearing a hat. Although, I was pretty confident the local fashion police wouldn't bother me. In Western Michigan men wear baseball hats inside casual restaurants. I figured it was better than having people stare at my banged up forehead.

A couple of my private-duty bodyguards were seated unobtrusively at the table next to us. I didn't like having them tag along, but I knew I had to get used to bodyguards again. They will be part of my life from now on. Sandy didn't seem to mind. She took it all in stride. The lady had a way of making everything seem easy.

I'm completely different. I make everything more difficult than it needs to be.

When we returned to the cottage after dinner, I decided it was time to talk. I couldn't put it off any longer. As much as I had been trying to avoid the subject, I needed to know what she was planning. Did she plan to stay? Did we have a future? Or was I just good for a couple of one-night stands?

Personally, I didn't want to lose her. It had been great being with her. We got along great. It was fun talking about old times. And, well, the sex was a bonus. I think we made love every day. I wondered sometimes if we were just trying to make up for all those frustrating dates we had as teenagers, acting like a couple of puppies in heat. It helped me forget my ugly past for a short time and gave me something to think about instead of Nue. I didn't see his dead man's eyes when I was with Sandy, not the way I did when I was with Ilana.

So, this was how it was for me. Sandy had become important. Despite my initial concerns, I had let her into my life again. I wasn't sure it was the right thing to do, but the truth was I hadn't spent a lot of time debating the issue in my mind. Probably should have, but didn't... Didn't because if I did, I would have to admit it was wrong. I was putting her in danger. But as I said, I didn't want to think about that. And besides, if she wasn't going to stay, then what difference did it make?

It was probably not the same for her. But then everything was always complicated when it came to being with that woman. Sex was a good example. She made love like she was enjoying a good meal, casual, easy, no fuss. She would take my hand and lead me to the bedroom, caress my face, smile, and touch me in places I had never been touched before. In my mind, in my spirit and body. The sex was pure joy, too good, too warm, too comforting. I didn't want it to ever end.

So, I had to know where I stood with her. I couldn't wait any longer. Couldn't just let it be. I had to know, even though subconsciously, I knew it was a mistake to ask. But I did it anyway. Like I said, I fight everything. It's my way.

We were sitting on the deck when I raised the subject. The sun had just set. It was not a particularly spectacular sunset. No clouds to make it interesting, just a reddish-pink glow across a barren lake horizon in the diminishing light. A glass of wine was in her hand. The lake was a shiny sheet of blue-gray glass. It was hot, but not too hot, the heat of the day receding with the sun. I felt good. I wanted to relax, but I could not. I did not. I asked her what her plans were.

She looked at me with a mischievous grin on her lips, the one she always seemed to conjure up at a time like this.

'John, I live in San Francisco. I have a life. I have friends and a home. I have to go back. This has been fun and you know I will always love you, but I can't stay.'

I started to object. I wanted to argue that I was not the person responsible for our previous teenage separation. It was by mutual agreement. It wasn't my fault completely. But she leaned over and put her finger on my mouth and said, 'Now, John, you know I don't blame you. I never did. We were young, and our love was too intense, too much for our tender age. Maybe if we had met when we were older, maybe then it could have been different. But the truth is we were just too young at the time.'

After she lifted her finger from my mouth, she waited for me to say something. But what could I say? She was right, of course.

She knew it. I knew it. I had done the only thing I thought made sense at the time. I had walked away. It was me after all, stupid me. It was not something I had ever admitted before. But she was right. I had just let her go, almost relieved she was gone.

I didn't say a word.

THURSDAY, SEPTEMBER 3, 5:40 P.M. JOHN

I stayed at my cottage for a few more days after she left, apparently unwilling to admit that Sandy was gone.

Most of my time was spent aimlessly wandering around an empty house, lacking motivation. I went swimming a few times to get my strength back, worked on my tan, and gave my forehead time to heal. The doctor said I would have no bad scarring. The cuts were mostly minor abrasions from flying glass and it was good I was wearing sunglasses at the time of the accident. Otherwise, my eyes might have been damaged.

'Lucky,' the doc said.

I didn't feel so lucky.

The morning after our inconvenient conversation, Sandy rose early and called her sister. I offered to take her wherever she wanted to go, but she refused my help. Said her sister would pick her up. I watched her pack her brown and black bag. It didn't take her long, not more than a few minutes, to stuff her meager belongings into the bag. We didn't communicate much after that. We didn't make any awkward promises we couldn't keep, just a few words on the deck overlooking the lake with a cup of coffee while she waited for her sister to arrive.

'You going to be alright?' she asked.

'What do you mean?'

'People are trying to kill you.'

'Yes.'

'So... are you going to be alright?'

'I don't know.'

She was silent after this brief exchange, just kissed me on the cheek when it was time to go and walked away.

That was it. She walked away, just like when she arrived.

The cottage was quiet after she left: no sounds of bare feet walking over the tile in the kitchen, no dishes clattering in the sink, no exchange of casual conversation... nothing... the place felt empty.

The weather changed. The wind increased.

Waves crashing on the beach sounded louder than before, maybe because there was no other noise, no other person, nothing available to erase the sound of the waves, which quickly became harsh and grating. No more peaceful, gentle, rhythmic lapping on the shore. Change was in the air. Autumn was coming. Life was in transition, and the lake was uncomfortably restless. The anxious noise of the wind and waves eventually made me feel uneasy. I decided it was time to call my charter jet service and schedule a pickup. Time to go, return to real life or whatever passed as real life for me. Vacation was over.

The local security company was informed I would be leaving. My bodyguards were scheduled to drive me to the airport in the morning, and then they were done. Security needs would be passed to my office. Helen had already made arrangements. We had been through this before. She knew the drill.

Only one hot afternoon remained before I was scheduled to travel in the morning. I decided to drive into town for a stroll and dinner. My cottage no longer felt like a place of refuge. With Sandy gone, the rooms were empty and uncomfortably quiet. I needed the noise of human drivel to drown out the ugly sounds in my head.

My bodyguards followed me into town driving their own car. I took the Mercedes. They had trouble keeping up. My internal engine was in an anxious gear. I drove fast down Lakeshore Avenue, a beautiful, curving road through the trees.

A walk on the cement sidewalk that runs parallel to the channel seemed as good an idea as any other. Maybe because this was where I met Sandy, maybe I hoped she would reappear again out of a daydream.

Summer was still in full swing. My hometown doesn't really quiet down until after Labor Day. Sidewalks were still filled with happy tourists: pretty girls in halter tops and sunglasses, guys in cutoff jeans and t-shirts, the usual summer scene. This was why some guy walking in front of me stood out in the crowd. For one thing, he wore long white shorts, and complimenting his Michael Jordan-style shorts were a pair of ugly black dress shoes worn over pulled-up white gym socks. Some sort of ugly shirt that looked like a relic from a Don Ho Hawaiian collection fulfilled his misguided sense of summer fashion. And these clothing miscues were not the only reason he looked ridiculously out of place. The color of his skin was a major giveaway. His legs and arms were oddly stark-white. It was August and he was the only guy on the sidewalk who had not been out in the sun long enough to achieve a semblance of a tan. He looked silly. But then something else about him struck me. It was the way he walked. He was kind of straight up, tall, and thin with a swagger like he was on stage. His gray ponytail bobbing in the wind was the final clue. No one else would think of looking this outrageous.

It had to be Phillip Palmer.

I should have turned around immediately and left as soon as I recognized him. My day had been depressing enough. I had gone into town to lift my spirits. Forget about Sandy and get on with my dreadful life. Dealing with my old nemesis, Phillip was the last thing I needed. I noticed Phillip was not alone. A young man was walking with him, seemingly immersed in conversation with Phillip. Or rather, it would be more accurate to say Phillip was having a one-sided conversation with this fellow. The young man would nod occasionally, maybe ask a question or two. Other than this, he spent his time taking in the scenery while Phillip rattled on, filling his ears with gibberish.

Phillip's walking companion was almost as tall as Phillip with neatly cut, straight black hair. He stood out in a sea of mostly fair-haired European descendants. He wore dark long pants, which were decidedly out of place for a casual walk along the channel on a hot afternoon, although he appeared unconcerned with the heat. A cream-colored linen short-sleeve shirt complimented his somewhat out-of-place but handsome appearance. The sun didn't seem to bother his dark skin. I couldn't help but wonder what his story was and why he was talking to Phillip. I continued behind them, catching an occasional brief glimpse of his face while maintaining two or three afternoon strollers between us at all times.

Boats cruised slowly in the no-wake zone of the channel as I continued down the sidewalk. Tied up to the cement retaining wall of the channel next to the sidewalk was a sailboat, which just happened to be occupied by a rather shapely young woman in a skimpy swimsuit getting a tan, seemingly unaware of the leering young men who eyed her as they slowly sauntered by. She was beautiful and so was the boat, tall masts and teak wood decks. It reminded me of my own sailboat in Belize, and I guess seeing the sailboat caused me to begin to daydream about my former life, which in turn led to a failure to notice that Phillip and his young friend had turned around and were headed in my direction.

Fortunately, Phillip didn't see me. He was more intent on maintaining his dominance in the conversation he was having with his walking companion. But his young friend appeared to be looking right at me. It was very disconcerting like he had singled me out in the crowd. He was a handsome boy, a foreigner from somewhere in the Far East. Something about his eyes immediately commanded my attention. I sensed I had seen those eyes before, like recognizing someone I could not remember. We connected briefly, this young man and I, only for a second, no longer than it took for a shot of panic to run rampant through my body, a shot of cold, hard fear.

I turned immediately to escape up a grassy hill, leaving behind the young man with the familiar eyes.

CHARLOTTESVILLE, VIRGINIA, WEDNESDAY, SEPTEMBER 9, 5:45 P.M. CHARLIE

Charlie entered my office as usual as if he owned the place.

Fine with me, Charlie had saved my ass on more than one occasion. He could have the run of the place as far as I was concerned. And besides, Helen, my secretary, liked Charlie. She always let him in without telling me he was coming.

But then, who didn't like Charlie? He was a tall, handsome, strong black man with a high degree of intelligence. After graduating from the University of Virginia Law School near the top of his class, he turned down some lucrative job offers from prestigious law firms and went to work for the CIA instead. Said it was his dream. I liked Charlie even though we didn't always get along. I assumed this was because we were both headstrong, alpha males who sometimes butted heads. We had gotten off to a bad start. It probably had something to do with my being jealous of my girlfriend, Monica. Mostly, this was my fault. I knew she had some kind of former relationship with Charlie, and there were times when I was afraid they were renewing an old romantic flame. But that had never been proved. And it didn't matter anymore. She was dead. Charlie and I have had a few skirmishes since then, but nothing that couldn't be worked out.

He promised to call after what happened in Grand Haven, and he finally did when I returned to Charlottesville. He knew I needed help. There was only so much I could do on my own. Charlie was the only guy who could possibly keep me alive.

Since returning to my office, I had spent my time ignoring my desperate situation by burying myself in work, falling into an old routine. Workaholic is what I guess you could call me. Helen has seen it all before: up early in the morning and going into the office with a cup of coffee. This is easy for me because my apartment is in the same building and right next door to my office. In the mornings, I go over reports, check out emails, and do the stuff that can only be done efficiently without interruption. I try to get most of my paperwork completed before the staff arrives, which is usually successful unless an occasional phone call gets in the way, which is not unusual. My company has Distribution Houses in New York, London, and Hong Kong, each in a different time zone. Miners all over the world are suppliers. They don't always wait until office hours to call. That's okay with me. The world is a big place, and time is fluid.

My business model was simple, really: control most of the world's supply of one particular commodity, the gemstone sapphire in my company's case. Next, improve market share through advertising, and finally, raise prices to reflect the scarcity and value of these beautiful natural gemstones.

Three Distribution Houses sell the stones. They are independent businesses that buy the gemstones from my office and sell them to clients in their part of the world. Even though they are independent, I have the final say over their pricing because each and every gemstone travels digitally through my Charlottesville office before being sold by the Distribution Houses. They buy the gems exclusively from me and sell them at prices I dictate for an add-on fee my company collects. Should a Distribution House ever decide to ignore my directives, I can simply cut them out of the supply chain immediately, effectively putting them out of business. However, I don't contemplate this possibility because the Houses are run by men who understand the marketing strategy of the company. It works for them, and it works for me.

All this has made my company very profitable. And that is good because it takes a lot of money to make everything work. For instance, a large portion of all our profits are returned to the miners through a nonprofit foundation that builds schools, runs health clinics, and generally improves the living and working conditions of the miners who sell their gems to us. In addition, we pay the miners higher prices for their products. It makes their life better. As a result, they are inclined to sell their product exclusively to us. And this is what we need; we need their product in order to survive. So it works. No one gets hurt. Everyone wins.

But it isn't easy. Maintaining a long supply network, which begins in many third-world countries and travels through cutting facilities in Sri Lanka before going to Distribution Houses in New York, London, and Hong Kong, is difficult. Getting everyone to cooperate is a juggling act. It takes constant attention. This is my job and the job is not an 'eight to five' job. Somewhere, someone always needs attention, needs to be educated or re-educated to the goals of the company, needs to have their hand held. It's why I spend most of my time on the phone or in the air traveling.

And if all this was not enough, I now had a new challenge that was not previously part of my previous job description, and that was to stay alive. Someone wanted to kill me, and this was why Charlie was here. I needed Charlie's help.

In truth, I had sort of given up, not completely, of course. It's just that I had begun to feel like a man who has been told by his doctor he has a terminal disease with no hope. But it is also true that no one ever stops thinking they will be the first one to beat an illness. I am no different. I am unwilling to fully acknowledge the fact I am a dead man walking.

So, the truth was I knew I had a death sentence hanging over my head, but I wasn't fully convinced I would die. Instead, I was running, running as fast as I could. In my case, this meant working hard because work was the one thing that kept my mind off my inevitable demise. But in the back of my mind, I knew my fate was fixed. I had dodged too many bullets too many times in the past. The odds of staying alive were diminishing fast.

Although... I have not given up. I am keenly aware of my situation. That's why the drapes in my office remain closed. No sniper's bullet will find me while I am slaving at my desk in plain view. But that makes my world visibly limited to nothing more than a room with a desk piled high with work. It is a nice room, a comfortable room, but a room that had become a claustrophobic cocoon: a compressing, stifling atmosphere with no freedom, just four walls with no windows.

In addition, two security men, bodyguards, rotate through my office/apartment complex at all times. I can go anywhere I want, but not without them. However, in reality, I seldom go out because they advise against it. They tell me to put off all business trips and schedule meetings only in my office. I have complied with their requests and gone nowhere since returning. I have not been a problem for them. I have stayed behind the walls of my office, behind my closed drapes, afraid to venture outside my self-imposed secure cocoon. As a result, I am alive, but it isn't much of a life, an existence only, and definitely not much fun.

'So, John, how are you doing?' Charlie sat down in the chair opposite my desk.

It was late in the afternoon and I was still in my office working, reviewing a new advertising campaign for the Christmas season, prepared for TV and magazines. It needed one final look before being approved. The ad agency which handled our marketing was scheduled in the morning.

Charlie was grinning when I looked up. The guy's smile was contagious. I couldn't help but force a smile in return. It was good of him to come, and I was happy to have a temporary diversion. Then I remembered why his happy face was grinning at me. I had been trying to bury this ugly subject deep in my subconscious so that I didn't have to think about it. I've been successful most of the time. Except at night, at night, the ugly thing came out of dark gloom to get me; like a slithering snake, it invaded my dreams with scenes of chaos and havoc. As a result, I wasn't spending much time in bed.

'I think you know,' I frowned in response to his question.

'Aw, come on, John, how bad can it be? You are alive and rich and handsome as ever.'

'Right, not bad for a dead man,' I said with a hint of sarcasm.

Charlie didn't respond so I continued. 'Charlie, you said it was over after South Carolina. Said I wouldn't have to worry anymore.'

'I think I was referring to the fact you would not have to worry about Nue ever again. I never said you wouldn't have to worry again,' Charlie responded. 'This sort of thing doesn't easily go away. Nue was just one man in a big organization, and it appears his organization doesn't like you.'

'So, is this what you came to tell me? Tell me Nue's organization is after me?'

'I didn't come to tell you anything. You were the one who called me, remember?'

'You know why I called. I don't have to tell you,' I said in disgust. 'My life is a mess. I stay inside where it is safe. I don't go out. I don't travel... I don't do anything but work in my office. It's not...' I paused without finishing my sentence, more in exasperation than anything else.

Now, it was Charlie's time to look glum. He didn't say anything; he just looked at the floor. 'John, I wish I could help you,' he finally responded. 'I wish I could wave a magic wand and make it all better. But I can't.'

'So what am I supposed to do, Charlie?'

'I don't know. I wish I did. But the truth is you have got yourself into a bad situation.'

'What are you talking about?'

'This thing you are involved in, it's international. It's big business, your business. It's one company against another, maybe even one country against another. It's about money and jobs. It's...'

'But I have created jobs in Thailand, maybe not as many as they desire, but as many as I'm able. What do they want from me?'

'Maybe they want more than you can deliver. Or maybe now it's just about the man you killed.'

'I couldn't help that. What was I supposed to do? Just let him kill Ilana's brother.' I fairly shouted at Charlie.

He just sat and looked at me. He knew nothing he could say would help. I also knew it. I needed to calm down. Our discussion was going nowhere. And it was frustrating because this was always what seemed to happen whenever Charlie and I got together. Not because I wanted to act like this when I was with him. Not because I didn't think about never letting this sort of thing happen again. I had promised myself I wouldn't get upset with him ever again. But it happened anyway.

I took a deep breath.

He wisely waited until he saw some semblance of composure return to my eyes.

'John, I will do what I can to help you. But the truth is, there's not much I can do.'

'Sorry, I didn't mean to get mad at you.' I responded. 'It's just ...'

'I know, don't bother apologizing.'

'So, do you have anything for me?' I asked, attempting to get our conversation back on track.

'I can tell you what I know,' Charlie said. 'But I'm not sure it will help. And stop me if you already know.'

'Okay.'

'Nue had a son. Sophon Nue is his name. The boy is in his early twenties, too young to take over the business. So, his great uncle, a man named Luang Nue, has returned to again take the leadership of the family business. He had it before he gave it to Nue when he retired. Now he is in charge again. Rumor is he's a level-headed guy, but who knows... Do you know him?'

'I called him once, but he wouldn't take my call.'

'So, you know as much as I do.'

I looked at the magazine advertisements lying on my desk. Suddenly, the ad campaign seemed completely useless. I had hoped Charlie would bring me some good news that would offer a glimmer of hope, but he had nothing. I took a deep breath.

'How is Ilana?' Charlie asked in an obvious attempt to change the subject.

'She's fine, living in Belize. I talk to her every few days.'

'Are you two still separated?' Charlie asked.

Charlie knew Ilana well. He had met her on several occasions. He knew we were deeply involved at one time.

'She wants to live in Belize, not here. I will probably go down to see her sometime. It's just...'

'You're afraid to travel?' Charlie stated.

'I have been advised not to travel for security reasons.'

'I understand. But do you want to travel?'

'Not really.'

'Because you are afraid?'

'I think it's a healthy fear.'

'Look, John, let me give you some advice. Life is a dangerous place. I know. I see and hear about death every day. It's part of my job. I know you're afraid, but you can't stop living. You need to get out. Take your bodyguards with you and be careful, but don't hole up in here. It's not healthy.'

I looked at him.

He smiled, one of his big broad grins.

I couldn't resist smiling back. 'I guess you're right, Charlie. Maybe that's why I needed you to come. I needed someone to tell me to get on with my life. Just one question first.'

'Sure.'

'Will you help me if I really need you?'

'I will, although I should probably just let you rot after all the trouble you have caused me.'

'True.'

'Will you do one thing for me?' he looked serious. 'Will you get some counseling? You know, we talked about this.'

I didn't have anything to say to him.

'It's called post-traumatic stress, John. You have all the classic symptoms,' he explained.

'I'll think about it.'

10:55 P.M. JOHN

We had a good time, Charlie and I.

Drank a few beers and talked about politics, the weather, sports, our golf games, and anything and everything except the painful memories we shared. We didn't discuss them. I didn't want to, and I didn't think he did either. We acted like a couple of old friends. And we were friends, but our friendship was a relationship cemented by a foul-smelling glue made from bad times and ugly scenes.

Still, it was nice to see him again. I enjoyed his company, and I think he enjoyed visiting me. But something unpleasant was always in the air when we were together, shadows of old sorrows floating through the back canyons of our minds, like the images of Monica's dead eyes. After he was gone, I worked for a few more hours, hoping work would relegate these memories to the subconscious caves in my brain where they belonged. Finally, I had to stop. I was hungry. I needed something to eat. After opening the door to my apartment, I hit the switch to turn off my office lights.

Helen had frozen meals delivered to my apartment so I wouldn't starve. All I needed to do was to heat the food in a microwave. She knew I wasn't a very good cook and her meals were far better than opening a can of soup or making a sandwich of lunchmeat and pickles which were two of my finer culinary talents.

I headed for the refrigerator to get some dinner but stopped first to pour a glass of wine. Ghosts from the past were still freely circulating in my brain at the time, swirling around like a bunch of unsupervised kids let loose on a playground, screaming and yelling, having fun at my expense. Charlie's visit had stirred up a pack of old, ugly memories, and they were in no mood to give me any peace.

My appetite was now gone, I went out on the deck in the back of the apartment with my glass of wine. It was dark. I first turned off the lights in my apartment. I didn't want anyone to know I was outside, exposed to a sniper's bullet. This may sound paranoid, but it has happened in the past. With the lights off, I felt reasonably safe in the darkness.

The air was warm, with a few clouds racing past a thin moon in a starry black sky. I decided it was time to let the ghosts from the past have their way. From experience I knew that trying to hold them down would result in their relentlessly attacking me until they were satisfied that I had not forgotten them. I sat in the dark, sipped wine, and let them come for me, first remembering how Charlie had carefully lifted Monica's dead body off me. I'm sure he thought she was dead at the time, but I didn't. I couldn't see the back of her head where she had been shot. I never looked, didn't want to see where a lead projectile had destroyed a beautiful mind. I didn't want to remember what that looked like.

She had fallen on top of me, fell face down as I lay beneath her in a kind of absurd last embrace. I believe she was trying to protect me at the time and pushed me down out of the line of fire. I made it, but she did not. The bullet hit her as we were falling. She never regained consciousness and died instantly in my arms. I held her as her warm blood dripped on my lips like a last kiss. When the shooting stopped, Charlie lifted her limp body off me and laid her on her on the floor as a tear glistened on the dark skin of his face. He took one last look before placing his jacket over her body, turning his back to me so I would not see him cry.

I was in love with her at the time of her death, but I had not acknowledged this fact to her. I had been avoiding the subject, afraid of the consequences of telling her how I felt. I was not mentally prepared to take the marriage plunge, even though I knew she was the person I wanted to live with for the rest of my life. Unfortunately, it was then too late to tell her. Too late for me and much too late for her.

Charlie's afternoon advice came to me as I thought about her. Life is a dangerous place, he had said. Don't live in fear, hiding. Get on with your life. He was right, but doing what he advised was not easy. Easy to say the words, but not easy to do. Because how does anyone go about the business of life when so much is uncertain, so much is unknown?

I like to plan.

I like to look at the future with a long-term focus. I like to work towards achievable goals. I think this is smart. And sure, I know life doesn't always go the way we think it should. Bad things happen, unforeseeable contingencies which can screw up a plan. I try to be prepared for unexpected consequences, but it never occurred to me before her death that so many unavoidable scenarios roam unchecked through what we call life, so many we can never ever fully plan for all of them. None of us can possibly anticipate all the inexplicable, unwelcome events that can bring us to our knees with unbearable sorrow. And worst of all, many of these unpleasant experiences may have nothing whatsoever to do with what we did. We are not responsible. They are like random bombs loaded with pain dropping out of a black night sky, falling on us with loud, mind-blowing anguish. One minute, our life is sunshine and success. The next it is filled with sorrow and weeping, sorrow so deep the caves in our minds containing the black sorrow have no end.

We are never the same after these events. They take a toll on our minds and bodies... a toll which never leaves us. Like our youth, once it is gone and you are old, you can never go back, no matter how hard you try.

I sipped my wine and stared up into the sky.

The night was black, and the stars were bright. I tried to imagine the wind of invisible particles that scientists tell us howls through the vast black voids of space, a wind of infinite dimensions. I mind-traveled on this wind, let my mind's eye ride on this silent wind to places I could not see, would never experience, to the edges of the universe. I wondered if a line existed somewhere on the edge of space, a line where our world stops and God's world begins. Or is it true we all live in one world together? Does heaven and hell exist folding over one another?

It certainly seemed that way. One moment, I was in heaven. And then Monica died... and I was in hell.

BANGKOK, THAILAND, THURSDAY,
SEPTEMBER 10, 1:15 P.M. LUANG

It was good, Luang thought, good to be home again living in the house where he had spent most of his life, as a boy, as an old man.

And it was good having people call and ask for his advice and help again. It was good to be needed. He no longer felt like a worthless old man.

All this was good, but he also had to acknowledge he missed some aspects of retired life. Mostly he missed his garden and his leisurely time to read and think. Now he never had enough time to enjoy his passions.

After trying to maintain the same work schedule before he retired, which meant spending ten to twelve hours per day in his office, he finally decided he was no longer capable of the stress. He would take some time each day to do other things. He was older now, and life was growing short.

After lunch, he spent time each day sitting in a garden, even if it was only for half an hour. No one could deny him. No one could tell him what to do. Phone calls could wait. Questions will be answered later. And did it really matter? How much could he really accomplish? Small changes maybe, but the big problems? Could he change these, the issues that really mattered? Was he really in control? Or was he, like us all, destined to ride a horse of many colors, a horse not of his own choosing?

He sipped his tea while looking around the garden. It was pleasant sitting in the shade, but it was difficult to keep his mind off work. Phillip Palmer was on his mind. The pest had called again. It seemed like this Phillip was always calling. At first, the old patriarch took his calls, but lately, Luang had started to avoid the persistent American. He had his secretary take a message instead. He didn't want to talk to Phillip every day. Especially since every call seemed to take an hour, it was obvious Phillip liked to talk.

The first time Phillip called, Luang accepted the call because he was told by his secretary an American was on the emergency line. This was the time Phillip had confirmed the truth about how his nephew died. The second time Phillip called, he asked about Sophon, several pointed questions designed to determine if Sophon was who he said he was. Luang had answered the questions slowly and deliberately until Phillip was fully convinced. Then Phillip asked Luang if he, Phillip, should help Sophon as Sophon had requested. Luang said yes, if Phillip was willing, he could help the young man. And what, Phillip wanted to know. What was in it for him if he cooperated with Sophon?

Just thinking about Phillip made Luang tired. He closed his eyes for a moment and rested. He missed his naps in the afternoon. Maybe he should include a nap every day in his garden. What did it matter if he took time for a nap? But instead of taking a nap, Luang's mind involuntarily returned to work, returned to thinking about Phillip and Phillip's question.

'What is in it for me?' Phillip had asked.

Wasn't this the question everyone asked, in different ways perhaps, but the same question? Business was simple. If you could answer this question in every situation, then you could conduct business with anyone.

Fortunately, the answer to Phillip's question was easy. Luang knew Phillip's history. Phillip's name had surfaced numerous times at previous family meetings. In fact, Phillip was probably startled to hear his question answered without hesitation. Luang simply told Phillip he would run the American division of a new company, which would be formed when John Van Laan's company was destroyed. This was the answer Phillip desired. So, this was the answer he was given. And Phillip had become very cooperative as a result.

Mr. Palmer had made himself instantly available to be one of the primary conduits in the family's desire to be rid of John Van Laan.

CHARLOTTESVILLE, FRIDAY, SEPTEMBER 11, 3:15 P.M. JOHN

Helen liked Ilana.

They had become good friends during the time Ilana lived with me in Charlottesville, a time when Ilana and I were lovers.

So, it seems whenever Ilana calls, Helen interrupts whatever I am doing to put her call through. And Helen does this even though she knows I don't like being interrupted. But apparently Helen has decided Ilana's needs and desires take priority over mine. It doesn't seem to matter that I am Helen's boss. Apparently, our relationship has changed. I suspect Helen, at this point in her career, considers her paycheck more of an entitlement than compensation for work.; something she deserves for years of past service. She shows up for work only as a favor to me, not to get paid.

In a way, she is right. I don't complain.

'John,' Helen buzzed.

'Yes, Helen,' I replied, trying to ignore her as I continued to read a report out of Zimbabwe.

Zimbabwe had one of the biggest and best emerald mines in the world. But unfortunately, Mugabe, the President, or should I say the dictator of Zimbabwe, had decided that all profit from his country's natural resources should benefit his country and therefore would allow any money to flow outside his country. Meaning... there was little to no incentive for a foreign company to develop the mines, even though this would have been a great benefit to his people in terms of investment and jobs. Finding a way to make him change his mind was the puzzle I had been trying to solve. It was not an easy task.

'John, Ilana is on the phone...

Pause

'John... did you hear what I said?' Helen repeated.

'Yes, Helen, you said Ilana is on the phone.'

'Well, are you going to answer the phone?'

'Yes, Helen, immediately, if not sooner.'

This was the game we played, Helen and me. She liked to interfere with my work, and I liked to piss her off by pretending to ignore her.

'John,' she repeated when I failed to immediately pick up the phone.

'Ilana, how are you?' I answered without responding to Helen.

'I am fine, John. But I am missing you. When are you coming to visit me?'

This was the question which had no easy answer. I loved seeing her. I loved Belize, the clear blue waters, the warm ocean breezes. I loved her big brown eyes and her smooth round body in her tight bikini. She was smart, intelligent, fun, everything I admired in a woman. In fact, at this moment, I would have given anything to step out of my office and take a leisurely dive into the warm emerald waters of the Caribbean Sea.

But she was not part of my life anymore. My work and my life were in Charlottesville while she was on her island because it was where she wished to be.

Plus, we shared a memory of the time we stood side by side together in a dark forest, looking at the dead body of the man I had just shot. And that memory is a problem because I associate it with Ilana and the association had badly soured our relationship.

Only a few people know me as a man who has shot and killed another man. Charlie knows, and Ilana knows. And unfortunately, Phillip knows. But to the rest of the world, I am the same man I was before. And I want to be this man again, a man who would never pull a trigger in anger. I try to forget what I did. But while looking into the eyes of Ilana, I will always see the man who pulled a trigger that killed another man.

I know that doesn't make her dislike me. She says I did it to save her brother. Nue had just ordered her brother's death. She insists I killed Nue to stop him from carrying out his order. And it would be nice to feel as she does, to think I did it for her. But I'm not sure that is true. Because as I have explained, Charlie's men were in the bushes behind me at the time. His CIA colleagues could have helped me stop Nue if I had asked. But I didn't ask.

So, I had another way to deal with Nue, a better way? But it was not the course I chose. I chose to take his life instead. I chose to kill him. So, I'm a killer whenever I see my reflection in the mirror of Ilana's eyes. And even though she tells me she understands, tells me I did it to save her brother, I can't accept that. I can't see it for anything more than what it was: an act of savage brutality that defied reason, an act that fails to stand up to the standards of a civilized society, an act of hate. And so I do not like the man Ilana sees and loves. And I don't want to be this man anymore. And this, more than anything, makes it difficult for me to be with Ilana. Even though it makes her unhappy, I cannot help her any more than I can help myself.

'Soon, Ilana, I will come down and see you soon,' I lied.

THURSDAY, SEPTEMBER 17, 2:05 P.M. JOHN

'Charlie is on the line,' Helen announced after peeking her head around the big oak doors at the entrance to my office.

Normally, she buzzes me through the intercom. But for important phone calls, the ones she wants to be sure I pick up, she often opens the door to my office and announces the call directly.

'Line two,' she added.

I didn't reply, simply picked up the phone and pushed the button which was blinking green. 'Charlie.'

'Got some news for you, old boy,' Charlie replied nonchalantly.

'I'm listening.'

'You remember I told you Nue had a son, Sophon. He is about twenty-two years old; a tall, handsome boy from the details on his passport. I think I told you he was too young to take over for his father, and his uncle has assumed the reins of power in the family business.'

'Yes.'

'Well, I thought you would like to know the boy is in the US. Seems he has been here for a few weeks.'

'Okay, why is this important?'

He paused. 'You know, John... sometimes you are a hard guy to understand.'

'Sorry, I just don't know why you are telling me.'

'Look, John, in my business, all information is important. You never know where it will lead you.'

'Okay, I'll bite. Where is this leading us?'

Charlie didn't answer immediately. Finally, he said with a hint of exasperation. 'John, I don't know where it is leading. I just thought it might be important for you to know. Do you understand?'

Like I said before, Charlie and I had a way of pissing each other off without even knowing we were doing it. Apparently, I had just made him mad again, and I needed to do something to make it right.

'Okay, I get it now. Thanks for the info.'

'Same to you,' Charlie replied sarcastically.

'Look, I apologize. I guess I'm just frustrated. I don't see any way out of this mess, and I was hoping you were calling with some really good news.'

'John, I'm doing everything I can.'

'I know. Sorry.'

'Look, forget it. Just tuck this information into the back of your head. If it means something to you someday, then call me. Okay?'

It took until he said this for my dumb brain to finally kick in and remember seeing a tall, good looking young foreigner talking to Phillip on the boardwalk in Grand Haven.

'Charlie, maybe I have something for you.'

I told him about the boy I saw.

Charlie didn't react right away. Finally, he said he would send the boy's passport photo over the internet. If I recognized his face, I should call.

Later in the day, the photo showed up on my computer screen. It wasn't a good picture, and I wasn't exactly sure it was the boy I had seen in Grand Haven, but it could have been. I called Charlie and told him. He didn't have to tell me this was not good news. I knew it. Then Charlie told me something else equally disturbing. He told me Phillip had disappeared. No one knew where he was. Charlie didn't have to say anymore. I could put the facts together as well as he could. Odds were Phillip and Nue's son were working together and no one knew where they were and what they were doing.

'Not good news,' I said to Charlie after taking a deep breath.

'No, not good.'

TUESDAY, SEPTEMBER 22, 11:15 A.M. JOHN

She walked right into my office on Helen's heels.

It was obvious Helen was completely unaware the woman had followed her inside because the look on Helen's face was priceless when Sandy announced from behind her back, 'Hi, John.'

I wasn't sure I had ever seen Helen look as flustered as she looked at that moment. First, a strange woman arrived at the office toting a suitcase, not a briefcase. Then, to make things even more interesting, the woman announced to Helen she had come to see her boss. And finally, when asked by Helen if she had an appointment, the woman said, 'no.' She did not have an appointment, but that didn't matter. She was certain Mr. John Van Laan would like to see her.'

Normally, Helen instructs all uninvited guests to take a seat. Then she summarily ignores them until they go away. But something about this woman was hard to ignore. Maybe it was because the woman was a statuesque blond with pretty blue eyes, and Helen knew I was a sucker for beautiful women. She must have decided it might be the better part of discretion to, at a minimum, check with me before sending the woman packing. Helen asked the woman to take a seat while she checked with her boss to ask him if he had time to see an uninvited visitor and not wanting the woman to overhear our conversation, Helen had come into my office rather than ask me over the phone. But what Helen had not anticipated was that Sandy would follow her into my office, simply walk right in without permission. And Helen was equally astonished to see the look of absolute surprise on my face when I saw Sandy standing behind her

For one extremely awkward moment, no one in the room said a word.

Sandy finally broke the standoff by passing a flustered Helen to take a seat in one of the chairs that faced my desk. 'You have a nice office, John,' she announced.

'Well gee, thanks,' I managed to reply. 'And what are you doing here?'

'Well... did you think you could make mad, passionate love to your old high school girlfriend and then expect she would never show up again for a repeat performance? Well, did you?'

When I looked at Helen. She had a... 'I don't believe I am hearing this,' look on her face.

Before she could hear another word, I waved at her out of my office.

'That will be all Helen.'

'You sure?' she smiled.

'Yes. I'm sure.'

Sandy sat grinning at me as I waited for Helen to close the doors.

Bob Anderson, the head of our New York Distribution House was scheduled to join me for lunch. Our meeting's agenda was a discussion of the next meeting of the Board of Directors. He was scheduled to arrive any minute. However, my immediate concern became Sandy, what to do with her while he was with me. I couldn't exactly put Bob off. He was flying in from New York.

'You don't look too happy to see me,' Sandy said.

'I'm very happy to see you. I just didn't expect to see you this morning. In fact, now that I think about it. I'm not sure I ever expected to see you again.'

'Oh, silly boy, did you think I would disappear forever?'

'You didn't exactly give me any clues to your intentions when you left.'

'I told you I had a life in San Francisco. I said I had things to do. I didn't say I would never see you again.'

'Yes, I guess that's true. But then you never said you would be returning either.'

She smiled.

I was lost. I knew I should be doing something other than arguing with her, but what?

'Well, do you want me to leave?' she asked.

It finally occurred to me there was at least one thing I could do. I got up and walked around the desk.

'No, that's the last thing I want you to do,' I said. 'Now stand up and give me a kiss and a hug, and let me tell you how pleased I am to see you.'

I held her, allowing the curves of her body to melt into mine. She felt good. It was like she was meant to be in my arms.

'John,' Helen barked through the intercom like a drill sergeant. 'Bob is here.' It was obvious from the tone of her voice that Helen was not pleased with what she assumed was happening in my office Sandy was not Ilana and Ilana was Helen's friend.

Sandy pulled back. 'I'm sorry. Am I in the way?'

'No, you're not in the way, but I have a luncheon meeting scheduled, and I can't put it off.'

'Oh, I will...'

My brain was scrambled. The close proximity of gorgeous curves was setting off a whole series of nervous messages to parts of my body that had nothing to do with business. What my body wanted and what I needed to do were two completely different activities.

'No... okay...' I stuttered, stalling for time, trying to solve my immediate problem. 'Hold on.' I pushed the intercom. 'Helen, give me a minute, then show Bob into my office and get lunch set up. Tell him I have a small matter to attend to first. I'll be back in about five minutes.'

Helen must have sensed the panic in my voice. She liked to tease me, but she was smart enough to know when that was not a good idea.

'I will take care of everything,' she said to my relief.

I quickly took Sandy by the arm. Grabbing her black and brown leather suitcase with my other hand, I ushered her towards the hidden door in my bookcase which opened to my apartment. Removing a book which covered the release, I hit a button and the door electronically opened.

'Oh, that is very clever, John Van Laan. Is this where you take all your girls?' she smiled.

'No, this is where I live.'

The door opened to a short hall leading to the main room of my apartment, a large room with a ceiling over a story and a half high. Behind closed drapes, tall sliding glass windows in the westerly wall overlooked a valley. They were separated by a stone fireplace which rose to the ceiling. Modern artwork I had collected from all over the world covered most of the other walls, which were painted white. The floor was wood covered by oriental and Native American Indian rugs. Leather seating surrounded the fireplace along with the usual assortment of lamps and tables, giving the room a modern but comfortable appearance. I hoped she was impressed, but she didn't show it.

I lead her through the room, past the dining room, and into a kitchen equipped with stainless steel appliances. It was a small but efficient kitchen with tile floors and smooth gray paneled cabinets. A dinette off to one side had sliding glass windows looking out toward a valley and mountains in the distance. A deck shaded by trees was outside the dinette. But none of this could be seen by Sandy because all the drapes in the apartment were closed as a precautionary, security measure. It would have been better for the drapes to be open at the time because the views outside were very impressive, but that couldn't be helped.

'Look, I'm sorry,' I said. 'But I have to return to my office to entertain a guest for lunch. There's food in the refrigerator. The bathroom is down the hall.' I pointed. 'Eat whatever you can find. Books and a TV are in a library on the other side of the kitchen. Relax; I'll be back as soon as I can.' Then I looked at her. 'That is if you can stay. I guess I should have asked first if you wanted to stay.'

She smiled. 'I came to visit you.'

'Great. My meeting could take time, at least an hour or two. But I'll be back as soon as I can.'

'Okay.'

'Will you be here when I return?'

'I think so,' she smiled.

'Say yes,' I pleaded.

'I'll think about it. Now run along to your meeting. I'll be fine.'

6:05 P.M. JOHN

If Bob didn't notice I was acting nervous, it was only because he was, as usual, oblivious to the obvious.

Bob was a New Yorker with a military background. And nothing in his history had educated him to the subtleties of human nature. And his inability to see past his narrow-minded point of view consistently got him into trouble. He had only one solitary concept of how the human race should be organized, and it was dictated by the military chain of command. Add his narcissistic New York insolence, and the problem of having a partner like Bob was easy to understand. These two mindsets added up to nothing good. Bob was simply not a caring, feeling person. For guys like Bob, the big boys make the decisions, and the grunts do the work. And when the short-sighted commands of the power elite fail to take into consideration the infinite disparity of human nature, even when men and women die because no one at the top is paying attention to anything but their personal shortsighted goals, even then, it is all about chain of command. Right or wrong, do what you are told. The big boys know better than you do.

This made it difficult to deal with Bob. But he was a major stockholder in my company and he ran our New York Distribution House. He was very important to my business. I had no choice except to work with him.

However, it was infinitely harder than usual to tolerate Bob this day. My head simply was not into our meeting. It was fixated on the presence of the beautiful woman in my apartment next door. The whole time I was talking to Bob, I was thinking about her. But unfortunately, big Bob was my schoolmaster that afternoon, and I was a schoolboy waiting painfully for the final school bell to ring. Time passed excruciatingly slowly; minutes seemed like hours. I couldn't stop daydreaming about Sandy. It was like when I was a teenager in high school, and all I could think about in class was walking my girlfriend home after school. Even though Sandy lived in the opposite direction from where I lived in town, I would walk her home. It was worth a long bus ride home just to be with her for a few hours. To see her smile in the sunshine. To hold her hand. To show the world she was my girl and make every guy along the road jealous.

To make matters worse, by the time I was finished talking to Bob, Helen had lined up a myriad of telephone calls like a freight train ready to roll down the track. Every time I thought I was done, another call would come in, which I simply could not ignore. I began to think Helen was doing this on purpose; sitting at her desk, calling everyone she knew and suggesting the best possible course of action designed to tie me up on the phone all afternoon. I sensed

Helen hoped Sandy would get bored and be gone by the time I finished.

At about six-thirty, I put down the phone one last time and headed for the door. The green lights on my phone consul were still blinking, but I didn't care. And I didn't bother to tell Helen I was leaving. I just got up and walked out; enough was enough.

My apartment was silent when I entered through the hidden door in my office.

Not good.

I don't like walking into a silent, empty apartment. In the past, I had a housekeeper who fixed my meals in the evening. He always played music while he was cooking, old jazz, which I loved. My apartment was never quiet when he was alive. But he was gone, killed by one of Nue's goons.

And Monica had lived with me for a short time before she died. She also made my apartment come alive. After Monica, Ilana came up from Belize. So, in the recent past, I seldom had to endure the silence of an empty apartment after work. And I didn't like it. It was one of the reasons I worked so much. I only went to my apartment to eat and sleep, nothing else.

That evening, I was hoping for more; actually, anxious to go to the apartment. It was strange in a way. It was like before when I looked forward to spending time with Monica or Ilana. It was a good feeling. But the silence that greeted me indicated nobody was home, only empty cold rooms. She was gone. Helen's plan had worked. I had told Sandy I would be busy for an hour or two. Instead, it had been more like five or six hours. I couldn't blame her for deciding not to wait.

The interior lights were all out. Only the receding light of the evening creeping through closed curtains cast some light in the form of dark shadows over the furniture. I walked slowly through every room looking for her, listening for any sound which would indicate her presence, but only an empty silence greeted my journey. When I didn't find her in in the kitchen or the main room or the small dinette, I began to accept the fact she was gone.

Then I spotted her brown and black leather overnight bag sitting near the door to the library. Next to it was her carryon bag with an airline label attached. An open book by Jim Harrison was lying on the floor beside the couch in the library where she lay sleeping.

Wearing tight jeans and a suede leather traveling jacket over a white tee shirt, her hair fell lazily over a pillow in soft blond curls, not too short and not too long, just comfortably stylish. She always had a flair for fashion. When we were together at the cottage, she mostly dressed in a bikini and summer shirt. But that was in August, and wearing almost nothing was the fashion of the day. I didn't take any notice of her wardrobe then. Now I remembered how well she dressed.

'So, do you like what you see?' she said without opening her eyes. As always, she had caught me off guard.

'I like everything I see.' I knelt down beside her.

'Good, because I'm hungry,' she smiled.

6:40 P.M. JOHN

While sipping wine at the kitchen counter of my apartment and amusing myself by observing her graceful body cooking our dinner, an overwhelming desire to hold her in my arms came over me.

Stealing around from behind while she was working at the stove with her back to me, a solitary ear looked especially tempting. I had no choice. I couldn't help myself. I leaned over her shoulder and gently kissed the elegant appendage. She didn't complain at first; she simply turned and smiled at me. Putting my arms around her waist, I took my time enjoying the quirky smile on her lips, the smile which always intrigued me, always took me in, as if she was saying, I know you, John Van Laan. I have known you since we were children. You have no secrets from me.

'Why don't you turn off the stove?' I suggested.

'Oh no, I've worked too hard preparing this meal. You're not going to spoil it.' She turned away.

I didn't argue with her; I simply held her firmly from behind so she could not get away, kissing her on the side of her neck while my hand fluidly explored the wonders that existed under her comfortable white tee shirt. She was not wearing a bra. It was easy to savor her soft breasts, the smooth flat of her tummy, and her luscious round shoulders. She didn't exactly fight my attention when I turned her to face me, although I could feel a certain resistance in the tight muscles of her back. I held my breath for a moment, looking anxiously into her eyes before gently kissing her lips. Her back muscles relaxed. The fight seemed to be going out of her. I buried my head on her shoulder and reached down to slowly undo the top button of her jeans and begin to push her zipper down.

Momentarily disregarding all my worried activity, she turned her back to me again and methodically turned off the burners on the stove and covered the pans while her jeans fell innocently to the floor. Slipping her panties down so I could caress her soft, warm bottom, I lifted her tee shirt over her head and gently kissed her once more on the back of her neck. Picking her up in my arms, I carried her naked body to the couch in the library, the place where I had found her earlier in the evening.

She lay on the couch and let me kiss the soft curves of her body while I was kneeling on the floor, allowing my mind to rest from the trials of work and become totally engrossed in the dream-like quality of her female body. Long and slim and wonderfully proportioned, I took my time enjoying her every fantasy, her breasts and the small round of her belly button as she undid the zipper of my pants and reached inside to hold me. I leaned over her body and slowly ran my hand up the smooth skin of her thighs until she arched her back to press her wet vagina against my hand.

Later, we sipped wine while the last light of the day receded behind mountains in the distance. Dinner was very good. Maybe a little less good than it would have been if it didn't need to be reheated, but still good. A simple meal really: pork chops, baked red skin potatoes, and beans, nothing fancy, a dinner our mothers made for us a hundred times when we were kids. And why not? She and I were two Dutch kids from Western Michigan. You can never change your genes or the place of your birth. It was special, going back to our roots.

A sense of comfort came with the meal like I was home again.

NEW YORK, N. Y., WEDNESDAY, SEPTEMBER 30, 2:55 P.M. JOHN

Bob Anderson, permanent board member and CEO of our New York Distribution House stood at the head of a long conference table, droning on and on and on about nothing especially pertinent.

Although his report to the Board of Directors was both accurate and exhausting, he could have said what he had come to say in about half the time. But the man liked to hear himself talk. His voice was clear and deep, authoritarian sounding to anyone who was still listening. Waving a pointer at a graph he had prepared to illustrate a point and acting like an Army officer of the rank, he naturally assumed his austere demeanor added credibility to a weak presentation. But it wasn't working. Most of the other directors had turned him off long ago.

The display board he had set up on his right at the head of the table had a line graph illustrating increased sales in certain sizes and colors. The point he was attempting to make, and I will admit, he had a talent for pointing out what was obvious, was that certain colors and sizes of sapphires sold better than others. The reason he was making this point was to force the company, meaning me, to buy more of these stones, which would make his job easier and put more money in his pocket. However, the problem was that the company had no control over what gemstones came out of the mines. I bought what the miners had to sell, and I didn't quibble. I paid a good price because I wanted them happy so they would not sell to anyone else. Therefore, I had no way of accommodating him. But I did understand him. He was a salesman at heart. And like all salesmen, he enjoyed selling products that were easy to sell. It took all the work out of his job.

I briefly thought about getting up and cutting him off. I could have. I was the Chairman of the Board, but I didn't. I let Bob enjoy his moment in glory. He loved giving his quarterly reports to the board.

Instead, I let my mind wander and think about Sandy when I should have been considering my responsibilities as the Chairman of the Board. She was in the city somewhere. We had come to New York because I needed to attend the board meeting. I was the Chairman. It was a job I couldn't hand off to someone else. So I sat dutifully listening to Bob's report while Sandy was having fun.

Nothing of great importance was planned for this meeting. No great drama was anticipated. It was simply the quarterly meeting of the board, one of my rigorous duties as CEO and Chairman of the Board. However, today, it seemed harder than usual to focus than normal. I assumed Sandy was the reason. I wanted to be with her, not sitting in this room with all these men and women around a long table filled with papers. I wanted to be roaming the streets of New York with Sandy, seeing her smile and enjoying the company of a beautiful woman.

When Bob was done, he smiled and sat down, satisfied he alone understood the needs of the company.

I sighed inside. The meeting would be over soon. I stood to introduce a report from Sri Lanka, which would be read by a member from that country. He rarely came to the meetings, always sending a representative instead. I could not blame him.

His brother had been murdered in this country.

5:55 P.M. SOPHON

The young man found it easy to blend into the crowded sidewalks of New York City.

People of all nationalities brushed shoulders in the city, pushing and shoving and darting around one another. The sidewalks were impatient places filled with constant commotion, people absorbed in their personal fantasies, their desires, and their obsessions for wealth and power. Shimmering dreams of fame danced in their heads as they walked. New York was a magical place, a place where dreams could come true. Where becoming a celebrity was only a heartbeat away, a chance discovery, a place to shine. Everyone seemed to be in a hurry to be somewhere, never content to rest; everyone except Sophon. He was in no hurry. He was a young man consumed by a different passion, and the absolute ambiguity of the restless streets of New York City fit his plans perfectly.

Phillip had informed Sophon that John Van Laan would be in New York today. Phillip told the young man that a meeting of the Board of Directors of John's company was scheduled. In fact, Sophon's great-uncle had a representative at this meeting. Sophon knew the man, but Sophon didn't plan to speak to him. Sophon had come to the city for another reason. He came to understand the man who had killed his father. Even though his primary mission was to kill John Van Laan, in a way he did not totally comprehend, Sophon was fascinated by this man. John Van Laan was someone who, in a very short period of time, had become disastrously important to his family... So, who was this man and how had he accomplished so much in so short a time? How could anyone who lived in a world so different from his have created a company that affected Sophon's family's business, a business that had existed for hundreds of years? How could this catastrophe have happened?

Sophon was young and like all young people he was naturally curious. He had asked Phillip to tell him about John Van Laan, but the answers he received from Phillip seemed shallow and unconvincing. He felt Phillip was holding something back, something he did not want to tell Sophon.

After he learned about the Board Meeting in New York, where the meeting was to be held and where to look for John, Sophon decided to go to New York to observe John in person. To help Sophon, Phillip had given him a picture, so he could easily identify his father's murderer.

After walking the restless sidewalks of New York, Sophon arrived midafternoon at the entrance to the club where Phillip said the Board Meeting would be held, hoping to see John leave the building.

It was a lonely vigil, waiting outside on the sidewalk. When he became tired, he had one of his men watch the entrance to the building while he rested in a car parked down the street. John Van Laan had to come out sometime. When he did, Sophon planned to follow him. In the meantime, he needed to be patient.

Fortunately, it was a sunny day, and the women of New York City were available to pleasantly occupy Sophon's bored attention. Dressed in everything from jeans to business suits, some of the women wore long skirts, and some chose short skirts. Some had long black hair, and some cut their blond hair short. Many of the ladies looked like models or actresses. Sophon was fascinated. He wondered about them. Wondered what it would be like to be with them, to make love to them. It helped pass the time. He was a young man, after all, and he did what all young men do. He looked, and he dreamed.

A dark blue Buick pulled up to the curb while Sophon was observing a tall woman with long straight black hair wearing a short skirt, stroll past a green awning which was one of only two visible clues to what resided inside the building. A brass plate mounted on the exterior of the building spelled the name of a club was the other clue. Other than these two identifiers, nothing indicated the old-world opulence which existed inside this old stone building.

Two men in suits exited the Buick and stood at the curb. A big Italian-looking chauffeur with curly black hair came around to open the back door. A man who looked like the picture of John Van Laan quickly arrived from inside the building and got inside the car after greeting the chauffeur with a handshake. The Buick headed uptown.

Sophon signaled his waiting car.

6:35 P.M. JOHN

It was still relatively early in the evening for high society New Yorkers. Plenty of empty tables were available in the uptown, upscale New York restaurant.

Sandy had been patient during the board meeting. As a reward I wanted to take her out to dinner, someplace special to show my appreciation.

The Board Meeting had gone well; boring with no surprises. And even though it was customary for the members to share a meal after the final meeting, I begged off, explaining with a smile that I had an out-of-town guest to entertain. I assumed most of the board members saw through my charade. Sandy had been seen with me at one time or another in the last few days. And I knew they noticed her. She was hard not to notice. I didn't think a more detailed explanation was necessary.

She looked good in the soft light of the restaurant wearing a simple black dress open at the neck. Her ears were highlighted by simple round silver earrings complimented by a silver necklace adorned with a topaz lying against the smooth skin of her neck. I wondered if she may have bought the dress while in New York because I didn't remember seeing it on her before. I complimented her on the dress and the necklace. She smiled and said the necklace was something she had found in a jewelry shop in San Francisco near where she lived.

Her blond hair flowed freely to her shoulders while she perused the menu. Occasionally, she brushed an errant strand off her forehead, a simple gesture executed with grace. She wore almost no makeup. Her face didn't require a disguise of cosmetics. I had to admit I felt proud to be in the restaurant with her. Trophy blond is what some might call her, but I knew she was so much more.

I had wanted to ask her how long she planned to stay ever since the first day she arrived in Charlottesville. And did the fact that she agreed to accompany me to New York for the board meeting, did this mean our relationship had moved to another level? These questions and others had been rummaging around in my brain all week. I wanted to know, but at the same time I was afraid to ask, afraid of being disappointed in what she might say.

She had been with me now for over two weeks and she didn't seem to be particularly eager to leave anytime soon. But at the same time, she hadn't said anything which would clue me to how long she planned to stay.

I kept remembering the last time she left. How she just packed her bag and walked away after only a short warning. Afterwards it occurred to me that her black and brown travel bag may have been the clue I desired to her intentions. The bag had never been emptied during its time at my cottage. It had resided on the floor of my bathroom, always available to be packed quickly without notice for a trip home.

This time was different.

This time her black and brown leather bag had made it all the way inside my bedroom. It sat on a chair beside the bed next to her carry-on; more inside than before, but still available for a quick exit if necessary. The contents of the bag had not been put away in a closet as I would have liked. But at the same time, the location seemed to indicate a natural evolution in our relationship.

After she arrived, I cleaned out one of my closets when she wasn't looking. I intentionally didn't say anything to her about it; I simply left the closet door open and empty for her to use. She took the clue without a word and hung up some of her clothes in the closet in the bedroom, a few things that she had ironed. So this was also different, and it was progress as far as I was concerned. A small bag containing her toiletries sat on a counter in my bathroom. I didn't complain about it, even though it was unsightly to have all her paraphernalia lying around. I would have preferred she put the stuff away on shelves behind closed doors. I like things neat. But in her case, I put up with the clutter.

Our time together in the evenings after work and errands, had been spent eating and talking mostly about old times. It was fun to reminisce about our youth, talk about old adventures. We purposely ignored the subject of our break up. We only talked about the good times. However, it wasn't all fun. We had some anxious times back then. I worried at one time she might be pregnant, something which may have driven us apart.

'What are you smiling about?' she asked as she sipped her wine while sitting across from me at dinner.

Our two bodyguards were already eating their meals at the table next to us. I guess they were hungry. Our menus were open on the table. We had not ordered. I wanted to relax and enjoy a drink first. The day had been long, and even though everything had gone well at the board meeting, it was still difficult work. Chairing a meeting where board members come from different countries was never easy. They all spoke English but with various dialects. Some were very difficult to understand. Oddly, the Brits were one of the worst. Their accents sometimes made it almost impossible to understand them.

We are two countries separated by a common language, as one of the Brits liked to say.

The Sri Lanka representative was easy to understand in contrast. He spoke very slowly with a rich English accent which was easier to understand than the Brits. The representative member from Thailand was also easy to understand. He had obviously learned his English in a US school and he took his time speaking.

Anyway, I was glad when the meeting was over, and I could finally relax.

'I was thinking about the time when we worried you might be pregnant,' I replied to her question.

She just smiled.

During one of our earlier evening conversations she had told me she had a relationship with a man who eventually went away when she told him she didn't want to have children. A question lingered in the air after she made this comment. It seemed she was asking me if it mattered to me. She didn't ask the question out loud, but I could feel she needed an answer. So, I simply said I had never considered the possibility of children. My life was too busy. I didn't have the time. It wouldn't be fair.

She had looked away after I said this as if she was looking for something that could never be, some vision of life that was more like a dream, a dream lost in the wind that could be felt but never held. She looked sad. But my answer seemed to satisfy her. It was what she needed to know. She tucked this bit of knowledge away and seemed content afterward.

'I learned my lesson,' she replied.

'What do you mean?'

'Always took precautions after our scare.'

'Always?'

'Always.'

I smiled.

'So why do you find that so funny?' she asked.

'Sorry, just wondering what I would have done if I had known that at the time.'

'You mean like screwing my brains out?'

'Yes, there is that. And perhaps I could have told my folks. You know something like Mom, Dad, don't worry. Sandy takes precautions. How do you think they would have reacted?'

'I think you would have been grounded for the rest of your life.'

'So, probably wouldn't have worked.'

'John, they never liked me.'

'They didn't like me either. You were just a phase of my bad behavior.'

'How did we survive those times?' she asked after a pause.

'Don't know.' I sipped my wine and thought about how strange life is, how some of the best times could also be the worst. But she was with me now, so maybe it didn't matter what happened in the past. I wondered again if she would stay this time. And I don't know why, but at that moment, I had to know. So, I just blurted out the question before I had a chance to consider the consequences.

As I waited for her answer, out of the corner of my eye, I noticed a tall young man with black hair sitting down with companions at a table near ours.

He looked familiar.

8:25 P.M. SOPHON

Sophon watched as his father's murderer, John Van Laan, signed the restaurant check and prepared to leave.

Sophon's two companions were still eating. He had only picked at his food, occasionally taking a sip of wine but mostly watching, trying to observe without being conspicuous.

The woman, the blond who was John's companion, she was beautiful. She smiled at her table companion often, talking occasionally, not too much, just enough to hold up her side of the conversation. John was doing most of the talking, obviously very interested in her. She seemed happy to be with him. They made an attractive couple.

From what Sophon could observe, his father's killer was nothing like Sophon imagined. He was handsome, dressed well, and seemed confident, nothing like the evil monster Sophon envisioned when he first heard about his father's death. He assumed his father's killer would be a large, ugly man, fat, maybe grossly fat, like the ugly Americans who visited his country looking for young girls to defile, or worse, young boys, something they would never do in their own country; sexual pleasures Americans traveled to Thailand to purchase.

The man he observed fit none of these images. He seemed kind and considerate to the blond woman. And she acted nothing like the American women he had met, the ones who roamed the streets of New York City offering services to young men who could pay. He had been solicited more than once as he walked the streets of this fine city at night. And he had been tempted, but he had turned down their offers. He had not come for this reason. He politely said no to all of them, even to the pretty ones who looked like they could use the money.

The blond was obviously not a paid prostitute. She did not look the part. She looked like she was John's girlfriend. Sophon found it strange that any woman would voluntarily be with a man who was a killer. Perhaps he never told her what he did, what he was. Maybe he would not want her to know what kind of man he had become.

When John got up to leave, Sophon waved at his waiter and placed several hundred-dollar bills on the table while pushing his chair away from the table. His men immediately put their forks on the table and stopped eating.

The trio stood in unison and left the restaurant together.

8:30 P.M. JOHN

The sidewalk was crowded, people milling around; some wanting to go inside the restaurant, some walking past, bumping and shoving.

This was New York after all. It is always crowded on the sidewalks of New York and it was a hassle, a necessary one if you wanted to be in the city. I took Sandy's arm and directed her towards the curb. Mike, the driver of our hired chauffeured car, was somewhere close. I had called him on my cell phone as we left the restaurant and asked him to pick us up.

My arm suddenly hurt. A hand, a strong grip, pulled me stumbling backward in surprise, half falling against a passing pedestrian who shouted at me to be careful, New York style. 'Watch it, buddy,' the man snarled.

Todd, one of our bodyguards, saw what was happening. Immediately, he stepped between me and the large man who was pulling my arm, swinging down hard, hitting the man's arm, forcing him to release his grip. The man swung back. Todd ducked. I turned to see anger on the large man's face, the man who had grabbed my arm. Another man hit Todd on the back of his neck from behind. Danny, our other bodyguard, was on him, instantly twisting the man's arm behind his back and turning him away. Todd looked stunned. A crowd formed around them. The large man stepped back when he saw Todd display a gun under his jacket. They stared at each other for a brief second, knees bent in a standoff.

I took Sandy around the waist and pushed her through the crowd towards the street. Mike's Buick slid up to the curb. I quickly opened the back door. Sandy stepped inside, and I got in behind her. Todd and Danny backed slowly towards the curb. Hands-on their guns under their jackets. The crowd stepped aside to allow them to pass.

The men who had tried to grab me were gone.

9:20 PM. JOHN

'So, do you mind telling me what happened back there,' Sandy asked.

The incident outside the restaurant had been verbally ignored on purpose while traveling to our hotel. I had silently fumed in the back seat of the car in a mad curse. Our bodyguards sensed I didn't want to discuss it. They didn't say anything. The drive to the hotel was completed in relative quiet, everyone decompressing after the scare. Outside, horns blared, ambulances screamed, and busses belched fumes while Mike, our chauffeur, stealthily weaved in and out of the traffic, inches from disaster, constantly checking his mirrors to make sure we were not being followed.

Mike and I had a history. He had saved my life once, the same day Monica had been killed. So I owed him big time. He was my driver of choice whenever I was in New York. I always made sure he got a big tip, cash his company, and the IRS would never see.

Although I hated New York traffic, I was never concerned when sitting in Mike's dark blue Buick. Mike was a great driver and the seats in the back were soft black leather and comfortable. It was a bit crowded with the two bodyguards in the car, one up front with Mike and one in the back seat with Sandy and me. I didn't mind. I tried to relax on the trip to the hotel after the incident outside the restaurant. I knew I needed to calm down. I didn't want Sandy to see my ugly, frustrated side.

Todd and Danny, our bodyguards stayed busy checking traffic, occasionally looking out the rear window, talking to Mike, asking if he saw anything troubling. Fortunately nothing concerned them. Apparently it was over. Our bodyguards had done their job.

'What,' I replied innocently to Sandy's question.

'That shoving match outside the restaurant, what was that all about?'

We were safe in our hotel room when she asked her question. A glass of wine was in her hand. I had suggested a nightcap as soon as we shut the door. I needed a drink. A sip of single malt whiskey felt warm going down my throat. I didn't really want to talk about it.

'I don't know,' I replied. 'Pickpockets, thieves maybe?'

'Out in the open on a crowded street?' she questioned.

I looked at her. I knew I couldn't dodge her question.

'It's possible they were trying to abduct me,' I said. 'The man who grabbed my arm didn't go for my wallet.'

'You sure do live a fascinating life, Mr. Van Laan,' she smiled

'I guess. You sure you want to live it with me?'

'For now.'

11:15 P.M.

Sophon put down his toothbrush, washed his face and stared into the mirror as he prepared for bed in his hotel.

It could have gone differently. It could have been over by now; his father's killer could have been dead, but he was not. His bodyguards had not been anticipated. The man had once more escaped death.

It was fate and Sophon could not control fate.

The young man was not entirely unhappy with the outcome. His evening had not been a total loss. It was the first time Sophon had been able to observe John Van Laan up close, and he had learned more than he could digest. He needed time to think about this man and decide what to do about him. Other opportunities would come. The man could not escape every attempt to kill him. Sophon simply needed to be patient and prepare better. It would happen. He would have his chance to confront his father's killer. It was just a matter of time before the murderer would be dead. For now, he had accomplished what he was necessary.

He would take his time, think about what he had learned and be better prepared for the next step in his revenge.

CHARLOTTESVILLE, FRIDAY, OCTOBER 2, 6:40 P.M. JOHN

'So, when were you planning to tell me about Ilana?' Sandy asked with an innocent look on her face.

We were sitting on the back deck off the dinette, having a drink at the time. The deck was sheltered by a stand of trees. A viewfinder on a sniper's rifle would have a hard time seeing through the trees. The other decks of the apartment were not as secure. They were out in the open with big, expansive views of the valley. I liked them better because of their views, but my security staff was not comfortable with me sitting on one of these open decks. So, I compromised. I told them I couldn't live like a mummy encased in a tomb. I needed to be outside some of the time. They said that if I had to go outside, they would prefer I sit on this deck, which was visually sheltered by trees. I agreed.

It was evening and cocktail time. Friday and the week was over, a long and tiring week. Going to New York for the Board Meeting had been draining. Sandy had come along, which helped. I don't think she minded. She seemed to like the Big Apple. She had become a big city girl since moving to San Francisco.

Charlottesville was okay with her. She visited historical sites while I was working, but she seemed far happier in New York. However, the security detail assigned to her did not share her enthusiasm. Their job was to keep her safe while she roamed the sidewalks, the museums, the shops and the parks. She didn't make their job very easy.

The incident on a sidewalk outside the restaurant on the last day of our trip was troubling. I still had not decided what to do about it. I thought about calling Charlie. But what could I tell him? A couple of guys had tried to grab me. But I really didn't know why. We were in New York. It could have happened for any number of reasons. I didn't want Charlie laughing at me. So I let it go. Sandy took it better than I could have anticipated, accepted it as a fact, and moved on. She was a remarkable woman.

A glass of Scotch was my choice on that Friday evening. I was beginning to relax after a long day of work when she asked me about

Ilana. More work was scheduled for Saturday morning, but my intentions were to devote most of the weekend to Sandy. I was looking forward to spending time alone with her.

Her question came out of nowhere and made me wonder where it originated. My first reaction was she had been talking to Helen. Helen liked Ilana, and I wasn't getting the same positive vibes from Helen about Sandy as I did with Ilana. So, it was possible Helen had been up to no good, spreading a few well-placed comments intended to put an end to my romance with Sandy. But then... I couldn't completely blame Helen for Sandys's question. Ilana had called several times when Sandy and I were together. I had taken the call each time. I didn't intentionally hide Ilana from Sandy, and I certainly didn't want to lie to Sandy about Ilana. On the other hand, I didn't volunteer information either. So, her question was inevitable.

I smiled. 'I guess I owe you an explanation.'

'Well, I know she calls you. And you do talk to her. So, I assume she is. ...'

'Have you talked to her?' I interrupted, suddenly concerned Sandy had talked to Ilana without my knowledge. It was important to know how much Sandy knew before I answered her.

'Well, yes, I answered the phone a few times when she called the apartment, and you were out.'

'And?'

'Well, she sounded nice, I guess.'

'So, did you two talk?'

'No, she didn't seem to want to talk to me. Just asked where you were.'

'I see. So now you want to know more about her.'

'I guess... although, you don't have to tell me. That is if you don't want to. It's really none of my business.'

I ignored her comment and instead asked her, 'Do you remember my telling you about a woman who helped me recover from Monica's death when I was in Belize?'

'You mentioned someone. But you didn't tell me you still had a relationship with her.'

'I guess I failed to mention that.'

'I guess you did,' she smiled.

I sipped some Scotch. She had me. It was time to tell her. It was the only thing I could do. I didn't begin at the beginning. I began at the end, first explaining to Sandy that Ilana was with me when I killed Nue and how that made me feel. Then I went back to the beginning and told Sandy the story of how Ilana had found me in Belize, where I had gone to drink away my sorrow after the death of Monica. I told her the whole story, a simplified version, of course, left out the intimate details, but for the most part, the story was accurate. It took a while, and Sandy didn't say too much. She didn't have to. It was a one-sided conversation. I finished by telling Sandy I had built a house on the sea in Belize and given Ilana money to live there. I admitted Ilana and I had been lovers, and we were still good friends.

When I was done, Sandy looked at me curiously and suggested visiting Ilana. She said she would like to meet Ilana and see my house on the sea. She had never been to Belize. It would be fun.

I looked at Sandy like she was out of her mind, but I could tell by the determined look in her eyes, she was serious. I was in trouble. I had no way out. Sandy could be very passive about some things, but persistent in others.

This was one of those times when she was resolute.

SATURDAY, OCTOBER 3, 8:30 A.M. JOHN

Her carry-on suitcase was sitting by the door next to the brown and black overnight bag when I went to look for her.

In the morning we had slept in and made love. I took a leisurely shower, shaved and got dressed. She was already dressed in jeans and a sweater when I found her. Her coat was lying on her bag near the door.

'Al will drive me to the airport,' she announced. 'I have to go.'

Al was one of the security staff, and apparently, Al knew more about the morning's activities than I did. I knew nothing. I just stood there like an idiot, looking rather stunned.

She spoke before I could say another word. 'I have some things I need to do at home. Don't worry, I will come back.'

'When?' I asked lamely.

'Oh, I'll call you. I won't just show up next time. I thought the first time would be a nice surprise.'

'Okay.'

'I promise I will call ahead next time so you can properly prepare for me. I wouldn't want you to have any strange women in the house the next time. The first time, I was prepared to take the risk. If someone had been here, I would have gone away. It was fun, really, the suspense, you know.'

'Yes, it was quite a surprise.'

'Did you like my surprise?'

'Sandy, you know I liked your surprise, but then you have always been full of surprises.'

'Yes, it would seem that way.'

'Are you going now?'

'I am, but I will come back, and then we can talk some more, you know, about us.'

'Okay.'

'And John, I'm serious about going to Belize. You will arrange it, won't you?'

'If that is what you want.'

'I do. Now kiss me goodbye. I need to get to the airport.'

I kissed her on the cheek and silently watched as she walked out the door with her brown and black bag over her shoulder, dragging her wheeled carry-on suitcase behind her.

8:55 AM. SANDY

It was time to return home.

Sandy needed time to think. As Al drove her to the airport, she considered her situation. What to do.

One possibility was to forget about John and move on. Her life was already complicated as it was. And being with him only added complications. Complications for her, complications for him; too many complications. Complications if she continued with him; far fewer complications if she didn't. One major complication was that she lived in San Francisco on the West Coast, and he lived near the East Coast in Charlottesville. Then there was the issue of housing. She owned a condo, and he lived in an apartment he owned attached to an office building. Complications, complications, so many complications; she just couldn't seem to find any easy solutions to all the complications.

And then there was the matter of John's girlfriend. Discovering he had another woman in his life only added to her long list of complications, making Sandy's decision even more difficult. Problematic, perhaps beyond any possibility that a solution was even remotely attainable.

Too many questions needed to be answered. Like what was his relationship with Ilana? What was it in the past? What was it now? Sandy could only guess.

And then there was the shooting incident in Grand Haven. What kind of person gets shot at these days? John didn't fit the description. He did not live in a big city. He wasn't part of the gang. He wasn't part of the mob. But apparently, he was a man who was involved in some sort of messy international business that involved a family in Thailand. And a man from this family had been killed. Shot by John for reasons that may or may not have been justified.

So... Who in their right mind gets involved in something like that?

Nothing made sense.

Everything told her to run, to hide, to avoid the complications. But one thought kept her from walking away. He held her back. He kept her from doing what she knew she should do because he was a man she could love. Despite all the complications, she could not get him out of her head.

However, one conclusion was altogether too obvious. Before she became any more involved with him, they needed to travel to Belize. Sandy could not imagine continuing with John without going to Belize first. Although she knew it was a big gamble, it had to be done. The other woman in his life, Ilana, could not be ignored. Sandy's relationship with John wasn't fair to Ilana. So Sandy did what she always did in situations like this. She met the situation head-on. Deal with it and move on. Never shy away from a problem. Because problems ignored have a habit of coming back to visit you sooner or later with disastrous consequences.

However, she wondered if any of this made sense. Given all the complications, wouldn't it be far simpler to give him a 'dear John' phone call? Or do it in person, fly back, and tell him face to face? Either way she would be honest with him.

Because honestly, it was just so complicated.

She sighed. It was time to go home, time to get away for a while, time to take some time to reflect and... decide later.

SUNDAY, OCTOBER 4, 4:05 P.M. JOHN

It was too early to fix a drink, and it was too late to start another work project.

I spent most of my weekend working. After Sandy's unexpected departure Saturday morning, I wandered around the apartment for a short time like a lost boy before eventually settling in my office. With nowhere else to go, my office became my designated place to retreat. I had work to do there, people to call, plans to make. I had hoped to put off most of this work until Monday and spend the weekend with Sandy, but she obviously had other plans. She had gone home. She had left me behind. So, I worked to hide from what was really bothering me. It was what I always did in situations like this.

But my subconscious wouldn't leave me alone.

My conversation with Sandy about Ilana kept playing over and over in my head. And a question, or should I say an uneasy feeling I had made a tactical error, kept strutting around in the back of my brain like a dancing clown. I just couldn't get the sucker to leave me alone. I kept wondering if my telling Sandy about Ilana Friday night had caused Sandy to leave on Saturday morning. I knew Sandy could be impulsive sometimes. So, yes, it was possible.

To hell with it, I thought. It was still early. I needed a drink. I missed her more than I wanted to admit, and I couldn't stop thinking I had caused her to leave.

Opening the shaded glass panel to my office liquor cabinet, I took out a bottle of Scotch and a glass. The office was empty at the time. It was Sunday, and except for two security personnel, the building was empty and quiet. My drapes were drawn. Security didn't want them open because, according to them, I was a sitting duck behind those open windows, like in the past, the time I had almost been killed by a sniper's bullet. So, I respected their caution, but it meant my office was a room with no windows and no view to the outside. I hated the closed drapes. But I did as I was told, although it felt claustrophobic.

A door on the left side of my office windows opened to a small deck. Stairs attached to the deck led to the ground one story below. The stairs were designed as a fire escape to please the local building inspector. The deck was only big enough for one chair.

Occasionally in the past, when I needed a break from work; I had gone out on the deck, left the door slightly open so I could hear my phone ring and breathed some fresh air. An old folding chair had been left out there for just this purpose: times when I wanted to be outside, needed to be outside, feel the wind, see no barriers in front of my eyes, only me and the vast expanse of forest valley below.

I briefly wondered if the chair was still there. I had not been out on the deck for months. Security didn't like it. Ignoring their directives, I stepped outside and placed my glass of Scotch on the railing. At that moment in time, I didn't care about being shot. I was not scared of dying. I was more afraid of living.

The old chair was where I left it, leaning against the wall, dirty and dusty but still usable. I brushed it off with my hand and sat down. A few puffy clouds roamed in a clear blue autumn sky as I sipped from my glass and tried to relax. Below the deck was the beginning of a trail through the woods. It was more or less flat for a short distance before climbing steeply up a long hill through the trees leading to another trail up a larger hill. I had often walked these trails to stay in shape, usually in the mornings before work. I would climb to the top of the second hill to enjoy the view. Take a moment to say a prayer and spend some time with God. It was my time to respect my roots and my upbringing in the church. I'm not an outwardly religious guy. I guess that's a fault, but that doesn't stop me from believing I have a relationship with God and thinking I need to honor this relationship. Sitting at the top of the hill was where I could be alone with God. Afterwards, I would return to my apartment for a shower, breakfast, and a long day of work.

I suddenly missed my morning walks.

I hadn't gone for a long time because it was not the same with some overweight security guy trying to keep up with me. I liked being alone. I liked walking at my own pace. I missed the solitude among the trees and rocks. This was the best part of the experience.

I quickly decided to walk up the trail; irrationally decided without taking time to consider the danger. I didn't care what the security boys thought. I needed to get out. I headed down the stairs with the glass of Scotch in my hand. Taking the glass with me was not ideal while walking, but I hadn't planned to go very far. Besides, I was in no hurry and an occasional sip of Scotch could help ease my restless mind.

I began by walking steadily, not at a strenuous pace.

GRAND HAVEN, MICHIGAN, 4:40 P.M. PHILLIP

Phillip Palmer was frustrated and alone in his office on a Sunday afternoon in Grand Haven, Michigan.

He had flown home after resigning himself to the fact that Sophon no longer needed him. Why travel a road which leads to nowhere? What for? Nothing was happening. Nothing was going to happen. He had been with the young man for weeks. They had accomplished nothing; nothing which would help Phillip achieve his goals.

Finally, Phillip had decided to go home.

Placing his feet on his desk, he leaned his cushioned leather chair back while trying to decide who to call. Phillip badly needed someone to call. Someone's ear he could bend because this was what he always did when he was bored. He called someone.

But who to call? This was his question. Maybe Sophon's uncle? But what good would it do? He had called the old man so many times he couldn't keep count them all. Most of his calls had been declined. A message was taken and ignored.

Phillip pondered his dilemma absentmindedly while playing with his ponytail, wondering why Sophon had delayed accomplishing his stated task, killing John Van Laan and avenging the death of his father.

It wasn't because Sophon didn't have the tools to do the deed. He had more tools than he could ever use. Phillip had done as he was told and placed the tools at Sophon's disposal as instructed by Sophon's uncle. Phillip didn't bother to tell Sophon where the tools came from. He didn't think he had to. He was pretty sure Sophon knew. Sophon was smart. He didn't ask questions that had obvious answers. He went along with the game Phillip and his uncle were playing. Men and guns, surveillance via satellite and other devices, Sophon was constantly updated concerning John Van Laan's location. He could have killed John on several occasions. And except for one time, the first opportunity, the weak attempt outside the restaurant, which failed; all other opportunities had been simply waved off by the young man. He said it was not the right time.

Phillip began to wonder if it would ever be the right time. Perhaps Sophon was incapable of killing. Perhaps he was only a watcher and not a killer, a person who would rather watch life pass him by, than participate in life's activity. Perhaps this was his weakness. Sophon was a watcher, watching John, mostly while they were in New York, in restaurants and hotels. Each time, he had veered away from acting.

Sophon offered no excuses to Phillip for his lack of action. Apparently, he didn't think he owed Phillip an explanation. When Phillip asked, Sophon had said he would kill him when he was ready and not before. Sophon had looked Phillip directly in the eye on this occasion and said nothing more.

It had been frustrating for Phillip. Sophon simply wouldn't talk to Phillip. Didn't seem to think it was necessary.

Phillip could tolerate many things, but silence was not one of them.

Phillip liked to talk, but both Sophon and his uncle seemed inclined to shut him out. And this infuriated him to the point he thought he might do the deed himself. He had access to the same tools Sophon's uncle had provided. Phillip knew how to contact the killers. He knew what to say. Surely, he had more than enough reasons to kill John. John had ruined his life, taken everything from him. With John gone, Phillip would have what rightly belonged to him. Sophon's uncle had promised him this would happen. Phillip had only to wait for John to die. Then it would all happen for him, riches, power, the life John had denied him.

But how long could he wait?

This was his question.

Phillip was a patient man. He had the self-discipline to wait. Waiting was not the problem. He could wait, but what for? If Sophon was never going to do the job, then maybe it was just a matter of prudence to do it himself, take the initiative, and move on. With John Van Laan gone, a good life would be his. Phillip could walk away from his cluttered two-room office in Grand Haven, Michigan, and move into the bright lights of big business to an office in New York City.

As he sat in his office on Sunday afternoon, Phillip dreamed about big offices in New York City with pretty secretaries. Phillip knew he deserved this life. He had planned for it. It belonged to him.

Only one obstacle remained in his way.

CHARLOTTESVILLE, VIRGINIA, 11:05 P.M.
SOPHON

Sophon's men rotated in and out of their motel rooms on a regular schedule, assigned to constantly watch John Van Laan's office building from locations hidden by trees.

A call from their base came to Sophon late that Sunday afternoon. Something unusual was happening. The target was sitting alone on a deck outside his office. It was an opportunity that none of his men had observed in the past. The target was making a mistake. Sophon was asked if he would like to have the man eliminated now. The situation was right. It would be an easy kill. One shot, and it would be over.

'No,' Sophon replied. 'Meet me on the road.'

After joining his man, Sophon asked him to bring him to the place where he was stationed so Sophon could see for himself.

As they walked together through the woods, each step was carefully taken, not a twig broken, not a bird disturbed; two shadows in the forest. The two men arrived at a location where a small deck outside John's office could be observed through the trees using binoculars. But by that time, John Van Laan was gone, on the move. Sophon's other man had called and said he was following. The target was walking alone up a trail not far from the building. A kill would be easy.

Sophon was perplexed. John never went out alone without a bodyguard. So why now, why was he making it easy? Did he not understand the danger he was in?

As his man waited, he took a silencer from a pocket in his vest and carefully screwed it on his pistol. He was good at his job. The shot would be quick and clean. The target would be dead before he hit the ground. He simply needed Sophon to approve the kill. But Sophon told him 'no' over the phone. Said to stay where he was and wait on the trail for him.

When Sophon arrived, he instructed the man to give him the gun and not follow. Sophon said he would go up the trail alone. Eventually, he saw John from a distance as John was slowly proceeding up a hill. Never too close, but close enough to catch partial views through the trees, Sophon could easily follow John because John seemed to be in no hurry. After a while, John stopped to rest along the trail, sat down, and put an empty glass on a rock. When John began to walk again, he forgot to take the glass with him. Or maybe he didn't care. Sophon eventually found the glass and put it in his pocket before continuing up the trail behind John.

When John reached the top of the hill at the end of the trail, Sophon observed him sitting down on a rock, looking over valleys to mountains in the distance. John seemed sad somehow; not overtly sad, no tears, no wringing of the hands; just something in his body language, something about the way he sat, kind of stooped over like he was resigned to being sad. His body language told Sophon John was not a happy man as he quietly stared into the distance, deep in thought.

Sophon felt the weight of the gun in his pocket as he searched the area for other hikers. Seeing no one at the top of the hill in the late afternoon, the place was completely deserted. No one would hear the shot. No one would care. No one would find the body until hours or perhaps days later.

His father's face came to Sophon, and his uncle's words spoke to him as he watched. This man had killed his father. His family's honor demanded revenge. A life taken in anger could not go unrewarded. A justified execution was the sentence for the crime. The man needed to die. The man had killed his father. Sophon hated this man.

The gun felt cold in his hand, heavy steel holding explosive death.

It was time.

This was the place.

It would be an easy over in a heartbeat.

He could walk away free to bury his father's memory forever.

Sophon rested the gun on a tree branch, took aim, and clicked the safety off. John's head was in his sights. The target was sitting quietly, an easy mark staring out into a vast void beyond the rocks. The trigger pressed uneasily against Sophon's finger; slow now, don't jerk... pull with even pressure, hold the gun firmly in both hands and wait for the recoil. The muscles in his forearms tensed, relaxed, and tensed again, the trigger lightly touching his finger.

A speck of dirt bothered his eye, an irritation. Sophon wiped his eye before once again concentrating on John's head through the gun sight. Something about John's sadness made Sophon hesitate. Something in his demeanor made Sophon want to know more about this man. He sensed he had something he needed to learn, something only John could teach him. Something he needed to know before he passed the sentence on to John.

Sophon took the gun off the branch and lowered it to his side. Changing his mind, he once again raised the gun and rested it on a branch, aimed, ready to pull the trigger until once again hesitating.

Why?

Why wait? This man had killed his father. It was simply a matter of justice. Simply a matter of serving this man with the fate justice demanded.

Sophon lowered the gun, clicked the safety on, and put the instrument of death in his pocket.

Sitting quietly, he watched John.

Two men alone, very close, close and yet far apart. One man sitting on a rock traveling endless mind journeys over valleys to distant mountains. And the other man, a young man, watching the older man through the trees, needing answers from a man he loathed, a man who represented everything he hated. And yet, a man who had become a mystery to him, a mystery he felt he needed to solve.

That night, as Sophon drifted off to sleep in his motel room in Charlottesville, he thought about the glass sitting on a table next to the TV in his room. About how he had found the glass, about how it had felt to touch the glass, a glass which only minutes before had been in the hands of the man who killed his father. The glass became a material link between the two men. The glass joined them together in a way he had not known before. The glass allowed Sophon to cross a physical divide between himself and this man who had previously represented nothing more than hate in his mind. His father's killer was a real man. The glass stained with whiskey and dirt was proof positive of his existence.

When Sophon finally went to sleep, it was a restless sleep filled with illusive dreams. Dreams of mountain cliffs, of falling through vast open spaces filled with endless shimmering fog disguising passing rock ledges in the sky.

He reached out to grab a ledge to stop from falling, but his hands touched nothing, nothing but thin air... falling, endlessly falling.

CHARLOTTESVILLE, 11:33 P.M. JOHN

Somewhere along the trail, I must have placed my empty glass on a rock.

Put it there while taking a break and I guess I forgot pick it up again before continuing up the trail.

I could have gone back to look for it, but it was dark by the time I remembered the glass. Plus, I wasn't sure I would ever find it again. Too many rocks, too many places where I could have left it. A transparent glass would be hard to see in the dark woods. So, I didn't return to look for it; I just left it where it was.

But the forgotten glass bothered me.

It wasn't because I needed the glass. I had plenty of glasses. It was because the lost glass represented the stupidity of my foolhardily walking the trail. The forgotten glass made me feel uncomfortable. I should not have been out on the trail in the first place. And drinking Scotch while walking a steep trail... not wise. A fall could have proven painful, the injuries potentially extensive.

Plus, it was dumb to be out on the trail alone without a bodyguard... dumb and untidy. And leaving the empty glass among rocks, spoiling a beautiful nature trial with human waste, broken glass which could cause harm. The empty glass became a symbol of my sloppy stupidity.

Yet, in a way, I was happy I had gone for a walk. I was sick of living afraid. Sick of living behind closed doors. Sure, I wasn't restricted to being inside all the time. I could travel. I go places, but always with bodyguards. Never alone, never free to be out on a whim, explore my world on my terms. It felt as if I lived with a glazed glass security shield placed between me and the outside world. It was a friendly shield. It was meant to protect me. But it obscured my view and made everything look dull and out of focus. It was as if the outside world was warped by my fears, like an oddly misshaped, old glazed glass window had been placed between me and the world, making everything appear to be slightly unreal.

After I reached the top of the hill, I didn't return immediately. I sat on a treeless rock outcropping, which stretched over the top of the hill. For a long time, I thought about my current state of affairs, mostly Sandy, the fact she was gone. In a way, I was glad she was gone. It meant I didn't need to be concerned about her. And the more I thought about her, the more I realized how much of my mental energy she had consumed.

Although I had to admit that it bothered me that she was gone. And it wasn't just that she was gone. It was how she had left without answering any of my questions. She had walked out the door without telling me what I wanted to know; like when she would return, or how she felt about me. An unknowing emptiness had followed in her absence and it forced me to reevaluate my situation.

As I sat on a rock at the top of the hill, I thought about my life, I didn't like what I saw. Death was all I envisioned for my future. Death was on my mind when I should have been thinking about something else. The scene from the top of the hill was spectacular, it should have been elevating. Instead, I spent my time obsessing about my problems, about my impending death.

Finally, I forced myself to thinking about death and and take a moment to enjoy the vast expanse that spread over the valleys in front of me. Trees were turning color, red oaks and pale-yellow maples blending with tall green pines as the sun dropped towards the horizon. As I rested, mountains in the distance began to fade into shades of blue-gray elegance.

I would have enjoyed staying longer, but it would not have been prudent. I had to get down the trail before it became too dark. Reluctantly, I gave up my rocky throne of glory at the top of the hill and turned my back on a deepening sunset. It was an awesome sight, but I had to go. It would have been foolhardy to try to navigate the steep trail down the hill in the dark. One bad fall on the rocks could cause a serious injury, maybe a broken leg. Spending the night lying injured on the cold ground waiting for help did not seem like an appealing prospect.

It was almost completely dark by the time I returned to my apartment. I didn't go inside immediately. I had no real need. No one was waiting for me in my apartment. No one knew where I was. My bodyguards didn't know. They assumed I was safely inside. They couldn't see me. My apartment was off-limits to their security cameras. They didn't like this, but I insisted. I didn't want them constantly looking over my shoulder. I needed a place that was mine, where I was free to do as I pleased.

I poured another glass of Scotch and took it out on the sheltered deck off the kitchen. Then I had another Scotch as night slowly swept all color from the horizon, and stars took possession of a black sky.

Normally, I find it easy to make decisions. But that evening, nothing came easy. The Scotch in my glass didn't help. Thinking about my problems didn't help. Nothing helped. I could see no way out of my dilemma. It wasn't because I was worried about Sandy or Ilana. I knew they could take care of themselves. It was me I was worried about. I had no escape from what seemed my certain fate.

It is too easy to be killed.

So many ways for it to happen. A man in a crowd, a face, any face in a sea of faces, a knife in his hand, the rush of his arm, pain, wild pain enveloping my chest, spreading out in waves of death wasting through my body until I become too weak to stand as life ride the waters of my blood oozing from a gaping wound; my body slowly evolving into nothing more than an unconscious cold shell, a vehicle no longer filled with visions or desires, no longer capable of dreaming. Or life could end from a rifle shot on a rooftop. A sudden explosion of anxiety and pain as my organs are ripped apart, bones crushed, heart muscles torn. Only a brief time to say a prayer, and then it is over.

Money is the ultimate weapon.

If you want someone dead, it is simply a matter of being willing to pay. Charlie explained this to me when he was in town. He didn't talk about me specifically; he just dwelled on the general topic of assassination. He did it to put the fear of God into me and make me abide by the rules my security guys had laid out. I didn't blame him. He was trying to protect me. But what he didn't see was the effect it had on me. Sure, if I played the game the way Charlie demanded, perhaps I could stay alive for a few years. But eventually, I would make a mistake, and then it would be over. He knew it. I knew it.

And in the meantime, what could I expect from life? This was my question for him. The question Charlie could not answer.

What kind of life would I live if I lived by Charlie's rules? Is simply preserving life an excuse for living? You sleep, wake up in the morning, eat. Your job is to do whatever it takes to stay alive. Is that a life? Or does life demand more? Is having a minimum level of love and joy required to be considered alive? Is living in fear, living in a state of constant anxiety, really living? Or is it simply surviving? And is simply surviving enough to justify the expense of living? The taking of the world's resources, occupying space, using time. Should life demand more from us if we wish to be alive?

I sipped the last of my Scotch and went inside, closing the door behind me. It was time to go to bed, enough for one day. I had taken a big chance. I had gone outside alone. If a killer was nearby, he could have killed me easily, my body lying at the top of the trail, blood slowly seeping into the crevices in the rocks, staining their natural gray with dark red stains.

In a way, that would have made everything easier because, as it was, I was alive, and I still had a problem I could not solve.

CHARLOTTESVILLE, WEDNESDAY, OCTOBER 21, 4:55 P.M. JOHN

Sandy called as promised.

It was early yesterday in the morning. I was working, deep into a report about mining operations in Zambia.

Zambia was a difficult place to do business. Not that the country didn't have gemstones. It was rich in gems, everything from emerald to sapphires and rubies, but the political climate was unstable. Still product could be had if I could solve Zambia's political puzzle.

Helen buzzed. 'That girl is on the phone,' she stated with a hint of disdain in her voice.

That was how Helen referred to Sandy as 'that girl.' It was obvious she didn't like Sandy. I assumed it was because Helen thought I had betrayed Ilana by being with Sandy. And maybe I had. So, I didn't make an issue of Helen's attitude. Just let it go.

'Do you want to take the call?' Helen asked impatiently.

I had been relegating Sandy to the back of my brain, trying not to think about her. Not completely, of course. I had called her several times in the past few weeks, but her voicemail was all I got in return. Oh, she didn't ignore me, not completely. She was smart. She returned my calls by leaving messages on the voicemail in my apartment. She knew that the phone was a separate line from my office. She also knew it was unlikely I would be in my apartment in the middle of the day. So, she conveniently called the apartment phone in the afternoon and left short, terse messages that told me nothing. Then, she would go silent.

I began to wonder if she was hiding something, something I had missed. Had I been so enamored with her when she showed up in my life that I had not considered she might have a life other than the life she shared with me? And what could be in her other life? Or, more importantly, who could be in her other life? Was she keeping someone, some male lover, from me? I had tried to be honest with her, but had she been completely honest with me? Or was it my fault because I never really asked her? Didn't ask because I was afraid to know. Was I so eager to return to what we had before we parted as teenagers? Did I so badly wish to time-travel backward to fulfill some exalted version of a personal fantasy of teenage puppy love that I had stubbornly ignored any possible reality that would keep me from accomplishing my mission?

Okay, but who could blame me?

Being with her was like living a dream. Like walking backward in time, eliminating everything between the day we parted and the present. I wanted to have everything I longed for then. Wanted to fulfill all my over-sexed teenage fantasies. I wanted to forget about everything that had happened between then and now, everything. Especially the horrendous memories I did not want to think about. And most of the time, that was what I did when I was with her. I forget about the dead man in the forest, the man I had killed. She helped me forget more than I could explain to her.

So, was I wrong to want to be with her?

It had been great. She had been great. But life is seldom simple. It's loaded with too many variables and too many obstacles. Now, I wondered what I had missed in my headlong attempt to relive my teenage dreams. Being apart from her for a few weeks had cooled the heat of love and sex, allowed my brain time to take a breather, and gave me an opportunity to logically consider all the potentially problematic considerations I had been ignoring.

I didn't like what I was thinking.

It would not be easy from now on. Or worse... maybe it was never meant to be, nothing more than a momentary fling into the past, the kind of unrealistic experience that can never be repeated. Maybe my wish for it to continue was just that, a wish and a prayer.

It could never be what it had been. Maybe it never really was. The future would be different. This was my thought process now.

And it was working because I wasn't constantly preoccupied with thoughts of Sandy. So, when she finally called, I took her call almost reluctantly. Although her initial absence had been a real letdown, I was over her in my mind.

She began our conversation by announcing she was scheduled to fly to Charlottesville tomorrow. She asked me if I was excited and could get all my other women out of the apartment by the time she arrived. Please, no lingering perfume smells, no panties hung on lampshades. Have your apartment cleaned and fumigated.

She said I didn't have a lot of time, only one day. I needed to get to work.

I replied in the affirmative to everything she asked, but apparently with a genuine lack of enthusiasm because she hesitated, suddenly unsure... And asked me if I wanted her to come.

I said I was looking forward to seeing her. Why did she ask?

She said she didn't know. Just sort of seemed to be the thing to do, you know, a polite, socially correct thing to do.

When I said she was always welcome, she didn't reply to my answer immediately. Apparently, I was acting too cool. I guess she was looking for something more positive, but she brushed it aside and asked me to send a car to pick her up at the airport. No need to come myself. She would see me late afternoon.

It was now the afternoon the next day, and my driver had reported in from the airport. Her plane was late, but it had landed. He said it would take time to get her luggage and drive to the office. He would call if any other problems caused a delay. I thanked him and went back to work, but I didn't accomplish much.

Sandy was on my mind.

THURSDAY, OCTOBER 22, 3:10 A.M. JOHN

The eyes of a sleeping woman can be very beautiful.

He blond hair fell softly over a pillow as she lay on her side with her face towards me. It was not a dark night. A perfect white orb of the moon in a cloudless sky spread its soft light through our bedroom window, making it possible for me to clearly see her lovely face.

I blamed the moon for why I couldn't sleep. After about an hour of restlessly trying to wander into dreamland, I finally gave in and got up. Slipping noiselessly out of bed so I wouldn't wake her, I wandered down the hall and into the kitchen. The refrigerator light was adequate to pour a glass of milk. Putting on a warm jacket over a tee shirt and pajama bottoms, I went out on the side deck to gaze at the moon through the trees like a love sick puppy.

Sleep was an illusion. Dreams were nothing more than journeys into a fantasy land. I was too keyed up to waste time trying to sleep. The evening had turned out to be everything I had hoped it would not be.

Earlier in the day as I waited for her to arrive at my apartment from the airport, I made the decision I had been putting off. I decided our next reunion should be more subdued. It wouldn't be wise to allow myself to slip again into some sort of wild, ecstasy world filled with teenage sex-crazed reincarnations. This time, her visit needed to be something more realistic, something less exotic, less engaging, less demanding, something that didn't approach perfection. Reality would bring us down and inform us that being together was something we could learn to live without. I decided my life would be far less complicated without her in it.

Initially, everything proceeded as I contemplated. In fact, when she arrived, I was still at work. I gave her a welcome kiss on the cheek and sent her packing to my apartment without too much fanfare.

'I need to finish a few tasks,' I explained. 'Food is in the refrigerator in the apartment. Help yourself, relax, have a beer. I'll come in a few minutes.'

Well, the truth was, it took over two hours to finish my work, not exactly what I promised. I felt slightly guilty for ignoring her, but what the heck? I had a job to do. I couldn't exactly ignore my work just because she decided to visit. However, everything changed the moment I opened the door to my apartment. Roaming freely through the air was the sweet smell of cooking food. Not that I minded, mind you. I didn't mind at all. The fact was, she was an excellent cook. Although I may not have been hungry before I opened the door, I sure as heck developed an appetite as soon as I smelled what she was preparing.

Nothing was said by way of an apology when I entered the kitchen. And she didn't seem to mind. She simply pointed to a glass of wine on the counter. I dutifully took the clue and sat down, silently watching her work as I sipped my drink.

She was wearing jeans and an old oversized blue sweatshirt with a gold M on the front, something she must have found in my closet. It was a University of Michigan sweatshirt I had purchased in Ann Arbor when attending a football game in the Big House. Although the sweatshirt was much too big for her lithe body and nothing special, I had to admit. It sure looked good on her as her blond curls fell over her dark blue shoulders.

'Go to the dining room,' she announced without fanfare. 'Dinner will be ready in a minute.'

We ate mostly in silence. I did manage to ask her about her trip home. She said it was fine. Said she had accomplished what she needed to do.

'So, what did you need to do?' I continued, looking for answers to some of the questions which had been circulating wildly in my brain.

'Oh, nothing special,' she replied.

'Just curious,' I dug for more information; like wondering if she had boyfriend who lived in San Francisco? 'Anything you want to tell me?'

'No. Just private stuff. Nothing you would be interested in.'

I guessed I could have probed harder, but I didn't want to appear too nosey. Our semi-strained question-and-answer session had an immediate limiting effect on our dinner discussion. We mostly ate in silence; very little table talk. I did say the meal was great and thanked her for making it. She apologized and said it was as good as she could do with what she found in my refrigerator. She asked me about my work. I didn't volunteer any real information; I just said the usual nonsense: lots to do and not enough time to do it all.

So, the truth was, the conversation was lagging badly, and I really thought we were off to the kind of let-down reality I had hoped for. The hot flames from our recent past felt like they had been reduced to something resembling the last limp warmth from a wood fire rather than the blast furnace heat of our previous torrid affair.

I helped her clear the table after dinner to be nice. I said it was the least I could do after a great meal. She stacked the dishes in the sink and waved me away, saying she would clean up the kitchen. I took the hint and went into the main room with a glass of wine. Despite all the warnings from my security guys, I opened the curtains covering the windows. The sun was going down, and a great sunset I didn't want to miss was spreading across the horizon. Retreating to a couch back away from the windows, I hoped I was safe as I relaxed with my drink while waiting for her.

The windows in the living room are a story and a half high, making it easy to view the sunset from the back of the room. I was very content. The meal had been great, and my preconceived desire for a more subdued relationship seemed to be holding. We had been cool toward each other all evening. Almost as if we both knew our recent reunion was an apparition leftover filled with teenage enthusiasm. This time our relationship would be conducted on an adult level. The spark would be more passive. The heat cooled, nothing to get excited about, great friends with a history, nothing more.

Then she came into the room, and everything immediately changed.

Although initially it was not exactly obvious what was different, for some reason, I didn't understand; I couldn't take my eyes off her. A mischievous grin covered her lips and I should have anticipated what would happen next after seeing that look on her face. I should have recognized the warning sign. Because in the past, her grin was a clue that had warned me I was in trouble. Like she knew something I didn't know. And, of course, she did. She knew what was going to happen next.

She curled up next to me, still wearing the big blue oversized sweatshirt with the gold M. It covered a large portion of her body, but not everything. Something was missing. Her jeans had disappeared, and her long, bare legs were peeking out from beneath the sheltering sweatshirt. She snuggled up to me and I raised my arm to allow her to move in closer. Turning to kiss her on the forehead, an overwhelming desire to touch her enticing leg took hold of me. I couldn't resist sliding my hand up her leg underneath the big blue sweatshirt across the gentle curve of a bare hip to the inner curve of her waist. She was naked under the sweatshirt, and I was... well... I was in love again. Despite my great resolve to avoid falling into a situation such as this, it was happening to me again, and I was... I was completely defenseless.

Beyond my apartment's tall windows, the sun set over distant mountains, filling the sky with streaks of glowing reds, purples, and blue grays, changing continuously as God painted pictures across his infinite canvases. Each picture lingered for only a moment, so elegant it could not be comprehended in the fullness of its beauty, too soon lost forever to new glowing colors of smoothly changing glory covering multiple canvases in time, each canvas so perfect it could not exist in an imperfect world for more than a brief memory. It was as if these glimpses of eternity were only meant to tease us with a taste of heaven and then move on, gone to places beyond the mountains as a cool dark night took over the sky.

I saw very little of the sunset that evening except for the colors that reflected off her pale skin, the soft colors her naked body absorbed from the sky, shades of dark reds, and deep purples glowing over her graceful curves. By the time the sky finally turned gray, it was over... as if our sexual energy had been played out across the sky. As if we had painted the sky with the glorious energy of our time together. As if our bodies had created so much excess energy, so much passion, that we alone had spread the warm colors of our love across the vast panorama of the sky. And then we rested in the cool gray half-light of the night.

I looked at her as she rested beside me after making love, her eyes closed. I didn't say anything. Standing to reach under her naked body, I carried her to bed so she could sleep.

Enough for this day, one more day in my life.

FRIDAY, OCTOBER 23, 6:35 P.M. JOHN

'So... when are we going to Belize?' she asked innocently.

She had only been in Charlottesville for a day and already I was adjusting to having her in my life again, happy again to have her living with me. Then, something in her complex brain compelled her to ask this impossible question, changing everything. It was just like her. She never gave me any rest.

My week had been mostly uneventful. That is until her arrival on Friday and all the baggage that came along with her, all the mental and physical baggage.

The truth was, she didn't arrive with much in the way of physical baggage, just a single carry-on suitcase and, of course, her black and brown overnight leather bag. And like before, nothing about the placement of her luggage gave me any clue as to how long she was prepared to stay: a day, a week, a month, forever, who knew? I feared her next surprise announcement of imminent departure could happen at any time, tomorrow for all I knew. However, I tried not to think about her leaving, just wanted to enjoy having her with me again. Plus, it served no purpose to press the issue with her because I knew she wouldn't tell me.

Unfortunately, the other baggage that came along with her, the mental baggage, that baggage was large and cumbersome, and it was a big problem. The question she asked was a large part of that rather weighty baggage.

I sipped a Scotch and looked at her. 'You sure you want to go to Belize?' I asked.

'Sure, why not? It's a beautiful place, isn't it? And it will be warm. We can go swimming in the sea.'

'Yes, Belize is a warm country beside a beautiful sea. But that isn't why you want to go, is it?'

'Why else would I want to go?' she smiled.

'You want to meet my friend, Ilana.'

She smiled again. 'It would be nice to meet her.'

'I don't think that is a good idea,' I countered.

The situation was out of control. I couldn't visualize being in the same place at the same time with two lovers, Sandy and Ilana. First and perhaps most important, because Ilana didn't know about Sandy. Or should I say I hadn't bothered to tell Ilana about Sandy, not yet? I knew I should tell her, but I wanted to wait. Do it when I am ready. And I wasn't ready, not yet. However, I couldn't speak for Helen. It was possible Helen had told Ilana all about Sandy. So maybe Ilana already knew, and maybe she didn't. Either way, it was not a good situation.

'Why not?' Sandy replied as she sipped a glass of wine.

We were sitting on the small deck outside the dinette of my apartment. The deck was sheltered by a stand of tall oaks which offered cooling afternoon shade. The weather had been warm and overcast but pleasant, with a gentle breeze. Sandy and I had plans to go to my club for dinner. It was all arranged. Two bodyguards would accompany us. I didn't like asking the guys to go out on a Friday night. I was sure they had better things to do, but without them, we could go nowhere. I was tired of eating in the apartment. I thought it would be fun to go out. I had a pleasant evening envisioned and the last thing I wanted was to have an unpleasant confrontation with her before dinner. But it seemed she wasn't going to let me dodge her question. Okay, perhaps it was best to get this issue settled once and for all. However, the more I thought about it, the more I didn't want to go to Belize. The idea of being in the same house with both Sandy and Ilana, I just couldn't picture it.

'You know who she is?' I finally asked.

'Yes, she is the girl who was with you when you killed a man.'

'Yes, and you remember why she was with me?'

'She was your girlfriend at the time.'

I looked at Sandy, wondering what she was thinking. I knew she could read me like a book, but I couldn't read her, never could. I was never really sure what she was thinking. Except I assumed that whatever was freely circulating in her brain was probably trouble. But then, that was part of her charm. Nothing was ever boring when I was with her.

'Well, yes, she was my girlfriend and my lover,' I replied.

'John, I didn't think you had been celibate for all the years since I last saw you.'

'Well, thanks for that.'

'You're welcome.'

'But some relationships are more than others,' I volunteered for no other reason than I knew it needed to be said.

'And this relationship, John, was it more?'

'It was. I was in a bad place mentally when she found me. She was good to me.'

'I'm glad she was good for you,' Sandy said with no malice in her voice. 'And now?' she asked. 'Is she still good?'

Okay, that was the question, and it was now out in the open. No escape is possible. But the problem was I didn't know the answer. I couldn't answer it for myself, much less for Sandy. I took a big sip of Scotch. The warm liquid slid down my throat, making me feel better, but it did nothing to help me find an answer.

'I'm sorry, John,' she said. 'I guess I shouldn't have asked. It's none of my business really.'

She was wrong.

It was her business. And worse yet, anything I said could be a problem. If I said Ilana was not important to me anymore, I might sound like a lying bastard and probably be one. But if I said Ilana was still important to me, then how would that go over? Would I look like a two-timing bastard? And how would Sandy react? Would my answer result in her imminent departure in the morning? Because why should Sandy stay if I was still in a relationship with another woman? Either way, I was in trouble.

I decided the truth was the only answer, no matter how complicated that made things.

'No, no, it is your business,' I began. 'The problem is I don't know the answer. It's complicated. So complicated I'm not sure I can answer it.' I paused. 'Look, Sandy, I should not have killed that man, and I don't like to think about what happened that night. And...'

'But Ilana didn't ask you to kill him, did she?' Sandy interrupted.

'No. No one asked. I just did it...'

I stopped, momentarily at a loss for words. The answer to why I shot Nue was still elusive, blowing in the wind through the trees somewhere.

'You don't blame Ilana for what happened, do you?' Sandy asked.

'No, of course not.'

'I'm sorry, John. What happened to you should never have happened. But things happen in life that shouldn't happen. But they do.' She continued, 'John, I lost a man I loved. That shouldn't have happened to me, but it did.'

I turned to face her. 'Okay, I get it. But that doesn't make it any easier, does it?'

Sandy took another sip of wine before saying, 'I think we need to go to Belize. I would like to meet Ilana.'

'Sandy, I don't think that is a good idea.'

'You said that before.'

'Okay, why don't you believe me?'

'Because this is something I think we need to do.' Then she paused before saying, 'More importantly, this is something you need to do.'

'Okay...' I half stammered as the implications of her last statement resonated through my brain in no logical order. 'It seems you have decided to give me no choice. We can go if you want to go. But first, I think I should tell you about Ilana as plainly as I can...and if my telling you causes you to get on a plane tomorrow morning and leave me forever... then okay. You should leave.'

I hesitated.

'You can tell me, John,' she interjected. 'I'm a big girl now. I'm not your teenage lover anymore. You can trust me.'

'Okay...' I paused, trying to find the right words. 'Ilana is a beautiful, intelligent woman with long black hair and a great body,' I began. 'We were lovers before I killed a man, and maybe we still are now. But there is this ugly experience that we share. The death of that man is not something I'm proud of. I don't blame her for it, but she was with me when it happened, and I can't stop thinking about it when I am with her. So, you see, our relationship is complicated. It's not fair to her, but it is what it is, and I can't change it.'

Sandy said nothing, just listened, waiting for me to finish.

'Then you showed up at... and how can I say this?' A tear formed in my eye. I tried not to get emotional. I couldn't help it. My voice audibly cracked. I continued anyway. 'I'm not sure you know how much you have meant to me. When I am with you, I don't think about being a killer. Well, not all the time, not like when I am with Ilana.'

'Okay.'

'The problem is I still have a relationship with Ilana... I don't know what it is, but it is not over.'

'Is being with me feel like you are cheating on Ilana?' Sandy asked with perfect clarity.

'Well, yes, I guess... maybe. I haven't thought about it much... but yes, in a way, that's true. Ilana is unfinished business.'

'What do you want to do about her?'

'Sandy, I don't know what to do.'

'Well then, why don't we go to Belize so you can decide what to do.'

'Sandy, don't you understand? How will taking my new lover to meet my old lover possibly solve my problem?'

'Is that what I am, your new lover?'

'Sandy, give me a break. You know what I mean.'

'It's okay. I think I like being your new lover. Is it bad to be your new lover?'

'No, no, it is not bad. The truth is I have always loved you. You know that. I don't have to tell you, do I?'

She smiled one of her mischievous smiles, and without saying a word, her smile spoke volumes. Most of the time I love to see her smile, but this time it drove me nuts because I had no idea what she was thinking.

'Okay, I have tried to be honest with you,' I said. 'Now, will you answer a question for me?'

'Sure.'

'Are you my... lover?'

She didn't hesitate. 'Yes, I am and will always be your lover.'

I looked at her. 'You said that pretty casually. What does it mean?'

'Well, I guess we will just have to find out, won't we?'

BANGKOK, THAILAND, SATURDAY, OCT 24, 9:25 A.M. LUANG

The flow of human greed, like a river, never pauses.

Even on weekends, visitors were constantly at Luang's door seeking favors, demanding favors. The heavy burden of the work was something the old patriarch had almost forgotten in his retirement. He had been retired for almost three years before returning to carry out his former duties in the family's mansion. During his retirement, the stamina necessary to put in the long days and nights that the job required had been lost. His body had become accustomed to being in a state of forced relaxation for so long that it was now difficult to endure the stress of the job. Somehow, he managed to keep up the pace, but for how long, he did not know.

When Sophon returned home, Luang talked to the young man about his problem, about needing help with the work. He told Sophon that helping him would be a learning experience for the young man and prepare him for his future. The boy said no. He was not ready, not yet. He had other tasks to accomplish first, and then they could talk.

When the old patriarch asked the boy when the boy thought he might be ready, Sophon had simply shrugged his shoulders and walked away. The boy's response, as much as anything, demonstrated to Luang that Sophon was still too young, too impulsive. Luang would have to wait. For now, he would have to find the strength to do the job alone. It was his duty to his family. No one could help him. The work needed to be done by him and him only.

As he sipped his tea in his garden, he thought about his nephew's son. The boy had been home for several weeks now. He appeared to be getting restless, but nothing was happening. Luang received the same reports Sophon was seeing. Their men in America were watching the office building in Charlottesville. Their reports indicated no change. John Van Laan was still holed up in his office. Nothing was happening.

It was curious, in a way. It should have been all over. Luang had been told about the day Sophon followed John Van Laan up a trail to the top of a hill. A detailed report on the incident had been written. The report indicated his nephew's killer was alone at the time. It would have been an easy kill. So easy that Sophon could have done it himself. Or the assassin assigned to the job could have accomplished it quickly and easily. It would have been all over now.

But it was not.

Something odd happened that day, something not easily explained. Sophon flew home within days of the incident. He said nothing to anyone. He spent his time wandering the mansion like he was lost. Apart from occasionally talking to his men in America, he did nothing.

So, they waited; the old man and the young boy waited together in the family mansion. They received the same reports from America. They talked to the same men across the seas.

But they did not talk to each other.

CHARLOTTESVILLE, VIRGINIA, MONDAY, OCTOBER 26, 11:05 A.M. JOHN

I put down my office phone and audibly sighed.

Working with the new head of the London Distribution House was not as much fun as working with my old buddy, Arthur.

Alan Jacobs, the new guy, was a good man, very meticulous, and extremely devoted to his job. But working with him was different from working with the previous head of the London House, Arthur. Arthur was much more fun. We always spent the first few minutes of phone conversation sharing a bad British joke or two. Brits have the weirdest sense of humor. Doing business with Arthur was enjoyable. In addition, Arthur knew the drill. We spoke the same language when it came to business. Our work could be accomplished in short order. It was not the same with Alan. He did not tell jokes, and my problem with Alan was that I had to be very specific with him and be absolutely certain he understood everything I told him. It took time, but it was something I had to do because my buddy Arthur was dead and gunned down on the streets of New York. Arthur had betrayed me, taken money from the Thai. His greed got in the way of his good judgment. His greed got him killed. So, I had no choice, I had to work with Alan. Alan would have to do it for now.

After my phone conversation with Alan, I reviewed my daily list of tasks. It was getting shorter. The day had gone well; most of my work was already done. The remaining items on the list would take time and study. All the short-order items and the easy tasks had been scratched off the list, and the other items were not pressing. They could wait until later in the afternoon. Everything that needed to be done immediately had been accomplished, everything except for one item, one small item at the top of the list. It still required my attention, and it was the most important item on the list, according to a certain blond. The importance of this item had been carved in stone into my brain by her. I knew I had to do it, but I had no idea how.

Our weekend had gone well.

Dinner at the club with Sandy Friday night was relaxing. On Sunday, she and I took a long ride through the city and into the mountains. I wanted to show her the area. We were followed closely by another car occupied by our two bodyguards. That didn't make the trip easy. Red lights and traffic were a problem. I had to slow down from time to time and wait for our security detail to catch up. They were constantly on the phone, yapping at me every time a gap opened between my car and theirs. They demanded I slow down and said I had to let them close the gap. For them to do their job, they needed to be on my tail. They made this perfectly clear. That was a pain. It wasn't easy to drive a Ferrari slowly on country roads. The car demanded exercise; go fast, test the breaks, and drive through the corners as a Ferrari was meant to be driven. Slowing down constantly to wait for another car took all the joy out of it.

The rest of the weekend was spent with Sandy and I wandering listlessly around inside the apartment, eating, sleeping, reading and watching a few DVD movies on my TV. I did some work and she did the cooking. A bodyguard went with her to the grocery store for supplies. She said it felt strange having him tag along, but not a problem; something she could get used to.

So, everything was good. Everything except for one item... the one task at the top of my to-do list. She wouldn't leave it alone. She used every moment of uninterrupted silence as an opportunity to reintroduce the subject of Belize. She would smile and remind me about how nice it would be to go swimming in the Caribbean Sea. Or she would ask if I had a boat on the island. Anything and everything was mentioned to remind me that she wanted to go to Belize, that we were going to Belize.

I patiently answered all her questions which satisfied her temporarily. I told her about the forty-five foot sailboat I owned. That really got her excited and it gave her an opportunity to tell me several times how much she was looking forward to sailing in Belize. I also described free diving on a reef in the sea. She liked this idea almost as much as sailing. I wasn't surprised. I knew she was a good swimmer.

This was how our weekend progressed, more or less in short fits of pain and pleasure. Pleasure when she wasn't bugging me about Belize and painful when she was. In a way, I couldn't blame her for wanting to go. Being cooped up inside my apartment could be claustrophobic. I could handle it for days on end because I was absorbed in my work. It wasn't the same for her. Apart from cooking and reading, she really didn't have much to occupy her day. We really needed to get away. I understood, and she reinforced the idea every chance she could. And she made it clear the place we wanted to visit was Belize. That, she made that imminently clear. That was not going to change. So, I had to make the arrangements. But I had been procrastinating. Mostly because I had one big issue to deal with first. I had to call Ilana and tell her I was coming, which, by itself, was not a problem. She wanted me to come. That wasn't the problem. The problem was I had to tell her I was not coming alone. I was bringing another woman with me, a girlfriend. I had no idea how she would react to my news, but I assumed her reaction would not be good, and I couldn't think of a way to tell her that wouldn't create a problem.

As I sat at my desk rehearsing one of the multiple possible ways of introducing the subject to Ilana, my phone seemed to be staring at me, demanding that I make the call. Still, I hesitated, hoping Helen would buzz me, anything that would allow me to justify putting off until tomorrow what I knew I should be doing today, which was to call Ilana. And my phone was reinforcing the idea, staring at me uncharacteristically and uncaringly silent as it waited.

Ilana's number had been programmed into my hardhearted phone. Helen had done this one day when I was out. I only had to hit two numbers, and a phone in Belize would begin to ring. The call would go directly to her cell phone. Usually, Ilana answered immediately when I called. She normally had her cell phone with her at all times. Unfortunately, this meant I couldn't leave a message and hoped to deal with her later. If I called, I knew I would have to talk to her.

I poured another cup of coffee and circled my desk, staring at the insensitive phone like it was my enemy, even though I knew the phone was not the problem. I was the problem. I had caused this mess, no one else. I had begun a relationship with Sandy before coming to a resolution with Ilana. I had no one to blame but me.

Impulsively, I hit the two speed-dial numbers and waited. Unfortunately, it didn't take her long to answer.

'Hi John,' Ilana said.

She spoke perfect English. Belize is an English speaking country. Something left over from colonial days. The Brits never lost control of Belize to Spain like the rest of Central America.

'Good morning, Ilana. How are you?' I began.

'I am fine, John, and you?' she answered curtly.

Our conversation felt way too formal from the beginning. Something was up. She either already knew about Sandy, or she was mad at me for some other reason, like why hadn't I called her recently? Either way, our conversation didn't get off to a good start, and it would, I assumed, deteriorate very quickly as soon as I told her why I was calling.

'I'm coming down to see you,' I began.

'Oh John, I am happy now. I have been hoping you would come soon.'

'Good, I plan to arrive on Friday if that is alright with you.'

'Yes, you know you can come anytime. This is your house, John.'

'No, it is your house, Ilana.'

'We share the house,' she answered, feisty as always.

'Okay, Ilana. It is my house, too.'

'Yes, John.'

'Can you have the boat cleaned before I arrive?' I asked, changing the subject.

'I will clean the boat myself.'

'That's not necessary; just hire some guys to do it. I'll pay for it.'

'John, you have given me more money than I can spend. You do not have to pay for it.'

'Okay, okay,' I began to get frustrated.

'I am looking forward to seeing you, John.'

'Me too. Okay then, Friday.'

'Call me when you get to Belize City. I will meet you at the airport on the island.'

'You don't have to do that. I can take a taxi.'

'John, I want to see you.'

'All right, I will call.'

'Good.'

'And Ilana, one more thing.'

'Yes, John.'

'I am bringing a friend with me. Her name is Sandy.'

My surprise announcement did not elicit an immediate response from Belize. My uncompromising phone went uncharacteristically silent. Finally, she spoke. 'And this friend, is she pretty?'

'Yes, she is pretty,' I replied, knowing I was a dead man if I lied.

'I see. And is she younger or older than I am?'

'She is older. She is my age.'

'And is she taller or shorter than I am?'

Twenty questions, this was going nowhere good. 'Ilana, she is taller with blond hair and blue eyes. She is an old schoolmate who I ran into when I was staying at the cottage.'

'I see. And were you good friends when you were in school? Or were you lovers?'

'She was my girlfriend,' I said without hesitation. 'But that was a long time ago.'

Ilana did not respond.

'She wants to meet you,' I added.

'Okay... I think we will have fun when you come to Belize, you and your pretty school friend Sandy. Tell her I am looking forward to meeting her.'

'Okay, I will see you on...'

My phone clicked off mid-sentence.

BELIZE, AMBERGRIS ISLAND, FRIDAY, OCTOBER 30, 4:55 P.M. JOHN

Closing my eyes in a vain attempt to stop worrying, it was impossible to get any rest while seated in the noisy bird.

A constant loud, beating racket from the helicopter's blades vibrated through the interior passenger compartment, offering no peace. I don't like helicopters. In contrast to planes, they seem bulky and clumsy... almost as if their big blades are muscling their way into the sky, never comfortable in flight, fighting constantly to avoid falling down.

Shadowed schools of fish swam swiftly and silently over the white sand under the sea, calming my troubled state of mind, offering a minimum visual relief from my immediate problem. The water was clear. From the air, endless patches of green seaweed could be viewed interspersed with areas of light brown sand. The surface of sea looked calm, like a crystal-clear sheet of rolling blue.

Sandy was sitting on the other side of the helicopter. She wore a tight white logo T-shirt and jeans. I assumed she was also wondering about what she would experience when she arrived on the island of Ambergris. I knew. I had lived on the island for many months. But what I didn't know was what would happen when we arrived. My conversation earlier in the week with Ilana had not ended well. I was pretty sure my hot-headed Latino girlfriend was mad when she hung up.

When I had tried to call her cell phone, to tell her we had arrived at the Belize City Airport, I got voicemail. This was not a good omen. I never got her voicemail. She always answered her phone. I assumed this meant hugs and kisses from my pretty island lady might not on her agenda when we met.

And what would happen next; well... this was anyone's guess. Ilana might not even come to the airport to greet us. Or worse, she might not be at the house when we arrived. She might be gone and the house empty, locked. It was possible we wouldn't be staying at the house. Even though I knew where the spare key was, under a potted plant near the back door, I wasn't the only person who knew its hiding place. Ilana also knew. Thus, the key might not be under the potted plant now. It might have disappeared, so I couldn't use it. And even if I found the key or took my key with me, which I forgot, perhaps the locks had been changed before we arrived, and the keys would be worthless. Any number of problematic scenarios raced through my head as the island appeared in the distance. None of them were good.

Behind us, Todd Brady sat quietly, looking out the window. Todd was our bodyguard for the trip. I considered one bodyguard enough. I was not concerned about security while on the island. It was a safe place, normally not much crime. The indigenous people were mostly Mayans, and they were good people, hard workers, and very friendly, not a threat to anyone's safety.

The island's main industry, besides fishing, was tourism. Many visitors come to dive on the offshore reef. Belize has the second largest reef in the world, eclipsed only by the Great Barrier Reef of Australia. The sea between the reef and the shore is normally a gently rolling, blue-green aquatic paradise, perfect for swimming and snorkeling. Water temperature is usually in the eighties, and air temperatures are about the same. It is a grand place to relax and enjoy nature's gifts. But I wasn't so sure it would be a relaxing place for me. I was feeling guilty and worried it was time to pay for my heated sins.

In contrast to me, Sandy had been very cheerful all day, happy to be out of the apartment. The prospect of meeting Ilana didn't seem to bother her at all. This was typical for Sandy. Nothing ever seemed to bother her.

Customs had been handled in Belize City. With formalities out of the way, we only had to retrieve our bags after the helicopter landed at the airport on the island of Ambergris. It was late in the afternoon when we touched down. The trip had been long but not difficult. Waiting in line in Belize City to go through customs was the hardest part. It was hot, upper eighties. The air conditioning inside the building wasn't working well. The heat was difficult to take. Our northern bodies were unaccustomed to it. I waited patiently in line, sweating and frustrated with the delay, all the time thinking this would not be the most difficult part of our journey today. The hard part would come when I was forced to confront Ilana with Sandy at my side.

Even though I left her a voice mail concerning our arrival time, Ilana was a no-show when our helicopter landed at the airport on the island of Ambergris, seeming to confirm my worst fears, which was not a good sign.

I said nothing to Sandy, let it go. What would happen would happen. I was not in control. This much was imminently apparent.

I asked Todd to find a taxi after explaining that taxis on the island were not new. Most were thirty year old clunkers, vintage cars out of the sixties or seventies. If the car ran and the trunk was not too rusty and could hold our luggage, then it was good enough.

The taxi ride to the house was uneventful. Sandy and I sat in the back of the old car, Todd up front, as we drove over a dirt road to the house. Nothing on the island is far from the sea. Bougainvillea plants could be seen growing up the sides of the stucco houses along the road. Palm trees and wildflowers were everywhere. I was tired and thirsty at the time. A Belican Beer sounded really good. I could almost taste its cool, refreshing liquid washing down my parched throat. But first, I had to face Ilana.

Pain before pleasure.

BANGKOK, SATURDAY OCTOBER 31, 5:06 A.M.
LUANG

He tried, but Luang could not sleep.

It was still dark. The sun would not rise for hours. It was that uncomfortable time in the night when the earth seemed to be waiting impatiently for dawn.

He thought about getting out of bed. Better than constantly turning over from one uncomfortable position to another. His old back muscles felt tight. He could not relax. He could not sleep. But he didn't want to get up either, not until it was light. Instead he lay in bed thinking all the uneasy thoughts which plagued him at night.

The boy was leaving in the morning. Sophon had informed him of his departure, nothing more. Luang suspected the reason for his going. A call had come from America with information. He was told that John Van Laan had left his office. It was not known where he had gone, not yet. But his spies were confident they would have the answer soon. It was easy to track a person, credit cards, airline tickets, and simple surveillance methods.

Sophon had been acting unusually restless lately. When Luang was told Sophon had purchased an airline ticket, he was not surprised. He was also not happy. The old patriarch would have preferred that his nephew stay home. Luang was more comfortable having the boy living with him where he could be supervised. The old man felt a sense of responsibility towards his younger relative. He had assumed the job of being the boy's guardian after the death of the boy's father. But Sophon was now old enough to do as he wished. Luang could not control the young man, not completely. The boy's fate was not in his hands.

Tired of listening to a constant ripple of ugly thoughts rummaging around in his head, Luang finally turned on the light beside his bed and sat up. Putting his robe over his shoulders, he went to a window in his bedroom, which overlooked his garden.

It was a windless night under a cloudless moonlit sky. Vague outlines of the garden plants could be seen in shades of gray; ghost-like, devoid of color; dead looking reproductions of their real images. It was as if this nighttime scene was made from the stuff of dreams. Real, but not really alive; more like imagined images, enough to identify the plants, but not enough detail and color to know if the plants were alive.

In his old age, it seemed to him as if his life was like his night garden: filled with forms without definition, shapes without color, without meaning or understanding; lost dreams of forgotten times.

AMBERGRIS ISLAND, 4:20 P.M. SANDY

It had been nerve-racking, the anticipation.

Sandy didn't know what to expect. She only knew John was concerned. She could read the signs, the look in his eyes, his lips pursed from time to time as they traveled. She knew he was uptight. But this had to be done because they couldn't continue together without going on this trip.

She had tried to stay positive. She knew she was good at disguising her emotions. In contrast to men, who were so easy to read, women can be much more elusive. And in a way it had been fun, watching him squirm. This was his mess after all. He had created it. He needed to deal with it. She was only facilitating what he needed to do.

When she was home in San Francisco, she had decided he needed this trip. More than she needed an answer for herself about him, she felt that he needed to resolve his relationship with Ilana. And that's exactly why she decided she should force him to do what he so obviously could not do for himself.

But then, wasn't it always like this? Women helping men do what they could not do for themselves.

Then she met Ilana.

Immediately, Sandy sensed they could be friends. Ilana was charming and warm, intelligent and funny. From the time they met, smiled, and talked, they quickly became friends. Not because Sandy could be friends with every woman. Some women were difficult, demanding, and impersonal. But Ilana was different.

Life was full of surprises.

Ilana was a happy surprise.

6:15 P.M. JOHN

Running down to the end of the dock, I jumped into the air, back arched, arms outstretched to break the water's resistance, slipping smoothly into the embracing arms of the Caribbean Sea.

A rush of liquid warmth quickly washed away a day of nervous, sweaty travel fatigue. Exhaling slowly, the momentum of my dive carried me into the sea as bubbles of life-giving air rose slowly behind me, disappearing at the surface into a gentle breeze. My body's momentum slowed as the weight of the water pushed against my unwelcome entry into a world I was never meant to inhabit for very long.

Intent on remaining below the surface of the water for as long as I could, I kicked hard, reaching with my hands to pull, propelling my body lower, rebelling against the sea's natural inclination to toss me towards the surface like an unwanted trinket. But I did not wish to rise too quickly. I wanted to live for a short time in this watery world, hide here among the creatures of the sea, here where life moved to the rhythm of the waves, always pulsing, pushing, seeking freedom in restless places.

The sea is never still. Gentle perhaps for a time, placid maybe for a day, but always in waiting for anticipation of the next storm, which could be only hours or days away; anxiously desiring the strength of the wind, the damning devastating rush of gale-tossed waves, desiring the mayhem of excited untamed energy which resides in a storm.

Finally, I relaxed to allow my body's natural buoyancy to push me to the surface before I couldn't hold my breath any longer. Rising above the water, I greedily inhaled the life-giving oxygen in the air. Even though I enjoyed being among the creatures of the sea, I knew I could not stay, not for long. The sea was not my home, maybe for a time, for a few brief minutes, for as long as I could hold my breath, no longer.

I rolled over on my back and let the sea hold me like a baby is held by its mother, enjoying its gently rocking, warm embrace. Hot sun and warm waters washed over my body as I gently kicked to remain floating horizontally on the surface, closing my eyes for a few minutes of tranquil freedom as I considered the recent unexpected events that had taken over my life.

Nothing had gone as anticipated, or rather as I had feared. But then, I guess I should have known better. It was a lesson I should have learned years ago. Never ever attempt to anticipate the actions of a woman. And when two women are involved in a given situation, doubts about possible preconceived conclusions should be doubled, perhaps squared like in an algebraic equation. Because once again, I had been totally wrong... Not just a little wrong... more like not even close. All my worries had been unnecessary.

When we arrived at the beach house from the airport, Ilana welcomed us, embracing Sandy, smiling, and helping with our luggage. Ilana apologized and said she was sorry she had been unable to meet us at the airport. Some emergency caused by her brother had kept her away.

I personally had my doubts about her excuse, but I said nothing. It was possible she was telling the truth. I just wasn't sure. Although she didn't act like she was lying. So, she could have been telling the truth. I didn't know.

I had been worried. I had dreaded how Ilana would act when she met Sandy. I feared they wouldn't get along. You know, two women existing together just this side of hell, completely ignoring each other in a cold, frigid, forced relationship, jealousy preventing them from even having a civil conversation. Didn't happen, not even close. They were having no trouble being together in the same house. Instead, it was me who appeared to be the odd man out. 'Man' being the operative word here. From the moment we arrived, I felt as if I was nothing more than an unnecessary ornament, an accessory to the decor that should have been discarded long ago. I was summarily ignored, dismissed, seen, but not heard, like a shunned, forgotten child.

Finally, after a few cold beers while listening to them chat like two reunited sisters, I decided to go for a swim. The water would feel good, washing off the sweaty travel from my weary body. Besides, it was clear my presence was not required inside the house.

The only obstacle I encountered when deciding to go for a swim was to find a room in the house where I could change into my bathing suit. Even though I knew the layout because I had helped design the house. It had a number of bedrooms, but I had slept in only one, always with Ilana in the master bedroom. However, Sandy was with me on this trip. So, I didn't think I would be sleeping with Ilana in the master bedroom. And I assumed, sleeping with Sandy would also not be approved behavior. So, I took my suitcase to one of the spare bedrooms upstairs and changed into my swimsuit. Grabbing a towel from a bathroom, I headed for the dock.

My sailboat, 'The Retreat', was tied at the dock. I took a moment to admire its tall mast and gleaming dark blue hull as I strolled by. The sun was setting in the west behind the house, but the air was still warm. This was Belize. It is not far from the equator. It never gets very cold here. This is one of the reasons I like it here.

After swimming until I became weary, I climbed up on the dock and placed my towel over the wooden deck. Laying down so my back could stretch, I rested, letting my mind wander over the miracle, which was a woman.

Not only had Ilana acted like she was not mad, she seemed to actually welcome Sandy with open arms. And Sandy took her caring gesture in stride, almost as if she expected it. She had not acted nervous before or during the trip. It was as if Sandy knew what to expect. She knew Ilana would kind.

This, however, was not my anxious expectation. I had expected the two of them to be jealous of each other. In fact, now, as I thought about them, I had to admit I was a little disappointed they weren't acting like a couple of alley cats fighting over me. Instead, it felt more like I didn't matter.

Truth was, I didn't understand any of this. And I felt slightly diminished by their apparent lack of attention. I could hear them laugh as I rested on the dock.

They were nearby on the deck in front of the house, having a good time, making new friends; girlfriends, drinking wine together, having fun.

SATURDAY, OCTOBER 31, 11:35 A.M. JOHN

Ilana lay with her eyes closed resting on the teak deck of my sailboat wearing a skimpy white bikini which left almost nothing to the imagination and everything to the sun's welcome energy.

Sandy was sitting across from me on the cushions, looking over the horizon in much the same negligent outfit. 'The Retreat,' my sailboat was making steady, slow progress through the sea towards a spot over the reef where Ilana and I had often come to free-dive in the past. Its broad white sails rose high in a perfect blue sky, occasionally flapping in a restless search for wind to push us toward our destination.

I was in no hurry.

The apparent lack of a reliable wind did not disturb me. When in Belize, everything slows. Time assumes a completely different rhythm. No longer craving to devour every second with tedious activity, time seems more content to wander aimlessly, enjoying the wonders of this island. This place is an absolute smorgasbord of delights. Everywhere you look, it says, come and enjoy me: the warm sea, the gentle breezes. Flowers grow naturally here. It is as if God is the gardener, and even the poorest broken down, old houses are richly framed in beautiful gardens of palm trees and indigenous blossoms.

Rolling over in bed earlier that morning, still not completely awake, I had instinctively reached to touch a body, wanting to be assured she was beside me, hoping to wrap my arms around her, curl up against her soft curves, and lounge for luxurious moments in her welcome embrace; maybe even to have sex. But, confusion was the only reality that captured my thoughts instead, wondering whose body I desired. Or where I was? Or who should be lying beside me? Was it the woman with long black hair or the woman with blond hair? Did my desirable lover have dark brown eyes or blue eyes?

I rubbed the sleep out of my eyes while blaming my temporary morning amnesia on jet lag. The trip yesterday had been long and tiring. I had gotten up early yesterday morning to finish a few necessary, work related tasks before leaving Charlottesville to fly to Belize. I think it was around four-thirty AM. By the time I went for a swim that evening in Belize, I was dead tired, and the two beers I drank before diving in the water did nothing to ease my fatigue. While relaxing on the dock after swimming, a lethargic state of being settled over my body and it was difficult to find the energy to drag my exhausted body to the guest bedroom in the house where I had taken my luggage and changed into my swimsuit. The bed looked inviting. I decided a short rest might be good, just a few minutes, thinking it would be prudent to lay on top of the covers. I didn't want to mess up the sheets. I wasn't really sure this bedroom was my assigned sleeping quarters for the duration of the trip. Nothing had been discussed. The ladies were too busy with other matters.

When I woke up in the morning, I was alone, under the covers.

Problem was I couldn't remember getting under the covers. Someone must have done it for me, covering my exhausted body. Dismissing this errant thought and all its implications, I dressed and wandered downstairs to the kitchen.

The house was quiet. I made some coffee, poured a cup, and headed for the front deck to enjoy the sunrise over the sea. Several cups of coffee and the morning newspaper later, the house was still quiet. Todd, our bodyguard, was out of bed. I found him in the kitchen having a cup of coffee. The two women were still absent, not in attendance. Todd informed me they had stayed up late talking.

I made some scrambled eggs. I was hungry and decided not to wait for the ladies. After popping a couple of pieces of bread in the toaster, I took my breakfast to the front deck under an umbrella. The sun was shining over the water. It was great to be outside. Life was good, mostly good, that is. I was still concerned about the ladies. Apparently, they had talked into the wee hours of the night. I wondered what was discussed. I was concerned that nothing good might come from their collaboration, but it was obvious by now I was not in control. For the moment, I simply enjoyed being in Belize again.

The house Ilana had built on the beach was wonderful. I had helped, but not much, some suggestions I gave to the architect like the general layout for the place, how many bedrooms, the size of the rooms, where to put the decks, that sort of thing. The details were left to Ilana. When it was done, I was very impressed. The house looked like it belonged in Central America. The main support structure was constructed from lightly varnished mahogany beams cut from the mountains in the west. The roof was covered with red tiles designed to collect rainwater in a cistern used for bathing and cleaning. The inside walls were stucco with naturally flowing round corners painted in shades of soft yellow, green, and tan. Hand-made furniture crafted in Belize, natural wood, and woven bamboo seating with large cloth cushions made the house comfortable. Locally created artwork adorned the walls. The living room was large, with wood-framed windows viewing the sea. An outside deck faced the ocean with a few palm trees offering natural shelter from the sun. The kitchen and dining room were open to the living room, giving the downstairs unobstructed ambiance. The master bedroom was off to the side in the back on the main floor. This is the one area where I disagreed with Ilana. I suggested that the master bedroom be located upstairs with a balcony looking out to the sea. But Ilana did not want to sleep upstairs. She wanted to sleep on the main floor in the back of the house, where it was sheltered from storms. She got her way.

A garden framed by palm trees grew in back where Ilana cultivated natural fruits and vegetables. A pond had been dug next to the garden with a patio under palm trees for shade. She loved to cook and she loved the natural fruits and vegetables which grew in her garden. She had grown up poor, but never hungry because her family always kept a garden.

The garden was her place to relax.

1:20 PM. JOHN

Rising in a rush, lungs screaming for air, water cascaded off my body; I inhaled as soon as my head broke the surface of the water.

It had been months since I had done any serious free diving, and it was painfully obvious that my ability to stay underwater for any length of time was severely restricted due to lack of exercise. In a futile attempt to quickly rebuild my stamina I had been forcing my body to stay underwater longer than it was capable. It was not working.

Resting for a few minutes while floating on my back in the sea, I eventually gave in to my pursuit of the depths and swam slowly to the sailboat. Climbing a rope ladder attached to the boat, I rested on deck in defeat, breathing deeply.

It had been fun swimming underwater by the reef, just as I remembered. Schools of small, colorful fish of all varieties darted in nervous flights away from what they perceived as my rather large intrusion into their wondrous world among the nooks and caves formed by the ever-reaching tentacles of a living reef. Their dashes for freedom in flashes of color created an underwater fireworks display. Nearly imperceptible shadows of gray barracuda flew overhead, ghostly gun-metal torpedoes in the blue water. Black stingrays could be seen floating below over the rippled white sands, seemingly unconcerned with my presence. Everything was as I remembered except for my ability to hold my breath as long as I desired. My body and my muscles quickly became strained and tired. Ears complained of pain from constant changes in pressure, diving into the depths of the sea, and returning too quickly to the surface for air. It seemed as if I had only been underwater for a brief few seconds when my lungs immediately called for, no... screamed for oxygen.

I had to admit, I was badly out of shape.

Before when I lived in Belize, I swam every day for exercise, I dived all the time building up my endurance slowly without thinking about it. Now I wanted to swim like in the past, but I could not. It was frustrating.

I toweled off and went down to the galley for a couple of beers, offering one to Todd even though he was on duty. He declined at first, but I convinced him to take the beer and relax. All afternoon, he had been sitting on the boat covered from the sun, his gun laying on a cushion next to him, instantly available in case of emergency. I knew he was doing his job, but it was annoying. I wanted to relax and it was hard to relax with him sitting there all tense, ready for action. I told him to loosen up. We were on vacation. Nothing was going to happen.

He smiled in response, ignoring me.

Eventually I stopped trying to convince him. It is difficult talking sense to military types. They live a different world.

After observing the ladies enjoying their time in the water for a few minutes, I leaned my head back and pulled an old baseball hat down over my eyes. Almost immediately sleep took control of my exhausted body until someone touched me gently, tracing her finger over my lips until I opened my eyes.

'You need to cover up, John,' Sandy said. 'This is our first day in the sun. You are going to burn.'

I blinked in the bright sun. Sandy was right. She was always right. She handed me a shirt and light khaki pants. I got dressed, knowing I had already been out too long in the sun. She was wearing a white linen shirt over her bikini. We found a place in the back of the boat to sit beneath the shade of the main sail. The breeze was down. The sail luffed lazily in the wind.

'Did you enjoy diving by the reef?' I asked.

She just smiled. 'It is wonderful here, John. How could you ever leave this place?'

'I have a job,' I said, knowing this was only half true. The real answer was far more complicated.

She looked at me like always, like she knew better. Draping her arm over the side of the boat, she lazily swirled her fingers in the water. 'I never knew a place like this existed. The water is so warm and clear,' she said. 'I love the color. It is so blue.'

'Not like Lake Michigan?'

'No.'

In silence we watched Ilana repeatedly rise and dive into the water. She had a spear gun in her hand. She was fishing for our dinner. It seemed an appropriate time to explore a few uneasy questions which had been wandering around unattended in my brain.

'Did you and Ilana have a nice time last night?' I inquired.

'Yes,' Sandy answered simply without volunteering any additional information.

'You two seem to be getting along?'

'Yes, she is a wonderful person.'

'What did you talk about?'

Sandy looked at me and smiled. 'I suppose you want to know if we talked about you.'

'Oh no, just making conversation.'

'Are you saying you don't care to know what we discussed?'

'Don't care,' I lied.

Sandy said nothing in response, silent, seemingly content, unwilling, or uninterested in continuing our conversation.

I waited, hoping for more as she quietly rested with her hand in the water.

'So, what did you talk about?' I finally asked. I couldn't help it. I had to know.

'Oh, you know, family, friends, that sort of thing.'

'Nothing more?'

'Like what?'

'Oh, you know.'

'Like, did we talk about boyfriends, maybe even you?'

'Well, okay, did you discuss me?'

'So, you really do want to know.'

'Yes.'

'That's it? Just yes, that's all you are going to say to me?'

Why, I wondered, do women frustrate men so? It is as if they have a God-given ability to find our weaknesses easily and exploit their talent relentlessly.

'What do you want me to say, John? Do you want me to say we both like you? You already know that.'

At that moment, Ilana swam to the boat with a fish on her spear.

I leaned over the back of the boat to help her with the wiggling fish.

10:05 P.M. JOHN

Red snapper grilled with butter, lemon juice, and breadcrumbs.

Red wine along with a salad made with fresh vegetables from Ilana's garden, coupled with cordial conversation at the dinner table. It was a pleasant evening. We ate in the shade of the front deck while the sun set in the west behind the house.

Our sail home from the reef had been uneventful. The inboard Volvo engine was forced into service, propelling the boat. Wind was down which was unusual. A breeze is a constant most days, but that afternoon the sea was calm and talk was almost nonexistent. I guess we were tired.

When we neared the dock, I signaled to Ilana. She stood in the bow, jumped to the dock when the boat was close, and tied off a line on a post. In the past, we had developed a well-established routine for lowering the sails and making the boat secure after arriving at the dock. It was something we had done many times. It didn't require a lot of conversation. It was a well-oiled routine. Sandy stood by and watched us work. Eventually, she stepped off the boat onto the dock and waited for us to complete our tasks. It was awkward having her do nothing, but it was easier than asking her to help. She would have just gotten in the way.

Todd seemed happy to be off the boat. He jumped to the dock as soon as he was able and stood sentinel while we worked. I didn't mind. He was doing his job.

The dinner routine was different from when it was only Ilana and me. Then I would help her. Now the ritual of making of a meal was orchestrated by ladies only. I was told to stay out of their way. I could hear them talk as I reviewed work related emails on my computer in the living room. Several messages required urgent replies. I wasn't quite finished when the ladies announced it was time to eat.

After dinner, I worked while they cleaned the dishes. Before I was finished, they retreated to the front deck with a glass a wine in hand. I joined them eventually, contributing very little to their conversation. Family history and childhood memories were the topics for discussion, not exactly my favorite subjects.

However, this was not true for them. Even though they came from completely different worlds, they had much in common. Both of them had lost parents at relatively young ages, Ilana earlier than Sandy. Ilana had lost her parents when she was around fourteen. Sandy's parents died in an automobile accident when she was older, away at college. This gave them a common bond. Both of them had been forced to become self-reliant long before they wanted the responsibility. In Ilana's case, her brother attempted to take over her parent's duties, but I knew from her stories that nothing but trouble came from his attempts to control her. She lived pretty much on her own from the time her parents died. Sandy's story was different in that she didn't have an older brother to care for her. The death of her parents forced her to be the parent, to find work to support her younger sister. Not for long; fortunately, her sister was not much younger, but still, it interrupted Sandy's life. She abandoned a college degree and graduate school, and instead of returning to college as planned after her sister was out of the house, a boy changed her life.

Ilana's childhood story was about a young girl who lived on the beach. Her father had died from a broken heart after her mother's death from an illness. Ilana did not wish to suffer the kind of pain her father had experienced. She rigorously avoided life-changing relationships with boys. Not because she wasn't offered the opportunity. She always shied away from relationships whenever they got serious.

I listened without comment as they compared personal histories. I also had stories to tell, but I didn't because it didn't seem as if my input was desired. This was girlfriend time. I was expected to remain silent.

A three-quarter moon cast a glow over the deck, illuminating their animated smiles. I realized, as I watched them, how much I adored them both. In different ways, maybe, but still, I loved them. Ilana was more animated than Sandy. She dominated the conversation with quick, excited stories from her past. Sandy was calmer, slower to tell a story, but still equally expressive.

Their conversation eventually moved to Sandy's questions about the island. Ilana was more than willing to answer. As the ladies continued to talk, I mentally slipped away, allowing their discussion to be music to my ears, listening to the chorus of their voices as I leaned my head back against a cushion and allowed my eyes to close in temporary contentment.

Crickets soon joined their choir, chirping like tenors in an opera. Rhythmic lapping of waves on the shore filled in the bass while soprano was sung in the pleasant sounds of their laughter. As much as I intended to rest for only a few minutes with my eyes closed, listening to their music, I must have slept much longer. When I woke, they were gone, and I was alone on the deck.

Tiptoeing quietly upstairs to my lonely bedroom outpost like a lost puppy, I once again slept by myself.

FRIDAY, NOVEMBER 6, 3:45 P.M. JOHN

'Ilana really is a lovely person,' Sandy said for no apparent reason.

I had just come from my bedroom hideaway on the second floor where I had been working.

For the first few days after we arrived, I tried to work on the main floor, in the dining room, the place where I had worked in the past when Ilana and I lived in this house together. But it quickly became obvious I had to move. With two women now occupying the house, the level of commotion increased exponentially. It was amazing, really. How could the addition of one more female body in a house be so disruptive? It wasn't like the amount of activity doubled. It was more like it quadrupled or worse. Once two female bodies occupy the same vicinity, they quickly multiply into something far more intensive. They were constantly in motion. From where I worked at the dining room table, I could see them and hear them. Their bantering discussions were relentless, and they were always in motion, either coming or going, in or out of the kitchen for food and drinks. Or changing their clothes, or wanting some fresh towels, or talking about going somewhere, or who knows what; always something to disturb my concentration. Finally, I gave up and took my computer and briefcase upstairs to my isolated bedroom outpost.

Todd helped me move a small desk and chair upstairs so I could be comfortable. It wasn't too bad once I was settled. I worked with a view over the ocean, which was great most of the day, except early in the morning when I had to pull the shades to shield a blinding sun. In the afternoon, the rolling seas were a visual relief when I needed a break. It was actually rather pleasant. And without the noise and interruptions of the female variety, I was able to get some work done.

Between emails, telephone conversations, and reports to digest, I stayed busy most of the day and sometimes into the night. This seemed to suit the ladies fine. It meant they were free to do their thing without having to bother about me. They spent their time going into town, swimming off the dock, or just talking. They were having fun, most of the time without me. If I was good for anything as far as the ladies were concerned, it was only to occasionally enrich their conversation at dinner. Otherwise, they summarily ignored me. I was simply there, available to make sure they were well cared for. And unfortunately, this did not mean in the carnal sense of the word.

Todd's situation was different. His job was security. He was a quiet guy. He stayed in a small attached apartment originally built for a live-in maid. I thought a maid would be necessary once the house was occupied. It was much bigger than any house Ilana had ever lived in before. I couldn't imagine Ilana cleaning it without help. But after we moved in, she never hired anyone. I suspected this was because she didn't want a local in her house, someone spreading unwarranted gossip around town about her. She said she liked taking care of the house herself. And that's why the apartment had remained unoccupied until Todd moved in. It had an efficient kitchen, a sitting room with a TV, and, of course, a small bedroom and bathroom. It suited Todd fine. He was a very self-sufficient guy. Most of the time, he stayed out of our way. Sometimes, he ate with us, but not often. He was content to be by himself and do his job, keep tabs on the ladies, and go with them when they went into town.

Ilana slept in the master bedroom. It was her room. It was where I used to sleep with her, just not now for obvious reasons. Sandy used a bedroom upstairs at the opposite end of the hall from my bedroom with a separate bathroom. And since we kept different hours, meaning I was up early and early to bed, and she was up late and late to bed, we seldom saw each other, except, as I explained, during my command performances at dinner.

It was a comfortable arrangement, at least for the ladies. It wasn't planned. We simply fell into it because it was easy, no conflicts.

My day had been filled with Trans-Atlantic telephone calls. By mid-afternoon, I needed a break. It was hot. The temperature had to be close to ninety. A window air conditioner was blowing in my room, but by late afternoon, the AC was insufficient. It was simply too hot to be upstairs for this Midwestern boy. A cold drink was required. I found some lemonade in the kitchen refrigerator downstairs, and I poured myself a glass, taking it out on the front deck to relax. Palms trees were swaying in the wind just off the deck and frigate birds could be seen floating on the thermals like great gliders. A few black-headed seagulls rose high in the clear blue sky before diving into the sea to catch a meal.

When I spotted Sandy lying on a lounge chair in the sand just beyond the deck, enjoying the late afternoon sun, I took a chair and sat down in the shade of a palm tree next to her. Thinking it was somewhat inappropriate to enjoy my cool drink while she was sweating in her bikini. I assumed the sociable thing to do would be to bring her a glass. After returning from the kitchen and offering her the drink, she sat up, and this was when she made her comment about Ilana.

'I can see why you like her,' she continued.

'Thanks.' I replied, not sure I was mentally prepared to discuss her chosen topic of conversation.

'I like her too.'

'Good. That's great.'

'You don't say it like you mean it. Aren't you glad I like her?' Sandy asked. 'Or is there some reason why you wouldn't want me to like her?'

'No, it's just...'

'Oh please, John, you don't have to make up lies to keep me happy. I see how she looks at you. And I see you looking back. I think you still like her.'

I didn't know what to say and apparently Sandy took my silence as an affirmation that she was right. And, of course, she was right. I liked Ilana. In fact, I still loved her. It was just that I had killed a man and she was with me when it happened. This was my problem. I didn't like thinking about what happened, and well... I guessed it poisoned our relationship. It was no one's fault, really. Certainly not hers. Maybe not even mine. It just was.

'Okay, so let's say you are right,' I volunteered. 'Is that a problem?'

'It doesn't have to be a problem,' Sandy replied.

'Does it change how you think about me?'

'No,' she said as she leaned over towards me to place her empty glass in the sand. She had beautiful, full breasts. And when she leaned over, her bikini top provided very little in the way of hiding the vision of their wonder. It had been almost a week since I last had sex with her, and I was getting horny. It's a male malady, I know. It can't be helped. And having two glorious beauties parading around wearing practically nothing all day was not making it easy.

She looked at me and immediately recognized the look of weak dependence on my face.

'Need something?' she asked with a smile.

'Let's not change the subject,' I replied, not wanting to allow her to avoid answering my question. 'Does it change our relationship?' I asked again.

'What relationship, John?'

'We have a relationship, don't we? At least I think we do,' I said, sensing it might be slipping away. I knew it was not a good idea to come to Belize. I knew it had the potential to ruin my relationship with Sandy. But I also knew any attempt on my part to delay the trip would have been seen as a lie by her, as if I was trying to compartmentalize my life, trying to keep two women in different worlds, being unfaithful to both of them. Sandy, if she was anything, was smart. She would easily have seen through my hypocrisy. So, I was dammed if I refused to take her to meet Ilana. And it appeared I was going to be dammed because I did.

'Well, let's talk about our relationship,' she continued. 'First, I think we enjoyed reliving some teenage fantasies for a week or two. Then, we spent some time exploring our present circumstances. And now, we are delving into your past to determine where we can go from here. Would you say that is an accurate assessment of our relationship to date?'

The woman never failed to confound me. Nothing was ever easy with her. She was very good at reducing everything to its simplest terms, which always seemed to complicate things on some level I could not control. I looked at her for a moment. I badly wanted to have sex with her right then and there on the deck. At the same time, I wanted to strangle her for being so damned smart.

'I guess what you say is accurate,' I replied feebly. 'So where does that leave us?'

'I not sure,' she smiled at me and lay down again to work on her tan.

Her skin glistened in the late afternoon sun, every inch of it; soft and smooth and wonderful in every way a woman's body can be wonderful.

I stood up when I couldn't stand it anymore and took my horny body to my self-imposed celibate place of exile, returning upstairs even though it was too sweaty hot.

SATURDAY, NOVEMBER 7, 12:10 A.M. JOHN

She must have gone for a late-night swim because when she slithered into my bed, her naked body felt cool and clean to the touch.

I wasn't sleeping at the time. A hot breeze had been blowing through my open bedroom windows keeping me awake. I don't like sleeping with the windows closed, not if I can help it. One of the things I love about Belize is sleeping with open windows, allowing the sounds of the night to wander into the bedroom and linger in half conscious dreams; the lapping of waves on the shore, the chirping of the crickets, the gentle rustle of palm leaves embraced by invisible night winds.

In Michigan where I lived as a boy, it was cold half the year. Windows needed to be closed to hold in heat. Sounds of the night were sealed away from early fall to late spring. Winter was a time of silence, snow falling in an empty quiet.

I never liked it. I never liked the silence of winter. Silence seemed to beckon bad dreams. It was as if the silent black void of a winter night waited with open arms to all sorts of mischief. Fear followed; nothing to keep it out, nothing familiar, nothing alive, nothing but an empty dark silence filled with childhood miseries. So wherever I can, I always sleep with windows open, even when it is hot.

Usually, the wind becomes calm during the night on the island of Ambergris and the air cools, but a storm must have been brewing because the wind was blowing hot and steady, making it difficult to sleep. My body was partially awake in anticipation of the storm. My mind relishing the coming rush of the wind and racket of the rain. I was half asleep, half awake, listening to the wind when her cool, damp body curled up against me like a refreshing breeze under the sheets.

She didn't move at first, resting beside me as I lay on my back. I turned over to face her, unsure in the dark who had come into my bed. Running my hands through her hair, her natural curls told me it was her. Even though her hair was damp from being in the water, I knew it was Sandy.

I rose up on one elbow and leaned over to kiss her on the lips. Running my hand over her full breasts and down across her naked thigh, I turned back the sheet to simply adore her body under the glow of the night sky. Smoothly flowing lines of desire greeted my gaze, her body resting under moon shadows creeping in through the bedroom windows. A million stars reflected in her eyes. Light from the moon raced in and out from behind flowing clouds, constantly changing the texture of her skin; at once, a soft and distant gray followed by a warm and sweet pale white highlighting the smile on her lips.

She ran her hands through my hair and touched me where men like to be touched. Sitting up to kneel over my waist. 'Is this what you wanted, John boy?' she asked innocently. 'Is this what you wanted this afternoon on the deck?'

I didn't say anything.

Finding the place between her legs, which was wet and inviting, I slowly moved inside her, allowing the moment to linger for an eternity in my wildest imagination.

7:05 A.M. JOHN

When I entered the kitchen the next morning, Ilana was there, casually sipping a cup of hot coffee with a mischievous smile covering her face like she knew something. Now, that was odd and potentially troubling. Or perhaps it was just my guilty imagination talking to me.

When I am home in my apartment on weekends, I don't often go into my office early, like on weekdays. Although I normally spend some time in my office every day; on weekends, I try to limit my office time. But that doesn't stop my biological clock from going off around the same time every day, around six a.m., regardless of what day it is. And I don't stay in bed any longer on weekends than weekdays.

When I first lived on the island with Ilana, I wasn't working. But this seemed to have little to no effect on my biological clock. Meaning I was often up well before for my sleepy-headed Belizean girlfriend. She liked her morning beauty rest. So, it was something of a shock to see her sitting at a table in the dinette off her kitchen when I came downstairs early for a cup of coffee.

After last night's amorous activity, my plan was to go to the kitchen for coffee and take it to my bedroom to spend a few hours working. I guess I was feeling guilty. Last night's adventure with Sandy had been great, but I wasn't sure it was an appropriate activity in Ilana's house. Therefore, it seemed that hiding out in my bedroom might be the most prudent, chicken-shit response to my current predicament. Assuming it would be good to let things settle down and hope all would be forgotten by late afternoon.

The dinette, where Ilana was sitting, had been built in the back of the house to take advantage of the morning shade. It was a small room with stucco walls painted pale yellow. A round wood table sat by a wide window overlooking Ilana's garden. She liked spending time sitting at the table in the morning. I knew this. I could have avoided to room, but I didn't expect to see her there so early.

'Did you sleep well, John?' she asked, smiling at me.

When I woke up, I had instinctively reached over, hoping to touch the long smooth body of Sandy. However, she was gone by this time. I remembered falling to sleep next to her after we made love, but I didn't remember hearing her leave. This seemed to indicate I had slept very soundly which was unusual because normally I wake instantly whenever I hear a noise. But apparently, not the case last night. Last night I must have slept like a baby.

'Yes,' I replied honestly, thinking I was glad Sandy had gone to her room during the night, meaning everything had returned to as it should have been by morning.

'It was very hot last night. I had trouble sleeping. Did you?' Ilana asked.

Now, this was a troubling question. My mind raced over the possible reasons for her asking. The master bedroom where Ilana slept was on the other side of the house from my bedroom. She couldn't possibly have heard us last night. The house was too big, and my bedroom was too far away for her to hear anything. But it was also possible she had been up because it was hot, walking around. She could have heard something, suspected something. And perhaps that's why she asked her question.

I looked at her, trying to read her mind, but I couldn't. She, like most women was very good at disguising her emotions.

'It was hot,' I finally replied. 'But I managed to get some sleep.'

'Did you dream last night?' she continued to probe. 'I usually dream when I don't sleep well. Sometimes my dreams are beautiful, and sometimes they are nightmares.'

'I guess I dreamed.'

'Was your dream beautiful?' she asked.

Now this was another odd question and even more troubling than the others, possibly leading to a topic I did not want to discuss.

'I don't remember,' I replied, hoping to end this conversation.

'Hi,' Sandy arrived in the kitchen at that moment, dressed in a robe over a nightshirt, open at the top. 'Sleep well?' she asked me, pinching my butt as she passed to get a cup out of the cupboard.

'Yes,' I replied, thinking they were now ganging up on me.

'Would you like me to pour you a cup of coffee?' Sandy asked.

'Yes, sure.'

I cautiously watched her slowly take another cup out of the cupboard and pour coffee into both cups, hers and mine. I desperately wanted to get out of the kitchen as fast as possible. No way was I prepared to deal with being interrogated by both of them.

'Why don't you sit down, John?' Sandy suggested.

'Yes,' Ilana chimed in. 'Sit down, John. It is nice to see you in the morning. We don't often get to see you in the morning.'

'Well... I have some work to do upstairs.' I half lied.

'Oh, you always have work to do. It's the weekend. Why don't you play with us today?' Sandy volunteered.

'Maybe later.'

They were smiling at me in the strangest way as I made a hasty retreat.

2:25 P.M. ILANA

When John called her to say he was coming to Belize, Ilana had been elated.

She knew he had serious problems. The shooting of that awful man had messed with his mind. He was having trouble dealing with it. And why not? It had been a terrible night, terrible for him and terrible for her. She understood. It had changed their relationship, and not for the best. However, she still wanted him and loved him even though she did not know if it would ever be the same. In fact, she was certain it would not be.

For this, she blamed herself. She thought about all the times she should have told John about that man, that bad man from Columbia who was always calling her, wanting her to do bad things. She had resisted telling John to avoid involving him, hoping to deal with the situation when she was ready. That had been a mistake, her mistake. And everything had gone wrong as a result, terribly wrong. It was her fault. It was her fault their relationship was not right, and there was nothing she could do now except wait and hope it would heal in time.

She hoped his coming for a visit was a good sign, hoped he was healing. Perhaps they could again be as they were before the awful night in the dark woods, hope they could again be lovers, talk about marriage. Not all at once, maybe, but eventually. However, when he said he was bringing a friend, a girlfriend, Ilana was confused. And then she was hurt, and then she became mad. How could he?

As his trip approached, she forced herself to become calm. She decided to wait and see what would happen. She knew John needed help. She knew he was badly wounded by what happened. Perhaps his new girlfriend was helping him. She decided it served no purpose to be mad. She could not change him any more than she could change the past.

She decided to wait until she could meet his girlfriend, then decide what to do after she knew more. It would be better to deal with John then, deal with him face to face. Tell him his new girlfriend must go.

When she met Sandy, Ilana was both surprised and confused. This American woman was not anything like she imagined, nothing like the American women she had met on the island, the haughty, arrogant tourist women who thought islanders should serve them because they were rich. Instead, Sandy was kind and thoughtful. Sandy had an easy smile and an easy way about her. Ilana immediately liked this Sandy.

Ilana never had a close girlfriend when she was young. The death of her mother that isolated her. Ilana had retreated from society after her mother died, afraid of the intimacy of friendship. Afraid to lose another person to death and the pain that had caused her. As a child Ilana retreated to the sea, the beach, a place where no one could hurt her. But now, she was older. Now she thought it might be good to have a friend, someone she could talk to, and Sandy was someone who could be that friend, someone who had become her friend.

As Ilana rested under the shade of a tall palm tree in her garden, she thought about Sandy, about John, about what to do, what not to do. It was all very difficult, complicated, made her feel tired. As she rested in the heat of the day, Ilana replayed the conversation she and Sandy had the previous afternoon.

This was going to be fun, Sandy had said. And it was. It was already fun.

Ilana liked her new friend, Sandy.

Ilana never had a friend like Sandy before.

6:25 P.M. JOHN

I could stay in my upstairs room for only so long.

Any longer might imply the appearance of guilt. And that would not be good.

In the morning, I had been able to avoid the ladies by working upstairs with the air conditioner on high. When I got hungry around noon, I timidly went downstairs for a sandwich and something to drink. Fortunately, the house was quiet. The ladies must have been out at the time, which meant avoiding an unpleasant confrontation.

After lunch, a storm promised by the hot winds during the night materialized from the northwest. Lines of rain swept down from dark clouds covering the horizon, eventually moving onshore and drowning the land in streams of muddy water. I took a break and sat outside on a protected balcony off my bedroom, watching the palm trees sway in a high wind. Lightning darted across the horizon in pinched radiant lines against a dark gray sky. Thunder rumbled in constant loud complaints. Wind whipped the ocean into a sea of frenzied white water, blowing the tops off the waves into a salt-water spray vanishing into the air.

The storm scrubbed all the Saturday afternoon activities planned for me by the ladies for me, which was good. It meant I could hide out in my bedroom a little longer. Great, because the more I thought about what happened the previous night, the more uncomfortable I was with it. Oh, don't get me wrong. It was wonderful. But, well, you know, feeling guilty always comes later.

Anyway, it was done, and I couldn't change it. I only hoped it would be forgotten and the inhabitants of the house would return to their peaceful, celibate lifestyle. Even though I wasn't really happy living in a sex-free, coed environment, which reminded me of frustrated college dorm life, I thought it was probably best under the circumstances. I decided to have a talk with Sandy. Tell her thanks, but let's wait until we return home. I hoped she would agree. I didn't want to seem ungrateful, and I wasn't. I just didn't think we should have a repeat performance.

However, that didn't mean that I wasn't still nervous. Ilana's comments in the morning were rumbling around in my head somewhere. I couldn't help but wonder what she knew or didn't know. And sooner or later, I would be forced to go downstairs where I would have to face the ladies which might just turn into a unpleasant experience. I couldn't exactly hang out in my bedroom for the rest of the trip.

It was almost cocktail time. The storm had passed, and the sky was beginning to lighten. I wandered downstairs, hoping everything had returned to normal.

The evening started out fine, meaning Ilana, Sandy, and I sat on the front deck with a drink as if nothing had happened. As was our custom, Ilana and I drank Belican beer, and Sandy liked her wine. Cocktail time conversation was casual. The air after the rain felt refreshingly clean and cool. The wind had died down, and it was very pleasant. Ilana eventually retreated into the kitchen to start dinner. Pan-fried fish was on the menu; I don't remember what kind. Sandy followed, offering a helping hand. I decided to assist by preparing a salad. I'm not much of a cook, but I can do salads. I cut up some romaine lettuce, chopped green peppers, added raisins, and some local fruit, along with shredded cheese. After choosing a poppy seed dressing, I was done. Salads are not difficult to make. It was my contribution.

Dinner was great, good food and a non-confrontational conversation. I was beginning to relax, thinking the crisis was over. Everything had returned to normal.

And then it wasn't, meaning nothing close to normal.

The sun was receding behind the house at the time; the sky quickly losing its radiant intensity. I decided to go on the dock. After being cooped up in my room all day, I felt the need for some exercise.

The end of the dock is about fifty feet from the shoreline. Not much in the way of human traffic normally roams the beach at this time of night. Raising my tee shirt over my head, I dropped it on the dock and let my shorts and underwear slip off before diving off the end of the dock, enjoying the warm liquid comfort of the sea, allowing the water to naturally cleanse my mind as well as my body as I swam. Muscles began to ache from exertion. Swimming became a rite of exorcism, penitence for my sins. Guilt was washed away as I pushed harder, swimming parallel to the shore until the dock was miniature in the distance.

Since I couldn't exactly walk back naked along the shore, a long, strenuous swim returning to the dock took about all the energy I had stored up during the day. Still, the exercise felt good as I pulled my tired body up the wooden stairs at the end of the dock and sat down to rest, breathing deeply. I had not planned on taking a swim. I didn't have a towel, so I let a warm breeze take care of drying my wet body with my back to the shore as the sky became dark.

'Hi, John.'

'Hi,' I replied, startled by Ilana's sudden appearance and just a little embarrassed. Although it wasn't like she hadn't seen me naked before, it was just the timing of the circumstances that seemed off somehow.

'Did you have a nice swim?' she asked while sitting down next to me.

'Yes, it was very refreshing.'

The moon cast a tail of soft light over the sea as we sat on the dock. Ilana looked great, her long black hair touched by a gentle breeze as she sat silently looking out over the ocean. Her silence was unusual. She was never quiet for very long, and her unusual behavior made me wonder if she was waiting for me to speak.

Still under the influence of a guilty conscience, I began to wonder if she was waiting for me to make a confession.

'Maybe I will go for a swim,' she suggested much my relief. 'Will you wait for me here while I take a short swim?'

'Of course.'

She was barefoot, wearing a one-piece linen dress. It was pale pink, elegant in its simplicity. After standing to lift it over her head, she handed me her dress. Braless, she slipped off her panties before diving into the water. Holding her clothes, I watched in guilty pleasure as her slim, naked body glided naturally over the water as only she could swim.

'Why don't you come in?' she asked from the sea.

'I don't know. I'm just getting dry,' I replied feebly.

'Oh, John, come on. We haven't gone swimming together for so long.'

Maybe because I was feeling guilty... Maybe I figured I owed her... I'm not sure why, but for whatever reason or lack thereof, I gave in. Placing her dress on the dock, I slipped off the dock into the water. She swam towards me and wrapped her arms and legs around me as I paddled to keep my head above the water. Then she kissed me, long and hard on my lips, in sweet proximity to the soft round curves of her glorious body.

'This is nice, John,' she said. 'Don't you think this is nice?'

It was very nice, and I could feel my body begin to react to her beauty as she held me and kissed me. I missed her. I really did miss her. As much as I wanted to forget her, put her memory and the associated ugly experiences we shared into a box to be forgotten, I could not. I wanted her. I wanted to be with her. She had not changed. She was still the same wonderful, beautiful woman I loved. She had done nothing worthy of incurring my rejection. It was simply the ugly killing that happened, changing how I saw her. It was not her fault I pulled the trigger. It was me. I pulled the trigger to kill a man. I created the problem. And now I was making the problem worse by forcing her to pay for my sins, my anger at what I had become, for being a man who killed another man in a horrible moment of insanity.

It was not right. I knew it. I knew I was wrong to make her share the consequences of my guilt. But what I didn't know was how to make it right.

She didn't stay in the water long, just long enough to cool off. Climbing the stairs, she sat on the dock as a warm breeze dried her wet body. I followed, sitting beside her.

Before I could say a word, she said. 'Okay, John, now it's my turn.'

'What.'

'Now it is my turn.'

'What is your turn?'

'Well, you were nice to Sandy last night. Now it's my turn. Now, you need to be nice to me.'

I was speechless.

I didn't understand.

It had to be this island, this wonderful place by the sea. A place where tomorrow will take care of itself, don't worry, just enjoy the moment.

'Well, don't you think it would be fair?' she asked. 'Don't you want to be nice to me?'

'Of course, I want to be nice to you. But I don't think...'

She got up on her knees and leaned over to kiss me.

'You don't have to think about anything,' she said. 'It is okay. It's okay with Sandy. We have talked. This is how it is to be. You get to love both of us. We are happy, and we don't mind sharing you.'

'You have talked about this?' I couldn't believe what I was hearing.

'Yes, we talked yesterday. We know you are hurting, John. You are suffering from what happened to you. You need to heal, John. So, we have decided to help you heal. Make it better for you.'

'Sandy knows about this?'

'Of course, you don't think I would do anything to hurt my friend Sandy.'

'I didn't know your friendship was that close.'

'John, Sandy, and I have become good friends. I like your Sandy, and she likes me. Now we have to make you well again.'

'Really,' was all I could stupidly say.

'Yes, John. Now, it is my turn to be with you.' And she kissed me again.

I didn't know what to say.

'John, I understand why you don't want to be with me, but I can't change that. I can't change what happened when you killed that man,' Ilana explained. 'It happened, and we cannot change the past, can we?' She paused... 'I'm not going to be jealous of your Sandy. Is this what you thought I would do?'

'Well, yes, I guess I did.'

'I will not be jealous because being jealous solves nothing. Being jealous will not change the past. If I have to share you now, then I will share you. I can do nothing more.'

I was speechless.

'Come on, John,' Ilana beckoned. 'Let's go to the boat. Make love to me like you did when we were on the boat to Mexico. Let's pretend we are sailing to Mexico again.'

She stood and took me by the hand, leading me to the boat like a lost child.

11:50 P.M. JOHN

Alone again in my self-imposed domicile of exile, my upstairs bedroom.

It was late in the night. I should have been sleeping, content with the events of the day. All things good; more than good, nothing like I feared. In fact, better than I could have ever imagined. But something bred by the guilt plagued society of my youth would allow me no rest.

It had been fun; sex had been great. They were wonderful, more than any man deserved. But then isn't it true, a woman is never deserved. They are always a gift. Love is by its nature undeserving. And was the love of these women diminished by the fact they freely gave me their gift? Did this make it impure, tainted, sinful?

I didn't know. But I did know that it came with some guilt. It was not what I had been taught from youth to expect. The church, the institution that dominates our thoughts and our culture, the church had bestowed on me a different standard, one not quite so understanding as my two lady friends. But I wondered if that was right. If love is the standard by which we are to be judged by God, then is it better to be loved by only one woman, or should we accept love whenever or wherever it is responsibly offered.

I rested in the dark unable to sleep, discontent.

I thought about the ladies, how different they were. They came from completely different backgrounds, educations. One was a product of my culture; the church, schools and college which gave me an interpretation of life. The other was a product of nature, a beach girl, a woman self-taught by the school of nature. One had blue eyes and curly blond hair. The other had big brown eyes and long straight black hair. They were so different and yet they were so very similar. I thought it must be their intelligence which made them similar, their strong will and their intelligent ability to see life for what it was. This was what unified them, gave them a common bond, something intrinsically understood from the moment they met. It was what made them friends. It was what they shared.

I loved them both. I had held them both in my arms for moments of exquisite pleasure. But I also knew I could never possess either of them forever. That much I understood. They were independent souls. They were not mine to have. To share, perhaps, to spend a few brief moments of time together with me when they chose to give me their love as a gift. They had come to me and loved me in times of great stress. Ilana and Sandy had come to me when I wasn't sure I could have made it without them.

Being with them, being in love with them became for me the only place on this earth where I did not see death.

THURSDAY, NOVEMBER 12, 3:25 P.M. JOHN

Ilana was the first to see the powerboat speed towards us.

It was one of those long, sleek offshore racing boats with a big white hull riding high in the water, sea spray rising off its bow. These expensive boats are not a common sight in the waters off the coast of Belize. I had seen a few, but not many. They are gas-guzzling hogs, consume fuel in gallons per mile, not miles per gallon. It was rumored some of these boats were owned by drug runners.

The boat was a long distance away. I ignored it at first, quite content to enjoy the sun and the sea. It had been a glorious day. We decided to go for a long sail and do some free diving. My stay in Belize was drawing to a close. I couldn't remain on the island forever. I had to return to my office soon, but no definite plans had been made.

When I first arrived, I was determined to see how the ladies would act. Maybe, I thought, maybe they would hate each other, and I would be forced to return immediately. Obviously that had not happened; quite the opposite. In fact I was beginning to think I never wanted to leave. Life in Belize was good, too good in fact: warm weather, beautiful place to live, and best of all... two wonderful lovers.

So why I would ever want to return to Charlottesville. But business was calling. Meetings had been postponed, and business trips rescheduled. I had to wrap my mind around the concept of returning. Before heading to the States, we unanimously decided one more day trip on the boat was required. Only one of our group would have disagreed with this decision if he had a vote, which he didn't, and this would have been Todd. It was discovered after a few rather unpleasant, gut-wrenching throw-up experiences that our fearless bodyguard was quite prone to becoming seasick. Trips on the sailboat were his least favorite duty. However, he wasn't a problem that day because he wasn't with us. His sister had called. His father was deathly sick and had only days to live. Todd was needed in the States in a hurry.

Everything had gone well during our stay. No signs of trouble. It was decided he should return; his family was important. I drove Todd to the airport in Ilana's jeep. And since we were not planning to stay much longer, I decided against finding a replacement for him.

We sailed along the coast in the morning towards a good diving spot over a reef, farther south than our usual destination. Ilana and I had been there before. We wanted to show it to Sandy.

That afternoon, we spent time diving, eating, and relaxing on the boat with three friends, good friends. Or it would be more accurate to say that Sandy and Ilana had become almost inseparable friends. My role was far less significant. I was more like an accessory after the fact. Or at least this was how I felt most of the time. It was difficult to determine if they were here for me or if I was here to serve them. Either way, I wasn't complaining. I had time to work. And I had two great ladies to keep me company. And they had me.

Or, again, it might be more accurate to say they had me when they were so inclined to spend time with me. And this was not often because most of the time, they were off on some adventure, and I was alone in the house working. Ilana was busy immersing Sandy in Belizean culture. I heard all about it at the end of the day when we had cocktails and dinner. They were having a great time.

It was late in the afternoon when we spotted the speedboat. Almost time to raise the sails. Free diving had been great, the reef beautiful, and schools of fish awesome in number and color.

I closed my eyes for a moment and rested, allowing my head to lean on a cushion. I think at the time, I was trying to imagine returning to work in Charlottesville. It was the middle of November. The weather would be cool in Virginia. Helen had been warning me work was piling up. I had talked to her on the phone the day before. The anxious tone in her voice was impossible to ignore. It was obvious she wanted me back. But I wasn't ready. In fact, I was spending more time daydreaming about the possibility of moving the office south to Belize than I was thinking about traveling north. I knew that was more or less impossible. Still, it was fun to dream.

The sun beat down as I rested, warming my body more than was prudent. I could feel my skin begin to overheat. It was time to put on a shirt and find some shade. Still, I lingered, wanting to remember the moment for future reference, for the times when I would be cooped up in my office during the ugly, cool, gray days of winter.

And I probably would have fallen to sleep except for the annoying noise of the speedboat's big engines grinding in the distance, reverberating across the water. The noise was loud. Sailboats make almost no noise. But these big, fuel-hogging behemoths are anything but inconspicuous. I never liked them.

Even though the boat appeared to be on a course to intercept our position at anchor, I wasn't concerned at the time. Our tall mast was clearly visible from a far distance. I was confident the speedboat would see us and veer away.

I found my tee shirt laying nearby on the deck, put it on, not wanting to be badly sunburned. Ilana was standing on the deck in her white bikini, looking towards the speedboat. I think Sandy was downstairs at the time in the galley getting something cool to drink. I'm not sure. All I remember is Ilana, her black hair blowing in the wind, looking at the boat.

'Hey, kid,' I called to her. 'What you doing?'

'I don't like these big boats, John. Bad people own these boats. Drug dealers and ...'

'Let's get the sails up.' It was time to go.

She nodded and turned to hit the switch for an electric winch, which raised the anchor. I attended to the self-reefing jib. Once the main sail was raised, it was only a matter of setting a course and allowing the wind to take us home.

'John, the anchor is up. Let's go,' Ilana said in a nervous voice, which seemed to express more concern than the situation dictated.

'Hey, what's the hurry?' I replied.

'I don't like that boat. I want to go.'

Ilana was a native of these waters. I always respected her opinion. I took another look at the speedboat and noticed it was not veering away, heading directly for us. I had heard stories about pirates. I guess everyone who sails in the Caribbean knows about them. Suddenly, Ilana's concern was mine. I started the engine to get the boat moving. Once the main sail was up, I cranked a winch to haul in the jib. A steady east wind off the ocean would make our journey home a good, fast one. It might take some tacking, but not much.

The bow immediately began to plow through the shallow waves inside the reef. We were underway. Sandy came up with a drink in hand, looking good in her yellow bikini. She sat down beside me as I set a course that would bring us closer to shore and hopefully out of danger. After adjusting the mainsail to the wind, our speed increased a couple of knots.

Sailboats are steady, efficient cruisers, but when it comes to speed, they are no match for high-powered boats. These lengthy, bullet-shaped boats are built for speed. Some have two or more huge engines churning out over five hundred horsepower each. The racing versions of these boats can travel over a hundred miles per hour. In contrast, I was more than happy to make speeds in the area of seven to eight knots per hour. It was no contest. My only advantage was I could travel for longer distances without stopping to refuel. I could outlast them, but I could not match them in speed.

Looking over my shoulder, it became obvious the powerboat was not veering away.

'Ilana, why don't you go below and get the gun out of the galley,' I said as calmly as I could. I didn't want to show too much alarm to Sandy in case my fears were unfounded.

Ilana was already concerned. I didn't need to ask her twice. She immediately went down to the galley.

Sandy looked at me, kind of funny.

'Nothing to be concerned about, just a precautionary measure,' I tried to reassure her.

'Are you worried about that speedboat?' she asked.

'A little,' I reiterated, raising my voice so I could be heard over the noise of the speedboat's obnoxiously loud engines.

Looking over my shoulder again, the big white hull raced towards us. I wondered if they wanted to have some fun. Do a fly bye. See if we had pretty girls onboard.

'Why don't you go down to the galley for a minute?' I said to Sandy.

'John?'

'Just do it, please. I don't want them to think we have valuable property on board. And tell Ilana to stay below.'

Sandy obediently went down the stairs to the galley as the big speedboat turned to run a course parallel to us. I was beginning to think I had overestimated the seriousness of the situation. In a minute, the boat would pass, and we would again be in paradise. No need for concern. But that was what happened. Instead it slowed to match our speed, running steady about fifty yards to port. Men onboard could be seen looking at me through binoculars. I waved in an effort to appear friendly, but it was hard to see their reaction. The sun was shining directly behind them.

All I could see was the silhouette of three men looking at me with binoculars while I was looking at them.

BANGKOK, THAILAND, 3:40 A.M. LUANG

Luang woke, his heart pounding, his mind working.

He would be unable to sleep any more that night.

A call had come in the morning.

Today was the day, the day he had anticipated for some time. Ever since his vision of Nue's death, this was the day he had desired more than any other day. But even though he had wished for this day, it was not a good day. It was not a day to be enjoyed. Revenge was never sweet. He knew this. But it was necessary, a means to set the world right again.

It had always been this way. The power his family held did not come easily. It had to be earned, and it took work plus constant vigilance to maintain. Never was power to be taken for granted. It was far more easily lost than gained. Hundreds of years of power were not a gift. It was the reward for years of hard work. Blood and sacrifice were continuously demanded.

So Luang was very aware. This day was necessary to fulfill destiny. If his family was to maintain their place in history, its position of power and wealth intact, then this day was required. And for this reason, plans were made, resources delivered, and money spent for outside help.

Now, it was only a matter of execution.

THE CARIBBEAN, 4:15 P.M. JOHN

It was simple, really.

It didn't take a great deal of effort for the thieves to catch us.

I tried to veer away, but it was a futile effort. Their powerboat was much faster than we were. It slowly eased towards us. They took their time. And why not? They could take as long as they liked. I was far from shore. I had no defenses.

'Put your sails down and turn off your engine.' A bullhorn demanded.

I tried to ignore them by steering away while increasing engine speed. But turning put my boat into the wind. Our speed slowed, not increased. That made no difference to them. Their engines were not affected by the wind. I could not escape.

'Stop, or we will shoot,' they demanded.

For the first time, I saw the outline of an automatic rifle in the hands of one of the men. It was an AK 47 or an M 16. Either way, their firepower was superior to ours. My options were few.

Ilana came on deck with the pistol. The gun helped, but not enough. We were no match for them. They sprayed a volley of bullets across our bow, tearing holes in the jib. Ilana reacted by aiming the pistol and firing a few shots in their direction. One of the men flinched when hit. Shots were immediately returned, ricocheting off the deck. Ilana and I dove for cover. She fired again wildly without looking. Bullets crashed against our bow just above the water line. Sandy screamed below.

I grabbed Ilana's gun and raised my hands in retreat. If they wanted our money, I reasoned, they could have it. It was not worth getting killed. I was more worried about the ladies. I didn't want them hurt. I told Ilana to take the gun and go below. Throw my wallet up first. Then stay below. Lock the door to the main cabin and don't come out until I tell you.

'I'll handle this,' I instructed.

'But...' Ilana started to say.

'Just do it, please.' I stared at her.

She went down the stairs and threw my wallet up on the deck after which I heard a door slammed in anger. After easing the throttle back and I turned the boat into the wind, her sails flapping uselessly in the breeze.

The powerboat coasted up alongside our boat. One of the men on board was kneeling over the man Ilana had shot. Blood drenched the injured man's white shirt just below his chest. He was not dead, still moving, but his wound looked bad, bleeding profusely. A towel covered his chest, and he was audibly groaning, his eyes closed tightly in pain. I could only watch helplessly, my hands in the air.

They threw gray rubber guards over the side of their boat to tie up to our boat. Very proficient in their work, as if they had done this more than once. I hoped that was a good sign. Hoped they were professional thieves, would take my money and leave. I could live with being robbed. My wallet held a couple of hundred dollars, some Belizean money and some American. And they could have my credit cards, whatever they wanted.

Then please go.

4:35 P.M. JOHN

They went about their work efficiently with no real need for conversation, almost as if they had done this many times before.

It didn't matter to me. I couldn't understand them. When they did speak, they spoke Spanish. I assumed they were from someplace in Central America. Dressed in clean, colorful new shirts and shorts, they looked prosperous. Perhaps pirating was a profitable business. It seemed a good sign. Hopefully they would conclude their nasty business quickly and be on their way.

After boarding our boat, they tied my hands behind my back with a coarse rope and shoved me onto an open cushion in the cockpit. I waited patiently, assuming they would eventually ask for money. They seemed to be in no hurry. One of the men went below. I heard him try to open a door. He rattled the handle several times before returning to the deck. After saying something to his companion, he jumped onto the speedboat. The other men remained on my boat, casually holding their automatic weapons pointed more or less in my direction.

I felt calm. I didn't know why. Given the potential for disaster, I kept wondering why I wasn't more worried, probably because there was nothing I could do. It did occur to me after the fact that I should have tried to call for help before being boarded and used the ship to shore radio. But it all happened so fast, no time to react.

And that's when he came on board. After a few minutes, a tall young man with dark black, closely cropped hair and a nice tan appeared. He looked familiar. He wasn't like the others, definitely not from Central America. More Oriental, although I didn't think he was Chinese. He smiled at me, and it was his eyes which betrayed him. I recognized his eyes. I had seen those eyes before. A burst of exaggerated energy exploded in my brain when I remembered where I had last seen those eyes. It was in a dark forest. The last time I saw those eyes, a smile had been on the lips of the man who possessed those eyes. The tall young man had his dead father's eyes, the eyes of the man I had killed.

It was then that I became very afraid.

Three additional men boarded with the tall young man. They were Thai or Chinese like him, dressed in neat white short-sleeved shirts and long pants. Their dress code looked out of place on a recreational boat. Too formal, not casual boat wear, more like clothes a businessman might wear. The men didn't smile, and they all had guns holstered in leather slings over their shirts.

The young man smiled at the two Spanish-speaking guys who were holding automatic rifles. He handed them a briefcase. They nodded and immediately returned to their speedboat. Lines attaching the speedboat to my sailboat were released, and the sleekly shaped craft drifted slowly away under power. Before it turned to leave, a body fell over the side, splashing into the sea. Something heavy had been tied around the waist of the body. It quickly slid into the deep blue-green water.

An involuntary shudder coursed through my shoulders as I watched the body disappear. I wondered if this was to be my fate. Closing my eyes to the horror, I leaned back on the cushions. It was uncomfortable sitting with my arms tied behind my back. My shoulders began to ache, and my wrists felt wet, bleeding from abrasions caused by the heavy, coarse ropes. A hot sun poured down as I contemplated my dire situation. Sweat beaded on my forehead. The salty perspiration dripped into the corners of my eyes and burned uncomfortably. I could do nothing to wipe it away.

The young man's crew of three restarted the engine and turned the wheel in the direction of shore, lowering the bullet-torn sails. We proceeded slowly under power. They seemed to know what they were doing.

As we headed towards the island in what promised to be a long journey at this speed, I wondered if I would still be alive when the boat was docked.

7:40 P.M. JOHN

It became apparent during our return journey to the island that our captors planned to wait until it was dark before docking.

Our beach house was visible when we got closer; a few lights were glowing through the windows, but the boat continued to slowly maneuver offshore in circles, waiting for the sun to set in the west behind the shadow of the island. From where I sat, the house looked good; it looked like a safe place, a place where I had been able to rest in the past. But not that night.

After the sky darkened, they headed for the dock to unload their human cargo, namely me, under the cover of night.

Before being dragged off the boat, the tall young man with black hair turned to me. 'I assume you know who I am,' were the first words I heard him speak.

By this time, my shoulders were sore, almost to the point of tying up in spasms of tight muscle agony, causing some pain in my back. I attempted to appear calm like nothing was bothering me, but that was becoming increasingly difficult under the circumstances. Two of the young man's accomplices were sitting next to him. The other one was down below in the galley. Fortunately, I didn't hear anything indicating a struggle coming from below. I assumed the ladies were still safe in their room. I was grateful for this, but nothing else.

'You are Nue's son,' I replied honestly, assuming I had no reason to lie. 'Your name is Sophon. Am I right?'

'Yes, you are well informed, Mr. Van Laan.' He replied in English with a slightly clipped oriental accent. It was easy to understand him.

'I have wanted to meet you for some time now. Ever since my father was killed while visiting you in America,' he added.

'You could have called and made an appointment,' I replied. 'This wasn't necessary.'

He looked at me for a long time before answering. 'Yes, I suppose I could have called, but I'm not sure you would have approved my agenda.'

'Why not?' I asked, thinking I probably didn't want to know the answer to my question.

'Perhaps we should talk about your lady friends first,' he ignored my question. 'We will be docking at your house in a few minutes. I'm sure they will be much more comfortable inside.'

'They are quite safe where they are. And you should know they have a gun. I advise you not to try to force them to come out.'

'They can stay down there as long as they like. But I assume they have no water or food. When they are ready to come out, I promise I will not harm them.'

'Why should I believe you?'

'You have no reason to trust me... Except, I give you my word. It's up to you to decide if you want to accept it.'

This seemed an unusual response. I expected him to be more forceful and angry. The power was on his side. I was helpless to defend myself or the ladies.

He could do with us what he wished.

11:20 PM. JOHN

I was getting tired.

Now, this may have seemed like the last thing I should have been feeling at the time. It would have been far more appropriate to be feeling scared, fearing I didn't have long to live. Sleep should have been the least of my worries. But I was bone-tired and fading fast. Probably because I was finally comfortable. The rough ropes holding my wrists had been removed, and I had been allowed to use the bathroom in the house to clean up. Not alone; one of Sophon's men accompanied me. He didn't carry a gun. But then he didn't need one. He was a big man with broad shoulders and hard muscles, probably trained in martial arts. I was no match for him. I could try, maybe run, but the bathroom had no windows, no way out. So nowhere to go. And two of his friends were waiting outside the bathroom door with guns. My chances were slim. I didn't try.

Handcuffs were placed on my wrists after exiting the bathroom. My ankles were shackled together with a rope, and I had no chance to run. Led away like a prisoner, I was directed to walk slowly back to the main living room, where I was instructed to sit down on a couch.

Sophon came in eventually and sat across from me in a chair. 'You are a very interesting man, John Van Laan. I have wanted to talk to you for a long time. But first I have something to tell you. And what I have to say to you may cause you to not want to talk to me. It is your choice, I suppose. And if you do choose to talk to me, you can lie... or you can tell me the truth. Again, your choice. But I am asking you to be honest with me.'

'Okay. Let's talk.'

'Before you answer my questions, you should know I intend to kill you. You are going to die. So, you have no reason to tell me lies because lying will do you no good.'

I said nothing. I had assumed he had come to kill me. I had killed his father, after all. My death sentence was not an unexpected announcement.

'You don't seem surprised.'

'Why should I be surprised?'

'I thought maybe you would try to tell me you did not kill my father, that he died in a helicopter crash.'

He paused, 'But you are not going to lie to me, are you?'

'No.'

'You killed him.'

I didn't answer.

'Do you want to know how I know you killed him?' he asked.

'Is that important?' I replied.

'Your friend Phillip told me,' he said, ignoring my question.

I sighed inwardly. 'He is not my friend.'

'Do you think I should kill you for killing my father?'

'That's your choice.'

'But do you think you should die? Do you think it would be just?'

I didn't respond.

'Okay, I didn't expect you to answer my question.'

I looked at him. Our conversation sounded almost like a business meeting. It seemed wrong, out of place. I didn't think that a conversation between a condemned man and his executioner was supposed to sound like this. But then, I didn't know what normal was in a situation like this.

'I will tell you anything you want to know,' I finally replied. 'But first, I would like to ask for something from you in return.'

'What can I give you? You already know I am going to kill you. You have only a short time to live. I can perhaps offer you more time. That is all. I am sorry, Mr. Van Laan, but you have brought this on yourself. Surely you know that.'

'I'm not asking for myself. I'm asking for the ladies in the boat. I want you to let them go.'

'What... let them go so they can run to the police?'

'Please do not harm them.'

'I have already given you my word.'

'If I know they are safe, I will tell you everything you want to know.'

'John, can I call you John?'

'Sure.'

'John, I cannot let them go. You do understand why.'

'Yes, I understand, but I am begging you. Please let them go. They have harmed no one.'

'John, you must know I can't let them go. They will bring the police, and I will have to run.'

'Then I will not talk to you.'

'Do you want to die now?'

'You are going to kill me anyway. What does it matter if it is now or later? Let them go. I will make them promise not to go to the police.' I stared at him. 'Please.'

He walked over to me, standing above me, staring down at me before speaking. 'You never gave my father time to prepare to die. Not like I'm giving you. You shot him without mercy. Why should I give you anything?'

I had no defense. His blow came fast, hitting me full force on the side of the head, causing a white-hot light to shoot through my brain, filled with shock and pain. I slumped over on the couch, barely conscious.

He walked away.

FRIDAY, NOVEMBER 13, 4:40 A.M. JOHN

Trying to sleep while tied to a bed is pure misery.

My arms lay stretched on both sides, bound to the bed frame with ropes. I simply could not move. Every time I fell asleep and unconsciously tried to turn over, pain shot through my arms, and I was instantly awake. Finally, I gave up trying to sleep and lay on my back, waiting for the dawn.

After a few hours of not being able to move, to adjust my position on the bed, forced to lie flat on my back in one position, my back muscles began to ach in agonizing knots. And my head hurt. When Sophon hit me, my head felt raw and tender. A headache, a bad headache, took control of my painful existence; the result of having my hands tied behind my back for hours, shoulders sore or head hurting, or both. What did it matter? A terrible black throbbing pulsed through my brain from the back of my eye sockets to the muscles in my neck. I couldn't open my eyes. It hurt so bad. My stomach became nauseous. I thought I was going to throw up. My shoulders quivered in a mass of tense, taut muscles. More than anything, I needed a couple of aspirin and a glass of water.

Relief was only a few short steps away. Aspirin and water were in the bathroom, but no way I could go to the bathroom. And I needed to pee. I badly needed to pee.

A windless night became still and torturously hot. Perspiration rolled down the sides of my salty, greasy face. I wanted to be somewhere else, anywhere else. I wanted this to be over. The hours hung on a dark night like a heavy lead weight dropped on my queasy gut. I considered yelling for Sophon to do me a favor, come and kill me now.

Then I tried thinking about something else, anything besides the throb in my temples, the weight in my gut. I wondered about the ladies and how they were doing. They couldn't last forever in the stateroom of the boat. They needed water more than anything.

I wondered why I was still alive.

And, of course, I wondered when I would die.

I couldn't help it. I couldn't stop thinking about the night, the horrible night which was the reason I was tied to this bed. The night I had killed his father in a fit of rage. Something had snapped deep inside me. Images from that night, like bad dreams, returned to my tortured brain over and over again as I lay in bed. The gun was in my hand. Pent-up anger had raced through my body until it ignited in my fingers like a high-voltage surge of energy. My arm had tensed. My fingers pulled the trigger. It wasn't a conscious action to pull the trigger. It was more of a reflex action that I could not control. It was not something I intended, not something justified, just something that happened.

The night I killed his father was a moonlit night. Tall pines, live oaks, and palm trees cast long gray shadows over a damp forest floor. I could not see his father clearly, but I could hear him. I clearly heard him order the death of Ilana's brother. In my mind, it was as if I was hearing him order my death sentence.

He had tried to have me killed on several occasions. I had been lucky. Death had not taken me. I could have been dead. I knew I could have died. The trauma from all those near-death experiences covered me with a blanket of pain. I could not stop; I did not stop. I pulled the trigger in wanton anger and killed him.

Despite all my endless excuses for killing him, I knew who was responsible. I was. I had broken. Something deep inside me broke. All the discipline, all the self-control, all the logic, all my religious upbringing, my faith did not save me that night. I broke.

In a moment of lost time, my mind rebelled in anguished fury, in a cataclysm of violence. Like an uncontrolled mass of hot flashing lava rushing bright red through my over stressed nervous system, anger and fear had burned too hot. A penetrating, propelling ship of fools overpowering my conscious mind. It was as if the bullet released by my curling fingers carried with it all the screaming frustration that had holed up deep inside me for too long.

Nue, the young man's father, had died, and I walked away a free man, my crime covered up by the CIA. But the fact that I got away with murder did not make me an innocent man. I knew what happened. I knew who killed another man. I knew it was me. I was guilty. And yet, I didn't feel guilty when it happened. It was more like I had been an observer, looking at the killing scene from the outside, watching someone else pull a trigger.

Someone else had done the guilty deed.

But in reality, this was not true. I knew it was me, whether I admitted it or not. I couldn't change that any more than I could change where I now lay with my hands tied to a bed. I was a man who had killed, who had pulled the trigger of a gun. I was the man Sophon wanted dead.

And in my torment, I wished more than anything else, I wished I had not killed his father. I wished I could do it differently, turn back time. But time is a ruthless master, never ever allowing one single act to be corrected. Once done, time never allows an act to be retracted. I could change nothing. I could deny nothing. I could only relive the murderous night over and over again as I sweated in agony.

Finally, I said a prayer to my God.

I had not prayed for a long time, but that night, I prayed, prayed like I had never prayed before. I didn't ask for myself, didn't ask to be forgiven. I was guilty, and I had nothing to forgive. I asked simply for them. I asked for Ilana and Sandy. I didn't want to see them get hurt. More than anything else, I didn't want them to die. Not because of me, not because of what I had done. Please, Lord, not because of me. I was guilty, not them. Do to me as you wish, but please save them.

Then I waited for the dawn. I waited, keeping watch for the dawn through the window in my bedroom. A dawn that seemed like it would never come. I lived in a world of perpetual agony for minutes, which became hours, hours, which became days. Time was stretched, ripped apart. Time is the great measurement of our lives; time, which, in science, is a constant measurement. Time spread its torturous wings over me and smeared me with agony that arched across the vast canyons of my mind.

My eyes closed to the dark night as I lay in painful anticipation of dawn, a dawn which no doubt would be the beginning of my last day on this earth, and yet, a dawn I dearly yearned for.

Yearning for a death that would finally release me from this hellish night of anguish.

5:55 A.M.

With a loud crash, the door broke open, waking Ilana and Sandy and separating them from their tortured dreams to a hellishly real nightmare.

Beams of light split the dark room, illuminating small useless images in the interior of the boat's main cabin, a book shelf, shoes on the floor, and Ilana's startled big brown eyes. She immediately reached for the gun on the floor next to the couch where she had been sleeping, but he was too fast. He kicked the gun, sliding across the floor out of her reach.

It hurt when he grabbed her arm. She swung her small, hard fist against his chest. His blow came out of the dark. She never saw his hand, only felt the dull, hard blow against her face.

Falling on the floor, she released an audible cry into the night air.

Across the room, Sandy screamed as she was dragged out of bed and across the floor, banging her leg on the door frame. The man took her forcefully out of the boat's bedroom, pulling her up the stairs by her arms and throwing her against the cushions in the boat's cockpit, where she sat whimpering uncontrollably, unable and unwilling to cry even though she badly wanted to yell. A man stood over her, perhaps begging her to fight. She did not move, fearfully listening to a commotion below.

Ilana was fighting, but it was no use. She soon emerged from below, was dragged up the stairs by two men, pushed across the deck, falling next to Sandy while holding the side of her bruised face.

BANGKOK, THAILAND, 5:40 P.M. LUANG

A folded white sheet of paper was placed on his desk without comment.

His assistant simply put the sheet where the old man would see it and walked out of his office.

It was late in the afternoon. Luang was still at his desk. Not because he had work to do but because he had been waiting. He had no desire to work. A report about Sophon's activities was due and he was in his office waiting for it because he was sure it would tell him his ordeal was over.

His garden was his place to rest.

Going to his garden was the only activity he had scheduled for his evening. He planned to enjoy a cup of tea while sitting quietly and thinking about Sophon. He would remember the days when his nephew's son had roamed this great house as a young boy. The boy loved to run through the many rooms playing imagined dramas in his head; dreams of glory and honor which would be his when he was older, when he was a man; battles he would win, enemies he would conquer, maidens he would subdue; all the great imaginary stories which occupy the minds of young boys as they play.

Tonight, while sitting in his garden, Luang planned to pay homage to the boy who was his nephew's son and who was also, in so many ways, his son.

Luang never had children. His wife had died at an early age. The pain of losing her had been too immense. It seemed easier and simpler to invite his brother's family to live with him instead. Luang had taken great pleasure in watching the boy grow bright and strong. He had taken time to teach the young boy like he was his son. He had tried to prepare the boy for the work which would eventually come to him. His family required a successor, a man who would run their many businesses, a man of great wisdom. Luang had taught Sophon many lessons and taken great pleasure in telling him the history and honor of the family.

Luang had been very successful in his time. He had seen the power and glory of his family grow under his direction. It had all been good. All good until it was not good until it began to fail. His nephew had been in charge during those dark days. Luang did not want to think about those bad times now. Failure was in the past. Luang had no plans to consider past failures. Instead, he planned to dwell tonight on what was good, thinking about the days when his life had been good, the days when the boy sat on his lap and smiled at his uncle.

Luang was confident everything would return to as it was after tonight. Everything would be good again. When the murderer was finally dead, it would be as it should be.

Luang slowly unfolded the paper on his desk and began to read the report. A dark frown crossed his face. The murderer was still alive.

He placed the paper on his desk and leaned back into his chair, deciding he would not go to his garden this evening as he had planned.

8:55 A.M. JOHN

Ilana was sitting on a couch in the main room of the house when I entered the room.

They dragged me downstairs in the morning, and I saw her before I saw anything or anyone else. Holding one side of a torn bikini top with her hand so it covered her breast; her face and arm were badly bruised, red and blue. Curled up on the couch like a hurt animal, yet the look on her face was still defiant. I knew when she was angry. I had seen this look before. Sandy sat next to Ilana, sitting upright. Also, dressed only in her bikini, she didn't appear to be hurt; she was more stoic, accepting, and not afraid. On the opposite side of the room was Sophon. I wondered what he was thinking when he looked at the women. They were beautiful, desirable women.

'You forced me to do this,' Sophon finally said to no one in particular, although it was obvious his words were directed at me. 'You were concerned about them. You wanted to know they were alright. I had them taken from the boat so you could see for yourself.'

He looked at me. 'They are fine as I promised... Now, can we talk?'

Ilana was clearly hurt. Her arm had dried blood from a cut near her shoulder, which had not been treated.

'You have injured one of them,' I replied.

'She would not come when she was asked. My men were as gentle as possible. She fought them. They had no choice but to take her by force.'

I believed him. I knew Ilana would fight. 'Let them go, and I will do what you ask.'

'Mr. Van Laan. We have been over this before. I cannot let them go.'

I stared at him.

'What do you expect from me, Mr. Van Laan? You are in no position to demand anything.'

He stood quickly as if he had suddenly made a decision.

Grabbing Ilana by the arm, which was already bleeding and bruised, he pulled her off the couch. She screamed, but he was too strong for her.

'Hold her,' he demanded.

Two of his men took her arms. Sophon ripped off her dangling bra. She stood half-naked in front of him. He hit her hard across the mouth with his open hand. She cried out weakly.

'Okay. Okay, I get it,' I shouted at him.

He turned and looked at me. I wasn't sure what he would do next. He looked back at Ilana as she squirmed, trying to get loose from the grip of his men.

'Do you want me to give her to my men? Is that what you want? Do I need to resort to violence to get your attention?' he asked. 'Is this what it will take for you to talk to me, Mr. Van Laan? Are we men of reason, or do we need to speak like savages who only communicate through violence?'

His question caught me off guard. I had no answer for him.

He raised his hand to hit her again across the side of the head. She turned away, crying a low, defiant moan.

'Stop, stop,' I yelled. 'I'll do whatever you say. Please leave her alone.'

He turned back towards me.

'So, it seems you understand the language of violence. But then, why would I expect anything different from you? You are a killer, after all.'

His words made me angry. I wanted to shout at him. I wanted to argue with him, but I was afraid for Ilana.

'Don't hurt her,' I begged.

He turned to her. She was naked and beautiful and defenseless. I looked away. I was ashamed. I had caused her agony.

'I will not hurt her,' he said defiantly.

'Thank you.'

'Do you believe me?' he shouted.

'I believe you.'

'Take him away,' Sophon ordered his men. 'I do not wish to speak to him now.'

He was angry, and even though he was young, it was obvious he was not a man who liked losing control of his emotions. He looked down in disgust.

A guard yanked on the chain connected to my handcuffs. My wrists were already sore from the tight cuffs. Pain shot up my arm as the man dragged me upstairs, tripping over a step when I turned to look at Ilana and Sandy. Ilana was still struggling, trying to get free, but Sophon's men held her tightly.

I was afraid for her.

BANGKOK, THAILAND, TUESDAY, NOVEMBER 17, 8:20 A.M. LUANG

His daily routine seldom changed.

A folded white sheet of paper was delivered to him same time, late in the afternoon. His assistant would enter his office, quietly place the paper on the old man's desk without saying a word, turn, and walk out, closing the door behind him.

Luang did not immediately read the report. He finished his work first. He had come to dread these reports. This had not been his response the first few days of Sophon's travels. He had eagerly unfolded the papers and read the reports as soon as they were delivered. But after days of disappointment, reading the information on the folded papers had become an arduous task he wished to avoid.

Eventually, he picked up the paper. After unfolding it carefully, he read every word, hoping, wishing for some sign that would give even the slightest indication that Sophon's work was finally coming to the desired conclusion. But to date, nothing in the reports stated it would be over soon. His nephew's killer was still alive.

Luang's work had become difficult in the last few days. He had trouble concentrating. His meetings often ended with quick, ill-considered conclusions... or with no conclusion, postponed for another day. Conversations with the old man were terse and abrasive. Petitions, which normally would have been granted, were denied without cause. Nothing of importance was accomplished. It was as if the world was waiting, waiting for a single event. Then, life could resume its journey. Pain and suffering would not be a priority.

But for now, time was wound up tight, straining, and agonizing.

BELIZE, MONDAY, NOVEMBER 16, 9:36 P.M.
JOHN

Every minute I was awake, I listened intently, afraid of hearing sounds of torture or rape coming from somewhere in the house.

But all I heard was the sounds of waves tiptoeing across the sandy beach, creeping in through my bedroom windows. That and the whisper of the wind rustling through palm leaves filled my painful, arduous nights and days. The sun would wander in through a window on the east side of the bedroom in the morning and lamely leave in the evening as if it was embarrassed for having accomplished nothing to relieve my pain.

Rain fell one night.

Usually, I love to hear rain in the night; especially when it is warm and windows are open, but not this night. Tortured, anxious dreams filled that night with slithering snakes and steep cliffs falling to foggy oblivion. Exhausted, I woke in a sweat, fear filling my mind.

My arms were still tied to the bed. They would twist and turn in unnatural ways whenever I involuntarily tried to turn over while sleeping. My body ached to be in a different position after hours of lying flat on my back. Spasms of agony ran through the muscles of my back, causing me to cry out in frustration.

Blood seeped into the sheets from cuts on my wrists where handcuffs had ripped the skin. A rough rope tied my ankles to the bottom of the bed and stretched my body full length, making it difficult to move. It was better to be awake. Nothing but nightmares occupied my sleep. Eventually, I would drift off to sleep before waking again after only a short time in pain, more afraid to be asleep than awake.

When I was awake, I would listen to the restless noises of the night. Days were better, filled with more activity, a boat out on the water, and laughter coming from the beach walkers. Unfortunately, I was unable to cry out to them or scream for help. Tape covered my mouth.

I heard no evidence of struggle in the house, no laughter or screams, nothing that could tell me what was going on. Even though I strained to listen to what was happening downstairs, I heard almost nothing other than an occasional conversation spoken in a language I could not understand: brief, stilted words spoken quickly in hushed tones that told me nothing. Then it would be quiet again, and in the still quiet, I was afraid, always afraid because quiet can be more fearful than screams. Quiet can be filled with invented fears. In my imagination, I feared Ilana and Sandy were already dead, beaten and raped, dropped off a boat like the wounded man Ilana had shot. A weight tied to their waists. Maybe still alive when they drifted down into the deep water, holding their breath until darkness closed around them, sinking slowly. Pressure increased in their ears as a searing pain exploded inside their skulls until their lungs cried out for oxygen, gasping for air, inhaling salty cold seawater from the ocean which would be their grave, choking until mercifully they became unconscious with only the memory of their brutal beatings still stinging the nerve ends of their minds.

I have a vivid imagination.

I have always had a vivid imagination. It serves me well on occasions when I need to be creative. But most of the time, my imagination is a burden filled with fear and longing. I am prone to imagine worst-case scenarios. I often wake in the night filled with fear, afraid, always afraid. I do okay during the day. And I am far better on sunny days than cloudy days. Reality, for the most part, gives me comfort. But not these days of pain, and surely not the nights I was tied to a bed. I was constantly afraid. No way could I lie on the bed without pain. Every muscle in my back ached. I longed to be allowed to stand and walk. Instead, I was trapped on the bed, completely unable to move more than a few inches. I pissed on the bed more than a few times when I could not hold it.

I feared my final eulogy would be nothing more than silence. No glory, no accolades, just a bed defiled by the dregs of my body, the smell and the agony overwhelming every other sensation. I waited to die. I longed to die.

My only reprieve was the few times the guards allowed me to use the bathroom and relieve myself. They would rip the tape off my mouth and shove a water bottle down my throat, water squirting everywhere. I tried vainly to drink in every precious drop rushing down my throat as I gagged, water choking my windpipe, coughing up more water than I drank. The guards laughed as the spilled water splashed over my face. I coughed and gagged, but I drank enough water to stay alive.

Why, I did not know.

TUESDAY, NOVEMBER 17, 1:10 A.M. SANDY

Sandy nudged Ilana on the shoulder.

'Something is happening,' she said.

Ilana was half asleep, half awake at the time.

The ladies had been deposited by their captors in the master bedroom in the back of the house, Ilana's room. It had a bathroom attached for their convenience. The only window in the room had been secured, nailed shut, covered with wood and a lock was put on the door. They were comfortable. They were fed. They were given water bottles, but they could not leave.

Ilana lay next to Sandy in bed and rubbed her eyes. 'What?'

'I hear something, noises.'

They were both silent for a minute, listening, wondering, worrying in the dark night. The house was quiet; no commotion, no noises, nothing to indicate a change.

They had talked over the last few days, expressing their fears. They thought, perhaps hoped, John was still alive because they had heard nothing, no yelling. No scuffle, no sounds of men dragging a body. A man fighting for his life would make some noise. But they had heard nothing which would lead them to believe he was dead. Yet the eerie quiet was almost as disconcerting as the noise of a violent, life-ending struggle.

They had been summoned several times, Ilana to answer the telephone and talk to her brother, who called. Sandy was asked to send an email to John's office explaining he would be gone sailing for a few days, don't worry, he would return shortly. The ladies had been warned to say one wrong word or ask for help in any way; if that happened, they would be killed instantly.

They had no choice.

They had cooperated.

When they had timidly asked their captures about their friend John; only silence returned their questions. So, they knew nothing.

And knowing nothing was almost as bad as knowing the worst possible outcome.

1:15 A.M. JOHN

He came in the middle of the night.

I was awake at the time.

But then I had been awake most of the time during those days and nights of suffering, unconscious for only short spans of occasional sleep. I never knew how long I slept. I assumed it wasn't very long.

Sophon came into my room and turned on an overhead light, half blinding me. When I could finally look at him through the blazing light on the ceiling, he looked bad like he had not slept any more than I had. His clothes were wrinkled and unkempt, as if he had been dozing in a chair. His white linen shirt was half tucked in and half out of his black trousers, not neat as I had always seen him in the past. He wore no shoes, and his black hair looked matted.

When he saw me, he turned away.

The smell must have been bad, sour piss and sweat-dampened sheets. He yelled at his men and told them to clean me up and get me into the shower immediately. Throw away my bed sheets. Clean the wounds on my ankles and wrists.

'Take him downstairs when you are done,' Sophon demanded. 'This is disgusting. How could you let this happen?'

His men looked at him wide-eyed. I guessed they thought it was okay to let me suffer. I had killed his father, after all. They must have thought I deserved nothing more. I was going to die anyway. What difference did it make?

I understood. I did not blame them. By this time, I had reconciled myself to the fact I was a dead man. I only feared for the ladies. I did not want them to suffer. They were not to blame. This was my fault. The guilt was mine alone.

Sophon left the room.

A man I had not seen before entered my bedroom. He loosened the ropes on my ankles and tied me to the handcuffs. He pulled me up out of the bed. It was difficult to stand. My muscles were tight and sore from lying in one position for long hours. Blood dripped where the metal handcuffs had cut my wrists. I tried to move and keep up with the man who was pulling on my handcuffs, but I stumbled. He held me and kept me from falling to the floor.

He was a large man, looked more Chinese than the other guards; thin eyes, big shoulders, very muscular, large round head, and long black hair to his shoulders. I will never forget him. He didn't talk. He did not need to talk to communicate.

It was dark outside my bedroom window; nothing to see. One light lit my room. He led me into the bathroom and turned the lights. I watched in fascination as he turned the shower faucet. The shower was like a dream. Soft, warm water fell over my body. I drank in as much as I could. Then I washed my body, feeling the stubble of new growth on my chin. My face itched. I wanted to shave, but it was enough to be clean. When I was done with my shower, the man handed me a towel. He removed my handcuffs and gave me cream for my cuts. I thanked him. He looked at me as I stood dripping wet, holding a towel.

'I will not try to escape,' I said quietly.

The large Chinese man nodded his head. He knew I was speaking the truth. I was too weak to run.

I dried my body and rubbed the cream on my wrists and ankles. Clean clothes were laid out on a chair when I walked into the bedroom. The mattress from my bed was gone and with it, the lurid smell. The room was clean.

A fresh breeze wandered in through the window, making it seem as if I was somewhere else as if my recent painful ordeal was only a bad dream.

2:35 A.M. JOHN

Food was placed on the dining room table.

The Chinaman, I did not know his name. I called him the Chinaman to give him a name. He walked behind me to the table, never more than a few feet from me. I assumed he would be with me for the rest of my short, painful life. The Chinaman was to be my constant companion, always at my side. Sophon must have brought him to the island for the express purpose of guarding me, and I assumed the Chinaman had the skills required to do the job, restrain me in case I tried to run. I didn't mind him. He was never mean or pushy. As I said before, the Chinaman never opened his mouth to speak, but I always knew what he wanted.

I could not eat most of the food on the table. My body was too weak to digest anything more than a small amount. I ate what I could and then simply looked at the rest of the food; bread and jam, cheese slices, cut fruit and some boiled eggs, very simple food. It all looked good. I wanted to continue eating, but I managed only to digest a piece of bread with jam and a banana. And a cold glass of milk which was very good.

After watching me stare at the food for a few minutes, the Chinaman stood and motioned for me to follow. I thought I was returning to a bed to sleep. It was the middle of the night. A clock on the wall told me it was nearly three in the morning.

The Chinaman walked behind me, directing me down the hall towards the stairs to the master bedroom on the main floor. He opened the door. The room was dark. He turned on the overhead light. They were sleeping together in a king sized bed, Ilana and Sandy. Both women looked instantly startled and afraid. I started to say something to them, but the Chinaman put his hand over my mouth and took hold of my injured wrist, pulling me quickly out of the bedroom into the hall. Shutting the door behind me, he locked it. Apparently, he wanted me to see the ladies, not talk to them. I guessed he wanted me to know they were alive, not dead. Then he shoved me in my back and pushed me down the hall towards the living room.

Sophon was waiting for me, sitting in a chair as if nothing had happened. He looked better than the last time I saw him. A clean, white, ironed shirt replaced the wrinkled one he had on before. His hair was combed and neat again. He seemed more at ease.

'Sit down,' Sophon said. 'It is time we talked.'

I did as Sophon requested. The Chinaman sat beside me on a couch.

'Would you like something more to drink?' Sophon asked.

'No.'

The room was lit by one light; a small table lamp with a shade sat in the far corner of the room, shedding dim light in shadows across the floor. Sophon sat between me and the light. The silhouette of his head was visible, but the details of his face were difficult to see in the shadows. His words sounded as if they were coming from a speaker across a room. I could not see his lips move. He sat very still like a statue. I longed to see his face, to understand the small movements of his eyelids, how he held his mouth, simple expressions which can often speak more than words. But I was unable to see his face.

'Can we turn on more lights?' I asked.

'That will not be necessary,' he replied.

I didn't argue. It didn't matter, really. I assumed this meeting was about my death, and it wouldn't take long.

'It is a mistake to underestimate your enemy,' Sophon began. 'Underestimating your enemy can often lead to assuming he is evil when in truth he is not. Do you know who wrote those words?'

'No.'

'They were written in the Tao. Do you know what the Tao is?'

His question seemed irrelevant, given it was coming from the man who intended to kill me.

'I have heard of the book, but I have never read it,' I answered truthfully.

'It is a book written by a Chinese Zen Master long ago. I have studied this book. It helps me understand how to live.'

I said nothing. Even though I couldn't see Sophon's face, I could feel his stare.

'Do you know why this book is important to you?' he asked.

'No, but I suppose you are going to tell me,' I was feeling weak and irritable. The small amount of food I had eaten had given me a limited amount of strength, not much, not enough to want to argue with him, only enough to answer his questions in simple terms. My wrists were hurting, and I had to constantly adjust my sitting position to avoid spasms of pain from shooting through my back. Every muscle in my body felt sore. I simply couldn't get comfortable. Plus, the prospect of my imminent death was far from relaxing. I was in no mood to have a casual conversation about philosophy with my executioner.

'It leads me to want to understand who you are before you die,' Sophon inexplicably continued on his intended mission. 'I want to know what made you shoot my father. I want to know who you are and what made you do this thing which has brought me so much sorrow.'

He paused.

'Why talk?' I asked. 'You are going to kill me. Isn't that enough?'

'No, it is not enough.'

'I don't really want to talk to you,' I replied weakly. 'Why don't you just kill me and get it over with?'

'No, first we talk,' Sophon said forcefully. 'And you will talk to me because if you do not, I will kill the women who are asleep in the bedroom.'

'If I talk to you, will you let them go?'

'Yes,' he said from behind the shadow of his face. 'But only after you have answered all my questions truthfully.'

'Why should I believe you?'

'Mr. Van Laan. You continue to exhaust my patience. You have seen your girlfriends. My friend took you to them. You know they are both alive and unharmed as I have promised. Is that not true?'

I didn't answer.

'Do you need more incentive to loosen your tongue? Because I can give you an incentive if that is what you require. I can choose one of the girls and kill her here while you watch her die. Then, if you are still unwilling to talk to me, I will kill the other girl. Then I will kill you.'

He waited.

He knew I could not refuse. Still, I did not want to do what he asked. I was becoming angry and irritated with this strange conversation. And I did not want to die. Even though I knew it was my fate, I still... I didn't want to die.

He continued. 'I do not want to kill them, but I will if that is what you choose. It's your choice. You can refuse to answer my questions. But if you refuse, they will die. So, decide now. Will you talk to me?'

I could not answer.

'Please understand I have gone to a lot of trouble to arrange this meeting,' he continued. 'I could have killed you and walked away many times. Like the time when you took a walk alone in the forest behind your office building. Do you remember?'

I looked at him, astonished he had seen me that evening.

'I didn't kill you then because I wanted to understand you first,' he answered my silent question.

His face was a shadow behind the light. I felt him staring at me, waiting for me to speak. Still, I could not open my mouth to talk. Maybe it was the lack of food and sleep for days. Cognitive thoughts seemed to wander in and out of my brain like strands of stardust in the sky. I stared back at him, trying very hard to concentrate. Perhaps it was something about not seeing his face. Or it could have been his voice; the tone and the inflection were similar to his father's but calmer, more caring. Something was different. Something I badly wanted to understand.

He was like his father in one respect: he was very unpredictable. I remembered the time Monica and I first sat across a table from his father. It was the night Monica died. His father had forced his way into our New York hotel room and demanded I sell him my stock. With ownership of my stock, he would gain control of my company. He demanded it like it was his birthright and belonged to him and his people.

And then there was a second meeting with his father, this time in Hong Kong, Ilana was with me then. Both times, his father had surprised me. He had offered me deals I did not want. Deals which were interesting but unacceptable. The deal he offered me that day turned out to be good only until my company was healthy. Then he planned to kill me. Seemed he had made up his mind I had to go. He just never enlightened me to this important aspect of the deal. Instead, he suggested we come to an agreement to work together. But it was a lie. A lie I didn't understand at the time. His father was a hard man to read.

His son appeared to be no different. They both offered me deals I could not refuse but didn't like. As I thought about his father now, I wished I had accepted his father's first offer. Monica would be alive now if I had taken his offer. And I wouldn't be sitting across from his son, my executioner ...

'I am waiting for your answer,' Sophon spoke very deliberately.

'I was thinking I wished I had taken your father's first offer,' I replied honestly.

'That would have been wise. But you did not, did you?'

'No.'

'And you still have my father's money, don't you? The money he offered you for stock in your company.'

'Yes, and my girlfriend is dead. Don't forget that. Your father took much more from me than he gave.'

'Do you blame my father for her death?' Sophon asked.

'He forced his way into my room. She would not have died if he had not come,' I argued. 'So yes, I blame him for her death.'

'Did my father pull the trigger of the gun which shot your girlfriend?' Sophon countered.

I stared at him. I didn't want to answer his dumb question. And I didn't want to be on trial for his father's death.

'Are you going to answer my questions,' Sophon demanded. 'Or do I need to kill one of your girlfriends to convince you to do what I ask?'

I looked at his face in the shadows. The Chinaman sat next to me. I had no choice.

I could not escape his demands.

4:05 A.M. ILANA AND SANDY

'Do you think they will kill John tonight?' Ilana asked.

They could hear men talking in the other room. The women's bedroom was on the main floor, the same floor in the house where Sophon and John were sitting. The rooms were not far apart. Their conversation could be heard but not completely understood. Only when someone shouted, only then did they understand the words. Although they could not understand everything the men were saying, they knew from the tone of the conversation that it was not a pleasant conversation. And they knew it was not going well for John.

Sophon was becoming frustrated. His voice was getting louder. John's words were softer, more subdued. They heard him get angry only a few times.

'I don't know,' Sandy replied honestly to Ilana's question.

They were sitting up in bed. The light in their room was on. It was obvious to them that this night was different. They were afraid, afraid it was going to happen tonight. John was going to die tonight.

'Do you think they will kill us too?' Ilana asked the question which had been plaguing their minds since their ordeal began.

Sandy did not reply immediately. Finally, she answered simply, 'I suppose they will.' This was the only conclusion she could imagine. Why would they leave evidence behind? She and Ilana had seen their faces. They could identify the men. They needed to die.

Ilana did not speak. She simply took Sandy's hand and gripped it tightly while listening to voices coming through the wall into their room.

4:50 A.M. JOHN

'Why won't you admit you are responsible for my father's death?' Sophon demanded. 'You pulled the trigger. You alone bear the responsibility.'

I stared at him with all the resolve I had. Our conversation had been long and tedious. Sophon was determined to go over the complete history of my relationship with his father, including all the failed attempts on my life which Sophon claimed were never meant to kill me, just intimidate me. He had an answer for everything.

Everything it seemed could be viewed in two ways, his way or mine.

We even discussed the death of my business partner, Arthur. He had been killed by assassins on the streets of New York, gunned down after his limo was forced off the road in broad daylight. I blamed Sophon's father for Arthur's death. But Sophon claimed Arthur's death was his own fault. Didn't Arthur betray me? Didn't he do it for money? And Arthur probably would have betrayed his father, given time, Sophon concluded. So why was I asking about Arthur? Arthur's death was Arthur's fault. Arthur was greedy.

'What about my friend Vidu,' I asked.

Vidu was a gem dealer from Sri Lanka who had been murdered on the streets of Chicago. A needle filled with poison was shoved into his back. He died in agony, lying on a cold sidewalk while people walked past.

'Vidu died because he broke a contract Thailand had with Sri Lanka. The contract stated that all mined Sri Lankan sapphire was to be sold exclusively to Thailand,' Sophon explained. 'Vidu knew what he was doing when he ignored the contract by cutting and selling gemstones mined in Sri Lanka. He knew the risk he was taking, and he paid the price.'

I remembered Vidu expressing something about this ancient contract to me. I knew there was some truth to it. Still, it was not right. Vidu did not need to die.

'The contract, if it existed, was an old contract,' I replied to Sophon. 'It did not justify murdering him.'

Sophon disagreed. He looked at me like I was a moron. He asked why the terms of a contract could be negated by time. This contract was well-known to every gem dealer in Sri Lanka. Vidu knew, and he chose to break the contract. He chose to take the risk. Contracts are contracts. Time does not make them invalid. Vidu paid with his life.

'How about my friend Arny?' I asked, becoming exasperated. Arny had died in my apartment from a bullet, which was probably meant for me. 'What about him? Did a century-old contract justify his murder?'

'I heard about your friend Arny. It was a tragic accident,' Sophon replied. 'Your friend was simply in the wrong place at the wrong time. Accidents happen every day. Life is a risk. We die from disease, from natural catastrophes, from accidents. Death is part of life.'

'Your father paid a man to shoot up my apartment. Doesn't this make your father responsible for Arny's death?' I asked.

'It was an accident.'

'It was no accident. It was the result of a deliberate attempt to kill or intimidate me. Either way, your father was responsible.'

'Collateral damage is, I believe, the term you Westerners use when someone dies as an unintended consequence of war.'

'We are not at war,' I replied.

'Oh, but we are,' Sophon answered.

I was getting nowhere.

I changed the subject. Once more, I brought up my girlfriend's death in New York. Monica's death had caused me the most pain. More than everything else, I blamed Sophon's father for her death. She was killed during an attempt to rescue us from his father. A gun battle had ensued. She died from a stray bullet.

'I loved her,' I said to Sophon. 'I wanted to marry her. She died because your father came into my hotel room to force me to do something I did not want to do. Your father told me he would kill me if I did not do what he asked. Kill me and my girlfriend. I believed him.'

'It was your right to believe him or not. Truthfully, I do not believe my father ever thought he would have to kill you,' Sophon said. 'He paid you money for your stock, a lot of money. Is this something someone would do if they intended to kill you?'

He paused before continuing, 'He threatened to kill you only if you did not sell him your stock. What were you going to do, Mr. Van Laan? Were you going to sell him the stock? Or were you going to refuse because you thought he was bluffing?'

Truth was I had been ready to sign the papers. I could have risked my own life, but I could not take a chance with Monica's life. I had to sign the papers. Sophon was right, but I said nothing, didn't want to admit that to him.

'It was the CIA who were responsible for your girlfriend's death,' Sophon continued when I did not answer his question. 'They forced the door to your hotel room and started shooting. Why do you think my father should be blamed for their stupidity? When your friends from the CIA stormed into the room, my father's life was at risk, as well as your girlfriend's. My father could have been killed. He was spared, and your girlfriend was killed. That was simply a matter of fate. Would you feel differently today if my father had been killed instead of your girlfriend?' he asked.

I had no answer for him. No answer that would serve any purpose.

No answer that would justify killing his father.

5:25 A.M. JOHN

The time shortly before the time when the sun rises in the morning can be the darkest, loneliest time of night.

Some nights are long, too long, as if night will never end.

We begin to worry the golden sun will never again spread its light and warmth over the vast reaches of the horizon while stars fade into a blue canopy, relinquishing their distant wonder to a brighter, clearer reality. We fear being enclosed forever in shadows, never again to see the gray light of dawn across the horizon and, with it, the promise of a new day. Imprisoned forever in a time of suffering under a cold, dark sky... night covering our minds with never-ending, restless remorse.

I was bone tired. I wanted this night to be done. The little strength I had gathered earlier from eating some bread and a banana had been exhausted hours ago. The relief I had felt after being finally freed from my dirty, stinky, piss-wet bed had long ago drained away. I was working on fumes. Still, I tried to hold up my end of the conversation. I was afraid once we stopped talking, it would be time to die.

I guess I still held some hope I could connect with Sophon, still believed he would let me live. Isn't it true that we spend very little time thinking about our death? We never really think this is the day we will die. Instead, we live every day as though death is not a reality. It is not until we have no hope. Only then are we forced to accept death.

Or... perhaps we never do; we are never able to completely wrap our minds around the fact our days are limited, even when the day of our death is inevitable.

I knew my desire to live was illogically founded, nothing more than a senseless drivel. Even so, I was trying, but it was becoming painfully obvious Sophon had one goal in mind, and that was to make me admit I was responsible for his father's death. I was guilty of murder. Then he planned to execute me for the crime I had confessed. Justice would be served.

I had been defending myself by trying to convince him his father's death was not completely my fault. But I was not winning. I began to wonder if I was unconvincing because I didn't really believe it myself. Because deep down, I knew he was right. I did feel responsible for his father's death. Or maybe it would be more correct to say I felt a heavy burden. Not that I was guilty of murder. More like I had a deep sense of regret. Regret for what happened. Regret it was my hand that had pulled the trigger. Regret I had been the agent of his father's death. Even though I thought his father deserved to die because he had been responsible for the death of so many innocent people, I wished it was not me who had been the instrument of his death. I should not have killed him.

During my long ordeal, I kept glancing out a window, hoping to see some sign of the sun rising in the east over the water. Hoping the light of a new day might give me strength. But every time I looked outside, it was dark, and I was wearing down. My eyelids were becoming heavy. Fear was the only emotion still motivating me. Every time I began to fade, a shot of adrenaline-induced fear would wake me. Stark adrenaline-dripping fear revived my lagging spirit. I feared if I went to sleep even for one moment, it would be over, our conversation done, and it would be time for me to die.

I had to stay awake.

'More than the watchman waits for the morning. More than the watchman waits for the morning.' The words of David's psalm keep running over and over in my head. I said a silent prayer to God for strength. I prayed for a way out of this mess. But I also prayed for my soul because I saw no way out.

'Are you willing to admit that you murdered my father?' Sophon asked again.

I do not know how many times he asked this question during that night. Over and over, he never seemed to tire of asking. In fact, he appeared to be gaining strength as I became more exhausted. Perhaps he sensed he would finally get the answer he desired if he asked his question enough times, and this prospect gave him energy.

'No, I am not willing to admit I am responsible for your father's death,' I argued. 'I am willing to say I regret it happened. I will tell you the memory of his death gives me nothing but sadness. I am even willing to admit I am very sorry it happened. But I will never be willing to agree I'm solely responsible for his death.'

'How can you say that?' Sophon asked in exasperation. 'You pointed the gun at my father. You alone pulled the trigger. By your own admission, you watched him die... Weren't you happy to see him die? Didn't you laugh inside when you realized that you had killed him? Didn't that make you happy?'

'No, I felt only sadness.'

'That is a lie.'

'No, it's not a lie,' I said as calmly as I could.

'You are a liar and a murderer. You just won't admit it?'

From somewhere deep inside my body, I gathered what strength I had left to make one last desperate argument. 'Sophon,' I began. 'We have been talking for hours. Your father's relationship with me was complex. From his perspective, my company created problems for him and your country. It took business from your country and gave it to people in other countries. It was not good for him, for you, for your family's business, for your country... But from my perspective, these things happen. Time changes things. Some businesses are successful, and some are not. Most eventually fail. It happens,'

'It didn't have to happen, Mr. Van Laan. You made it happen. It was your fault. You should have understood the consequences of your actions before you started your company. You should have considered what would happen before you destroyed so many lives.'

I took a moment before answering. 'Maybe that's true. Maybe I was naïve. But I had the right to start a business just as you do.'

'Do you have a right to throw people out of work? Do you have a right to take their food from them and cast them out of their homes? This is what you did, Mr. Van Laan. Your company made beggars out of many people in Thailand.'

'Yes, but I helped many other people. There are workers in many parts of the world who have a better life today because of my company.'

'People in my country are starving because of your company,' Sophon countered from behind his dimly lit shadow.

I looked out the window again, vainly attempting to see some strain of gray light near the horizon over the sea. Nothing but darkness hung over the restless waters. My eyelids dropped. I looked down, almost unable to hold up my head.

'I did what I thought I had a right to do,' I said wearily.

'So did my father. He did what he needed to do to bring work back to his country. He did it because he loved his country.'

'No, he did it because he loved money and power,' I said in a whisper.

'What did you say?'

'Nothing.'

'Do not say such a thing. I will kill you now if you say this one more time. My family has always treated our people with great respect,' Sophon exclaimed. 'It is you who did this for money. Not my father.'

My eyes wanted to close. I was losing the argument. It was useless.

'Are you finally ready to answer my question truthfully?' he asked.

'You want me to admit to murdering your father.'

'Yes.'

'I cannot.'

'Why?'

'Because you are wrong.'

I suddenly became angry, and anger gave me one last semblance of strength. 'Because if you look at the events we have been discussing individually; sure, you can rationalize excuses for what your father did. But if you step back for a moment and put all the events together, if you take the time to consider everything that happened between your father and me, then you must come to a different conclusion, the same conclusion I came to the night I killed your father.'

I paused.

Sophon did not interrupt me as I expected, so I continued. 'Think about all the times your father hired assassins to kill me. Think about all the times I thought I was a dead man. Like when I almost died when men hired by your father rammed my car, and it almost fell off a cliff in the mountains. Or when men shot at my car, causing me to lose control and hit a truck. Or when they shot into my apartment. Think about how you would feel if you found your best friend dead in a pool of blood in your apartment... Do you know how that feels?'

I stared at him, strength coming from somewhere deep inside me.

'You don't know, do you, Sophon?' I pushed ahead. 'And you don't know how it feels to have your girlfriend die in your arms...'

He said nothing.

'Another friend died from a poisoned needle in his back.' My voice began to rise. 'Think about all these times, Sophon. Put them all together. Then force yourself to think about the time your father's men dynamited a dam, which should have killed me. How many people in your country died when that dam broke, hundreds? Think about those people.'

'That was an accident,' he responded.

'I don't think so, and I don't believe you do either. He was trying to kill me. Those people, those villagers who drowned in the river, they meant nothing to him.' I said, remembering the day a dam broke, causing a high wave of water to rush down a valley in Thailand, killing hundreds of villagers and almost killing me and my friend. In my mind's eye, I could still see the dead faces of the villagers floating in the river.

'That is a lie. It was an accident,' Sophon said emphatically.

'Really, are you telling me it was just a coincidence I happened to be in the river valley the day the dam collapsed? And it is also a coincidence your father just happened to be somewhere else at the time?'

'Don't say things you cannot prove,' Sophon replied angrily.

'How many innocent people died in that disaster?' I pressed my case, thinking this was the one incident Sophon could not justify. 'I almost drowned. And even if you don't believe he did it, I do. Think about how that made me feel.'

'I cannot pretend to know how you feel. You are a murderer.'

'Well, try. Think about all the terrible things that have happened to me, all of them caused by your father.'

I pressed on. 'One of the women in the bedroom across the hall was beaten in front of my eyes the night I killed your father. Get her in here if you don't believe me. Ask her about that night. Ask her if your father ordered the death of her brother.' I shouted at him.

Sophon was silent.

'You say he was just trying to influence me all the times I almost died. Well, maybe you are right. Maybe he never intended to kill me. Maybe they were all an effort to get me to give in to his demand to take control of my company. Maybe this was his intention, and maybe not. But either way, everything he did had an effect and its effect grew in my mind every day, grew until it exploded. All the pain, all the fear, all the sorrow erupted inside my brain the night I pulled the trigger... Am I sorry for what I did? Yes... But do I feel totally responsible? No... Except I wish I had been stronger... I wish I had been able to resist the insane urge to kill him. I wish I had walked away. But I did not... I was weak. I regret killing your father in a moment of weakness, and I am sorry for that... But I am not totally responsible... No, your father bears most of the responsibility. He created the circumstances which led to his death. He is the man you should blame, not me.'

I stopped.

I had stepped over the line, and I knew it. Sophon could never blame his father... I waited. Sophon would retaliate now. I expected to die.

Up until this time, he had been acting calm. Now Sophon appeared to be agitated, apparently frustrated he had not achieved what he came for. I sensed he would want to end it now. I feared it would happen before the sun rose. I had hoped to see the light of one more day. Now, I feared I would die in the night. I almost didn't care. I felt so bad, so weak, so tired I thought I might die even if he didn't kill me. Every sinew attached to my bones wanted to collapse. It felt like my organs were producing a poison and were shutting down one after another until finally, my heart would stop, and it would be over. The only thought which seemed to keep me going was a strange desire to see one more sunrise. I did not want to die at night. I do not like the night. I wanted to die during the day.

'My father was not responsible,' Sophon said slowly as if he had given up trying to convince me. He said the words as if he were a judge issuing a prepared statement before passing a sentence. 'My father did what he did to convince you to sell your company. He did it for his country.'

I was exhausted, but something in me wouldn't give in.

'Sophon, your father marched into my life followed by a path flowing in blood: the blood of my girlfriend, the blood of my friend from Sri Lanka, the blood of my best friend, and my business partner. Blood on a hotel room floor in New York, blood on the streets of New York and Chicago, bodies strewn along a river valley in the mountains of your country. No matter what his intentions are, the trail of blood he created is his legacy. Blood follows blood; blood flows, no turning back, no peace, no good could come from what your father did, only death and sorrow.'

'No, my father was a peaceful man. He did what he did because he cared for his people.'

'Doesn't matter, don't you understand? Because I saw only pain and death. I thought he was going to kill again. I had to stop him.'

'He was not going to kill your girlfriend's brother. It was just a threat.'

'I didn't believe that.' I said, my voice rising even though I was trying to stay calm.

'You killed my father.' Sophon delivered his verdict. 'You alone are responsible.'

'No, he killed himself,' I argued. 'Violence and death walked with him in everything he did. You speak of your country. You speak of a peaceful man. But I saw another man, a man consumed by blood and pain. The violence he created was like a friend who walked at his side. And in the end, it was his friend who killed him, not me.'

'How can you say that?' Sophon stood up and shouted at me.

'Because it is the truth!' I screamed back at him with every ounce of energy I had left in my body.

Sophon's face was a shadow standing in front of a lamp, the only light in the room. Turning slowly, he whispered something quietly to the man guarding me, the man I called the Chinaman. I didn't know the Chinaman had a gun. I hadn't seen the gun before, but I was not surprised to see it. The gun had been carefully disguised behind folds of cloth in his shirt. He gave the gun to Sophon without looking at me.

Sophon took the gun from him while facing the front windows filled with a black night sky over the sea.

I wanted to run, to hide, but I could not move.

Sophon turned and looked at me as if he had finally made up his mind. The gun in his hand rose, the barrel pointed directly at my chest. I waited, too tired to react, simply waited for a flash of light at the end of the barrel, a flash which would end my life; I waited and watched.

The gun wavered imperceptibly. Sophon's body trembled. His arm fell to his side as if the gun was too heavy. It was a burden he could not hold. Each time he attempted to raise the gun, his arm again fell limp against his side.

I focused on the gun, watching it fall several times. I could not see his eyes. His eyes were in the shadows. I desperately wanted to see his eyes, see something in his eyes that would warn me.

Sophon raised the gun one final time, holding it steady without wavering.

5: 45 P.M. ILANA AND SANDY

The ladies were listening, trying to understand the words coming through the walls of their bedroom, the shouting, the arguments John could not win.

They could not comprehend every word, but they knew John was losing. They heard it in his voice. He was wearing down, becoming harder to understand.

The discussion had been long and exhausting, but they had nowhere to go. They had remained in bed, awake in the night, riveted by a conversation coming from another room. Holding hands under the sheets, gripping their new friend's hand, they listened and waited.

Ilana's eyes were closed, hoping, holding Sandy's hand tightly.

Sandy didn't complain, even when her hand hurt. She said nothing, lying beside Ilana, wanting to comfort her. Because what could she say? What could either of them do to give comfort? Nothing... nothing except wait.

They had heard John's last words. He shouted something about the truth, about it being the truth. They sensed the end was near. He was out of words. Nothing more to hear, nothing but a deathly silence; no more words, no more arguments... nothing.

Sandy gripped Ilana's hand, tears forming in her eyes.

5:50 A.M. CHARLIE

Charlie woke early, too early to get out of bed.

He had been dreaming.

He couldn't remember his dream, but he knew it woke him out of a deep sleep. Something about it was troubling. And then it came to him. It wasn't his dream that was bothering him, which woke him in the middle of the night. It was something he had learned late the previous afternoon. An agent friend in Thailand had called and told him Sophon Nue had left the country, the young man was traveling. His fellow agent in Thailand had apologized for not calling Charlie sooner and said he had been busy, some big deal at the embassy, lots of VIPs in town, senators and congressmen on a junket. All bullshit, of course, but it took his time and concentration.

Charlie said he understood and thanked the agent for calling and giving him a heads-up. Then Charlie called Buddy, the head of John's security staff at his office in Charlottesville. Charlie asked Buddy if everything was alright, any signs of trouble. This was when Charlie discovered John was in Belize with two girlfriends. Charlie had chuckled when he learned that John was with his two girlfriends in Belize. Charlie wished he could witness this debacle. Then Charlie asked Buddy if John had taken bodyguards with him to the island.

Buddy said he did, one bodyguard, but the man had returned. His name was Todd, and Todd's father had a heart attack. His father had almost died and needed open heart surgery. It was touch and go for several days. Fortunately, Todd had returned to the States in time for the surgery. His father survived, but post-surgery had been difficult. Several times, his father's heart had stopped, and he needed to be resuscitated. So, Todd was not with John. He knew he should be, but his father was his main concern.

Anyway, Todd's father was doing fine now. Crisis was over. Todd had called Buddy and apologized for not calling sooner. He told Buddy everything was fine in Belize, with no signs of trouble. John had ordered him to go home to his family. John said not to worry. Todd had flown home to be with his family. He was happy he did. He almost lost his father. He was glad he had been able to be at his mother's side to help her through the crisis.

'So, John and his two lovely girlfriends are down in Belize alone and unprotected?' Charlie asked Buddy.

'Yes, but Todd said he had seen no signs of trouble,' Buddy responded.

'That is your assessment.'

'I'm not in Belize. I don't have an assessment,' Buddy answered coldly. 'John told Todd to go home without waiting for backup, not me.'

'I see,' Charlie replied. Without further editorial comment, he thanked Buddy and hung up the phone.

The conversation replayed again in his mind now as Charlie lay in bed. He knew it was all wrong. John had made a mistake, an inexperienced rookie mistake. But then, Charlie could not protect John from every mistake.

He hoped John was okay.

BANGKOK THAILAND, 6:35 P.M. LUANG

The dreaded report came in late.

Luang had waited. Something in the previous day's report indicated Sophon was ready. His men had communicated and said it would happen soon, maybe even today. Luang had been eagerly anticipating the report.

When his assistant arrived with the report, nothing in the man's demeanor was different from the past, no smile, no emotion. The assistant simply placed the folded paper on Luang's desk without saying a word; turned and walked out of the room as was his custom, closing the door behind him.

Luang could have assumed from his assistant's actions, his lack of joy; he could have feared the report was not good, but he did not. He wanted to be positive, think good thoughts, hope it was finally over.

He didn't wait. He took the paper immediately and unfolded it, reading every word. Then he slumped into his chair.

The murderer was still alive.

Not possible.

The man should be dead.

Luang crumbled the paper tightly in his hands, throwing it on his desk in disgust.

He would not visit his garden tonight. He would not sip tea and think about better days ahead.

His personal nightmare was not over.

BELIZE, 5:00 P.M. JOHN

Ilana and Sandy lay curled around me in bed, holding me, sleeping and not sleeping.

When I finally opened my eyes, they stared at me in wonder, happy I was awake. But not as surprised as I was to see them. They told me I had been dragged into their room and thrown on their bed. I didn't remember any of it. All I remembered was fearing I was going to die. A fear so strong, it alone had kept me awake during the night talking to Sophon. When the crisis was finally over, I must have succumbed to my weakened physical condition and completely collapsed. They were afraid I was dying because they could not wake me. All they could do was hold me, talk to me softly, and wait, hoping I would eventually open my eyes.

I tried to move. That was a mistake. Every bone, every muscle in my body hurt. I was thirsty. I asked for water, although I was too weak to drink. Water fell like drool in streams from my chin. They wiped the water and washed my face with a cool, wet cloth, which felt good. I thanked them. Just their sweet act of washing my face was an incredible kindness. After days of torturous neglect, this simple gesture was like being in heaven. I smiled at them; then I closed my eyes and slept.

Eventually I had to wake up, couldn't sleep any longer. Their eyes were closed when I opened mine to look at them. They were resting beside me. I touched their faces to be sure they were real. They opened their eyes and smiled at me.

'Are you alright?' I whispered.

'We are fine,' Ilana replied.

'Can you help me sit up?' I asked, feeling too weak to move.

They propped me up with pillows.

'How long did I sleep?' I asked.

'It's past four in the afternoon,' Sandy replied. 'We were afraid you were dying.'

'I feel like I have died and gone to heaven, and you are two angels... except... I don't feel very good.'

'You don't look very good either,' Sandy, the realist, replied.

'Thanks.'

'My pleasure.'

I smiled.

'We have a problem,' Ilana interrupted. 'We have heard nothing outside our room since morning. They have not come to check on us. And we have had nothing to eat since yesterday.'

I looked at them. They looked better than I felt. 'Have you been getting regular meals?' I asked, wondering if they had been treated badly.

'Yes, twice a day,' Sandy said. 'They brought us food.'

'Was the food good?' I asked, even though the thought of food made me nauseous.

'Good enough,' Sandy replied.

I remembered Sophon's promise. He said he would not harm them. I wasn't sure he was telling the truth, but apparently, he had been true to his word. I guess I underestimated him and missed something in his character.

'And you, Ilana, did you like the food,' I smiled, knowing her finicky tastes.

'It was not good food,' she said. 'I ate it because I was hungry, but I did not like the food.'

Sounded like Ilana. She liked her food, her way, the food she made, food native to her Belize. It didn't matter if she was kidnapped or in a hurricane. She wanted her food. Nothing else was good.

'Could I have some more water?' I asked.

Ilana went into the bathroom to get a glass of water. I drank it slowly, this time allowing the cool water to run down my throat. It helped. I felt better.

The house was quiet. A bedroom window drew my interest. As I looked out of the window, the memory of the previous night's ordeal came back to me, every horrifying detail, especially the dark window to a lifeless black night sky. More than anything, I wanted to see the light of a new day through that window. I remembered praying, asking God for nothing more than the ability to see the dawn of one more day before I died.

Bright sunshine shone through the bedroom window as I stared in disbelief. I had lived to see another day against all odds. I never thought I would see the sun again.

I thanked God.

It was afternoon. The sun had traveled to the west side of the house, reflecting off the pool outside Ilana's bedroom window. Being able to see the light was a blessing beyond imagination. An almost iridescent glow rose from the pool. I was drawn to the water and to the flowers that surrounded Ilana's pool, to her garden, to her lush green garden so full of life and vibrant colors under an afternoon sun. I got out of bed slowly and walked over to a sliding glass door to the outside. My ladies helped me, wondering what I was doing. A lock had been placed on the door by Sophon's men, locking the ladies inside the bedroom during their captivity.

Ilana tried the door, and to her amazement, it opened.

My legs felt like lead. Every joint ached, but I pushed my body to move. The colorful flowers drew me outside the door to a small deck off the bedroom. I walked slowly like an old man on shaky legs. I wanted to feel the breeze. I wanted to feel everything alive around me. I felt like I had returned from being dead. I couldn't describe it to the women. It was as if everything outside was a living, breathing organism. The water in the pool appeared to be a shimmering life-form, shining at me. For a brief time on the deck, I simply immersed my senses in all the life-giving forces surrounding me, letting them wrap their loving arms around me, welcoming me back to life.

Ilana and Sandy held me, one under each arm, held me so I wouldn't fall, held me so I could feel the wind in my face. I eventually asked them to take me to a chair on the deck. As I rested there, they waited patiently, saying nothing, watching and waiting.

Finally, Sandy asked me what we were going to do.

'Do about what?' I replied. 'Isn't it enough to be alive.'

THE END

For excerpts from book 6, see below.

GRAND HAVEN, MICHIGAN, FRIDAY, NOVEMBER 20, 11:35 A.M.

The phone rang just as Phillip was getting ready to leave his office for lunch.

His intuition told him Sophon was on the line. He had tried all week to call Sophon. He knew where Sophon had gone and he knew why the young man went there. Sophon had informed Phillip he would be traveling to Belize to locate John and it didn't take a genius to understand that the visit would not be good for John. Phillip assumed Sophon intended to kill John.

Nothing like that had been suggested by Phillip. That was not his MO. Instead, he made the case for John's execution. Like a lawyer to the jury, Phillip had primed Sophon to the point that Phillip had no doubt about what the young man would do when he confronted John.

Phillip was the one person who was fully capable of making his case. He had been at the scene the night Sophon's father was shot dead by John. Phillip was a first-hand witness. He told Sophon that John had come out of the darkness and killed Sophon's father at close range. Point blank, pulled the trigger. Phillip saw it all. John had killed Sophon's father in cold blood. John was a murderer. It was only because the CIA had decided to cover up the murder; that was the only reason John was not on death row. That is what Phillip told Sophon.

It was easy to make the CIA the bad guys. The agency had a bad reputation in Thailand. So that part was easy. In fact, it was all easy.

The only unanswered question, the question that was important to Phillip, the one question that mattered most, was who was going to take control of John's company after he was gone. And even though Phillip was not absolutely assured of getting the job, he had no doubt about that either. Again, he had laid the foundation carefully, regaled Sophon with story after story, illustrating his experience in the gem business while patiently demonstrating his technical knowledge of gemology. Sophon was told stories from the history of gems in Thailand, stories that even Sophon didn't know. For a few weeks, Phillip had become Sophon's mentor, his instructor, and his friend. Like an actor on a stage, Phillip had played his part until he was confident that Sophon would naturally turn to him to run the company as soon as John was gone.

Now, it was only a matter of time until it all happened, as Phillip anticipated it would. He had only to wait.

But Phillip hated waiting. Not that he couldn't wait; Phillip had taught himself to be a patient man. Patience was just a matter of discipline. And Phillip had learned discipline.

Phillip had waited patiently all week for the phone call he knew would come from Sophon. But when it seemed to be taking longer than it should, Phillip got curious and his curiosity took control of his patient brooding. His patient patience broke down, and although he knew this was a bad idea, he called Sophon's cell phone. And when that failed, he tried calling Sophon's uncle in Thailand. The old man refused to take his calls, so he called John's office in Charlottesville, thinking someone there might tell him what he wanted to know.

He was told that John Van Laan was not returning his calls. And he assumed that meant John was dead.

After that he called anyone and everyone he could think of calling to learn the details of John death. For a whole week he learned nothing more. Every call was unproductive. When the phone rang just before lunch on Friday, Phillip naturally assumed it was Sophon.

And Phillip was confident that Sophon would tell him what he wished to know.

BANGKOK, THAILAND, SUNDAY, NOVEMBER 22, 5:30 P.M.

Sophon's great-uncle never got a call.

Luang didn't need one. He had received word of what happened in a daily report. One of his men assigned to be with Sophon had called it in.

The report was then written on a folded white sheet of paper which was delivered daily by a young assistant to Luang, simply placed on his desk. The assistant never spoke to the old man. That was not his place. He retreated from of his office quietly, closing the door behind him.

Luang was frustrated but not completely surprised by what he read in the report. However, after days of disappointment, he had come to assume this might happen. His nephew's son was unpredictable.

The boy's father on the other hand was never hard to read. Luang always knew what his nephew would do. The challenge in dealing with his nephew was different. Luang had tried to council him, to moderate his rash behavior, tried to calm him down from time to time. His nephew was always rushing off on some sort of mission, never content, always looking to make things right, never afraid or aware of the consequences, just intent on achieving his goals no matter what the cost.

His nephew's son, Sophon, had his father's impulsive character. But also predominant in his character were some of his mother's qualities. She was more introspective, more aware of her world and all that existed in it. She saw the complexity of life. She was content to enjoy its beauty, less ready to want to change it. Luang had liked Sophon's mother. He was sad when she died at a young age. Sophon had never known his mother. Never had a chance to be educated by her, taught to see the world in a different way, through her eyes instead of his father's. Luang was sure the boy would have loved his mother. They were very much alike. And now that Sophon was growing up, the qualities that had shone in his mother were beginning to be seen in her son.

But it was hard for the boy. Hard because what his heart told him to do was often polar opposite of what he had been taught by his father. So his behavior was erratic. Kind of like a bouncing ball, bouncing this way and that. The old patriarch could never really predict what Sophon would do.

When Luang heard about what happened on an island far away, he was not surprised, but he was very frustrated.

11:50 P.M. JOHN

Alone again in my self-imposed domicile of exile, my upstairs bedroom.

It was late in the night. I should have been sleeping, content with the events of the day. All things good; more than good, nothing like I feared. In fact, better than I could have ever imagined. But something bred by the guilt-plagued society of my youth would allow me no rest.

It had been fun; sex had been great. They were wonderful, more than any man deserved. But then, isn't it true that a woman is never deserved? They are always a gift. Love is, by its nature, undeserving. And was the love of these women diminished by the fact they freely gave me their gift? Did this make it impure, tainted, sinful?

I didn't know. But I did know that it came with some guilt. It was not what I had been taught from youth to expect. The church, the institution that dominates our thoughts and our culture, the church had bestowed on me a different standard, one not quite so understanding as my two lady friends. But I wondered if that was right. If love is the standard by which we are to be judged by God, then is it better to be loved by only one woman, or should we accept love whenever or wherever it is responsibly offered?

I rested in the dark unable to sleep, discontent.

I thought about the ladies and how different they were. They came from completely different backgrounds and educations. One was a product of my culture: the church, schools, and college, which gave me an interpretation of life. The other was a product of nature, a beach girl, a woman self-taught by the school of nature. One had blue eyes and curly blond hair. The other had big brown eyes and long straight black hair. They were so different and yet they were so very similar. I thought it must be their intelligence that made them similar, their strong will, and their intelligent ability to see life for what it was. This was what unified them and gave them a common bond, something intrinsically understood from the moment they met. It was what made them friends. It was what they shared.

I loved them both. I had held them both in my arms for moments of exquisite pleasure, but I knew I could never possess either of them. That much I understood. They were independent souls. They were not mine to have. To share, perhaps, to spend a few brief moments of time together with me because they chose to give me their love as a gift. They had come to me and loved me in times of great stress. Ilana and Sandy had come to me when I wasn't sure I could have made it without them.

Being with them, being in love with them became for me the only place on this earth where I did not see death.

THURSDAY, NOVEMBER 12, 3:25 P.M. JOHN

Ilana was the first to see the powerboat speed towards us.

It was one of those long, sleek offshore racing boats with a big white hull riding high in the water, sea spray rising off its bow. These expensive boats are not a common sight in the waters off the coast of Belize. I had seen a few, but not many. They are gas-guzzling hogs. They consume fuel in gallons per mile, not miles per gallon. It was rumored some of these boats were owned by drug runners.

The boat was a long distance away. I ignored it at first, quite content to enjoy the sun and the sea. It had been a glorious day. We decided to go for a long sail and do some free diving. My stay in Belize was drawing to a close. I couldn't remain on the island forever. I had to return to my office soon, but no definite plans had been made.

When I first arrived, I was determined to see how the ladies would act. Maybe, I thought, maybe they would hate each other, and I would be forced to return immediately. Obviously that had not happened; quite the opposite. In fact I was beginning to think I never wanted to leave. Life in Belize was good, too good in fact: warm weather, beautiful place to live, and best of all... two wonderful lovers.

I began to wonder why I would ever want to return to Charlottesville.

But business was calling. Meetings had been postponed, and business trips rescheduled. I had to wrap my mind around the concept of returning. Before heading to the States, we unanimously decided one more day trip on the boat was required. Only one of our group would have disagreed with this decision if he had a vote, which he didn't, and this would have been Todd. It was discovered after a few rather unpleasant, gut-wrenching throw-up experiences that our fearless bodyguard was quite prone to becoming seasick. Trips on the sailboat were his least favorite duty. However, he wasn't a problem that day because he wasn't with us. His sister had called. His father was deathly sick and had only days to live. Todd was needed in the States in a hurry.

Everything had gone well during our stay. No signs of trouble. It was decided he should return; his family was important. I drove Todd to the airport in Ilana's jeep. And since we were not planning to stay much longer, I decided not to bother finding a replacement for him.

We sailed along the coast in the morning. A good diving spot over a reef, farther south than usual, was our destination. Ilana and I had been here before. We wanted to show it to Sandy.

That afternoon, we spent time diving, eating, and relaxing on the boat with three friends, good friends. Or it would be more accurate to say that Sandy and Ilana had become almost inseparable friends. My role was far less significant. I was more like an accessory after the fact. Or at least this was how I felt most of the time. It was difficult to determine if they were here for me or if I was here to serve them. Either way, I wasn't complaining. I had time to work. And I had two great ladies to keep me company. And they had me.

Or, again, it might be more accurate to say they had me when they were so inclined to spend time with me. And this was not often because most of the time, they were off on some adventure, and I was alone in the house working. Ilana was busy immersing Sandy in Belizean culture. I heard all about it at the end of the day when we had cocktails and dinner. They were having a great time.

It was late in the afternoon when we spotted the speedboat. Almost time to raise the sails. Free diving had been great, the reef beautiful, and schools of fish awesome in number and color.

I closed my eyes for a moment and rested, allowing my head to lean on a cushion. I think at the time, I was trying to imagine returning to work in Charlottesville. It was the middle of November. The weather would be cool in Virginia. Helen had been warning me work was piling up. I had talked to her on the phone the day before. The anxious tone in her voice was impossible to ignore. It was obvious she wanted me back. But I wasn't ready. In fact, I was spending more time daydreaming about the possibility of moving the office south to Belize than I was thinking about traveling north, even though I knew that was more or less impossible. Still, it was fun to dream.

The sun beat down, warming my body more than was prudent. I could feel my skin begin to overheat. It was time to put on a shirt and find some shade. Still, I lingered, wanting to remember the moment for future reference, for the times when I would be cooped up in my office on ugly, cool, gray days.

And I probably would have fallen to sleep except for the annoying noise of the speedboat's big engines grinding in the distance, reverberating across the water. The noise was loud. Sailboats make almost no noise. But these big, fuel-hogging behemoths are anything but inconspicuous. I never liked them.

Even though the boat appeared to be on a course to intercept our position at anchor, I wasn't concerned at the time. Our tall mast was clearly visible from a far distance. I was confident the speedboat would see us and veer away.

My tee shirt lay nearby on the deck. I put it on, not wanting to be badly sunburned. Ilana was standing on the deck in her white bikini, looking towards the speedboat. I think Sandy was downstairs at the time in the galley getting something cool to drink. I'm not sure. All I remember is Ilana, her black hair blowing in the wind, looking at the boat.

'Hey, kid,' I called to her. 'What you doing?'

'I don't like these big boats, John. Bad people own these boats. Drug dealers and ...'

'Let's get the sails up.' I decided it was time to go.

She nodded and turned to hit the switch for an electric winch, which raised the anchor. I attended to the self-reefing jib. Once the main sail was raised, it was only a matter of setting a course and allowing the wind to take us home.

'John, the anchor is up. Let's go,' Ilana said in a nervous voice, which seemed to express more concern than the situation dictated.

'Hey, what's the hurry?' I replied.

'I don't like that boat. I want to go.'

Ilana was a native of these waters. I always respected her opinion. I took another look at the speedboat and noticed it was not veering away, heading directly for us. I had heard stories about pirates. I guess everyone who sails in the Caribbean knows about them. Suddenly, Ilana's concern was mine. I started the engine to get the boat moving. Once the main sail was up, I cranked a winch to haul in the jib. A steady east wind off the ocean would make our journey home a good, fast one. It might take some tacking, but not much.

The bow immediately began to plow through the shallow waves inside the reef. We were underway. Sandy came up with a drink in hand, looking good in her yellow bikini. She sat down beside me. I set a course that would bring us closer to shore and hopefully out of danger. After adjusting the mainsail to the wind, our speed increased a couple of knots.

Sailboats are steady, efficient cruisers, but when it comes to speed, they are no match for high-powered boats. These lengthy, bullet-shaped boats are built for speed. Often, they have two or more huge engines churning out over five hundred horsepower each. The racing versions of these boats can travel over a hundred miles per hour. In contrast, I was more than happy to make speeds in the area of seven to eight knots per hour. It was no contest. My only advantage was I could travel for longer distances without stopping to refuel. I could outlast them, but I could not match them in speed.

Looking over my shoulder, it became obvious the powerboat was not going away.

'Ilana, why don't you go below and get the gun out of the galley,' I said as calmly as I could. I didn't want to show too much alarm to Sandy in case my fears were unfounded.

Ilana was already concerned. I didn't need to ask her twice. She immediately went down to the galley.

Sandy looked at me, kind of funny.

'Nothing to be concerned about, just a precautionary measure,' I tried to reassure her.

'Are you worried about that speedboat?' she asked.

'A little,' I reiterated, raising my voice so I could be heard over the noise of the speedboat's obnoxiously loud engines.

Looking over my shoulder again, the big white hull raced towards us. I wondered if they wanted to have some fun. Do a fly bye. See if we had pretty girls onboard.

'Why don't you go down to the galley for a minute?' I said to Sandy.

'John?'

'Just do it, please. I don't want them to think we have valuable property on board. And tell Ilana to stay below.'

Sandy obediently went down the stairs to the galley as the big speedboat turned to run a course parallel to us. I was beginning to think I had overestimated the seriousness of the situation. In a minute, the boat would pass, and we would again be in paradise. No need for concern. But that was when the boat did something unexpected. It slowed, slowed to match our speed, running steady about fifty yards to port. I could see some men onboard looking at me through binoculars. I waved, trying to act friendly. It was hard to see them. The sun was shining directly behind them.

All I could see was the silhouette of three men looking at me with binoculars while I was looking at them.

BANGKOK, THAILAND, 3:40 A.M. LUANG

Luang woke, his heart pounding, his mind working.

He knew he would be unable to sleep any more that night.

A call had come in the morning.

Today was the day, the day he had anticipated for some time. Ever since his vision of Nue's death, this was the day he had desired more than any other day. But even though he wished for this day, it was not a good day. It was not a day to be enjoyed. Revenge was never sweet. He knew this. But it was necessary, a means to set the world right again and put affairs back in balance.

It had always been this way. The power his family held did not come easily. It had been earned, and it took work plus constant vigilance to maintain. Never was power to be taken for granted. It was far more easily lost than gained. Hundreds of years of power were not a gift. It was the reward for years of hard work. Blood and sacrifice were continuously demanded.

So Luang was very aware. This day was necessary to fulfill destiny. If his family was to maintain their place in history, its position of power and wealth intact, then this day was required. For this reason, plans were made, resources delivered, and money spent for outside help.

Now, it was only a matter of execution.

THE CARIBBEAN, 4:15 P.M. JOHN

It was simple, really.

It didn't take a great deal of effort for the thieves to catch us.

I tried to veer away, but it was a futile effort. Their powerboat was much faster than we were. It slowly eased towards us. They took their time. And why not? They could take as long as they liked. I was far from shore. I had no defenses.

'Put your sails down and turn off your engine.' A bullhorn demanded.

I ignored them and steered away while increasing engine speed. But turning put my boat into the wind. Our speed slowed, not increased. That made no difference to them. Their engines were not affected by the wind. I could not escape.

'Stop, or we will shoot,' they demanded.

For the first time, I saw the outline of an automatic rifle in the hands of one of the men. It was an AK 47 or an M 16. Either way, their firepower was superior to ours. My options were few.

Ilana came on deck with the pistol. The gun would help, but we were no match for them. They sprayed a volley of bullets across our bow, tearing holes in the jib. Ilana reacted by aiming the pistol and firing a few shots in their direction. One of the men flinched when hit. Shots were immediately returned, ricocheting off the deck. Ilana and I dove for cover. She fired again wildly without looking. Bullets crashed against our bow just above the water line. Sandy screamed below.

I grabbed Ilana's gun and raised my hands in retreat. If they wanted our money, I reasoned, they could have it. It was not worth getting killed. I was more worried about the ladies. I didn't want them hurt. I told Ilana to take the gun and go below. Throw my wallet up first. Then stay below. Lock the door to the main bedroom and don't come out until I tell you.

'I'll handle this,' I instructed.

'But...' Ilana started to say.

'Just do it, please.' I stared at her.

She went down the stairs and threw my wallet up on the deck after which I heard a door slammed in anger. After easing the throttle back and I turned the boat into the wind, her sails flapping uselessly in the breeze.

The powerboat coasted up alongside our boat. One of the men on board was kneeling over the man Ilana had shot. Blood drenched the injured man's white shirt just below his chest. He was not dead, still moving, but his wound looked bad, bleeding profusely. A towel covered his chest, and he was audibly groaning, his eyes closed tightly in pain. I could only watch helplessly, my hands in the air.

They threw gray rubber guards over the side of their boat to tie up to our boat. Very proficient in their work, as if they had done this more than once. I hoped that was a good sign. Hoped they were professional thieves, would take my money and leave. I could live with being robbed. My wallet held a couple of hundred dollars, some Belizean money and some American. And they could have my credit cards, whatever they wanted.

Then please go.

4:35 P.M. JOHN

They went about their work efficiently with no real need for conversation, almost as if they had done this many times before.

It didn't matter to me. I couldn't understand them. When they did speak, they spoke Spanish. I assumed they were from someplace in Central America. Dressed in clean, colorful new shirts and shorts, they looked prosperous. Perhaps pirating was a profitable business. It seemed a good sign. Hopefully they would conclude their nasty business quickly and be on their way.

After boarding our boat, they tied my hands behind my back with a coarse rope and shoved me onto an open cushion in the cockpit. I waited patiently, assuming they would eventually ask for money. They seemed to be in no hurry. One of the men went below. I heard him try to open the bedroom door. He rattled the handle several times before returning to the deck. After saying something to his companion, he jumped onto the speedboat. The other men remained on my boat, casually holding their automatic weapons pointed more or less in my direction.

I felt calm. I didn't know why. Given the potential for disaster, I kept wondering why I wasn't more worried, probably because there was nothing I could do. It did occur to me after the fact that I should have tried to call for help before being boarded and used the ship to shore radio. But it all happened so fast, no time to react.

He came on board after a few minutes. A tall young man with dark black, closely cropped hair and a nice tan. He looked familiar. He wasn't like the others, definitely not from Central America. More Oriental, although I didn't think he was Chinese. He smiled at me, and it was his eyes which betrayed him. I recognized his eyes. I had seen those eyes before. A burst of exaggerated energy exploded in my brain when I remembered where I had last seen those eyes. It was in a dark forest. The last time I saw those eyes, a smile had been on the lips of the man who possessed those eyes. The tall young man had his dead father's eyes, the eyes of the man I had killed.

It was then that I became very afraid.

Three additional men boarded with the tall young man. They were Thai or Chinese like him, dressed in neat white short-sleeved shirts and long pants. Their dress code looked out of place on a recreational boat. Too formal, not casual boat wear, more like clothes a businessman might wear. The men didn't smile, and they all had guns holstered in leather slings over their shirts.

The young man smiled at the two Spanish-speaking guys who were holding automatic rifles. He handed them a briefcase. They nodded and immediately returned to their speedboat. Lines attaching the speedboat to my sailboat were released, and the sleekly shaped craft drifted slowly away under power. Before it turned to leave, a body fell over the side, splashing into the sea. Something heavy had been tied around the waist of the body. It quickly slid into the deep blue-green water.

An involuntary shudder coursed through my shoulders as I watched the body disappear. I wondered if this was to be my fate. Closing my eyes to the horror, I leaned back on the cushions. It was uncomfortable sitting with my arms tied behind my back. My shoulders began to ache, and my wrists felt wet, bleeding from abrasions caused by the heavy, coarse ropes. A hot sun poured down as I contemplated my dire situation. Sweat beaded on my forehead. The salty perspiration dripped into the corners of my eyes and burned uncomfortably. I could do nothing to wipe it away.

The young man's crew of three restarted the engine and turned the wheel in the direction of shore, lowering the bullet-torn sails. We proceeded slowly under power. They seemed to know what they were doing.

As we headed towards the island in what promised to be a long journey at this speed, I wondered if I would still be alive when the boat was docked.

7:40 P.M. JOHN

It became apparent during our return journey to the island that our captors planned to wait until dark before docking.

I could see our beach house when we got closer; a few lights were glowing through the windows. The boat maneuvered offshore in slow circles while the sun set in the west behind the shadow of the island. From where I sat, the house looked good; it looked like a safe place, a place where I had been able to rest in the past. But not tonight and perhaps never again.

After the sky darkened, they headed for the dock to unload their human cargo, namely me, under the cover of night.

Before being dragged off the boat, the tall young man with black hair turned to me. 'I assume you know who I am,' were the first words I heard him speak.

By this time, my shoulders were sore, almost to the point of tying up in spasms of tight muscle agony, causing some pain in my back. I attempted to appear calm like nothing was bothering me, but that was becoming increasingly difficult under the circumstances. Two of the young man's accomplices were sitting next to him. The other one was down below in the galley. Fortunately, I didn't hear anything indicating a struggle coming from below. I assumed the ladies were still safe in the bedroom. I was grateful for this, but nothing else.

'You are Nue's son,' I replied honestly, assuming I had no reason to lie. 'Your name is Sophon. Am I right?'

'Yes, you are well informed, Mr. Van Laan.' He replied in English with a slightly clipped oriental accent. It was easy to understand him.

'I have wanted to meet you for some time now. Ever since my father was killed while visiting you in America,' he added.

'You could have called and made an appointment,' I replied. 'This wasn't necessary.'

He looked at me for a long time before answering. 'Yes, I suppose I could have called, but I'm not sure you would have approved my agenda.'

'Why not?' I asked, thinking I probably didn't want to know the answer to my question.

'Perhaps we should talk about your lady friends first,' he ignored my question. 'We will be docking at your house in a few minutes. I'm sure they will be much more comfortable inside.'

'They are quite safe where they are. And you should know they have a gun. I advise you not to try to force them to come out.'

'They can stay down there as long as they like. But I assume they have no water or food. When they are ready to come out, I promise I will not harm them.'

'Why should I believe you?'

'You have no reason to trust me... Except, I give you my word. It's up to you to decide if you want to accept it.'

This seemed an unusual response. I expected him to be more forceful and angry. The power was on his side. I was helpless to defend myself or the ladies.

He could do with us what he wished.

11:20 PM. JOHN

I was getting tired.

Now, this may have seemed like the last thing I should have been feeling at the time. It would have been far more appropriate to be feeling scared, fearing I didn't have long to live. Sleep should have been the least of my worries. But I was bone-tired and fading fast. Probably because I was finally comfortable. The rough ropes holding my wrists had been removed, and I had been allowed to use the bathroom in the house to clean up. Not alone; one of Sophon's men accompanied me. He didn't carry a gun. But then he didn't need one. He was a big man with broad shoulders and hard muscles, probably trained in martial arts. I was no match for him. I could try, maybe run, but the bathroom had no windows, no way out. So nowhere to go. And two of his friends were waiting outside the bathroom door with guns. My chances were slim. I didn't try.

Handcuffs were placed on my wrists after exiting the bathroom. My ankles were shackled together with a rope, and I had no chance to run. Led away like a prisoner, I was directed to walk slowly back to the main living room, where I was instructed to sit down on a couch.

Sophon came in eventually and sat across from me in a chair. 'You are a very interesting man, John Van Laan. I have wanted to talk to you for a long time. But first I have something to tell you. And what I have to say to you may cause you to not want to talk to me. It is your choice, I suppose. And if you do choose to talk to me, you can lie... or you can tell me the truth. Again, your choice. But I am asking you to be honest with me.'

'Okay. Let's talk.'

'Before you answer my questions, you should know I intend to kill you. You are going to die. So, you have no reason to tell me lies because lying will do you no good.'

I said nothing. I had assumed he had come to kill me. I had killed his father, after all. My death sentence was not an unexpected announcement.

'You don't seem surprised.'

'Why should I be surprised?'

'I thought maybe you would try to tell me you did not kill my father, that he died in a helicopter crash.'

He paused, 'But you are not going to lie to me, are you?'

'No.'

'You killed him.'

I didn't answer.

'Do you want to know how I know you killed him?' he asked.

'Is that important?' I replied.

'Your friend Phillip told me,' he said, ignoring my question.

I sighed inwardly. 'He is not my friend.'

'Do you think I should kill you for killing my father?'

'That's your choice.'

'But do you think you should die? Do you think it would be just?'

I didn't respond.

'Okay, I didn't expect you to answer my question.'

I looked at him. Our conversation sounded almost like a business meeting. It seemed wrong, out of place. I didn't think that a conversation between a condemned man and his executioner was supposed to sound like this. But then, I didn't know what normal was in a situation like this.

'I will tell you anything you want to know,' I finally replied. 'But first, I would like to ask for something from you in return.'

'What can I give you? You already know I am going to kill you. You have only a short time to live. I can perhaps offer you more time. That is all. I am sorry, Mr. Van Laan, but you have brought this on yourself. Surely you know that.'

'I'm not asking for myself. I'm asking for the ladies in the boat. I want you to let them go.'

'What... let them go so they can run to the police?'

'Please do not harm them.'

'I have already given you my word.'

'If I know they are safe, I will tell you everything you want to know.'

'John, can I call you John?'

'Sure.'

'John, I cannot let them go. You do understand why.'

'Yes, I understand, but I am begging you. Please let them go. They have harmed no one.'

'John, you must know I can't let them go. They will bring the police, and I will have to run.'

'Then I will not talk to you.'

'Do you want to die now?'

'You are going to kill me anyway. What does it matter if it is now or later? Let them go. I will make them promise not to go to the police.' I stared at him. 'Please.'

He walked over to me, standing above me, staring down at me before speaking. 'You never gave my father time to prepare to die. Not like I'm giving you. You shot him without mercy. Why should I give you anything?'

I had no defense. His blow came fast, hitting me full force on the side of the head, causing a white-hot light to shoot through my brain, filled with shock and pain. I slumped over on the couch, barely conscious.

He walked away.

FRIDAY, NOVEMBER 13, 4:40 A.M. JOHN

Trying to sleep while tied to a bed is pure misery.

My arms lay stretched on both sides, bound to the bed frame with ropes. I simply could not move. Every time I fell asleep and unconsciously tried to turn over, pain shot through my arms, and I was instantly awake. Finally, I gave up trying to sleep and lay on my back, waiting for the dawn.

After a few hours of not being able to move, to adjust my position on the bed, forced to lie flat on my back in one position, my back muscles began to ach in agonizing knots. And my head hurt. When Sophon hit me, my head felt raw and tender. A headache, a bad headache, took control of my painful existence; the result of having my hands tied behind my back for hours, shoulders sore or head hurting, or both. What did it matter? A terrible black throbbing pulsed through my brain from the back of my eye sockets to the muscles in my neck. I couldn't open my eyes. It hurt so bad. My stomach became nauseous. I thought I was going to throw up. My shoulders quivered in a mass of tense, taut muscles. More than anything, I needed a couple of aspirin and a glass of water.

Relief was only a few short steps away. Aspirin and water were in the bathroom, but no way I could go to the bathroom. And I needed to pee. I badly needed to pee.

A windless night became still and torturously hot. Perspiration rolled down the sides of my salty, greasy face. I wanted to be somewhere else, anywhere else. I wanted this to be over. The hours hung on a dark night like a heavy lead weight dropped on my queasy gut. I thought about yelling for Sophon to do me a favor, come and kill me now.

I tried thinking about something else, anything besides the throb in my temples, the weight in my gut. I wondered about the ladies and how they were doing. They couldn't last forever in the stateroom of the boat. They needed water more than anything.

I wondered why I was still alive.

And, of course, I wondered when I would die.

I couldn't help it. I couldn't stop thinking about the night, which was the reason I was tied to this bed because I had killed his father in a fit of rage. Something had snapped deep inside me. Images from that night, like bad dreams, returned to my tortured brain over and over again as I lay in bed. The gun was in my hand. Pent-up anger raced through my body until it ignited in my fingers like a high-voltage surge of energy. My arm had tensed. My fingers pulled the trigger. It wasn't a conscious action to pull the trigger. It was more of a reflex action that I could not control. It was not something I intended, not something justified, just something that happened.

The night I killed his father was a moonlit night. Tall pines, live oaks, and palm trees cast long gray shadows over a damp forest floor. I could not see his father clearly, but I could hear him. I clearly heard him order the death of Ilana's brother. In my mind, it was as if I was hearing him order my death sentence.

He had tried to have me killed on several occasions. I had been lucky. Death had not taken me. I could have been dead. I knew I could have died. The trauma from all those near-death experiences covered me with a blanket of pain. I could not stop; I did not stop. I pulled the trigger in wanton anger and killed him.

Despite all my endless excuses for killing him, I knew who was responsible. I was. I had broken. Something deep inside me broke. All the discipline, all the self-control, all the logic, all my religious upbringing, my faith did not save me that night. I broke. In a moment of lost time, my mind rebelled in anguished fury, in a cataclysm of violence. Like an uncontrolled mass of hot flashing lava rushing bright red through my over stressed nervous system, anger and fear had burned too hot. A penetrating, propelling ship of fools overpowering my conscious mind. It was as if the bullet released by my curling fingers carried with it all the screaming frustration that had holed up deep inside me for too long.

Nue, the young man's father, had died, and I walked away a free man, my crime covered up by the CIA. But the fact that I got away with murder did not make me an innocent man. I knew what happened. I knew who killed another man. I knew it was me. I was guilty. And yet, I didn't feel guilty when it happened. It was more like I had been an observer, looking at the killing scene from the outside, watching someone else pull a trigger.

Someone else had done the guilty deed.

But in reality, this was not true. I knew it was me, whether I admitted it or not. I couldn't change that any more than I could change where I now lay with my hands tied to a bed. I was a man who had killed, who had pulled the trigger of a gun. I was the man Sophon wanted dead.

And in my torment, I wished more than anything else, I wished I had not killed his father. I wished I could do it differently, turn back time. But time is a ruthless master, never ever allowing one single act to be corrected. Once done, time never allows an act to be retracted. I could change nothing. I could deny nothing. I could only relive the murderous night over and over again as I sweated in agony.

Finally, I said a prayer to my God.

I had not prayed for a long time, but that night, I prayed, prayed like I had never prayed before. I didn't ask for myself, didn't ask to be forgiven. I was guilty, and I had nothing to forgive. I asked simply for them. I asked for Ilana and Sandy. I didn't want to see them get hurt. More than anything else, I didn't want them to die. Not because of me, not because of what I had done. Please, Lord, not because of me. I was guilty, not them. Do to me as you wish, but please save them.

Then I waited for the dawn. I waited, keeping watch for the dawn through the window in my bedroom. A dawn that seemed like it would never come. I lived in a world of perpetual agony for minutes, which became hours, hours, which became days. Time was stretched, ripped apart. Time is the great measurement of our lives; time, which, in science, is a constant measurement. Time spread its torturous wings over me and smeared me with agony that arched across the vast canyons of my mind.

My eyes closed to the dark night as I lay in painful anticipation of dawn, a dawn which no doubt would be the beginning of my last day on this earth, and yet, a dawn I dearly yearned for.

Yearning for a death that would finally release me from this hellish night of anguish.

5:55 A.M.

With a loud crash, the door broke open, waking Ilana and Sandy and separating them from their tortured dreams to a hellishly real nightmare.

Beams of light split the dark room, illuminating small useless images in the interior of the boat's main cabin, a book shelf, shoes on the floor, and Ilana's startled big brown eyes. She immediately reached for the gun on the floor next to the couch where she had been sleeping, but he was too fast. He kicked the gun, sliding across the floor out of her reach.

It hurt when he grabbed her arm. She swung her small, hard fist against his chest. His blow came out of the dark. She never saw his hand, only felt the dull, hard blow against her face.

Falling on the floor, she released an audible cry into the night air.

Across the room, Sandy screamed as she was dragged out of bed and across the floor, banging her leg on the door frame. The man took her forcefully out of the boat's bedroom, pulling her up the stairs by her arms and throwing her against the cushions in the boat's cockpit, where she sat whimpering uncontrollably, unable and unwilling to cry even though she badly wanted to yell. A man stood over her, perhaps begging her to fight. She did not move, fearfully listening to a commotion below.

Ilana was fighting, but it was no use. She soon emerged from below, was dragged up the stairs by two men, pushed across the deck, falling next to Sandy while holding the side of her bruised face.

BANGKOK, THAILAND, 5:40 P.M. LUANG

A folded white sheet of paper was placed on his desk without comment.

His assistant simply put the sheet where the old man would see it and walked out of his office.

It was late in the afternoon. Luang was still at his desk. Not because he had work to do but because he had been waiting. He had no desire to work. A report about Sophon's activities was due and he was in his office waiting for it because he was sure it would tell him his ordeal was over.

His garden was his place to rest.

Going to his garden was the only activity he had scheduled for his evening. He planned to enjoy a cup of tea while sitting quietly and thinking about Sophon. He would remember the days when his nephew's son had roamed this great house as a young boy. The boy loved to run through the many rooms playing imagined dramas in his head; dreams of glory and honor which would be his when he was older, when he was a man; battles he would win, enemies he would conquer, maidens he would subdue; all the great imaginary stories which occupy the minds of young boys as they play.

Tonight, while sitting in his garden, Luang planned to pay homage to the boy who was his nephew's son and who was also, in so many ways, his son.

Luang never had children. His wife had died at an early age. The pain of losing her had been too immense. It seemed easier and simpler to invite his brother's family to live with him instead. Luang had taken great pleasure in watching the boy grow bright and strong. He had taken time to teach the young boy like he was his son. He had tried to prepare the boy for the work which would eventually come to him. His family required a successor, a man who would run their many businesses, a man of great wisdom. Luang had taught Sophon many lessons and taken great pleasure in telling him the history and honor of the family.

Luang had been very successful in his time. He had seen the power and glory of his family grow under his direction. It had all been good. All good until it was not good until it began to fail. His nephew had been in charge during those dark days. Luang did not want to think about those bad times now. Failure was in the past. Luang had no plans to consider past failures. Instead, he planned to dwell tonight on what was good, thinking about the days when his life had been good, the days when the boy sat on his lap and smiled at his uncle.

Luang was confident everything would return to as it was after tonight. Everything would be good again. When the murderer was finally dead, it would be as it should be.

Luang slowly unfolded the paper on his desk and began to read the report. A dark frown crossed his face. The murderer was still alive.

He placed the paper on his desk and leaned back into his chair, deciding he would not go to his garden this evening as he had planned.

8:55 A.M. JOHN

Ilana was sitting on a couch in the main room of the house when I entered the room.

They dragged me downstairs in the morning, and I saw her before I saw anything or anyone else. Holding one side of a torn bikini top with her hand so it covered her breast; her face and arm were badly bruised, red and blue. Curled up on the couch like a hurt animal, yet the look on her face was still defiant. I knew when she was angry. I had seen this look before. Sandy sat next to Ilana, sitting upright. Also, dressed only in her bikini, she didn't appear to be hurt; she was more stoic, accepting, and not afraid. On the opposite side of the room was Sophon. I wondered what he was thinking when he looked at the women. They were beautiful, desirable women.

'You forced me to do this,' Sophon finally said to no one in particular, although it was obvious his words were directed at me. 'You were concerned about them. You wanted to know they were alright. I had them taken from the boat so you could see for yourself.'

He looked at me. 'They are fine as I promised... Now, can we talk?'

Ilana was clearly hurt. Her arm had dried blood from a cut near her shoulder, which had not been treated.

'You have injured one of them,' I replied.

'She would not come when she was asked. My men were as gentle as possible. She fought them. They had no choice but to take her by force.'

I believed him. I knew Ilana would fight. 'Let them go, and I will do what you ask.'

'Mr. Van Laan. We have been over this before. I cannot let them go.'

I stared at him.

'What do you expect from me, Mr. Van Laan? You are in no position to demand anything.'

He stood quickly as if he had suddenly made a decision.

Grabbing Ilana by the arm, which was already bleeding and bruised, he pulled her off the couch. She screamed, but he was too strong for her.

'Hold her,' he demanded.

Two of his men took her arms. Sophon ripped off her dangling bra. She stood half-naked in front of him. He hit her hard across the mouth with his open hand. She cried out weakly.

'Okay. Okay, I get it,' I shouted at him.

He turned and looked at me. I wasn't sure what he would do next. He looked back at Ilana as she squirmed, trying to get loose from the grip of his men.

'Do you want me to give her to my men? Is that what you want? Do I need to resort to violence to get your attention?' he asked. 'Is this what it will take for you to talk to me, Mr. Van Laan? Are we men of reason, or do we need to speak like savages who only communicate through violence?'

His question caught me off guard. I had no answer for him.

He raised his hand to hit her again across the side of the head. She turned away, crying a low, defiant moan.

'Stop, stop,' I yelled. 'I'll do whatever you say. Please leave her alone.'

He turned back towards me.

'So, it seems you understand the language of violence. But then, why would I expect anything different from you? You are a killer, after all.'

His words made me angry. I wanted to shout at him. I wanted to argue with him, but I was afraid for Ilana.

'Don't hurt her,' I begged.

He turned to her. She was naked and beautiful and defenseless. I looked away. I was ashamed. I had caused her agony.

'I will not hurt her,' he said defiantly.

'Thank you.'

'Do you believe me?" he shouted.

'I believe you.'

'Take him away,' Sophon ordered his men. 'I do not wish to speak to him now.'

He was angry, and even though he was young, it was obvious he was not a man who liked losing control of his emotions. He looked down in disgust.

A guard yanked on the chain connected to my handcuffs. My wrists were already sore from the tight cuffs. Pain shot up my arm as the man dragged me upstairs, tripping over a step when I turned to look at Ilana and Sandy. Ilana was still struggling, trying to get free, but Sophon's men held her tightly.

I was afraid for her.

BANGKOK, THAILAND, TUESDAY, NOVEMBER 17, 8:20 A.M. LUANG

His daily routine seldom changed.

A folded white sheet of paper was delivered to him same time, late in the afternoon. His assistant would enter his office, quietly place the paper on the old man's desk without saying a word, turn, and walk out, closing the door behind him.

Luang did not immediately read the report. He finished his work first. He had come to dread these reports. This had not been his response the first few days of Sophon's travels. He had eagerly unfolded the papers and read the reports as soon as they were delivered. But after days of disappointment, reading the information on the folded papers had become an arduous task he wished to avoid.

Eventually, he picked up the paper. After unfolding it carefully, he read every word, hoping, wishing for some sign that would give even the slightest indication that Sophon's work was finally coming to the desired conclusion. But to date, nothing in the reports stated it would be over soon. His nephew's killer was still alive.

Luang's work had become difficult in the last few days. He had trouble concentrating. His meetings often ended with quick, ill-considered conclusions... or with no conclusion, postponed for another day. Conversations with the old man were terse and abrasive. Petitions, which normally would have been granted, were denied without cause. Nothing of importance was accomplished. It was as if the world was waiting, waiting for a single event. Then, life could resume its journey. Pain and suffering would not be a priority.

But for now, time was wound up tight, straining, and agonizing.

BELIZE, MONDAY, NOVEMBER 16, 9:36 P.M.
JOHN

Every minute I was awake, I listened intently, afraid of hearing sounds of torture or rape coming from somewhere in the house.

But all I heard was the sounds of waves tiptoeing across the sandy beach, creeping in through my bedroom windows. That and the whisper of the wind rustling through palm leaves filled my painful, arduous nights and days. The sun would wander in through a window on the east side of the bedroom in the morning and lamely leave in the evening as if it was embarrassed for having accomplished nothing to relieve my pain.

Rain fell one night.

Usually, I love to hear rain in the night; especially when it is warm and windows are open, but not this night. Tortured, anxious dreams filled that night with slithering snakes and steep cliffs falling to foggy oblivion. Exhausted, I woke in a sweat, fear filling my mind.

My arms were still tied to the bed. They would twist and turn in unnatural ways whenever I involuntarily tried to turn over while sleeping. My body ached to be in a different position after hours of lying flat on my back. Spasms of agony ran through the muscles of my back, causing me to cry out in frustration.

Blood seeped into the sheets from cuts on my wrists where handcuffs had ripped the skin. A rough rope tied my ankles to the bottom of the bed and stretched my body full length, making it difficult to move. It was better to be awake. Nothing but nightmares occupied my sleep. Eventually, I would drift off to sleep before waking again after only a short time in pain, more afraid to be asleep than awake.

When I was awake, I would listen to the restless noises of the night. Days were better, filled with more activity, a boat out on the water, and laughter coming from the beach walkers. Unfortunately, I was unable to cry out to them or scream for help. Tape covered my mouth.

I heard no evidence of struggle in the house, no laughter or screams, nothing that could tell me what was going on. Even though I strained to listen to what was happening downstairs, I heard almost nothing other than an occasional conversation spoken in a language I could not understand: brief, stilted words spoken quickly in hushed tones that told me nothing. Then it would be quiet again, and in the still quiet, I was afraid, always afraid because quiet can be more fearful than screams. Quiet can be filled with invented fears. In my imagination, I feared Ilana and Sandy were already dead, beaten and raped, dropped off a boat like the wounded man Ilana had shot. A weight tied to their waists. Maybe still alive when they drifted down into the deep water, holding their breath until darkness closed around them, sinking slowly. Pressure increased in their ears as a searing pain exploded inside their skulls until their lungs cried out for oxygen, gasping for air, inhaling salty cold seawater from the ocean which would be their grave, choking until mercifully they became unconscious with only the memory of their brutal beatings still stinging the nerve ends of their minds.

I have a vivid imagination.

I have always had a vivid imagination. It serves me well on occasions when I need to be creative. But most of the time, my imagination is a burden filled with fear and longing. I am prone to imagine worst-case scenarios. I often wake in the night filled with fear, afraid, always afraid. I do okay during the day. And I am far better on sunny days than cloudy days. Reality, for the most part, gives me comfort. But not these days of pain, and surely not the nights I was tied to a bed. I was constantly afraid. No way could I lie on the bed without pain. Every muscle in my back ached. I longed to be allowed to stand and walk. Instead, I was trapped on the bed, completely unable to move more than a few inches. I pissed on the bed more than a few times when I could not hold it.

I feared my final eulogy would be nothing more than silence. No glory, no accolades, just a bed defiled by the dregs of my body, the smell and the agony overwhelming every other sensation. I waited to die. I longed to die.

My only reprieve was the few times the guards allowed me to use the bathroom and relieve myself. They would rip the tape off my mouth and shove a water bottle down my throat, water squirting everywhere. I tried vainly to drink in every precious drop rushing down my throat as I gagged, water choking my windpipe, coughing up more water than I drank. The guards laughed as the spilled water splashed over my face. I coughed and gagged, but I drank enough water to stay alive.

Why, I did not know.

TUESDAY, NOVEMBER 17, 1:10 A.M. SANDY

Sandy nudged Ilana on the shoulder.

'Something is happening,' she said.

Ilana was half asleep, half awake at the time.

The ladies had been deposited by their captors in the master bedroom in the back of the house, Ilana's room. It had a bathroom attached for their convenience. The only window in the room had been secured, nailed shut, covered with wood and a lock was put on the door. They were comfortable. They were fed. They were given water bottles, but they could not leave.

Ilana lay next to Sandy in bed and rubbed her eyes. 'What?'

'I hear something, noises.'

They were both silent for a minute, listening, wondering, worrying in the dark night. The house was quiet; no commotion, no noises, nothing to indicate a change.

They had talked over the last few days, expressing their fears. They thought, perhaps hoped, John was still alive because they had heard nothing, no yelling. No scuffle, no sounds of men dragging a body. A man fighting for his life would make some noise. But they had heard nothing which would lead them to believe he was dead. Yet the eerie quiet was almost as disconcerting as the noise of a violent, life-ending struggle.

They had been summoned several times, Ilana to answer the telephone and talk to her brother, who called. Sandy was asked to send an email to John's office explaining he would be gone sailing for a few days, don't worry, he would return shortly. The ladies had been warned to say one wrong word or ask for help in any way; if that happened, they would be killed instantly.

They had no choice.

They had cooperated.

When they had timidly asked their captures about their friend John; only silence returned their questions. So, they knew nothing.

And knowing nothing was almost as bad as knowing the worst possible outcome.

1:15 A.M. JOHN

He came in the middle of the night.

I was awake at the time.

But then I had been awake most of the time during those days and nights of suffering, unconscious for only short spans of occasional sleep. I never knew how long I slept. I assumed it wasn't very long.

Sophon came into my room and turned on an overhead light, half blinding me. When I could finally look at him through the blazing light on the ceiling, he looked bad like he had not slept any more than I had. His clothes were wrinkled and unkempt, as if he had been dozing in a chair. His white linen shirt was half tucked in and half out of his black trousers, not neat as I had always seen him in the past. He wore no shoes, and his black hair looked matted.

When he saw me, he turned away.

The smell must have been bad, sour piss and sweat-dampened sheets. He yelled at his men and told them to clean me up and get me into the shower immediately. Throw away my bed sheets. Clean the wounds on my ankles and wrists.

'Take him downstairs when you are done,' Sophon demanded. 'This is disgusting. How could you let this happen?'

His men looked at him wide-eyed. I guessed they thought it was okay to let me suffer. I had killed his father, after all. They must have thought I deserved nothing more. I was going to die anyway. What difference did it make?

I understood. I did not blame them. By this time, I had reconciled myself to the fact I was a dead man. I only feared for the ladies. I did not want them to suffer. They were not to blame. This was my fault. The guilt was mine alone.

Sophon left the room.

A man I had not seen before entered my bedroom. He loosened the ropes on my ankles and tied me to the handcuffs. He pulled me up out of the bed. It was difficult to stand. My muscles were tight and sore from lying in one position for long hours. Blood dripped where the metal handcuffs had cut my wrists. I tried to move and keep up with the man who was pulling on my handcuffs, but I stumbled. He held me and kept me from falling to the floor.

He was a large man, looked more Chinese than the other guards; thin eyes, big shoulders, very muscular, large round head, and long black hair to his shoulders. I will never forget him. He didn't talk. He did not need to talk to communicate.

It was dark outside my bedroom window; nothing to see. One light lit my room. He led me into the bathroom and turned the lights. I watched in fascination as he turned the shower faucet. The shower was like a dream. Soft, warm water fell over my body. I drank in as much as I could. Then I washed my body, feeling the stubble of new growth on my chin. My face itched. I wanted to shave, but it was enough to be clean. When I was done with my shower, the man handed me a towel. He removed my handcuffs and gave me cream for my cuts. I thanked him. He looked at me as I stood dripping wet, holding a towel.

'I will not try to escape,' I said quietly.

The large Chinese man nodded his head. He knew I was speaking the truth. I was too weak to run.

I dried my body and rubbed the cream on my wrists and ankles. Clean clothes were laid out on a chair when I walked into the bedroom. The mattress from my bed was gone and with it, the lurid smell. The room was clean.

A fresh breeze wandered in through the window, making it seem as if I was somewhere else as if my recent painful ordeal was only a bad dream.

2:35 A.M. JOHN

Food was placed on the dining room table.

The Chinaman, I did not know his name. I called him the Chinaman to give him a name. He walked behind me to the table, never more than a few feet from me. I assumed he would be with me for the rest of my short, painful life. The Chinaman was to be my constant companion, always at my side. Sophon must have brought him to the island for the express purpose of guarding me, and I assumed the Chinaman had the skills required to do the job, restrain me in case I tried to run. I didn't mind him. He was never mean or pushy. As I said before, the Chinaman never opened his mouth to speak, but I always knew what he wanted.

I could not eat most of the food on the table. My body was too weak to digest anything more than a small amount. I ate what I could and then simply looked at the rest of the food; bread and jam, cheese slices, cut fruit and some boiled eggs, very simple food. It all looked good. I wanted to continue eating, but I managed only to digest a piece of bread with jam and a banana. And a cold glass of milk which was very good.

After watching me stare at the food for a few minutes, the Chinaman stood and motioned for me to follow. I thought I was returning to a bed to sleep. It was the middle of the night. A clock on the wall told me it was nearly three in the morning.

The Chinaman walked behind me, directing me down the hall towards the stairs to the master bedroom on the main floor. He opened the door. The room was dark. He turned on the overhead light. They were sleeping together in a king sized bed, Ilana and Sandy. Both women looked instantly startled and afraid. I started to say something to them, but the Chinaman put his hand over my mouth and took hold of my injured wrist, pulling me quickly out of the bedroom into the hall. Shutting the door behind me, he locked it. Apparently, he wanted me to see the ladies, not talk to them. I guessed he wanted me to know they were alive, not dead. Then he shoved me in my back and pushed me down the hall towards the living room.

Sophon was waiting for me, sitting in a chair as if nothing had happened. He looked better than the last time I saw him. A clean, white, ironed shirt replaced the wrinkled one he had on before. His hair was combed and neat again. He seemed more at ease.

'Sit down,' Sophon said. 'It is time we talked.'

I did as Sophon requested. The Chinaman sat beside me on a couch.

'Would you like something more to drink?' Sophon asked.

'No.'

The room was lit by one light; a small table lamp with a shade sat in the far corner of the room, shedding dim light in shadows across the floor. Sophon sat between me and the light. The silhouette of his head was visible, but the details of his face were difficult to see in the shadows. His words sounded as if they were coming from a speaker across a room. I could not see his lips move. He sat very still like a statue. I longed to see his face, to understand the small movements of his eyelids, how he held his mouth, simple expressions which can often speak more than words. But I was unable to see his face.

'Can we turn on more lights?' I asked.

'That will not be necessary,' he replied.

I didn't argue. It didn't matter, really. I assumed this meeting was about my death, and it wouldn't take long.

'It is a mistake to underestimate your enemy,' Sophon began. 'Underestimating your enemy can often lead to assuming he is evil when in truth he is not. Do you know who wrote those words?'

'No.'

'They were written in the Tao. Do you know what the Tao is?'

His question seemed irrelevant, given it was coming from the man who intended to kill me.

'I have heard of the book, but I have never read it,' I answered truthfully.

'It is a book written by a Chinese Zen Master long ago. I have studied this book. It helps me understand how to live.'

I said nothing. Even though I couldn't see Sophon's face, I could feel his stare.

'Do you know why this book is important to you?' he asked.

'No, but I suppose you are going to tell me,' I was feeling weak and irritable. The small amount of food I had eaten had given me a limited amount of strength, not much, not enough to want to argue with him, only enough to answer his questions in simple terms. My wrists were hurting, and I was constantly adjusting my sitting position in an attempt to avoid spasms of pain from shooting through my back. Every muscle in my body felt sore. I simply couldn't get comfortable, and the prospect of my imminent death was far from relaxing. I was in no mood to have a casual conversation about philosophy with my executioner.

'It leads me to want to understand who you are before you die,' Sophon inexplicably continued his intended mission. 'I want to know what made you shoot my father. I want to know who you are and what made you do this thing which has brought me so much sorrow.'

He paused.

'Why talk?' I asked. 'You are going to kill me. Isn't that enough?'

'No, it is not enough.'

'I don't really want to talk to you,' I replied weakly. 'Why don't you just kill me and get it over with?'

'No, first we talk,' Sophon said forcefully. 'And you will talk to me because if you do not, I will kill the women who are asleep in the bedroom.'

'If I talk to you, will you let them go?'

'Yes,' he said from behind the shadow of his face. 'But only after you have answered all my questions truthfully.'

'Why should I believe you?'

'Mr. Van Laan. You continue to exhaust my patience. You have seen your girlfriends. My friend took you to them. You know they are both alive and unharmed as I have promised. Is that not true?'

I didn't answer.

'Do you need more incentive to loosen your tongue? Because I can give you an incentive if that is what you require. I can choose one of the girls and kill her here while you watch her die. Then, if you are still unwilling to talk to me, I will kill the other girl. Then I will kill you.'

He waited.

He knew I could not refuse. Still, I did not want to do what he asked. I was becoming angry and irritated with this strange conversation. And I did not want to die. Even though I knew it was my fate, I still... I didn't want to die.

He continued. 'I do not want to kill them, but I will if that is what you choose. It's your choice. You can refuse to answer my questions. But if you refuse, they will die. So, decide now. Will you talk to me?'

I could not answer.

'Please understand I have gone to a lot of trouble to arrange this meeting,' he continued. 'I could have killed you and walked away many times. Like the time when you took a walk alone in the forest behind your office building. Do you remember?'

I looked at him, astonished he had seen me that evening.

'I didn't kill you then because I wanted to understand you first,' he answered my silent question.

His face was a shadow behind the light. I felt him staring at me, waiting for me to speak. Still, I could not open my mouth to talk. Maybe it was the lack of food and sleep for days. Cognitive thoughts seemed to wander in and out of my brain like strands of stardust in the sky. I stared back at him, trying very hard to concentrate. Perhaps it was something about not seeing his face. Or it could have been his voice; the tone and the inflection were similar to his father's but calmer, more caring. Something was different. Something I badly wanted to understand.

He was like his father in one respect: he was very unpredictable. I remembered the time Monica and I first sat across a table from his father. It was the night Monica died. His father had forced his way into our New York hotel room and demanded I sell him my stock. With ownership of my stock, he would gain control of my company. He demanded it like it was his birthright and belonged to him and his people.

And then there was a second meeting with his father, this time in Hong Kong, Ilana was with me then. Both times, his father had surprised me. He had offered me deals I did not want. Deals which were interesting but unacceptable. The deal he offered me that day turned out to be good only until my company was healthy. Then he planned to kill me. Seemed he had made up his mind I had to go. He just never enlightened me on this particular aspect of the deal. Instead, he suggested we come to an agreement to work together. But it was a lie. A lie I didn't understand at the time. His father was a hard man to read.

His son appeared to be no different. They both offered me deals I could not refuse but didn't like. As I thought about his father now, I wished I had accepted his father's first offer. Monica would be alive now if I had taken his offer. And I wouldn't be sitting across from his son, my executioner ...

'I am waiting for your answer,' Sophon spoke very deliberately.

'I was thinking I wished I had taken your father's first offer,' I replied honestly.

'That would have been wise. But you did not, did you?'

'No.'

'And you still have my father's money, don't you? The money he offered you for stock in your company.'

'Yes, and my girlfriend is dead. Don't forget that. Your father took much more from me than he gave.'

'Do you blame my father for her death?' Sophon asked.

'He forced his way into my room. She would not have died if he had not come,' I argued. 'So yes, I blame him for her death.'

'Did my father pull the trigger of the gun which shot your girlfriend?' Sophon countered.

I stared at him. I didn't want to answer his dumb question. And I didn't want to be on trial for his father's death.

'Are you going to answer my questions,' Sophon demanded. 'Or do I need to kill one of your girlfriends to convince you to do what I ask?'

I looked at his face in the shadows. The Chinaman sat next to me. I had no choice.

I could not escape his demands.

4:05 A.M. ILANA AND SANDY

'Do you think they will kill John tonight?' Ilana asked.

They could hear men talking in the other room. The women's bedroom was on the main floor, the same floor in the house where Sophon and John were sitting. The rooms were not far apart. Their conversation could be heard but not completely understood. Only when someone shouted, only then did they understand the words. Although they could not understand everything the men were saying, they knew from the tone of the conversation that it was not a pleasant conversation. And they knew it was not going well for John.

Sophon was becoming frustrated. His voice was getting louder. John's words were softer, more subdued. They heard him get angry only a few times.

'I don't know,' Sandy replied honestly to Ilana's question.

They were sitting up in bed. The light in their room was on. It was obvious this night was different. They were afraid it was going to happen tonight. John was going to die.

'Do you think they will kill us too?' Ilana finally asked the question which had been plaguing their minds since their ordeal began.

Sandy did not reply immediately. Finally, she answered simply, 'I suppose they will.' This was the only conclusion she could imagine. Why would they leave evidence behind? She and Ilana had seen their faces. They could identify the men. They needed to die.

Ilana did not speak. She simply took Sandy's hand and gripped it tightly while listening to voices coming through the wall into their room.

4:50 A.M. JOHN

'Why won't you admit you are responsible for my father's death?' Sophon demanded. 'You pulled the trigger. You alone bear the responsibility.'

I stared at him with all the resolve I had. Our conversation had been long and tedious. Sophon was determined to go over the complete history of my relationship with his father, including all the failed attempts on my life which Sophon claimed were never meant to kill me, just intimidate me. He had an answer for everything.

Everything it seemed could be viewed in two ways, his way or mine.

We even discussed the death of my business partner, Arthur. He had been killed by assassins on the streets of New York, gunned down after his limo was forced off the road in broad daylight. I blamed Sophon's father for Arthur's death. But Sophon claimed Arthur's death was his own fault. Didn't Arthur betray me? Didn't he do it for money? And Arthur probably would have betrayed his father, given time, Sophon concluded. So why was I asking about Arthur? Arthur's death was Arthur's fault. Arthur was greedy.

'What about my friend Vidu,' I asked.

Vidu was a gem dealer from Sri Lanka who had been murdered on the streets of Chicago. A needle filled with poison was shoved into his back. He died in agony, lying on a cold sidewalk while people walked past.

'Vidu died because he broke a contract Thailand had with Sri Lanka. The contract stated that all mined Sri Lankan sapphire was to be sold exclusively to Thailand,' Sophon explained. 'Vidu knew what he was doing when he ignored the contract by cutting and selling gemstones mined in Sri Lanka. He knew the risk he was taking, and he paid the price.'

I remembered Vidu expressing something about this ancient contract to me. I knew there was some truth to it. Still, it was not right. Vidu did not need to die.

'The contract, if it existed, was an old contract,' I replied to Sophon. 'It did not justify murdering him.'

Sophon disagreed. He looked at me like I was a moron. He asked why the terms of a contract could be negated by time. This contract was well-known to every gem dealer in Sri Lanka. Vidu knew, and he chose to break the contract. He chose to take the risk. Contracts are contracts. Time does not make them invalid. Vidu paid with his life.

'How about my friend Arny?' I asked, becoming exasperated. Arny had died in my apartment from a bullet, which was probably meant for me. 'What about him? Did a century-old contract justify his murder?'

'I heard about your friend Arny. It was a tragic accident,' Sophon replied. 'Your friend was simply in the wrong place at the wrong time. Accidents happen every day. Life is a risk. We die from disease, from natural catastrophes, from accidents. Death is part of life.'

'Your father paid a man to shoot up my apartment. Doesn't this make your father responsible for Arny's death?' I asked.

'It was an accident.'

'It was no accident. It was the result of a deliberate attempt to kill or intimidate me. Either way, your father was responsible.'

'Collateral damage is, I believe, the term you Westerners use when someone dies as an unintended consequence of war.'

'We are not at war,' I replied.

'Oh, but we are,' Sophon answered.

I was getting nowhere.

I changed the subject. Once more, I brought up my girlfriend's death in New York. Monica's death had caused me the most pain. More than everything else, I blamed Sophon's father for her death. She was killed during an attempt to rescue us from his father. A gun battle had ensued. She died from a stray bullet.

'I loved her,' I said to Sophon. 'I wanted to marry her. She died because your father came into my hotel room to force me to do something I did not want to do. Your father told me he would kill me if I did not do what he asked. Kill me and my girlfriend. I believed him.'

'It was your right to believe him or not. Truthfully, I do not believe my father ever thought he would have to kill you,' Sophon said. 'He paid you money for your stock, a lot of money. Is this something someone would do if they intended to kill you?'

He paused before continuing, 'He threatened to kill you only if you did not sell him your stock. What were you going to do, Mr. Van Laan? Were you going to sell him the stock? Or were you going to refuse because you thought he was bluffing?'

Truth was I had been ready to sign the papers. I could have risked my own life, but I could not take a chance with Monica's life. I had to sign the papers. Sophon was right, but I said nothing, didn't want to admit that to him.

'It was the CIA who were responsible for your girlfriend's death,' Sophon continued when I did not answer his question. 'They forced the door to your hotel room and started shooting. Why do you think my father should be blamed for their stupidity? When your friends from the CIA stormed into the room, my father's life was at risk, as well as your girlfriend's. My father could have been killed. He was spared, and your girlfriend was killed. That was simply a matter of fate. Would you feel differently today if my father had been killed instead of your girlfriend?' he asked.

I had no answer for him. No answer that would serve any purpose.

No answer that would justify killing his father.

5:25 A.M. JOHN

The time shortly before the time when the sun rises in the morning can be the darkest, loneliest time of night.

Some nights are long, too long, as if night will never end.

We begin to worry the golden sun will never again spread its light and warmth over the vast reaches of the horizon while stars fade into a blue canopy, relinquishing their distant wonder to a brighter, clearer reality. We fear being enclosed forever in shadows, never again to see the gray light of dawn across the horizon and, with it, the promise of a new day. Imprisoned forever in a time of suffering under a cold, dark sky... night covering our minds with never-ending, restless remorse.

I was bone tired. I wanted this night to be done. The little strength I had gathered earlier from eating some bread and a banana had been exhausted hours ago. The relief I had felt after being finally freed from my dirty, stinky, piss-wet bed had long ago drained away. I was working on fumes. Still, I tried to hold up my end of the conversation. I was afraid once we stopped talking, it would be time to die.

I guess I still held some hope I could connect with Sophon, still believed he would let me live. Isn't it true that we spend very little time thinking about our death? We never really think this is the day we will die. Instead, we live every day as though death is not a reality. It is not until we have no hope only then are we forced to accept death.

Or... perhaps we never do; we are never able to completely wrap our minds around the fact our days are limited, even when the day of our death is inevitable.

I knew my desire to live was illogically founded, nothing more than a senseless drivel. Even so, I was trying, but it was becoming painfully obvious Sophon had one goal in mind, and that was to make me admit I was responsible for his father's death. I was guilty of murder. Then he planned to execute me for a crime to which I had confessed, and justice would be served.

I had been defending myself by trying to convince him his father's death was not completely my fault. But I was not winning. I began to wonder if I was unconvincing because I didn't really believe it myself. Because deep down, I knew he was right. I did feel responsible for his father's death. Or maybe it would be more correct to say I felt a heavy burden. Not that I was guilty of murder. More like I had a deep sense of regret. Regret for what happened. Regret it was my hand that had pulled the trigger. Regret I had been the agent of his father's death. Even though I thought his father deserved to die because he had been responsible for the death of so many innocent people, I wished it was not me who had been the instrument of his death. I should not have killed him.

I kept glancing out a window, hoping to see some sign of the sun rising in the east over the water. Hoping the light of a new day might give me strength. But every time I looked outside, it was dark, and I was wearing down. My eyelids were becoming heavy. Fear was the only emotion still motivating me. Every time I began to fade, a shot of adrenaline-induced fear would wake me. Stark adrenaline-dripping fear revived my lagging spirit. I feared if I went to sleep even for one moment, it would be over, our conversation done, and it would be time for me to die.

I had to stay awake.

'More than the watchman waits for the morning. More than the watchman waits for the morning.' The words of David's psalm keep running over and over in my head. I said a silent prayer to God for strength. I prayed for a way out of this mess. But I also prayed for my soul because I saw no way out.

'Are you willing to admit that you murdered my father?' Sophon asked again.

I do not know how many times he asked this question during that night. Over and over, he never seemed to tire of asking. In fact, he appeared to be gaining strength as I became more exhausted. Perhaps he sensed he would finally get the answer he desired if he asked his question enough times, and this prospect gave him energy.

'No, I am not willing to admit I am responsible for your father's death,' I argued. 'I am willing to say I regret it happened. I will tell you the memory of his death gives me nothing but sadness. I am even willing to admit I am very sorry it happened. But I will never be willing to agree I'm solely responsible for his death.'

'How can you say that?' Sophon asked in exasperation. 'You pointed the gun at my father. You alone pulled the trigger. By your own admission, you watched him die... Weren't you happy to see him die? Didn't you laugh inside when you realized that you had killed him? Didn't that make you happy?'

'No, I felt only sadness.'

'That is a lie.'

'No, it's not a lie,' I said as calmly as I could.

'You are a liar and a murderer. You just won't admit it?'

From somewhere deep inside my body, I gathered what strength I had left to make one last desperate argument. 'Sophon,' I began. 'We have been talking for hours. Your father's relationship with me was complex. From his perspective, my company created problems for him and your country. It took business from your country and gave it to people in other countries. It was not good for him, for you, for your family's business, for your country... But from my perspective, these things happen. Time changes things. Some businesses are successful, and some are not. Most eventually fail. It happens.'

'It didn't have to happen, Mr. Van Laan. You made it happen. It was your fault. You should have understood the consequences of your actions before you started your company. You should have considered what would happen before you destroyed so many lives.'

I took a moment before answering. 'Maybe that's true. Maybe I was naïve. But I had the right to start a business just as you do.'

'Do you have a right to throw people out of work? Do you have a right to take their food from them and cast them out of their houses? This is what you did, Mr. Van Laan. Your company made beggars out of many people in Thailand.'

'Yes, but I helped many other people. There are workers in many parts of the world who have a better life today because of my company.'

'People in my country are starving because of your company,' Sophon countered from behind his dimly lit shadow.

I looked out the window again, vainly attempting to see some strain of gray light near the horizon over the sea. Nothing but darkness hung over the restless waters. My eyelids dropped. I looked down, almost unable to hold up my head.

'I did what I thought I had a right to do,' I said wearily.

'So did my father. He did what he needed to do to bring work back to his country. He did it because he loved his country.'

'No, he did it because he loved money and power,' I said in a whisper.

'What did you say?'

'Nothing.'

'Do not say such a thing. I will kill you now if you say this one more time. My family has always treated our people with great respect,' Sophon exclaimed. 'It is you who did this for money. Not my father.'

My eyes wanted to close. I was losing the argument. It was useless.

'Are you finally ready to answer my question truthfully?' he asked.

'You want me to admit to murdering your father.'

'Yes.'

'I cannot.'

'Why?'

'Because you are wrong.'

I suddenly became angry, and anger gave me one last semblance of strength. 'Because if you look at the events we have been discussing individually; sure, you can rationalize excuses for what your father did. But if you step back for a moment and put all the events together, if you take the time to consider everything that happened between your father and me, then you must come to a different conclusion, the same conclusion I came to the night I killed your father.'

I paused.

Sophon did not interrupt me as I expected, so I continued. 'Think about all the times your father hired assassins to kill me. Think about all the times I thought I was a dead man. Like when I almost died when men hired by your father rammed my car, and it almost fell off a cliff in the mountains. Or when men shot at my car, causing me to lose control and hit a truck. Or when they shot into my apartment. Think about how you would feel if you found your best friend dead in a pool of blood in your apartment... Do you know how that feels?'

I stared at him, strength coming from somewhere deep inside me.

'You don't know, do you, Sophon?' I pushed ahead. 'And you don't know how it feels to have your girlfriend die in your arms...'

He said nothing.

'Another friend died from a poisoned needle in his back.' My voice began to rise. 'Think about all these times, Sophon. Put them all together. Then force yourself to think about the time your father's men dynamited a dam, which should have killed me. How many people in your country died when that dam broke, hundreds? Think about those people.'

'That was an accident,' he responded.

'I don't think so, and I don't believe you do either. He was trying to kill me. Those people, those villagers who drowned in the river, they meant nothing to him.' I said, remembering the day a dam broke, causing a high wave of water to rush down a valley in Thailand, killing hundreds of villagers and almost killing me and my friend. In my mind's eye, I could still see the dead faces of the villagers floating in the river.

'That is a lie. It was an accident,' Sophon said emphatically.

'Really, are you telling me it was just a coincidence I happened to be in the river valley the day the dam collapsed? And it is also a coincidence your father just happened to be somewhere else at the time?'

'Don't say things you cannot prove,' Sophon replied angrily.

'How many innocent people died in that disaster?' I pressed my case, thinking this was the one incident Sophon could not justify. 'I almost drowned. And even if you don't believe he did it, I do. Think about how that made me feel.'

'I cannot pretend to know how you feel. You are a murderer.'

'Well, try. Think about all the terrible things that have happened to me, all of them caused by your father.'

I pressed on. 'One of the women in the bedroom across the hall was beaten in front of my eyes the night I killed your father. Get her in here if you don't believe me. Ask her about that night. Ask her if your father ordered the death of her brother.' I shouted at him.

Sophon was silent.

'You say he was just trying to influence me all the times I almost died. Well, maybe you are right. Maybe he never intended to kill me. Maybe they were all an effort to get me to give in to his demand to take control of my company. Maybe this was his intention, and maybe not. But either way, everything he did had an effect and its effect grew in my mind every day, grew until it exploded. All the pain, all the fear, all the sorrow erupted inside my brain the night I pulled the trigger... Am I sorry for what I did? Yes... But do I feel totally responsible? No... Except I wish I had been stronger... I wish I had been able to resist the insane urge to kill him. I wish I had walked away. But I did not... I was weak. I regret killing your father in a moment of weakness, and I am sorry for that... But I am not totally responsible... No, your father bears most of the responsibility. He created the circumstances which led to his death. He is the man you should blame, not me.'

I stopped.

I had stepped over the line, and I knew it. Sophon could never blame his father... I waited. Sophon would retaliate now. I expected to die.

Up until this time, he had been acting calm. Now Sophon appeared to be agitated, apparently frustrated he had not achieved what he came for. I sensed he would want to end it now. I feared it would happen before the sun rose. I had hoped to see the light of one more day. Now, I feared I would die in the night. I almost didn't care. I felt so bad, so weak, so tired I thought I might die even if he didn't kill me. Every sinew attached to my bones wanted to collapse. It felt like my organs were producing a poison and were shutting down one after another until finally, my heart would stop, and it would be over. The only thought which seemed to keep me going was a strange desire to see one more sunrise. I did not want to die at night. I do not like the night. I wanted to die during the day.

'My father was not responsible,' Sophon said slowly as if he had given up trying to convince me. He said the words as if he were a judge issuing a prepared statement before passing a sentence. 'My father did what he did to convince you to sell your company. He did it for his country.'

I was exhausted, but something in me wouldn't give in.

'Sophon, your father marched into my life followed by a path flowing in blood: the blood of my girlfriend, the blood of my friend from Sri Lanka, the blood of my best friend, and my business partner. Blood on a hotel room floor in New York, blood on the streets of New York and Chicago, bodies strewn along a river valley in the mountains of your country. No matter what his intentions are, the trail of blood he created is his legacy. Blood follows blood; blood flows, no turning back, no peace, no good could come from what your father did, only death and sorrow.'

'No, my father was a peaceful man. He did what he did because he cared for his people.'

'Doesn't matter, don't you understand? Because I saw only pain and death. I thought he was going to kill again. I had to stop him.'

'He was not going to kill your girlfriend's brother. It was just a threat.'

'I didn't believe that.' I said, my voice rising even though I was trying to stay calm.

'You killed my father.' Sophon delivered his verdict. 'You alone are responsible.'

'No, he killed himself,' I argued. 'Violence and death walked with him in everything he did. You speak of your country. You speak of a peaceful man. But I saw another man, a man consumed by blood and pain. The violence he created was like a friend who walked at his side. And in the end, it was his friend who killed him, not me.'

'How can you say that?' Sophon stood up and shouted at me.

'Because it is the truth!' I screamed back at him with every ounce of energy I had left in my body.

Sophon's face was a shadow standing in front of a lamp, the only light in the room. Turning slowly, he whispered something quietly to the man guarding me, the man I called the Chinaman. I didn't know the Chinaman had a gun. I hadn't seen the gun before, but I was not surprised to see it. The gun had been carefully disguised behind folds of cloth in his shirt. He gave the gun to Sophon without looking at me.

Sophon took the gun from him while facing the front windows filled with a black night sky over the sea.

I wanted to run, to hide, but I could not move.

Sophon turned and looked at me as if he had finally made up his mind. The gun in his hand rose, the barrel pointed directly at my chest. I waited, too tired to react, simply waited for a flash of light at the end of the barrel, a flash which would end my life; I waited and watched.

The gun wavered imperceptibly. Sophon's body trembled slightly, and his arm fell to his side as if the gun was too heavy. It was a burden he could not hold. Each time he attempted to raise the gun, his arm again fell limp against his side.

I focused on the gun, watching it fall several times. I could not see his eyes. His eyes were in the shadows. I desperately wanted to see his eyes, see something in his eyes that would warn me.

Sophon's arm raised the gun one final time, holding it steady without wavering.

5: 45 P.M. ILANA AND SANDY

The ladies were listening, trying to understand the words coming through the walls of their bedroom, the shouting, the arguments John could not win.

They could not comprehend every word, but they knew John was losing. They heard it in his voice. He was wearing down, becoming harder to understand.

The discussion had been long and exhausting, but they had nowhere to go. They had remained in bed, awake in the night, riveted by a conversation coming from another room. Holding hands under the sheets, gripping their new friend's hand, they listened and waited.

Ilana's eyes were closed, wishing to herself, hoping, gripping Sandy's hand tightly.

Sandy did not complain, even when her hand hurt. She said nothing, lying beside Ilana, wanting to comfort her. But what could she say? What could either of them do to give comfort? Nothing... nothing except wait.

They heard John's last words. He shouted something about the truth, about it being the truth. They knew he was out of words. Then they heard nothing, only a deathly silence; no more words, no more arguments... nothing.

Sandy gripped Ilana's hand, tears forming in her eyes.

5:50 A.M. CHARLIE

Charlie woke early, too early to get out of bed.
He had been dreaming.
He couldn't remember his dream, but he knew it woke him out of a deep sleep. Something about it was troubling. And then it

came to him. It wasn't his dream that was bothering him, which woke him in the middle of the night. It was something he had learned late the previous afternoon. An agent friend in Thailand had called and told him Sophon Nue had left the country, the young man was traveling. The agent in Thailand had apologized for not calling Charlie sooner and said he had been busy, some big deal at the embassy, lots of VIPs in town, senators and congressmen on a junket. All bullshit, of course, but it took his time and concentration.

Charlie said he understood and thanked the agent for calling and giving him a heads-up. Then Charlie called Buddy, the head of John's security staff at his office in Charlottesville. Charlie asked Buddy if everything was alright, any signs of trouble. This was when Charlie discovered John was in Belize with two girlfriends. Charlie had chuckled when he learned that John was with his two girlfriends in Belize. Charlie wished he could witness this debacle. Then Charlie asked Buddy if John had taken bodyguards with him to the island.

Buddy said he did, one bodyguard, but the man had returned. His name was Todd, and Todd's father had a heart attack. His father had almost died and needed open heart surgery. It was touch and go for several days. Fortunately, Todd had returned to the States in time for the surgery. His father survived, but post-surgery had been difficult. Several times, his father's heart had stopped, and he needed to be resuscitated. So, Todd was not with John. He knew he should be, but his father was his main concern.

Anyway, Todd's father was doing fine now. Crisis was over. Todd had called Buddy and apologized for not calling sooner. He told Buddy everything was fine in Belize, with no signs of trouble. John had ordered him to go home to his family. John said not to worry. Todd had flown home to be with his family. He was happy he did. He almost lost his father. He was glad he had been able to be at his mother's side to help her through the crisis.

'So, John and his two lovely girlfriends are down in Belize alone and unprotected?' Charlie asked Buddy.

'Yes, but Todd said he had seen no signs of trouble,' Buddy responded.

'That is your assessment.'

'I'm not in Belize. I don't have an assessment,' Buddy answered coldly. 'John told Todd to go home without waiting for backup, not me.'

'I see,' Charlie replied. Without further editorial comment, he thanked Buddy and hung up the phone.

The conversation replayed again in his mind now as Charlie lay in bed. He knew it was all wrong. John had made a mistake, an inexperienced rookie mistake. But then, Charlie could not protect John from every mistake.

He hoped John was okay.

BANGKOK THAILAND, 6:35 P.M. LUANG

The dreaded report came in late.

Luang had waited. Something in the previous day's report indicated Sophon was ready. His men had communicated and said it would happen soon, maybe even today. Luang had been eagerly anticipating the report.

When his assistant arrived with the report, nothing in the man's demeanor was different from the past, no smile, no emotion. The assistant simply placed the folded paper on Luang's desk without saying a word; turned and walked out of the room as was his custom, closing the door behind him.

Luang could have assumed from his assistant's actions, his lack of joy; he could have feared the report was not good, but he did not. He wanted to be positive, think good thoughts, hope it was finally over.

He didn't wait. He took the paper immediately and unfolded it, reading every word. Then he slumped into his chair.

The murderer was still alive.

Not possible.

The man should be dead.

Luang crumbled the paper tightly in his hands, throwing it on his desk in disgust.

He would not visit his garden tonight. He would not sip tea and think about better days ahead.

His personal nightmare was not over.

BELIZE, 5:00 P.M. JOHN

Ilana and Sandy lay curled around me in bed, holding me, sleeping and not sleeping.

When I finally opened my eyes, they stared at me in wonder, happy I was awake. But not as surprised as I was to see them. They told me I had been dragged into their room and thrown on their bed. I didn't remember any of it. All I remembered was fearing I was going to die. A fear so strong, it alone had kept me awake during the night talking to Sophon. When the crisis was finally over, I must have succumbed to my weakened physical condition and completely collapsed. They were afraid I was dying because they could not wake me. All they could do was hold me, talk to me softly, and wait, hoping I would eventually open my eyes.

I tried to move. That was a mistake. Every bone, every muscle in my body hurt. I was thirsty. I asked for water, although I was too weak to drink. Water fell like drool in streams from my chin. They wiped the water and washed my face with a cool, wet cloth, which felt good. I thanked them. Just their sweet act of washing my face was an incredible kindness. After days of torturous neglect, this simple gesture was like being in heaven. I smiled at them; then I closed my eyes and slept.

Eventually I had to wake up, couldn't sleep any longer. Their eyes were closed when I opened mine to look at them. They were resting beside me. I touched their faces to be sure they were real. They opened their eyes and smiled at me.

'Are you alright?' I whispered.

'We are fine,' Ilana replied.

'Can you help me sit up?' I asked, feeling too weak to move.

They propped me up with pillows.

'How long did I sleep?' I asked.

'It's past four in the afternoon,' Sandy replied. 'We were afraid you were dying.'

'I feel like I have died and gone to heaven, and you are two angels... except... I don't feel very good.'

'You don't look very good either,' Sandy, the realist, replied.

'Thanks.'

'My pleasure.'

I smiled.

'We have a problem,' Ilana interrupted. 'We have heard nothing outside our room since morning. They have not come to check on us. And we have had nothing to eat since yesterday.'

I looked at them. They looked better than I felt. 'Have you been getting regular meals?' I asked, wondering if they had been treated badly.

'Yes, twice a day,' Sandy said. 'They brought us food.'

'Was the food good?' I asked, even though the thought of food made me nauseous.

'Good enough,' Sandy replied.

I remembered Sophon's promise. He said he would not harm them. I wasn't sure he was telling the truth, but apparently, he had been true to his word. I guess I underestimated him and missed something in his character.

'And you, Ilana, did you like the food,' I smiled, knowing her finicky tastes.

'It was not good food,' she said. 'I ate it because I was hungry, but I did not like the food.'

Sounded like Ilana. She liked her food, her way, the food she made, food native to her Belize. It didn't matter if she was kidnapped or in a hurricane. She wanted her food. Nothing else was good.

'Could I have some water?' I asked.

Ilana went into the bathroom to get a glass of water. I drank it slowly, this time allowing the cool water to run down my throat. It helped. I felt better.

The house was quiet. A bedroom window drew my interest. As I looked out of the window, the memory of the previous night's ordeal came back to me, every horrifying detail, especially the dark window to a lifeless black night sky. More than anything, I wanted to see the light of a new day through that window. I remembered praying, asking God for nothing more than the ability to see the dawn of one more day before I died.

Bright sunshine shone through the bedroom window as I stared in disbelief. I had lived to see another day against all odds. I never thought I would see the sun again.

I thanked God.

It was afternoon. The sun had traveled to the west side of the house, reflecting off the pool outside Ilana's bedroom window. Being able to see the light was a blessing beyond imagination. An almost iridescent glow rose from the pool. I was drawn to the water and to the flowers that surrounded Ilana's pool, to her garden, to her lush green garden so full of life and vibrant colors under an afternoon sun. I got out of bed slowly and walked over to a sliding glass door to the outside. My ladies helped me, wondering what I was doing. A lock had been placed on the door by Sophon's men, locking the ladies inside the bedroom during their captivity.

Ilana tried the door, and to her amazement, it opened.

My legs felt like lead. Every joint ached, but I pushed my body to move. The colorful flowers drew me outside the door to a small deck off the bedroom. I walked slowly like an old man on shaky legs. I wanted to feel the breeze. I wanted to feel everything alive around me. I felt like I had returned from being dead. I couldn't describe it to the women. It was as if everything outside was a living, breathing organism. The water in the pool appeared to be a shimmering life-form, shining at me. For a brief time on the deck, I simply immersed my senses in all the life-giving forces surrounding me, letting them wrap their loving arms around me, welcoming me back to life.

Ilana and Sandy held me, one under each arm, held me so I wouldn't fall, held me so I could feel the wind in my face. I eventually asked them to take me to a chair on the deck. As I rested there, they waited patiently, saying nothing, watching and waiting.

Finally, Sandy asked me what we were going to do.

'Do about what?' I replied. 'Isn't it enough to be alive.'

THE END

For excerpts from book 6, see below.

GRAND HAVEN, MICHIGAN, FRIDAY, NOVEMBER 20, 11:35 A.M.

The phone rang just as Phillip was getting ready to leave his office for lunch.

His intuition told him Sophon was on the line. He had tried all week to call Sophon. He knew where Sophon had gone and he knew why the young man went there. Sophon had informed Phillip he would be traveling to Belize to locate John and it didn't take a genius to understand that the visit would not be good for John. Phillip assumed Sophon intended to kill John.

Nothing like that had been suggested by Phillip. That was not his MO. Instead, he made the case for John's execution. Like a lawyer to the jury, Phillip had primed Sophon to the point that Phillip had no doubt about what the young man would do when he confronted John.

And Phillip was the one person who was fully capable of making his case. He had been at the scene the night Sophon's father was shot dead by John. Phillip was a first-hand witness. He told Sophon that John had come out of the darkness and killed Sophon's father at close range. Point blank, pulled the trigger. Phillip saw it all. John had killed Sophon's father in cold blood. John was a murderer. It was only because the CIA had decided to cover up the murder; that was the only reason John was not on death row. That is what Phillip told Sophon.

It was easy to make the CIA the bad guys. The agency had a bad reputation in Thailand. So that part was easy. In fact, it was all easy.

The only unanswered question, the question that was important to Phillip, the one question that mattered most, was who was going to take control of John's company after he was gone. And even though Phillip was not absolutely assured of getting the job, he had no doubt about that either. Again, he had laid the foundation carefully, regaled Sophon with story after story, illustrating his experience in the gem business while patiently demonstrating his technical knowledge of gemology. Sophon was told stories from the history of gems in Thailand, stories that even Sophon didn't know. For a few weeks, Phillip had become Sophon's mentor, his instructor, and his friend. Like an actor on a stage, Phillip had played his part until he was confident that Sophon would naturally turn to him to run the company as soon as John was gone.

Now, it was only a matter of time until it all happened, as Phillip anticipated it would. He had only to wait.

But Phillip hated waiting. Not that he couldn't wait; Phillip had taught himself to be a patient man. Patience was just a matter of discipline. And Phillip had learned discipline.

Phillip had waited patiently all week for the phone call he knew would come from Sophon. But when it seemed to be taking longer than it should, Phillip got curious and his curiosity took control of his patient brooding. His patient patience broke down, and although he knew this was a bad idea, he called Sophon's cell phone. And when that failed, he tried calling Sophon's uncle in Thailand. The old man refused to take his calls, so he called John's office in Charlottesville, thinking someone there might tell him what he wanted to know.

He was told that John Van Laan was not returning his calls. And he assumed that meant John was dead.

After that he called anyone and everyone he could think of calling to learn the details of John death. For a whole week he learned nothing more. Every call was unproductive. When the phone rang just before lunch on Friday, Phillip naturally assumed it was Sophon.

And Phillip was confident that Sophon would tell him what he wished to know.

BANGKOK, THAILAND, SUNDAY, NOVEMBER 22, 5:30 P.M.

Sophon's great-uncle never got a call.

Luang didn't need one. He had received word of what happened in a daily report. One of his men assigned to be with Sophon had called it in.

The report was then written on a folded white sheet of paper which was delivered daily by a young assistant to Luang, simply placed on his desk. The assistant never spoke to the old man. That was not his place. He retreated from of his office quietly, closing the door behind him.

Luang was frustrated but not completely surprised by what he read in the report. However, after days of disappointment, he had come to assume this might happen. His nephew's son was unpredictable.

The boy's father on the other hand was never hard to read. Luang always knew what his nephew would do. The challenge in dealing with his nephew was different. Luang had tried to council him, to moderate his rash behavior, tried to calm him down from time to time. His nephew was always rushing off on some sort of mission, never content, always looking to make things right, never afraid or aware of the consequences, just intent on achieving his goals no matter what the cost.

His nephew's son, Sophon, had his father's impulsive character. But also predominant in his character were some of his mother's qualities. She was more introspective, more aware of her world and all that existed in it. She saw the complexity of life. She was content to enjoy its beauty, less ready to want to change it. Luang had liked Sophon's mother. He was sad when she died at a young age. Sophon had never known his mother. Never had a chance to be educated by her, taught to see the world in a different way, through her eyes instead of his father's. Luang was sure the boy would have loved his mother. They were very much alike. And now that Sophon was growing up, the qualities that had shone in his mother were beginning to be seen in her son.

But it was hard for the boy. Hard because what his heart told him to do was often polar opposite of what he had been taught by his father. So his behavior was erratic. Kind of like a bouncing ball, bouncing this way and that. The old patriarch could never really predict what Sophon would do.

When Luang heard about what happened on an island far away, he was not surprised, but he was very frustrated.

www.ingramcontent.com/pod-product-compliance
Lightning Source LLC
Chambersburg PA
CBHW060433310726
48977CB00001B/169